The Second Woman

The Second Woman

Kenneth Cameron

FELONY & MAYHEM PRESS • NEW YORK

All the characters and events portrayed in this work are fictitious.

THE SECOND WOMAN

A Felony & Mayhem mystery

PRINTING HISTORY
First UK edition (Orion): 2010
Felony & Mayhem edition (first US edition): 2019

ISBN: 978-1-63194-196-2

Manufactured in the United States of America

Library of Congress Cataloging-in-Publication Data

Names: Cameron, Kenneth M., 1931- author.
Title: The second woman / Kenneth Cameron.
Description: Felony & Mayhem edition. | New York : Felony & Mayhem Press,
2019. | "A Felony & Mayhem mystery."
Identifiers: LCCN 2019010750| ISBN 9781631941962 (softcover) | ISBN
9781631941986 (ebook)
Subjects: | GSAFD: Mystery fiction.
Classification: LCC PS3553.A4335 S43 2019 | DDC 813/.54--dc23
LC record available at https://lccn.loc.gov/2019010750

To
Patrick O'Connor
First editor, longest friendship

ACKNOWLEDGEMENTS

As with the earlier Denton books, the contribution of my editor, Bill Massey, has been essential; so, too, has that of Tim Waller, who copy-edited and rode herd on period language.

Several books have given me useful detail: Arthur Hertzberg's *The Zionist Idea*, Walter Laqueur's *The History of Zionism*, and Jonathan Schneer's *London 1900: The Imperial Metropolis*. I'm sure that my opening scene was affected by Isabel Colegate's *The Shooting Party*, a novel (later a film) of which I'm very fond. I continue to use a number of works for material on the Metropolitan police, particularly here J. F. Moylan's *Scotland Yard and the Metropolitan Police*, Hargrave L. Adam's eight-volume *The Police Encyclopedia*, and H. Childs's *'Police Duty' Catechism and Reports* (11th ed.). For details of London's streets, I relied on several editions of Baedeker's *London and Its Environs*, the latest 1906. For period language, especially slang, I went to John Ayto's *Oxford Dictionary of Slang*, the *OED*, and the 1902 edition of Chambers's *Twentieth Century Dictionary*.

The icon above says you're holding a copy of a book in the Felony & Mayhem "Historical" category, which ranges from the ancient world up through the 1940s. If you enjoy this book, you may well like other "Historical" titles from Felony & Mayhem Press.

For more about these books, and other Felony & Mayhem titles, or to place an order, please visit our website at:

www.FelonyAndMayhem.com

Other "Historical" titles from

FELONY&MAYHEM

ANNAMARIA ALFIERI
City of Silver
Strange Gods

KENNETH CAMERON
The Frightened Man
The Bohemian Girl

FIDELIS MORGAN
Unnatural Fire
The Rival Queens

ALEX REEVE
Half Moon Street

KATE ROSS
Cut to the Quick
A Broken Vessel
Whom the Gods Love
The Devil in Music

CATHERINE SHAW
The Library Paradox
The Riddle of the River

LC TYLER
A Cruel Necessity
A Masterpiece of Corruption

LAURA WILSON
The Lover
The Innocent Spy
An Empty Death
The Wrong Man
A Willing Victim
The Riot

The Second Woman

CHAPTER 1

'What a dreadful breakfast—simply appalling! Nothing but cold porridge and toast without butter. Might be the worst breakfast I've ever had, and I've been to some disgusting places.'

'An hour ago there were eggs, gammon, that fish stuff—'

'There was kedgeree? I love kedgeree!'

'You should have got up earlier. What kept you in bed, some duchess?'

'Duchess, indeed! I went to bed at ten with a red dispatch box, and I was up with it again at six!'

'Funny tastes you've got, Hector.'

The two men were walking down a muddy lane between dense hedges, the morning air chilly and damp, with frost on the yellow grass like grey velvet. Behind and ahead of them, other men were moving, some with guns broken at the breech, their breath faint smoke.

The man named Hector—moustached, well-bellied, straight-backed—frowned at those ahead, then at those behind. 'All of them had a proper breakfast, I'm sure. So much for the rewards of virtue. I suppose the kedgeree wasn't very good, in fact. Fenniman is famous for his bad food.' Fenniman was their host. 'Has a very rum cook, said not to pay enough. But luncheon will be spectacular, I promise you—has it catered in London and brought out by rail, everything down to the extra servants and the tables and chairs. Marquee in case it rains. Likes to make a show for the higher echelon of guests.' He snorted, became sorrowful. 'I shall be starved by luncheon.'

'Good for you.' The other man tapped his friend's waist-coat. 'Well-filled starvation.' He was tall and lean and had an American accent. He had a huge nose, as well, and a greying moustache that hung down each side of his mouth, his face rather weary and battered-looking, as if he had been walking against the wind for too long.

'Don't poke me like that!' Sir Hector Hench-Rose sucked his belly in and put a hand where the American had been tapping. 'It's undignified.' Amused as suddenly as he had been irritated, he said, 'I am a baronet, after all. We're very dignified creatures—unlike you, Denton. Authors have no more dignity than—than artists. Big hats and earrings and Spanish capes and—when are you going to change your clothes, by the way? You're the only one of us in mufti.'

'Change into what?'

'Your shooting clothes.'

'These are my shooting clothes.' He was wearing a rather old lounge suit, green-brown tweed, and a soft hat that had been through a good deal of rain.

'You're joking.'

'You said to wear shooting clothes. These are clothes I can shoot in.'

'I said "shooting suit"!'

'This is a suit.'

'But it's not a *shooting* suit! Look at me. *I* am wearing a shooting suit. Doesn't your man know better than to let you come on a shooting weekend without a shooting suit?'

Denton stopped and looked his friend up and down. 'You're wearing knickers.' Too late, he remembered that 'knickers' meant something different in England.

'They're breeks, and they're part of a shooting suit! Everybody's wearing them—look around you!'

Denton looked at the other men, some of whom were squeezing against the hedges to go around. All of them were wearing tweed breeches and Norfolk jackets, stiff collars and neckties. 'The lot of you look like a cycling club,' he said.

'We look nothing of the kind! Cyclists wear funny little hats.' Hench-Rose was in fact wearing a tweed hat that might have been considered funny, but it was different from the caps that cyclists wore with *their* breeches and Norfolk jackets. 'Denton, what *were* you thinking of?'

'You said we'd be tramping over wet moors behind dogs.'

'Um, well—not that it makes any difference to the clothes question, but we're not going to be shooting over dogs.' Hench-Rose cleared his throat, stretched his neck from his collar, put his hand again on his waistcoated belly. 'Butts, in fact.'

'What're butts?'

'Place you stand for driven birds. Now, before you go off half-cocked, listen to me! The plans changed; our host suddenly had the chance to entertain several very important persons who are also first-rate shots, and so he—between you and me and the gatepost, he's rather a collector of personages, our Fenniman, the very reason he wanted you, in fact a bit of a bum-sucker—so he waved his magic wand and transformed a rough shoot into driven birds. It's a far more elegant sport, Denton! His Majesty does it!'

'His Majesty does all sorts of things.'

'He makes huge bags.'

'At some of his other pastimes, too, I hear.'

'Now, now, this is too bad of you—I shan't let you impugn my sovereign, much less—' He clutched Denton's arm as another man passed them, murmuring a hello as he stepped around. Beautifully turned out in the required shooting suit, he was carrying an open shotgun in the crook of his right arm. As he went ahead of them and out of earshot, Denton murmured, 'Handsome gun.'

'Do you know who that is? Held, the financier—one of Fenniman's catches. He's a Jew, of course, but the right kind.'

'What's that supposed to mean—the rich kind?'

'You know what I mean—one of *us*. Cultured. Not—you know—Jewy.'

'You certainly wouldn't want a Jew to be Jewy.'

'You know what I mean. Don't be flippant, Denton. Held is a millionaire. At least. Quite welcome in the very best houses.'

'I wish I could say as much for myself. You were telling me about butts.'

Hector frowned and then gave a quick sketch of shooting driven birds from prepared positions while as many as a hundred beaters drove everything that could fly or run towards them. 'Mostly Chinese pheasant now, but there'll be some partridge from last year, plus the odd rabbit or hare. Wonderful bags are made, Denton—Prince Nordeep Singh regularly shoots in the middle hundreds. I have on occasion bagged three hundred myself. No telling how it will go here, of course: Fenniman had stocked for rough shoots, but when he snared Held and a couple of others, he slung in thousands of pheasant from a breeding place, so the count will be well up.'

'I think I'm more the rough-shoot type, Hector.'

'You *look* more like one of the beaters, but in for a penny, in for a pound. I would remind you that I suggested you to Fenniman, and in a sense I'm responsible for you. You *have* to shoot driven birds today, Denton.' His voice had taken on a hint of appeal. Like a parent with a fractious child, he said, 'Perhaps I can get you a rough shoot tomorrow.'

'If I'm a good boy. Hmp.' Denton patted his friend on the shoulder. 'I'll behave, Mother.'

Denton found that he had been placed near the right-hand end of the line of butts, not quite at the end (it was explained to him that a proven good shot would be there to pick up birds he or others missed) and nowhere near the middle, where the person-ages would shoot and where, it was hoped, the birds would come the thickest.

'First shoot, sir?' a bearded man in a wine-red velvet jacket said to Denton. The man was holding two shotguns, one in each hand. 'I'm Feather, sir, under-keeper. Be loading for you today.' He was eyeing Denton's clothes. 'Used a shotgun before, have you?'

Denton had in fact used a shotgun—to kill four men, but that had been thirty years before, and he wasn't about to talk about it now. He passed over years of hunting everything from buffalo to prairie hens in the American West, and a year with Cody's Wild West as a 'crack pistolero', said only, 'I know which end the shot comes out of.'

The under-keeper grunted. He insisted on demonstrating the safety device on each gun, the method of raising the gun, of sighting. He explained what it meant to lead the bird. 'These are ejector guns, sir. Open them after shooting, the spent cartridges fly out. Don't you do that, sir. I'll do that. You pass the gun to me after one or both barrels are fired—the gun has two barrels, remember—and I'll hand you the newly loaded gun and then crack the first gun and eject, and by the time you've fired number two, I'll have number one loaded and we'll make the exchange again. Now let's practise, please, sir.'

'Shoot, you mean?'

'No, sir, the exchange. The goal is to keep shooting, bang-bang-bang-bang. The birds come very fast and often. Exchange has to be fast and smooth.'

Denton saw that the under-keeper despised him. In his eyes, Denton was an interloper, an American and an ignorant one, at that, who knew nothing about shooting driven birds and would be useless when the shooting started. Now, Feather said, 'Don't mind if you miss, sir. Everybody does, at first.'

'Where do I pee?'

The under-keeper blinked, frowned. He didn't like having the shooting taken less than seriously. Still, he bobbed his chin towards a stand of trees behind them. 'Couple of privies beyond it if the call is serious. Less important thing, do it in that wood. Another for ladies over the cart-track there. We'll rehearse the exchange now, if you please, sir.'

'After I pee.'

Denton strolled up to the little wood, hardly deep enough to give cover to a standing man, but he knew that this class of British were quite offhand about it: so long as his back was turned or one sapling stood between him and onlookers, propriety was satisfied. Discharging the breakfast tea in a cloud of steam, he heard somebody else come up next to him, glanced over to see the millionaire, Held—the unJewy Jew—unbuttoning his flies.

'Not shooting today?' Held said.

'I am, apparently.'

'I suspect you're rather good at it. You're Denton, aren't you? I'm Henry Held.' He smiled. 'You'll forgive me if we don't shake hands.' He gave his penis a shake and chuckled. 'I read your last book—I think it was your last, *The Love Child*? Rather wonderful. I always marvel that such sad things aren't depressing, but that's the art of it, isn't it? You can do in a book what we can't do in life. How I wish I could do it!' He buttoned himself up and turned away. 'Shoot well. I'm sure you will.'

He knows, Denton thought. Many people did.

He strolled back to the butt, which was really only a waist-high mound of earth pushed up by a horse-drawn scraper.

'We must practise the exchange, sir. The beaters are coming.'

'Is that what I hear—that racket?'

'Yes, sir, the beaters hitting the trees with their sticks. The first birds will appear any moment, sir.'

Denton took a shotgun and passed it back and was handed another; they went through it again, Denton desultory, the under-keeper insistent and quick, and then the first shots sounded from well off—one, and then two almost together—and then there was a second of silence and then a fusillade.

'Now, sir!' Feather was cramming cartridges into one of the guns. He thrust it at Denton. 'Remember to lead, sir—shoot what you can hit; leave the high ones and the fast ones for the good shots—'

A bird came sailing high, high above them, going fast at an angle across the butt. Denton raised the shotgun and killed it, then swung and took a bird that was crossing fast and low from left to right.

'Good shot, sir! Oh, good again—!'

Denton broke the gun and the spent cartridges popped out. He put the gun in the crook of his arm and looked up the line of butts, watching birds come sailing over the treetops into the range of the guns. Little more than dark dots with the flutter of their wings as a kind of halo, they moved into the open space before the butts and then, more often than not, collapsed in the air as if they had been squeezed by a fist. Feathers burst into a tiny puff and the bird would come pelting down at an angle, cartwheeling, wings useless, abruptly pathetic.

'The gun, sir—give me the gun! Sir! You've broken the gun yourself—Take the gun, sir!'

Denton turned and looked at him. The under-keeper's face was red, perhaps with anger or perhaps simply with excitement. He had a gun held out almost in Denton's face, and he was trying to wrench the empty one out of his arm.

'I'll tell you when I'm ready for the next gun,' Denton said.

'You must shoot, sir!'

Denton turned back towards the wood, picked off a fast bird with one barrel and then went up and back and caught a high flier that was actually behind him. A voice he didn't recognize shouted, 'Oh, well shot,' from his left. A spattering of applause followed; he turned and saw half a dozen women leaning on parasols or sitting on uncomfortable-looking folding stools.

'Gun!' Feather cried. 'Sir, you *must* shoot!'

'Why? I've got four birds; that's enough.'

'You let that one go—and that one—sir—there's another—!'

'They're too easy.'

'*Shoot!*' The keeper's red face was almost touching Denton's. Denton put his hand on the man's chest and pushed him back as he said very low, 'If you tell me to shoot one more time, I'll belt you one.' He took the loaded gun, let five birds go by as too easy, picked off a fast partridge that had just been missed by the clean-up shooter on his right, and then stood with the gun ready, waiting for another sporting shot.

'Shoot, sir—*please.*' Feather's voice all but broke, as if he were near tears.

Denton held the shotgun out. 'You shoot,' he said.

'No, please—you must—'

'Like hell.' Denton broke the gun, ejecting the spent and the unspent cartridge, and leaned the shotgun against the berm of dirt. 'You want them dead so much, you shoot them. I've had more sporting times throwing black-powder bombs into fish-ponds.' He turned and started up towards the women, who were staring at him with horror and a kind of sensual fascination.

'You're leaving the butts!' the under-keeper cried.

'So I am.' He strode on. The hostess, Mrs Fenniman, was one of the group that was watching him. He knew he must have done an unforgivable thing; he knew that Hench-Rose would suffer for having brought him there. But enough was enough.

Removing his hat, he said, 'Mrs Fenniman—'

'You have been taken ill, I am sure.' She was the third daughter of somebody in Salisbury's government, one of his titled crew; her tone was arch, hard, withdrawn, as if he were a boy who couldn't possibly have thought up all by himself the atrocious thing he'd just done.

'Only sick of shooting sitting ducks, ma'am. I'm sorry, but this isn't for me.'

'But you shoot so magnificently,' another woman said.

Mrs Fenniman looked severely at the woman, then at Denton. 'You must, of course, please yourself. As you already have.'

'I'm very sorry. I didn't understand—' He never had to explain what he didn't understand, and it was just as well, as he didn't think he could explain to a woman of her sort what disgusted him about killing the helpless; instead, movement from his left distracted him, and he saw a figure running towards him with a yellow something fluttering in one hand. The figure became his soldier-servant, Atkins, ex-British army, and the something became a telegram that read 'COME TO MY HOUSE AT ONCE STOP J'.

'I must return to London,' he said.

'Of course you must,' Mrs Fenniman said in the voice of a woman who has had the self-sent-telegram trick played on her a hundred times. 'Do not linger out of some misplaced idea of courtesy.'

❊ ❊ ❊

The Fenniman Panhard bounced along the unmetalled road. Wind reddened the passengers' faces. Denton had forgone goggles; Atkins, beside him, wore them below his bowler hat, with a grin below the goggles.

'Won't this thing go any faster?' Denton shouted at the driver.

'Unlawful to go more than twenty miles per hour, sir. Mr Fenniman quite strict about it.' He avoided a rutted place and pulled back into the centre of the road, his passengers swaying to one side and then the other. With a bang, a rear tyre burst.

'Oh, hell!' Denton shouted.

'Not to worry, sir. Happens all the time.' The chauffeur climbed down and asked that they do the same, then began to unload the tyre-changing tools from the boot.

'Couldn't you have borrowed a motor car that worked?' Denton snarled to Atkins as they huddled beside the road, a light drizzle beginning to fall on their heads.

'Only one on offer. If you'd ordered your own motor car in time, we'd have it now.'

'It's due any day.'

'Lot of good that does us.'

'You look ridiculous in those goggles.'

'One of us has to be able to see where he's going.'

'Her telegram said to come to *her* house. Not my house. Why?'

'Daresay she wants you to come to her house and not your house.' The 'her' was the *J* of the telegram, Janet Striker, with whom he didn't quite live but with whom he had an intense and constant relationship: their houses backed on each other, separated only by back gardens, allowing for a veneer of propriety over an entirely scandalous—and delightful—intimacy.

'You know, Atkins, if Job advertised for a comforter, I'd write you a character.'

'Only trying to calm the frantic employer.'

'I'm not frantic! What the hell, how long does it take to change a tyre?' Denton jumped into the road and shouted, 'Do you need help?'

The chauffeur waved a hand and said he'd be done at any moment, thank you, sir. He had yet to remove the old tyre.

On the road again, Denton glowered into the drizzle and was silent. At the railway station, he let Atkins lead him inside, then to the platform, then to a bench. Suddenly he said, 'We should have telephoned.' Janet Striker had the telephone now; his own was to be installed in a week or two, despite his misgivings.

'No telephone at Fenniman's, General. Just like the hot water and the central heating—doesn't exist.'

In time, he let Atkins push him into a railway carriage, where they rode side by side, although custom said he should have gone to first class. Denton disliked the marks of privilege; Atkins knew it and indulged it. Encouraged by Denton, he had manufactured a somewhat cheeky persona that mocked the normal master-servant behaviours. Included in this were the military titles that flickered through Atkins's conversation: Denton, who had been only an acting lieutenant at the end of the American Civil War, got called General, Colonel, Major or Captain by the former sergeant. The fact that Denton paid Atkins half-again as much as any manservant in London encouraged him to be offhand.

In London at last, Denton paid a cab driver to 'go as fast as you can', meaning he didn't go very fast at all because of the traffic. It was by now the middle of a busy Saturday, horses and motor cars everywhere, pedestrians crossing in packs like herd animals swimming a river. The traffic smell—urine and horse dung, mixed now and then with petrol fumes—was so strong that some women walked with perfumed hankies at their noses, while, behind them, Commissionaires carried their packages and, hankie-less, inhaled the smells as if they were their native air. Here and there some woman of means was followed by her carriage as she shopped, its walking pace a frustration to Denton as his cab got behind it.

'Damn these women!' he growled. He shouted up at the driver, 'Can't you stay off the damned shopping streets?'

'Not if you want t' get where yer going, I can't.' He sniffed and flicked the horse's back. The horse flicked its tail and kept at the same speed. A few streets later, they came on an entire stretch of road that had been torn up, men in shirtsleeves and caps moving through the rubble with shovels and hods of cement. The cab stopped altogether.

'What now?' Denton roared.

'Bloody telly-phone lines. Bloody Post Office can't keep to its proper business but has to use our bloody money to lay down telly-phones!'

At last they got around Russell Square and into Guilford Street, where the horse, without encouragement, picked up speed, actually achieved a slow trot as they passed the end of Lamb's Conduit Street, where Denton was able to look to his right and see, halfway along, his own house. On the front steps was the unmistakable uniform of a London policeman.

'Uh-oh,' Atkins said.

'Judas Priest.'

'That'll be the least of it.'

The driver put the horse into a lope, and they careered into Millman Street, as if speed over the last sixty yards would make up for the delays. Denton jumped down before the cab had stopped at Janet Striker's door, left the vehicle swaying on its springs as he shouted back to Atkins, 'Pay!'

He pulled the bell, pounded on the door and shouted. Then he kicked the door. Even though he could hear quick footsteps, he shouted and pounded again. His foot was back for another kick when the door opened and Janet Striker was standing there, swaying aside as a huge dog rushed out, barking, and made for Atkins. She looked him in the face, looked down at his foot, smiled, then gasped as he put his arms around her and threatened to break her ribs.

'Denton, you idiot—!' She pushed him back. 'People will see.'

'Are you all right?' He held on to her arms as if ready to shake the truth out of her. *Are you all right?*'

'I was until you grabbed me. Really—'

'Janet, what's happened?'

She looked down her walk at the cab, at Atkins, now boosting down the luggage, then left and right up the street as if for eavesdroppers. And then she said in a perfectly normal voice, 'I'm afraid there's a corpse in your back garden.'

CHAPTER 2

A brick wall separated his own back garden from Janet Striker's; in the wall was a door, with a lock to which she kept the key. Usually, the door was unlocked, the traffic between the two houses fairly constant.

Now, the door was locked from Denton's side.

He pounded on it. He kicked it. A voice shouted at him to give over; he paid no attention, kicked it again, got a threat of immediate arrest, started to shout an obscenity, then thought better of it and hoisted himself up the bricks and hung there looking into his own garden.

'Hi there now, that's enough!' A grey-haired constable was standing among the rows of autumn vegetables. He pointed a truncheon at Denton. 'Down you go, or I'll run you in, my lad!'

'I'm as old as you are, *my lad*. That's my garden you're standing in!'

'I don't care if it's the garden of the Queen of the Fairies—I'm in it and you stay out!'

'I have a right to get into my own garden!'

'This here is a crime scene and now the province of the Metropolitan Police. Get your head off that wall!'

Another head appeared beside Denton's. 'Them's my swedes you're trampling on with your big boots, you ape!' The vegetables had been Atkins's idea, the winter crop his special pride.

The policeman waved the truncheon and took a step towards them. 'I'll have you both in, then—'

Atkins screamed. 'Don't move! You're heading for my cold frames!'

Denton's grip was slipping. Trying to muster an air of hurt dignity, he said, 'New Scotland Yard will hear about this.' He slid down the wall.

'And about them swedes!' Atkins added as he dropped beside Denton. 'That bastard. Begging your pardon, General. But to stand on my vegetables and wave his great calabash and—'

'Did you see any corpse?'

'No. Did you?'

'It's too close to the wall, I suppose.'

'That's where the cold frames with the lettuces are!' Atkins tilted his head back and bellowed at the wall, 'If you're into my lettuces, Bobby Peel, I'll have your helmet for a chamber pot!'

'Enough, enough—' Denton pulled him away. 'No more—'

'Bloody hell, Major, I raised them from little sprigs!'

'If they've ruined them, they've ruined them. Let's stick with the corpse.'

He crossed Janet Striker's garden and bounded up the steps to the rear door. He knew the house well, had once, before she had bought it, gone into it in the dark after a man who was stalking him. She had transformed it, turned it back into the little eighteenth-century house it had once been. In the basement, once a huge kitchen and storerooms, she had installed a couple to take care of her; upstairs now had white walls and uncurtained windows, and she moved through this brightness, uncorseted, in flowing dresses made of Liberty silks and cashmeres. Outdoors, she was drab in greys and blacks; in her own house, she was a many-coloured bird.

'My God, you're so beautiful,' he said to her now, seeing her suddenly in the room where she kept her piano. He put his hands on her face. 'I thought something had happened to you.'

'Don't be silly, Denton.' She put her hands over his. 'I'm a plain woman, and you know it.'

'Not to me.'

'Ah, that's a different thing altogether.' She grinned at him. The long scar that ran down the left side of her face, faded now, gave him its own ironic smile—*Don't forget me*. It had been made with a knife. Denton had shot the man who held the knife, but too late to save her face.

'They won't let me into my own house.'

'Call Munro.' Without letting go of his hands, she put the toe of her left shoe behind her right ankle and rubbed. Scratched, in fact. 'Damn the fleas!' she said. Letting go of one of his hands, she bent sideways to scratch with her fingers. 'There's every sort of vermin in Europe in the Isle of Dogs!' She was doing a survey of income and outgo in four poor streets; he had made the mistake of saying he thought that Charles Booth had already done that very thing. It had made for a chilly day or two.

'If I call Munro, he won't like it. Anyway, I hate the telephone.' He was getting one to please her and Atkins; he planned to use it only to talk to her—if it worked.

'Munro likes you.' Munro was a CID detective at New Scotland Yard. Denton told her that it wasn't Munro's stamping ground; this was E Division. The police were jealous of their territories. But she got the operator and placed the call, and he found himself listening to the peculiar muted explosions of the lines and, muffled as if somehow offstage, another conversation about horses. Then he got the big room where, he knew, three telephones hung on a wall and, far away, Munro had a desk. Whoever answered sounded as if he was hung-over; then it took half a minute to get Munro to the telephone.

'Detective Inspector Munro here, sir.'

'Don't sir me, Munro—it's Denton.' He was shouting because of the telephone.

'Oh, cripes, I should have known. It's about your house, isn't it? And stop shouting; I can hear.'

'You know?'

'It's all over the Yard. Dead woman in her knickers, famous man's house—you'd think we were one of the cheap papers. Well, what?'

'They won't let me into my garden.'

'Quite right.'

'Munro, it's my house! The whole house can't be a crime scene!' Denton realized he was still shouting. He could be heard all over the street, he thought.

'"Course it can. Anyway, not my bailiwick; it's—'

'E Division, I know, I know. At least get me into my own quarters, Munro. My God, man, I live there!'

'Well, she may have died there, so you're out of it. Stay out. Sorry, truly, but this is police business, Denton. You'll probably be let back in tomorrow.'

'Tomorrow!'

'I'm sure you can find somewhere to stay.' Munro knew about Janet Striker and the two houses. However, he was careful not to sound sarcastic, or perhaps that tone didn't carry over the instrument.

'Hell.'

'Good to talk to you.'

'Hell again.'

He put the mouthpiece back on its hook and looked at Janet Striker. Atkins, who had been lurking in the doorway with the enormous dog, which was still in an ecstasy of tail and tongue at seeing him, muttered something about lettuces and turned away.

'Munro implied I should stay with you.'

She raised her eyebrows.

Denton chewed his lower lip. As if he had been running ever since first seeing her telegram and now had the first chance to catch his breath, he stood very still. He folded his arms. He was thinking that he hadn't given her time to tell him what she knew, if anything, about the body in his garden. He said, 'Munro says it's a woman. In her underclothes. Who found her?'

'One of the men putting in your heating.' Denton was having central heat installed, another enthusiasm of hers and Atkins's. He had said he'd have it torn out if it did anything to upset his peace of mind.

'How did you hear about it?'

'A detective came to question me. I suppose they saw the gate in the garden wall and thought the woman might have come from here.'

'And you told him she hadn't.'

'I told him I'd been out most of the morning, at my class at University College.' She was studying economics after half a life-time of, as she said, knowing nothing; the project in the Isle of Dogs was a result. 'He of course said he'd "verify my statement".' She smiled a little grimly.

'Nothing else? Nothing he could——?' He gave a one-sided shrug and a questioning look: *Nothing they could smear you with?* She had a past—prostitution, commitment to a prison for the criminally insane, although she had been neither criminal nor insane—and they both knew that she would be vulnerable in a police court and the press.

'Nothing.'

He looked at her and said, 'You know I love you.' It was a way of saying that she could tell him anything, and that now was the time to tell it.

'Yes, I know.' The tone committed her to nothing. She had dark eyebrows, rather thick; large eyes, beautifully shaped but often inscrutable. Now, she looked at him steadily and said, 'There is something. But it isn't about me.'

'What?'

She looked down at her hands, which were tented in front of her. 'The woman could be one Dr Bernat saw this morning.' Bernat was Denton's doctor and had a surgery at the corner.

'I don't follow you.'

'Bernat saw her early—before eight. His wife's away; he wanted a woman in the surgery with him and he sent for Mrs Cohan, but she was off doing the shopping so I went.' Mrs Cohan was her cook, housekeeper and seamstress; she lived in the basement with her husband.

Puzzled, Denton said, 'There's nothing wrong in that.'

'I didn't say there was.'

'Did you tell the detective that?'

'No.'

'Good God, why not? Janet, you know the police—'

'I told you, because of Bernat. Bernat's a friend as well as our doctor.'

They stared at each other. Denton surrendered to her seriousness. He said, 'What happened?'

'Bernat performed an illegal operation on her.'

'What illegal operation?'

'Oh, really, Denton! What operation is illegal?' She was quickly angry, then calm again. 'He aborted a pregnancy.'

'My God!'

'Oh, do grow up! You look like a parson who's just learned how to gamahuche. He aborted a pregnancy! And don't say "How could he do such a thing"! She said she had to get rid of it; he did it. What was the woman supposed to do, go to Harley Street and pay the rate the great ladies of society pay? My God, Denton, come into the real world—what do you suppose women do?'

'But—but—the law.'

'To hell with the law. Would you rather the woman carried the thing and had a child and then gave it away to God knows what? Would you rather she had half a dozen children before she's twenty-five, half of them dead before they're two?'

He flinched. He had been married once; his wife had carried four children, lost two, and killed herself while pregnant the last time. Janet knew all this; what she had said might not have been deliberate, but of course it had not been mere coincidence. He saw her regret what she had said, start to speak; he waved a hand and walked to a window, his left hand curled at his mouth, then turned back to her. 'Did she die at Bernat's?'

'Of course not.'

'What happened?'

She hesitated, then came to him. 'Bernat had to go to the Jewish Infirmary. The woman was afraid to be alone—not a childish sort of fear, something more real, maybe some*body*. I thought she was afraid of her husband; I'm not sure why. I couldn't understand her terribly well; she spoke some French and, I think, Russian. Anyway, I said she could come and rest here.'

Denton frowned but held his tongue; nothing could be changed now. After a silence, he said, 'Who saw you?'

'We walked up the street and came into your house and through the gardens—it was shorter. She was feeling weak. Denton, I didn't see the harm!'

'All right, through my house—were the heating men there?'

'Not yet, I think.'

'And to your house.'

'I put her in the Cohans' extra room. She didn't want to climb the stairs. Then Mrs Cohan came back and I told her the woman had been ill and needed to rest.' She shrugged. 'I went to my class.'

'That's everything?'

She nodded. He knew better than to ask again; when she said something, she had said it, and that was that. She played no games, no *Are you really sure?* or *Truly nothing?* He looked out of the window and then back at her. 'If it's the same woman, the coroner's autopsy will find out about the abortion—won't it?'

'I think so. It's what I worry about. She was only about two months along; I don't know how much evidence it would leave. But will they examine her womb?'

'It depends on the doctor and what they think happened. Probably they'll want to know if there was rape or sex of some kind. Probably, yes. Does Bernat know?'

'I sent Cohan with a message for him.'

Denton thought about what she had told him. 'If it's the same woman,' he said.

'How would I know? But how could it not be?'

He tried to think about that, shrugged. 'I have to get into my house. I have to know where we are—what Bernat's going to walk into. Janet, if they find out about the abortion—*and they will*—they'll find about you bringing the woman to my house. Somebody along the street saw you. Somebody always does. Then they'll track it back to Bernat.' He raised his eyes to meet hers. 'But you'll be in it.'

She said nothing.

'So they'll have you involved in the abortion and keeping evidence from the police. Then they'll try to make it you and Bernat killing her. Depending on what they've got in my garden.' He shook his head.

'I'd do it again the same way.'

'I know you would.' He kissed her forehead. 'If Bernat shows up, keep him away from the police—away from his surgery, too. Is your lawyer on the telephone? Call her and tell her to stand by. You're going to need her if the police want to talk to you again.' He held her against him. 'We've got through other things. We'll get through this.' He went out, snatching a hat from the waiting Atkins's hands and telling him to stay there.

CHAPTER

3

Denton was still wearing the old suit he had worn for the shooting, and he supposed he looked seedy and perhaps untrustworthy. Not, certainly, like a successful novelist who could afford to have central heating installed.

He walked back down to Guilford Street. He fumed over what she had done. He saw no way out of it, and he knew what a prosecutor would make of her in front of a jury—*Is it not true, Mrs Striker, that your husband committed you to an institution for the criminally insane? Is it not true, Mrs Striker, that you worked for years in a house of prostitution? Is it not true, Mrs Striker, that you assisted at the hideous procedure called abortion?* And she would say yes because she was honest and courageous. *Damn her.*

He turned into Lamb's Conduit Street, seeing his own house and beyond it the Lamb, debouching its midday clientele, afternoon closing almost on them. He had let most of the ground floor of his house to a draper; his own entrance was beyond it on the Lamb side, set back behind an iron gate. A policeman stood on his steps, probably the same one he had glimpsed earlier from the cab. Around his gate lounged half a dozen dispirited-looking men who would be, he supposed, journalists. His own face was not a well-known one, although his name was, but they surely would know whose house the police had taken over; still, Denton strode around them without hesitation or hurry and opened his gate and went in.

'Now then, sir.'

'Aha, Constable.' Denton smiled. Denton kept his voice too low for the journalists to hear.

The policeman scowled. 'You another newspaper scribbler?'

'I hope I don't look that bad.' He was trying to seem a cheerful, blind-to-the-obvious optimist: Hench-Rose came to his mind.

'One of the heating men?'

'Certainly not!' Denton forced a laugh. 'Heating man, indeed!'

'If you was one of the heating men come to go in and get his tools, you could have done.'

Oh, dammit! 'I just spoke with Detective Inspector Munro at New Scotland Yard.'

'Oh, yes?' The policeman squinted, possibly a sign of poor vision, more likely utter contempt for any interference from the Yard. 'Your name Allinson?'

Not to be caught out a second time, Denton hesitated. To be Allinson or not to be Allinson, that was the question—was Allinson, whoever he was, to be allowed in, or was he somebody to be arrested on sight? Denton temporized. 'I own this house, Constable.'

'That's very fine, sir, but you can't go in it today. Police order. If you don't like it, take it up with E Division. Superintendent Masham.' The constable, who appeared to be about forty and disappointed with the world, stared him in the eye without pity.

'But I—'

'Not a hope. Please leave the premises, sir.'

Denton sighed and turned around. Most of the journalists were hanging on his gate now, glad for any novelty. When they saw he had been defeated, they cheered and hooted; one waved his hat. Denton walked slowly back to them to find that they took him for one of their own. One shouted, 'Good try!' another, 'He's on to all our tricks.' As Denton pushed through them, one said, 'What paper?'

'*The Daily Crapper.*'

'We all write for that one!' Weak huzzas and haw-haw laughter.

Denton turned back towards Guilford Street and found Atkins waiting in front of the drapery shop. Denton shook his head.

'Thought I'd stay back,' Atkins said. 'Might be mistaken for one of them.'

Denton looked at the drapery shop's door. 'What do you think of trying the cellar?' A common cellar lay under both the shop and Denton's part of the house.

'Draper's got no cellar access.'

'Unless the heating men have made one.'

Atkins screwed up his face, then said, 'Aha. Pipes, and so on. Right, Colonel—good tactics. But if you think I'm going down a heating pipe, you got another think coming.'

'There wouldn't be a fire yet; what's the difficulty? Let's see if there's an opening, and then we'll talk about who's going into it.'

Atkins said he definitely was not going into any pipe, but Denton was already on his way up the drapery shop's steps. At the top, he said, 'Coming?' and held the door. Atkins came up but said again as he passed inside that he wasn't Meshach nor Abednego and wasn't going into any furnace, fiery or otherwise.

'Mr Henson!'

'Mr Denton!' The draper smiled and looked vaguely terrified to find his landlord inside his shop. A short, square man in his fifties, he was probably aware that the rent was lower than it might have been and that he didn't want it pegged where it probably should be. 'To what do I owe the honour of this visit, sir?'

'The central heating.'

'Ah, oh, the heating.' Mr Henson's facial tic suggested that he thought that heating might add to the rent. 'None yet, I'm afraid. Months yet.'

'Oh. I thought they might have installed a—pipe, register, whatever it is.'

'Oh, yes! Oh, indeed. The register. Yes. But there's no pipe yet and of course no heat.' Henson smiled. 'We're actually rather proud of our register. The clientele comment upon it—quite possibly the first in the trade. Several ladies told me they're looking forward to coming here in the cold months and standing on it.' Henson grinned, looked away in case the grin could have been taken as suggestive, muttered, 'Not that it won't cost me a good deal in coal—expenses frightful just now...' and then stared moodily at a display of velvets as if he regretted saying anything good about the central heating. He tried to shift the subject to the police and the rumours about the back garden, but Denton cut him off.

'Where's the register?'

'Right behind the bombazines. You see it there, near the cutting table—? Yes. Yes.'

Denton strode to it, Atkins behind him. At their feet was an ornate iron casting covering a two-by-three-foot hole in the shop floor; black iron branches and leaves curled and twined inside the rectangle to form a grating strong enough to bear human weight but with plenty of openings to let the heat rise.

'Fine register,' Denton said. 'I just wanted to make sure it was being done right.' He knelt; one knee gave a crack. He found the screws that held the register in place. He looked up at Atkins. 'Turn-screw?'

Atkins produced a stag-handled knife (Army and Navy Stores, 10/6, a Christmas gift from Janet Striker), opened a short screw blade at one end and held it out.

'You're a source of never-ending satisfaction.' Denton started in on the screws, which were bigger than the designer of the knife had expected and well sunk in the joists beneath. In time, however, he got them out, assuring Mr Henson along the way that he wanted only to check the supports under the register. When the last screw came free, he and Atkins lifted the register upside down, revealing that the underside was in fact a shallow box with louvres that could be moved from above to control the flow of heat, and laid it on the floor.

Denton took his hat off and put his head into the opening. A smell of damp and earth rose up. He put his head in farther and tried to look around: gloom greeted him. A dozen feet away, however, he could make out the bulk of a metal furnace, round, squat, already sprouting connections for pipes meant to go all over the house. 'Excellent,' he said. He rolled on his front and put his legs into the opening.

'You're going down there?' Henson said. The idea seemed to frighten him.

'We both are.'

'But—the hole—'

'Put the register back when we're down.'

'How will you get out, sir?'

'Cross that river when we get to it.' And Denton swung down, caught his weight on his hands and dropped to the cellar floor. Seconds later, Atkins's legs appeared; Denton embraced them, took Atkins's weight and lowered him until his feet touched the floor, too. Denton waved up into the hole. 'Close it up, Mr Henson. We're fine—all's well.'

'But hold the screws,' Atkins shouted. 'Just in case.' He muttered to Denton, 'I for one don't want to spend the bleeding night down here.'

Denton made his way towards the furnace and felt his way around it. It smelled of the foundry still, copperish and oily. Pieces of pipe lay higgledy-piggledy, and he nudged them aside like a swimmer moving through cluttered water.

'Light,' Atkins said behind him. Indeed, light was coming from uneven gaps in boards above their heads now; yet another, smaller hole was off to their right. The boards had been laid over a sawn opening so nobody would fall through.

'Oh, hell,' Denton said. 'That's my front hall up there. They've cut a damned hole in my front hall!'

'Two, Major.'

'What the hell!'

'The big one's for a register; the little one, my guess is, is for a pipe to the floor above.'

'They said the pipes would go in the walls!'

'Them pipes we just kicked about wouldn't fit inside a meat safe, much less a wall. My guess is, you're going to have pipes *in* the rooms. For company.'

Denton swore again and set about finding something to stand on. They both rummaged about the cellar, Denton discovering two more holes in the floor above, both towards the back of the house; through one, the rumble of men's voices came.

'Coppers,' Atkins whispered.

'Not very happy coppers.' Indeed, the voices sounded angry.

A table with three legs was found against the rear wall. They put it under the largest of the openings and Atkins held up the legless corner while Denton hoisted himself on the other end, first his buttocks and then his feet.

'Not very steady,' he said.

'Get on with it, General, it's destroying my back.'

Denton stood, slowly and uncertainly, then pushed the rough boards apart and grasped the edges of the hole, now level with his eyes. 'Here I go,' he said.

'In the name of God, go!'

Denton bent his knees and jumped; the table clattered into pieces; Atkins swore and lurched forward, and Denton heaved his abdomen up to the floor above, then flailed and squirmed and got his thighs up and at last his feet.

'Nothing to it.'

'My hat. What about me?'

'Find something else to stand on, then put up a hand.'

'Oh, yes, I will. Oh, in for a penny...' Atkins went off into the gloom. While he was gone, Denton looked around his downstairs hall, standing still because the police voices, now louder, were coming from beyond the door to Atkins's quarters. What he saw didn't please him: the carpets had been rolled back; the paintings—large, mostly bovine, bad (as he now knew)—had been stacked against a wall. The smaller hole near the house's front wall was matched, he saw, by another just like it in the ceiling. 'They're butchers!' he muttered.

'I'm back,' came a voice from the bigger hole. 'I found a crock.'

Denton lay down again, his torso canted into the hole, and extended an arm. Atkins was there; they clutched each other's wrist, and up Atkins came. He was both gamer and stronger than he let on: once he was drawn to the level of the floor, he swung up his other arm and a leg and scrambled the rest of the way like a boy. He lay on the floor on his back. 'We're now guilty of breaking and entering.'

'It's my house, so we didn't break.' They were both whispering.

'Crime scene. Probably hang the both of us.'

Denton indicated the stairs. 'Up.'

'I lost my hat down there. Object of virtue.'

'We'll get it later.'

They pushed the boards back over the hole. Denton tiptoed up the stairs that led to his rooms above. A voice from below was shouting something about lawyers. Atkins whispered, 'Bloodshed soon, from the sound of it.'

To Denton's surprise, his door was unlocked. Frowning, he put a finger to his lips, then slowly pushed the door open. The heavy curtains on the front window had been drawn—he had left them open—and the room was dim. Denton stepped in, turned to Atkins and heard a sudden exclamation and the clatter of something falling. He whirled and saw a large figure scrambling out of his own favourite armchair.

'What the hell!' He went one way, Atkins the other, Denton with an eye on the poker and Atkins apparently for a small chair, which he had picked up by the time the figure, now seen as a youngish man in an overcoat, said, 'Now, then!'

Denton's left foot struck something on the rug; he bent, his eyes still on the man, and felt a bottle by his shoe; he picked it up and started to brandish it as a weapon but at the same moment recognized the man. 'Sleeping on duty, Detective Constable Mankey?'

'Oh, it's you is it, Mr Denton! No need to be sarcastic, is there?'

'Perhaps you'd like another beer while you're here.' Denton held up the bottle—Fremlin's Elephant Brand (Special Quality). He tossed the bottle down the room to Atkins and yanked the curtains open, letting in a clouded light that nonetheless made the detective blink. The light revealed the room, a long one made before his ownership by knocking two rooms together: opposite the door, a fireplace and the armchair, books filling the wall above; far down, an alcove that served as a pantry, undoubtedly where the detective had found the beer; then a head-high porcelain stove (unused) and the stairs to the rooms above. At the far end was a large window that overlooked the garden; Denton had been making for it to try to see the dead woman when the detective had woken and jumped out of the chair. Nearer, in the wall opposite the pantry, was a dumb waiter, into whose open doors Atkins was now staring.

'Bloody hell!' Atkins whispered. 'They're putting a stovepipe up my dumb waiter!' He stared down the room at Denton. 'I will *not* carry a back-breaking load of dishes up and down them stairs!'

'Later, Sergeant, later!' He turned back to the detective. 'It is Mankey, isn't it? E Division?'

'Remarkable memory you have—make a good witness. Detective Constable Mankey, yes, sir. And I know you're Mr Denton. Two years ago, wasn't it? Attempted assault on you.'

'It was.' Denton jerked his head at the door. 'Let yourself in?'

'Quite proper, Mr Denton. This is a crime scene. I employed established procedure to effect entry.'

'You picked the lock, you mean. You have a warrant?'

'Warrant not necessary in the immediate vicinity of a crime of this magnitude.'

'Beer authorized under the same statute?'

'I'll pay you for the bloody beer!' Mankey pushed a large hand into his suit-jacket pocket.

'No, no, no—only ragging you, detective. Have another, if you like. It isn't a sin to catch a catnap when nothing's going on.' Atkins had disappeared into the pantry, now put his head out and murmured, 'Pale ale or lager?'

'Not for me,' Mankey said, trying for a pious tone. 'I was only washing down my bit of lunch.' He began to stuff into his overcoat pocket several pieces of tan paper, some with grease stains, that lay on and around the table beside Denton's armchair. Denton laughed. He waved at Atkins to leave the beer where it was. Mankey said huffily that Denton had no business being there and how had he got in, and he'd better leave at once or it would be a police matter.

Denton pulled over a small chair and sat. 'How was she killed?'

Mankey stopped stuffing papers and said, 'How do you know it's a she?'

'Munro told me.'

'Oh, so the Yard's putting its nose in, is it!'

'I called him; get off your high horse. Come on, Mankey, you know me, you know I'm not a suspect or even a witness—I was in the country shooting little birds, and thirty people can vouch for it.'

Mankey stood as if guarding the armchair against assault, sniffed, growled, 'That's to be verified.' He sniffed again. 'I interviewed the female in the house behind. *She* said you were shooting at some posh spot or other. I note that she was the same female that you saved from a murderer two years past by shooting him. Last year a madman put two bullets in your back. Now there's this. Things seem to happen to you, Mr Denton.'

'Some of the police think I'm actually a decent citizen. Friend of the force.'

'Hmp.'

'Oh, sit down, Mankey. I'm here now—it isn't going to do the Metropolitan Police any good to throw me out of my own house.'

Mankey stood for two seconds longer to show that he was not to be soft-soaped, and then he lowered his bulk back into the armchair. He was a wide man, almost bald; his round face was divided by a dark moustache that was so straight it looked like an iron bar he was carrying between nose and upper lip. Seated, Mankey kept his head up, his look severe: perhaps because essentially unsure—Denton had several volumes of the latest scientific psychology on the shelf above the detective's head and knew what deep insecurity was—he was trying to be outwardly overbearing. The unsureness showed, however, when he said, 'I suppose you'll spread it about that I was having forty winks and some refreshment up here.'

Denton waved a hand. 'I don't care if you ate the cheese and toasted the last loaf of bread. What I want to know is, how the hell did a dead woman get into my back garden?'

'So would we.'

'How did she die?'

'Waiting for the doc to tell us—if he ever gets here.' He frowned at Denton, then grunted and, looking around as if for spies, lowered his voice. 'Between you and me, I think her neck was broke.' He did a quick imitation of somebody whose head had been twisted so far to the side that the neck was broken— mouth open, tongue out, eyes wide—and snapped back to himself. 'And not out there, is my guess.'

'Where?'

'Can't say yet. Your house, I'd think.' He wiped fingers over his mouth. 'She was wrapped in an old tarpaulin and stuffed behind that outhouse of yours in the corner of the back garden. Wouldn't of been found for God knows how long if one of the workmen hadn't gone back there to pee.'

'He couldn't use the WC?'

'Habit, probably. Or maybe the water was off. Anyway, whoever killed her must of dragged her out there, but of course there's been boots all over the garden so I couldn't see what the hell went on. This case is a complete and utter hash.' He patted his head and combed a few hairs over the top with his fingers. 'Shouldn't be telling you this. Improper. I suppose you'll go to Munro with it.'

'Where's the medical man? When are they going to examine her?'

Mankey gave a sarcastic laugh. 'That's what all the carry-on's about downstairs.' He leaned forward, suddenly confidential, and Denton realized that Mankey was eager to talk, even to him. 'We'd have had a medico in here three hours ago if there wasn't two gents—I *don't* think—came busting in here, acting like little tin gods visiting the unwashed, and demanding the deceased! I ask you! It's been a right comedy.'

'From the Yard?'

'The Yard, my arse, pardon my French. They *say* they've got special authority from the Home Sec, but all they did was wave a bit of paper at us and come the high and mighty. I'd of thrown the pair of them out, but Steff—you don't know him, I think, new-made inspector—says no and tiptoes about like he don't want to hurt their feelings. Kept whispering to me about "protocol". I'd have given them protocol! Anybody can wave a bit of bloody paper!'

'I don't get it.'

'And nor do I! Steff went off and found a telephone and got on to our super, who's also, pardon me, a bit cautious, and *he* called some great man and he apparently called their lawyers, and the word came back that nobody's quite sure, it may be and maybe not, but it could be, or not, or perhaps, but we're to be nice to these two chaps until everybody makes sure his own arse is out of the line of fire.'

'You mean they may be legitimate.'

'And I may be the Prince of Wales. Legitimate what?'

'Special Branch?'

Mankey made a rude sound.

'I don't get it, Mankey.'

'I came up here to get away from them—talking about "their" body and "their" investigation. I needed that bottle of beer after an hour with them.'

'Are they still downstairs?'

'What d'you think the argy-bargy's about? It's a right disaster—I got a pile of cases working, four people to question in Red Lion Square, court appearance first thing Monday, and promised the wife to be home early to spade up the garden. I don't need two la-di-das waltzing in and wasting time when this investigation should have been open and closed in a morning! Now look at the time—' He pulled a fat watch from his waistcoat. 'After half-two. Tomorrow a Sunday, and I'll have to work to be where I should have been today. It's like the what-d'you-call-it. In that book. Running fast to stay in place. Judas Priest!'

'Will they do a post-mortem, do you think?'

'How would I know? If we ask for one, I suppose. No reason to right now—plain as your face how she died.'

'Sex thing? Raped?'

Mankey shrugged. 'Nothing obvious. Still has her knickers on.' Mankey stared at Denton, sucked on a space between two front teeth, and seemed to make a decision. 'Look: here's how I think it was. I think she was in this house, and I think she took her own clothes off and I think she had herself a lie-down. There's a black dress and a coat hanging up in a room downstairs, plus a bed's been laid on but not between the sheets, only somebody rumpled it and pulled up an old military blanket from the foot. That doesn't say rape to me, nor probably somebody having herself a morninger, either. What I see is a woman that hung up her outer clothes and lay down in her stockings and knickers and top, and somebody broke her neck and dragged her into your back garden and rolled her in a tarp and hid her.'

'That makes no sense.'

'Not yet, it doesn't. If we could get rid of the two milords, we might make some sense. I'd be out questioning the neighbours this minute if these two pips hadn't put the kybosh on it.'

'Why would they?'

'I'm damned if I know. They just keep saying it's confidential and they'll do their own questioning. Bastards.'

'Have you been over my whole house?'

'Hadn't anything else to do.'

'The attic? The one who assaulted me a couple of years ago got in through my attic, you remember.'

'I looked. Nothing. No sign of entry anywhere. So how did she get in? How did the killer get in?' Mankey eyed Denton. 'Lot of keys to your house floating about, Mr Denton?'

'Me, Atkins—the man who was with me.' He didn't want to say anything about Janet, but as quickly as he thought that, he realized that holding something back would return to hurt him. Or her. He mumbled, 'And a set at a neighbour's.' He added in a near-whisper, 'The house behind.'

'That'll bear looking into, then.' If he had formed any idea of Denton's relationship with the house behind, Mankey showed nothing. He got to his feet, fighting with the chair and his overcoat, then pulling himself up to his full height, though not quite as tall as Denton. 'Want to see her?'

Mankey started down the room; Denton followed. He was aware as he passed the dumb waiter that the doors, which had been open, were closed—he had wanted to look in to see what damage the heating men had done—and then he realized that Atkins had disappeared and that he had probably closed the doors. The open dumb waiter was Atkins's means of listening in from downstairs on what was said in Denton's sitting room; he must have closed the doors to prevent Denton's conversation with Mankey from being heard. Worth every penny, Atkins.

At the far end of the room, Mankey was parting the curtains just enough to allow them to look down into the back garden. The constable was huddled by the cold frame now, leaning against the wall and looking bored and miserable. In the left-hand corner of the garden from where they stood was an old brick privy, now a tool shed. A stained tarpaulin covered a mound next to it, from which poked on the side towards the house two rather heavy legs in black stockings.

'Can't see much,' Denton said.

'All you're going to see.'

'What's she like?'

'Hasn't seen forty. Bit on the heavy side. Underclothing fairly good quality. Wedding ring.'

'Shoes?'

'In with the dress and coat. Hat, too.'

'Handbag?'

Mankey glanced at him. 'Haven't found it yet. Thought it might have gone over the wall into the garden behind, but no such luck.'

'Robbery?'

Mankey shrugged and dropped the curtains. Denton parted them again with three fingers and looked down. 'I might know her.'

'What's that?'

'She may have known my house. Even had a key. I have one or two former female, mm, friends.' In fact, he had several, but he had never given any of them a key. He realized he had told Mankey earlier that only Atkins and 'a neighbour' had keys.

Mankey, however, was off on his own tack. 'The face is not the one you knew, if you knew her. Right ugly now. Still—' Mankey thought it over. 'Help no end if you knew her.' He took Denton by only the fabric of his suit jacket and pulled him towards the door, down to Atkins's part of the house. 'The lords of creation will raise merry hell if they see us, so—a word to the wise.'

But the lords of creation and, presumably, Detective Inspector Steff had moved their argument to the front of the house, because now the raised voices were coming from the downstairs hall. Somebody new at the door, Denton guessed, maybe the medical man. Or the journalists.

Mankey said, 'Be quick now.' They passed through Atkins's little sitting room in three strides and then were out in the garden, Mankey signalling the constable to remove the tarpaulin.

The constable pointed at Denton and said, 'That chap was up on the—'

'He's a witness.'

The constable dragged the tarpaulin partway off but left the face mostly covered. Mankey bellowed, 'We want to see her face, you bloody fool, not her cunt!'

Denton went around the stockinged feet—surprisingly small, he thought—and knelt by the head. The face was twisted towards him, as Mankey had pantomimed. It was, indeed, grotesque.

She lay on her back in a part of the garden that Atkins had already dug over and manured. The smell of wet earth and horse dung mixed with a smell that came from her, urine and eau de cologne. The V of drawers was dry but discoloured below her corset, that shade called Isabella after the Spanish queen who wouldn't wash her underclothes until the Moors left. Denton looked up at Mankey.

Mankey grunted. 'She pissed herself. Not uncommon. But somebody may have cleaned her up. God knows why.'

Denton reached to touch her hair.

'Don't touch her! Do you know her, or don't you?'

The hair was black, a few grey hairs sprinkled through it. Not too old to be pregnant, but still—He reached to touch the wedding ring and Mankey hissed, 'No!'

'Might be initials in it.'

'That's for us to find out. Do you know her or don't you?'

He looked again at the V where the plump thighs came together. What sign would an abortion leave? He really knew nothing. He saw no blood there, but...

The underclothes were better, he thought, than Mankey had said. Denton knew a bit about underclothes, had removed some quite expensive ones; these were of that sort, although perhaps not new.

He stood and brushed grains of dirt from his fingers. 'No,' he said. 'I don't know her.'

'Off you go, then.'

Mankey indicated the wall and the door in it with a sideways nod of his head.

'Door's locked,' the constable said as he dragged the tarpaulin back over the body and tucked it around her with surprising delicacy.

Mankey flushed. 'Well, who the hell's got the key?'

'Inspector. Wouldn't trust me with it, oh, no—'

'Hell and damnation!' Mankey turned back towards the house. 'You stay out here!' he shouted at Denton over his shoulder. Denton waited until the detective had cleared the doorframe, then went after him, ignoring something called out by the constable. Once in Atkins's sitting room, he made for the stairs but stopped as Mankey, preparing to open the door into the downstairs hall, was flung back by the door's sudden opening in his face. Atkins seemed to fall into the room; behind him, a large blond man had Atkins's left arm up behind his back and was pushing him forwards in a pained crouch.

'You want your arm broken, arsehole, keep giving me sauce!' the blond man said, adding as he came by Mankey, 'Get out.' He let go of Atkins's wrist and pushed him at the same time, and Atkins almost fell into Denton before pulling himself up, tears in his eyes and trying to straighten his left arm.

'Who the hell are you?' the blond man shouted. He was almost as tall as Denton, heavier, at least fifteen years younger. His skin was red with sun; Denton thought *soldier* and said, holding Atkins upright, 'I'd ask the same of you.'

'Don't you give me any lip! I asked who you are!' His accent was lower than middle class; Denton had learned that much of England. Behind him, another, only slightly smaller man came in to stand in the doorway as if blocking it.

'I own this house. You're trespassing.'

'My arse! Let go of that little runt; he's under arrest.'

'Are you a policeman?'

The blond head came forward, bullish, the eyes narrowed. 'I'm anything I want to be, dad. Now sit over there in the corner before I put you under arrest, too.'

Denton stepped in front of Atkins. 'Show me your warrant card.'

Mankey was looking at one and then the other. Behind the man in the doorway, another figure, possibly that of Steff, the inspector, appeared and then as quickly disappeared.

'I'll show you my bloody fist if you don't sit down!'

'If you don't have a warrant card, you're not a policeman. Show it to me or get out.'

'This is my warrant card—' The blond man closed the space between them and began to swing his right hand, his left going out backhanded to grab Denton's shirt-front. Denton blocked the right hand and hit the reddened face with his left, a straight, short blow that knocked the man backwards and down. Blood began to spurt from his nose.

Mankey said, 'That tears it.'

The man in the doorway came into the room. His hands, closed into fists, were raised partway. Seeing that his partner was not going to get up, he stopped.

'Want to show me your warrant card?' Denton said.

'Now, now, what's all this?' a voice said from the doorway. The voice was big, cultivated, slightly brutal in the way that politicians' can sometimes seem brutal. He moved into the now crowded sitting room, pushing the standing man aside with the back of one hand, not even looking at him. As if they were meeting at a dinner, he said, 'It's Denton, isn't it? I thought so. We've met.'

He held out his hand. Denton pulled the face—bearded, sixty, fleshy—and a name from rather distant memory: 'Mr Freethorne, I think.' He allowed his hand to be taken, squeezed.

'We met at the Anselms', in fact.' Freethorne smiled, the smile meaningless, heartless, practised. He was a solicitor who had made a good deal of money out of vigorous assertions of novel, usually successful, interpretations of the dimmer recesses of the law.

'What's going on here, sir?' He glanced at the man on the floor, who was now sitting up with his head hanging back, pinching the bridge of his nose in big fingers.

'These bullies seem to have invaded my house.'

Freethorne laughed. 'No, no, that won't do. They're here officially.'

'They behaved in a way that no British policeman behaves. They were brutalizing Atkins, and that one on the floor tried to assault me. Detective Mankey was a witness.' Mankey flinched.

'Resisting arrest,' the standing one of the pair said. He was still staying well back from Denton.

Denton whirled on him. 'You're not policemen! You can't make arrests!'

'Now, now, you don't know that, Denton.' Freethorne had slid into the voice of sweet reason that he sometimes used with difficult clients. 'Things are not always what they seem. The power to arrest in fact resides in citizens——III Henry, 2.174——under many circumstances, and who is to say without examination what powers these men possess? If a minister signs a paper asserting certain powers for certain persons as officers of the Crown, they then are possessed of those powers.' He smiled again.

'If either of them lays a hand on me or Atkins, I'll put him on the floor again.' The one with the bleeding nose had got to his feet but now took a step backwards and leaned against the wall. Denton said, 'If you bleed on Atkins's floor, I'll damned well pitch you out into the garden.'

'Now, now, now——!'

'And what's your interest here, anyway, Freethorne?'

'I have been brought in to assure the police that in fact the Home Office authorization carried by these two is genuine. I am the legal adviser to the Home Secretary.' He held up a rather pale, puffy hand. 'I should warn you not to make statements that may complicate matters, Mr Denton. Although of course welcome here, you are a guest in this country; I shouldn't like to see you endanger that status.' He looked around as if studying a distant landscape. 'And am I not correct that a Mrs Striker occupies the house behind? She, it would seem to me, would also be vulnerable if——if...' He smiled.

'One more word, and it's slander.'

'No, no, no.' He chuckled. 'Let me be the judge of what is and isn't slander.' Freethorne laughed. 'We're a long, long way from slander.' Turning suddenly on the second of the two younger men, he said, 'Clean him up.' The first one was holding a doily from one of Atkins's side tables to staunch the blood still oozing from his nose. He muttered, 'Broken.' Freethorne seemed not to hear him; turning back to Denton, he said, 'I suggest you let well alone. We'll simply forget that anything happened here, shall we? An Englishman's home is his castle, even an American-in-England's home; you were defending your castle and didn't understand the situation, perhaps. Detective Mankey saw nothing remarkable, I'm sure. Nor did you,' he said to Atkins, the tone loud with the trumpets of class.

'I saw, and I felt. Sir.'

Freethorne's eyes swivelled to Denton, seemed to expect something, were disappointed. Freethorne gave a small shrug and a smaller smile. 'I think if you would remove to some other part of the house...?'

'Gladly.' With a look at Mankey, Denton took Atkins's arms and piloted him towards the stairs, pushing him ahead. Freethorne turned away and beckoned towards the doorway.

Passing the dumb waiter, Atkins opened the doors and looked up into the well as if examining it, then shook his head and went on up ahead of Denton.

At the top, Denton closed the door behind him, saw Atkins already standing at the rear window. Denton said, 'I'm sorry.'

Atkins turned from looking into the back garden. 'I've had worse done to me in the non-coms' mess. Nasty tykes, though, those two. I'd nipped down behind you and the detective to find myself a hat, and they grabbed me. Going to "question" me, oh yes.' He glanced again through the window. 'Garden's a complete ruin. Bloody cops are the real criminals hereabouts.'

'Did you see anything down there?'

'Just poked my head into my bedroom when they grabbed me. Saw a black dress hanging on a hook, bed a bit rumpled. That was it.'

Denton chewed on his lower lip. 'I ought to have a look.'

'Don't chance your arm, Major—that's a pair of very nasty boys. Every regiment's got them—adjutant's bullyraggers.'

Atkins raised his head at a sound, put a finger to his lips and went to the dumb waiter, opened one door and put his head in. Without removing his head, he beckoned Denton with a finger, opening the other door with his free hand. Denton went to stand next to him and leaned into the dark shaft. From below, Freethorne's rich voice floated up, hollowed a little by the space. He sounded patient but authoritative, menacing because so unemotional: he was cautioning somebody—presumably the two younger men—to go slowly and less violently. 'Kings,' he said with the unction of a man who had advised kings, 'don't have to insist; their being kings is all the insistence they need. Practise to be quiet.'

Then there was the rumble of another voice, and then footsteps going away. After a silence, two voices spoke at once, then one, and then, seeming to come closer as it spoke, the rough voice of the man Denton had put on the floor said, '...getting precisely nowhere.' *Getting* sounded like 'gedding' because of his damaged nose. Atkins nudged Denton. A second voice murmured something and the first one said in the same denasalized way, 'Id's a disaster. I say we go back to Bard's.'

The other voice muttered something that sounded like 'Gorman.'

'Gorban'd bedder try it! Bloody duffer! Hib and his "rules of war". One more like this and I'll go right over that brick he has for a head and straight to M.'

The murmur seemed to disagree.

'He couldn't think fast if you poured petrol down his throat and set fire to his arsehole. Let him come and try to argue it out with this inspector clod. Bloody stolid idiot! We never should have done id this way. Bring our own hearse right off was what we should have done, couple of strong boys, tell the coppers to suck eggs and take her away. *Fade accomply!* They don't like id, show them what a revolver looks like. These bloody abateurs make me puke.'

Then the other voice murmured for almost a minute, and at last the rough one said, 'All right, all right. But if I ever see that tall American shit again, I'll fucking kill him.' The other voice said something sharp, the word 'hearse' perhaps understandable, and there were footsteps, and a door slammed.

Atkins threw himself back from the dumb waiter and hurried to the front window. Denton came behind a little more slowly, joined Atkins at the corner of the window, where it was possible to look down at the front steps and, by shifting a little more towards the middle, the gate and the street.

The scene had changed since he had been out there—when? an hour ago? A police hearse was drawn up at the kerb now, and the journalists, formerly draped on fence and gate, were penned up across the street by three constables. Two men with a rolled stretcher were standing between Denton's gate and his front door, one leaning on the stretcher's poles, the other back on his elbows against the iron fence. They looked at each other and shook their heads, then fell into their same positions. A second hearse, plain but more clearly civilian, was parked in the middle of the street. The neighbours' servants stood in little clusters, enjoying the spectacle.

On Denton's front steps, Mankey, foreshortened but recognizable, stood with a heavier man, also recognizably a police type, almost certainly Detective Inspector Steff. In the doorway, the two 'bullyraggers', as Atkins had called them, were just making their appearance; a bulk behind them seemed to be Freethorne. They gave the odd impression that they were in possession of the house; the police, lower down and outside, seemed to be suing for permission to enter—a little tableau of No Room at the Inn.

'The nasty boys,' Atkins muttered, jabbing a finger at the pair.

'I don't get it. What do you think he meant by "Bart's"? The hospital? It makes no sense that they're from a hospital.'

'Right, and who's Gorman or Gorban? And who's M? Gorman/Gorban is a bleeding idiot, I got that much, but if we gathered together all the idiots who answered to Gorman or Gorban, we'd have ourselves a mob.'

Denton recognized the face turned half towards him as the owner of the rougher voice of the dumb waiter: he was flushed, his nose swollen, and, even seen partly from above, contorted with feeling—one of those people who use anger, always on call, as a weapon. 'A bullyragger, indeed,' Denton said aloud. The man was better dressed than the detectives, clothes proclaiming a better class, whatever the truth of him. The shoe on the top step was distinctly a good one. 'Little tin gods' and 'milords' had been what Mankey had called the pair.

'Gent?' he muttered to Atkins.

'Gent, my hat. Anybody can wear a gent's shoes.'

The man was wearing an overcoat, open, over a dark double-breasted suit, in the lapel of which something glinted. 'What's that in his buttonhole?'

'Badge. Looks like a V. Greek to me.'

Afraid that one of the four would look up, Denton said, 'We'd best go.'

'Might miss something.'

'You're welcome to stay.'

'Look there!'

The man with the bruised nose was gesturing towards the street. The detectives turned and looked. The police stretcher-men looked, as well, and one opened the gate and stood behind it as if he were the gatekeeper. From the civilian hearse came two more men and another stretcher. Ahead of them the detectives parted; the bruised nose stood aside; the stretcher-men progressed up Denton's front steps and in the front door.

'Coppers have given up,' Atkins said. 'Serves them bloody right for savaging my garden.' He hurried to the back window, Denton following more slowly. He reached the window in time to see the stretcher-men come out through the rear door. Exiting behind them, the bruised nose waved the constable out of the way, and, seconds later, the stretcher was down on the ground next to the body and the tarpaulin had been whisked away.

'Shows the power of not taking no for answer,' Atkins whispered.

The two men lifted the body to the stretcher, rubbed dirt from their hands, placed themselves between the handles and picked up their burden.

'What price police procedure now, eh?' Atkins said. 'What a lot of duffers!' He hurried back to the front window. Denton, still at the back, watched his rear garden empty, the constable coming last, pausing to look back at the door as if checking that everything was in order, then vanishing.

'Are they out of the house?' he said.

'Just clearing the front door.'

'Time to go, then—strike while the iron is hot.' He gestured towards the empty garden. He walked up the room and took a derringer from a small box near his armchair, checked that it was loaded and put it in his jacket pocket. 'Just in case.'

'Right—shoot a policeman, the end to a perfect afternoon.'

CHAPTER 4

Hyam Cohan was a stocky man with a battered face he had earned as the Stepney Jew-Boy a dozen years before: he had taken the insult 'Jew-boy' and pounded it back into gentiles' faces in the boxing ring. Born in Stepney, he sounded 'Cockney' (Denton's word for anybody who didn't sound upper class). Now, he and his wife lived downstairs in Janet Striker's house and worked for her, and Hyam was opening a boxing school in east London: 'Masada—for Jews Who Want to Fight!'

'I been chasing Dr Bernat all over the East End,' Cohan was saying. 'I come on him finally in Limehouse Cut, putting ointment on a baby got burned when the kettle fell over. Not the way for an observant Jew to spend *Shabbat*—which I ain't.'

It was an hour since Denton had come over the back wall from his own house. He said, 'Did you tell him about the dead woman?'

'I told him, right, somebody found a woman dead in Denton's garden, so come straight to Mrs Striker's, she wants you. I didn't know nothing more; what am I supposed to say?'

Janet Striker patted his shoulder. 'You did just right. You go to Leah now.'

'She still bad?'

'One of her spells. One of her days. You go and stay with her.'

'I knew it. The instant I heard "dead woman", I knew it. It'll last a week, it will.' He looked at Denton and shook his head. 'I'd rather go twenty rounds with Bob Habbijam.'

'How's the boxing school?'

'Opening tomorrow, six in the after, everything ready but some paint that's still wet.' Cohan pulled a folded paper out of a deep coat pocket. 'The neighbourhood's champing at the bit, but some people don't like us.' He unfolded the paper, which turned out to be a four-page tabloid sheet, at the top 'THE COMMAND!' and yesterday's date, then 'Your Marching Orders for Britain's Deliverance!' Below that, in italics, a quotation:

> *Modern imperialism is really run by half a dozen financial houses, many of them Jewish, to whom politics is a counter in the game of buying and selling securities and the people are convenient pawns.*
>
> Robert Blatchford

'Who's Robert Blatchford when he's at home?'

'A noted socialist,' Janet said, her voice metallic. She had told him she thought she was a socialist now.

In smaller type, heading a block of text that ran right across the page, was a large headline, 'The Jews Forget What Happened at Masada!' Denton looked up from reading.

'Everybody in Masada committed suicide,' Cohan said. 'But the Romans never conquered them, that's the prize in the cracker.'

The article ranged from attacks on 'a hook-nosed Rothschild behind every sweater' (a sweater being what Denton would have called a sweat shop) to 'long-bearded Ikeys tailoring cheap clothes to steal jobs from British seamstresses!' Cohan's boxing club, however, was the article's springboard and also its climax: 'Let no

Asiatic invader of our shores mistake: tho' we know Jews cannot fight in fair contest, we know too that banded together in their garlic-smelling bands, they will threaten the hard-working men and women of a purer race. Let them beware, therefore! We will not let them arm! We will not let them learn to use their fists! THIS IS A COMMAND!'

Denton crumpled the paper. 'Who writes this stuff?'

Cohan shrugged. 'They call themselves "The Commando". Like they was Boers. They march up and down the Jewish streets singing hymns and shouting "Jews out!" and other nice things. Quite a fine lot of fellas.'

Janet Striker had taken the page and was spreading it flat again. 'You haven't lived there, Denton; you don't know what they're like. It's ugly, ugly.'

'The police?'

'The police have better things to do. Some of them *are* the police, anyway; that's how they're allowed to march. A lot of them are dockworkers, courtesy of Ben Tillett.' She handed the paper back to Cohan. 'It's disgusting.'

'Why d'you think I'm starting a place for Jews to learn to fight?'

'Be a mite careful,' Denton said.

'The *gentiles* want to fight, I'll give them fight. Present company excepted.'

'Now, now...' Denton followed him to the door that led downstairs. 'Are you and I sparring tomorrow? I can't give it the time today.' He had been working with Cohan for several months, adding the lay science of boxing to a life of rough and tumble.

'Not tomorrow, guv; I've lost today and still a gobbet of things to do. Come Tuesday, say half-four.'

Denton smiled. 'No gentiles to be found on the premises during business hours?'

'No offence, guv, but I want my lads to see the place is for yids.' He tapped Denton lightly on the chin with a fist and went off towards his part of the house.

'Poor Hyam—one of Leah's spells is just what he doesn't need right now.' Janet Striker watched him go. 'She's sitting down there in the dark with an apron over her head. I tried to talk to her; she simply mutters in Yiddish.'

'You understand Yiddish.'

'Not when she's like this. Anyway, I don't understand much.' She had lived for a dozen years in the East End when she was on her uppers, knew some Yiddish and some Italian and a little Chinese, the way travellers know enough of a language to survive. 'Hers is sufferers' Yiddish.'

'Will she really be like that for a week?'

'She's always on the verge of one of her spells. She's never got over the pogroms. They did something to her mind, or her spirit, whatever it is. Her sister was burned alive with a lot of other children. Leah will never get over it.'

Denton hesitated and then said, 'Where was she when the woman in my garden was killed?'

'Oh, Denton!'

'They're going to ask her, Janet! They're going to lean on everybody from our two houses—that dead woman didn't fall out of the sky.'

'Somebody must have come in off the street. It could have been one of the workmen.'

'So what was she doing in my house?'

'I don't know. I don't know!' She touched his arm. 'Don't say it—don't say I never should have brought her there.'

He shrugged. The doorbell clanged; footsteps sounded overhead, then clattered down a flight of stairs—the one maid she employed. 'That'll be Bernat,' he said.

'Or the police.'

The house was silent as they waited. The dog barked from her back garden: Atkins was out there, throwing a ball for it. Denton said, 'Rupert's happy, anyway.'

The footsteps came towards them, and the maid knocked and put her head in and said, 'The doctor, ma'am. Mr Bernat.' She was young, rather wispy, Scottish. She was seventeen, looked fourteen, had been living rough on the street, believed in ghosts and witches, seemed to fear everything and everybody and always had some sort of foolish weapon about: a stick propped in a corner; a kitchen knife used to pare apples; a stone.

'In here, Annie.' The frightened face vanished.

'You should fatten that girl up.'

'It isn't food, Denton. She's a stray.'

A few seconds later, Dr Bernat pushed the door fully open, stood there looking at the two of them, and came slowly in. He nodded at Denton, gave a crooked smile to Janet Striker.

'We have a dead woman, it is being said.'

She told him it quickly—the body, the tarpaulin, the workman. When she was done, she said, 'I think it's the same woman, doctor. The same dress.'

He looked at Denton, then at her. 'He knows?'

'Of course I know. The—illegal operation this morning. But she didn't die of that. Her neck's been broken.' His anger showed.

Bernat frowned and sighed and looked at his hands. He was a large man, bald on top with abundant black hair, very curly, around the sides and back. His face was made to smile; now, sombre and frightened, it seemed to collapse. He said, 'I am so sorry I brought Mrs Striker into it.' His Rs were guttural, 'sorry' coming from far down in his throat.

'It wasn't your doing! I offered.'

Bernat almost whispered, 'I could have refused you.' He looked at Denton, his face miserable. 'I did not think.'

'Why? Why did you do such a thing? The money?'

Bernat stared at him, clearly not understanding, then seeing what was meant. He tried to smile. 'Not for money, no. For—she was very frightened. Of her husband. Of, of—losing her job. Of life, you know?' His face collapsed again. 'And now she is dead?'

Mrs Striker began to walk up and down. 'The trouble will come if they do a medical examination. Any competent medical man will know she had an abortion, isn't that right?'

'Yes, yes—anybody competent.'

'She'll have been seen, either going into your surgery or coming along the street with me.'

'It was very early. It was morning, still not good light. Maybe nobody saw.'

Denton sneered at him. 'Somebody always sees when you don't want them to. You can't waste time expecting miracles, doctor.' He bent forward, hands on his knees. 'Look, Janet and I have been talking. I have a first-rate legal man I can bring in. Janet has a good solicitor, too, a woman. The sooner you start to work out a defence, the better.'

'What *defence*?' Bernat smiled. 'That I did not do it? But I did do it! I had to do it! What am I to do, go before the justice and say "My lord, I am too pure, too good to do that thing"? And deny what I believe, and what I practise? No, no, I did it. My regret is Mrs Striker.'

She turned on him. 'Mrs Striker can take care of herself. The police will come back here soon, today or tomorrow; they'll come to you, too. Denton says we should say nothing to them and have a legal person with us when we're questioned.'

'That is like saying we did something, Mrs Striker.'

Denton interrupted them. 'What was she wearing, the woman on whom you operated, doctor?'

'Oh—maybe—black? I think black.'

'I've told you—' Janet Striker began; Denton waved her silent. 'What was her underclothing?'

'Oh, I don't—she removed, you know, her clothes—' He looked at Janet Striker. 'Did she not?'

'I didn't see the procedure; you wanted a woman there, you said, but I didn't watch. But, yes, she took her clothes off. Denton, her underclothes were—'

Again, he waved her silent. 'Doctor?'

Bernat shook his head. 'I didn't see. I saw her nude; I saw her all dressed. I didn't see her halfway.'

Denton glanced at Janet. 'Old or young?'

'Mmm—maybe some of each. But, I think, more young, perhaps—thirty? More?'

'Doctor, would the operation have left any sign on the woman's body? On the outside, I mean?'

'No, of course not. What sign? No, this is the simplest of things. In the womb, yes—they will know.' He tapped the knuckles of his fists together. 'They will send me to prison, yes?'

Denton went to a window that looked down into the back. Atkins was still out there with his dog. He looked much younger, happy, uncaring. Denton said, 'I hate lying to the police.'

'There have been no lies yet, Denton!'

'Not of commission, no.'

'Ah, I see—because I didn't tell them about bringing her here, I lied—is that it?'

'Yes!' His voice was bitter. 'And I hate it that you felt you had to!'

She didn't spit; she didn't erupt. She looked at him for several seconds and then turned away. 'We're on our own, doctor.'

Denton went after her. 'That isn't what I meant!'

'You meant you won't lie for me! Isn't that it?'

He faced her, her strength, her independence. He sagged. 'Yes, I would. I'd lie for you. And I'd hate it.' He stopped himself from saying *And I'd hate you.*

She put her right hand on his chest, then patted it twice, so lightly he didn't feel it through his jacket and waistcoat. 'So that three of us may go to prison,' she said.

'No.' He caught her hand. 'We won't let it come to that. It can't!'

'And what do I tell them I did to this woman this morning?' Bernat said.

Janet released Denton's hand. 'You tell them she complained of "women's trouble" and you did a pelvic examination and found signs of a recent miscarriage. I had come to the surgery to consult with you about Mrs Cohan, whose mental state isn't of the best— and that's true, of course—and when your patient said after the examination that she felt ill, I offered to bring her home with me so she could lie down. You had to go to the hospital—which is true.' She looked at Denton. 'That'll do, won't it?'

Denton nodded. 'Doctor?'

Bernat smiled. 'Unlike you, Mr Denton, I can lie. It is part of the practice of medicine. Yes, Mrs Striker, that will do. Maybe I will look in my ledger to see what I wrote of the patient, although in fact I do not use the word "abortion", ever.' Still seated, he looked up at Denton. 'I know you do not approve, Mr Denton. You are a moral man—as am I. It is a moral matter, each way—mine and yours. The law—?' He shrugged. 'The law is not a moral matter; it is—Shakespeare says the law is an ass, yes?'

Denton thought it was foolish to correct him at such a time. 'I think the author wasn't being serious. But, yes, mm, somebody said that.'

Bernat stood. 'Maybe I have seen more of the law being an ass than you. Being a Jew, I have seen the Hungarian law that says that a Jew cannot be a member of the parliament; I have seen the Berlin law that says a nice hotel can put up a sign, "No Jews." I have seen the Russian law that says Jews cannot live except in what they nicely call the "Pale of Settlement". I see the English law that says a woman cannot abort a pregnancy, even if she has six children and a drunken husband. The law is an ass.' He put out his hand. 'I am sorry, sorry in the depth of my heart, to involve this lady in my crime. And I am sorry to involve you in lying. I know it gives you pain. But to do it for her—that is a great thing.'

Bernat went out. Janet seemed not to notice that he was gone; she began to move around the room as if it were somebody else's, picking up things and putting them down, staring at a small watercolour of boats. Then she said, 'I'll never go back to prison. Never—never!' She whirled to face him. 'I'll kill myself first!' When he said nothing—what had she expected, approval?—she said, 'Would you kill me if I asked you?'

He felt sick. 'You know I never could. Never would.' He was sick because he thought he was losing her: it was as if she were shrinking as he looked at her, disappearing into herself. She had started to disappear when she had told him about the abortion.

She turned away from him. 'I'll find my own way to do it if I have to.'

The institution to which her husband had condemned her had been a prison for the 'criminally insane'. She had been neither criminal nor insane, but only a woman not yet twenty, made desperate by her husband's brutality. He had been older, had 'bought' her from her mother—'bought' was Janet's word—and had used her as a sexual toy and victim. When she had revolted, too late, and tried to push him down a flight of stairs, he had her put away: the court had understood and disapproved of 'unwomanly violence' and 'irrational disobedience'.

Now, evening coming on, Denton was walking, thinking of her, her past, then of their shared present and the abortion. She had, perhaps not meaning to, made it a test; he had failed. Then his only grudging willingness to lie for her; then this about killing her. It was all unlike her, he thought, then admitted it was unlike only one part of her; there was another, lurking part of Janet Striker that was less brave, less stoic than the Janet he mostly knew. At her core was a Janet of ferocious independence and a crippling fear of its loss. In the terms of one of Denton's novels, that fear was her demon—one that might drive her even to suicide.

'I thought love would be enough,' his wife had said to him a year before she killed herself. 'It ain't, though—love ain't ever enough for what happens.' She had been grey-faced from coming off a binge when she had lain in bed for days, drinking whiskey from bottles she thought he didn't know about, not understanding that he had given up. He had already discovered that love was not enough. He was twenty-five.

And now Janet Striker.

He passed the front of his own house. The hearses and the constables and the journalists and the housemaids were gone, the show over. He nodded at the lone policeman who stood at his front door; the man touched a finger to his helmet. The house was dark. Denton remembered that he had decided to fire the heating installers; how would he restore the house to what it had been? Holes everywhere, the dumb waiter jammed into its blocks—

He walked down Great Ormond Street, picked his way to the Museum, then down to Soho, and the narrow streets there. It was Saturday evening; the French and Italian restaurants were filling, carriages and cabs trying to thread what little way was open, drivers shouting. He'd have brought her here, other nights; tonight it was useless even to ask her.

He tried to think of the dead woman. Puzzles interested him, criminal puzzles most of all. Now, his brain could focus only on Janet. The dead woman was merely a curiosity, a quirk, somehow a cause but not real.

He went into Kettner's and ate a little and drank too much.

CHAPTER

5

tkins and Rupert had gone off to one of Atkins's pals. Denton slept in an extra bedroom in Janet's house, not in her bed. The sense of separation was worse than when he travelled. Both of them lived in both their houses, always until now comfortable in crossing the back gardens and going in and out. Atkins and Hyam Cohan gardened together; Mrs Cohan, when she was out from under her dark cloud, was often at Denton's, fitting a dress to Janet or quietly sewing while they talked. Janet and Denton slept now in his bed, now hers. And here he was, sleeping alone in a narrow room that smelled of camphor.

And there she was, alone with her door closed.

The old dream returned after an absence of almost a year—his wife's suicide. He had thought it had left him for good, as if Janet had exorcised it. Now it showed that it had been only quiescent: he was standing inside the window of the farmhouse he had built in Iowa, four crude rooms. He was watching his wife walk away into the meadow where in life he had found her, the mostly empty lye jug beside her. She had lived for three terrible days, no doctor near, but in the dream he went after her and found her dead, diseased-looking bones, but this time the corpse of the unborn baby she had been carrying lay near her. A huge, gaunt horse loomed over it; as Denton came close it lowered its head to the baby and began to eat it.

He woke trying to shout, strangled, coughing. Cold sweat covered him.

The house was silent. Had anyone heard him? Had he made any sound? He stripped off his nightshirt and stood by the window, the room cold. He stared down into the blackness of her garden.

The horse in the dream frightened him. Horses often came into his dreams of her, always threatening. He shuddered.

'The baby,' he whispered. *The abortion.*

In the morning, Janet went off to church. He went around to his own house again, found another constable, went back to her house. In the middle of the afternoon, he went to her sitting room, where she was playing something on her antiquated piano. He stood behind her and said, 'Janet, I can't be in the same house with you like this.'

She took her hands from the keys, turned around and stood slowly. She put her face into the shoulder of his jacket. She was tall; her hair was close to his face. 'Just don't talk to me about love, Denton.' She put her head back and looked him in the eyes. 'I spent an awful night. I was horrible to you yesterday, but I'm frightened. I'm sorry you saw me like that. I'm sorry I hurt you. But that was the real Janet.' She sighed. 'I'd say, "Let's go to bed," if I didn't think the police were coming back. And perhaps I'd just be trying to distract myself, anyway. I'm *afraid*, Denton.'

'It'll come right.'

'Maybe not. Life has no interest in coming right. But you stick by me and maybe it will.' She was holding on to the fabric of his jacket with both hands. 'I thought I might hear from Bernat by now, but of course that's silly. The police won't get to him until they've been up and down the street and found somebody who saw a woman in a black dress going into his place.' She shuddered. 'Then it will start.'

'You have to tell them about bringing the woman here.'

'I've worked that out. I'll tell them I was embarrassed to talk about "female troubles" to a man. They'll believe that. They'll believe anything stupid about a woman.'

He thought Mankey probably would. Mankey was what Denton's police friend Munro called 'one of the dimmer coppers'. Munro himself wouldn't have accepted her tale so easily, but Munro wasn't on this case.

She shuddered again. 'Somebody walking on my grave. Let's go to bed, anyway; to hell with the police.' He made himself seem delighted, but he felt a stab of doubt because she had been a prostitute. Usually he was able to shut that threat out, but now it was insistent: prostitutes are used to faking pleasure, used to proposing sex. What if she was doing this only for his sake, or for the sake of peace?

They went to her bedroom, fell into bed as if they were twenty years younger, made love quickly and rather roughly, as if to prove to each other that they'd made up; then they started again, slowly and quietly, Denton waiting for the front door ring that would be Mankey's, but the ring didn't come until almost five, and by then they were sleeping, naked and wrapped around each other like old trees.

'Bless my lies,' she said when she was dressed and Mankey was waiting downstairs. 'Make me glib.' She kissed him. She had put on a veneer of cheerfulness, but he knew her too well.

'I want to be with you.'

She shook her head. 'I want to seem defenceless. And not very appealing to men. Do I look as if I've been spending the afternoon doing illicit but pleasurable things?' Her eyes were puffy, and a slight flush spread up to her face from her collar. She was wearing one of her severe outfits, a mannish suit of dark grey with a boxy cut.

'More like you're going to address a temperance meeting after not enough sleep.'

Incredibly, she winked at him and went out.

'Detective Mankey took it like a man. He blushed at "female troubles" and said that I had shown very poor judgement. I promised never to do it again, and he said I could be up on a charge, if he so chose. I did my best to look as if I might faint, and he said that he would put in his report that I had withheld information "without malicious intent". Evidently malice is nine points of the law.'

'Don't take Mankey too lightly. He's dim, but he's a cop, and I think he tries, meaning that he's persistent and he won't forget.'

'He insisted on talking to Annie, who of course was terrified and sat with her apron between her teeth the whole time, slumped down on her spine like a rag doll. Mankey sent me out but called me back in when, as I take it, she did nothing but moan. All we got out of her was that she hadn't seen anything, neither woman nor corpse. She did tell him that the house was haunted; he said that was "not relevant", which to Annie was like speaking French.' She sighed. 'He asked about "the others downstairs". I'd forgotten I'd mentioned the Cohans yesterday. Cohan was out again, off to his boxing school this time, and Leah's almost a corpse herself. Mankey says he'll come back tomorrow to talk to them. When I said she was hardly capable of speaking, he said he'd be the judge of that. Poor Leah.'

'Hard on you.'

'Me?' She made a sound with breath and lips, *puhhh*.

'Maybe you've taken in too many strays.'

'Don't mind my business for me, Denton.' She put out a hand, took one of his. 'I waited a long time to have money. I mean to do what I want with it.' After she had come out of the institution, she had sued her husband and had been on the verge of winning when he had killed himself and left everything to his Oxford college. It had taken her a dozen years to break the will and get half of the estate. She squeezed his hand. Her smile was brittle. 'Bedding me isn't a warrant to dispense advice.'

He smiled, shaking his head at her. 'But are we all right again?' Asking even though he knew the answer.

She took her hand away and looked towards a window and was silent so long he thought she wouldn't answer. Then she said, 'You are what you are; I am what I am.'

'That sounds pretty hopeless.'

'This afternoon was nice—wasn't it? Why ask for more?'

So he knew that they were not all right again.

In the evening, Denton walked round to his own house and found no constable. He went in; the hall was cold, the paintings against the walls ghostly in the near-dark. He lit the gas and went into Atkins's quarters: the dress that Atkins had seen was gone. There were remnant hints of a search, a turned back rug and two chairs set at odd angles, but things were in remarkably good order except for the garden mud tracked all over the downstairs. Up in his own rooms, things were just as he and Mankey had left them.

'Hoy!' a voice said from below. Denton looked down. Atkins and Rupert were looking up at him. 'Saw the light,' Atkins said. Rupert, gasping, started up the stairs.

'Coppers are gone from the front door,' Denton said. 'Looks like E Division—down, Rupert, dammit—or the bullyraggers searched your place. Rupert, get down!'

'Don't bode well for the Met, if you ask me.'

Rupert was trying to lick Denton's face, his paws almost on Denton's shoulders. He weighed more than a hundred pounds. Denton put him down by main force, spoke sternly, watched Rupert sit with a foolish grin on his face, his stump of tail wagging. 'This dog is undisciplined.'

'Free spirit. Best kind. You want me to fetch something to eat from the Lamb?'

'I'm having supper with Mrs Striker.'

'Spending the night? I ask as one who brings up a tea tray at seven if you're here.'

'You mind sleeping here alone?'

'What, because somebody was murdered practically in my bed? General, I slept in a ruined Hindoo temple where the ghosts of dead whores howled like banshees. Except it was the wind. Any road, I got Rupert, who isn't afraid of anything.' Atkins had come upstairs, was pouring sherry for Denton and, at a nod, one for himself.

Taking his glass, Denton said, 'You should lend Rupert to Annie. She says Mrs Striker's house is haunted.'

'Oh, Annie sees spooks in church! She runs to the other housemaids ten times a day to tell them what she saw in the clothes press or the pantry. You be careful of Annie—she's got no brain and a wagging tongue.'

Denton was looking around the shadowed room. 'Damned mess the workmen left. I've decided to fire the lot.' He sipped the sherry. 'So Annie runs about with tales, does she?'

'Like the town crier.'

'Detective tried to talk to her today—she didn't say boo to him. Saving it for the other housemaids, maybe. Not that she knows anything. But I'd better tell you what's going on—Mrs Striker brought a woman through this house yesterday, then through the garden to her house. The dead woman.'

Collecting the glass, Atkins bobbed his head towards Janet Striker's house. 'She in trouble?'

Denton hesitated. 'Maybe. I can't tell you all of it.'

Atkins nodded as if his own worst doubts had been confirmed. 'You're going to get involved, aren't you! Off on another wild hare, instead of writing the way God meant you to!' He sighed. 'Playing detective!'

Denton started down the stairs. 'Mind your manners. And teach some to Rupert while you're at it.'

He left Janet's house early the next morning, again in the grip of a bad dream, this time one he couldn't remember. Worry about her was like a bad taste in his mouth, a tightness in his gut. She was off to the Isle of Dogs as soon as she'd dealt with Mankey and the Cohans. The truce between them was fragile, he thought: they hadn't 'made it up' yesterday, only come to an unspoken acceptance of distance. Knowing that she had to deal with Mankey again that morning had them both on edge.

Crossing her garden and then his own, he looked at the houses on each side, wondered how much could be seen from their windows: nothing from the side where the Lamb stood, he thought, because of the garden wall on that side and, along it, a decrepit grape arbour overhead, old grape vines, now leafless, grasping across it like gnarled arms. On the other side, a weed tree—regularly cursed by Atkins because it shaded his vegetables—masked much of his property, despite its lack of leaves. Somebody might have nonetheless been able to get a glimpse of whatever had happened there, he thought, from two of the houses. The likelihood of somebody having actually been at a window when something was going on, however—the woman, maybe somebody else, going from Janet's house to his; the killer dragging the body out to his garden shed, improbable as that seemed—was imponderable.

Atkins was awake and out of bed, brewing tea in the ancient kitchen but not yet dressed, wearing instead an extremely seedy floor-length robe that had once been covered with coloured curlicues, and was now napless and faded. 'Employers not supposed to poke their noses below stairs before eight,' he muttered.

'I see Rupert's already left a steaming pile in the garden.'

'Meaning to get to that soon as I'm decent. Never know who's looking out of a window.'

'Just what I was wondering as I came through. You might ask around among the housemaids whose hearts you've captivated, see who saw what Saturday.'

'Such as?'

'How the woman got here from Mrs Striker's. And how the body got out behind the garden shed.'

'Walked, maybe.'

'Mankey thought she was killed in here.'

'But he doesn't know, does he! Could of been thrown over the wall from the next garden for all he knows. Could of fallen off the wall and broke her neck that way. What ever happened to the idea of evidence?' He finished making the tea and grabbed a covered plate that smelled like toast from the huge wood range (now cold, used only as a support for a gas ring). 'Up you go.'

Settled in his armchair with the tea and toast and preserves from his pantry, Denton said, 'Have a cup.'

Atkins shook his head. 'Had mine. You going out for the day?'

'Have to finish a piece for the *Strand,* want to work up an idea for a story.' Writing short stories was new to him, but he had no novel in train. 'It's money.'

'Glad to hear of it.' Atkins was always concerned that Denton would run out of money. Atkins's own ambition was to get enough money to escape from servitude; it explained his infatuation with money-making schemes and his fear of Denton's going bust and Atkins's losing his place. Now, as Denton ate, Atkins said, 'Chap here has an advert in the *Graphic* for a clock-work alarm and teamaker. What's your opinion of that, Colonel?'

'Don't give me one for Christmas.'

Atkins put on his public-reader's voice. '"Will make tea, prepare shaving water, hot water for any purpose. Warms infants' food, et cetera, et cetera." His et ceteras, not mine.' Denton chewed a piece of toast, said nothing because he was thinking about Janet and the abortion and the murdered woman. Atkins, after a short silence, tried again. '"The clock calls the sleeper at the hour desired, and a few minutes afterwards he is drinking a hot cup of tea. The machine works with a spirit lamp, which it lights automatically, boils water, tips up gently, puts out lamp, and finally rings a second gong to notify that tea is made." Says it's tested by experts and fully recommended.'

'Does he want you to invest?'

'"Agents Wanted."'

'Can you imagine what the commission on a tea-making clock would be?'

Atkins sighed. 'Probably doesn't work, anyway. The spirit-lamp part sounds dangerous.' He produced the morning newspaper from under an arm. 'You're in the papers.' He handed it over, pointing at a column:

VIOLENCE STRIKES FAMED NOVELIST'S HOME—AGAIN!
DEAD WOMAN IN REAR GARDEN

Denton read the piece, which was short and thin on facts, long on his own past: 'Mr Denton's association with violent death is of long term, dating to his famed elimination of four badmen in the American West long ago. In recent years, in London, he has been responsible for the death of Harold Satterlee, who had butchered his own daughter, and that of the murderer of Erasmus Himple, R.A., and Captain Heseltine. Whether a propensity for brutality exists in the novelist, whose books are full of such scenes, remains to be...' Denton made a rude sound.

The only new thing in the newspaper was a name: 'The victim was a woman believed to be one Rebecca Shermitz, an immigrant.' He looked up at Atkins. 'I wonder where they got the name.'

'Coppers.'

'They didn't take the body.'

'Maybe they found her handbag.' Atkins disappeared down the stairs to the lower hall, reappeared with the early mail and put it on Denton's tray. 'Chatting up the housemaids takes time,' he said. 'You want me to chat them up, you said.'

'I take it that's a hint. Yes, you can have the morning to visit.'

'I'll dress.'

'What do the housemaids' mistresses say while you're chatting up their employees?'

'What they don't know can't hurt them.'

The Second Woman

Among the bills and the unwanted invitations was a squarish envelope, heavy paper, with a crest on the back. The contents amused and surprised Denton: an invitation, practically a command, from Hector Hench-Rose—'You *must* lunch with me tomorrow at the Kestrel—twelve sharp—*very important!!!* No excuses—time of the essence—shall be most hurt if you fail me!! Hector Hench-Rose, Bt.'

It made Denton smile, then frown. Hench-Rose wanted to scold him for leaving the shoot on Saturday, of course. The shooting party had been forgotten in the furore over the dead woman; now it came back to him, bringing shame with it. He had let Hector down.

Hector was his oldest English friend. He had first appeared in Denton's life as a young subaltern in the West in the early eighties, wanting somebody to take him buffalo hunting on the cheap. They had made an odd pairing, but it had become a friendship, maintained for years by letters. Now Hench-Rose was a baronet. And Denton had behaved badly towards him.

He scribbled a reply. 'See you at the Kestrel at noon on Tuesday, when I will make a proper apology for my recent behaviour.'

He went upstairs to his bedroom, also his workroom, and changed into an ancient pair of rat-catchers and a greeny-brown velvet jacket as napless as Atkins's robe. He tried to finish the article for the *Strand*, kept sliding away from it to Janet and Mankey's return visit to her house. It took two hours to do an hour's work, and he sent the piece off by a Commissionaire to his typewriter; another hour saw the new short story scarcely blocked out, so that he wrinkled his nose at the pages and sat staring out of the grimed window at the upper back of Janet's house. That view reminded him of his curiosity about who could see what from the houses; he stood, leaning forward over his desk, looking down. He could see surprisingly little, in fact, more of Janet's than of his own garden. Still, somebody from one window or another, one house or another, could have seen into part of both gardens, but no one person from one window could have seen everything.

He threw down his pencil and went up to the attic and exercised with a hundred-pound dumb-bell and a rowing contraption, then practised with his parlour pistols. After an hour, he came down again and sat at his desk and stared at the wall. He was still sitting there when he heard a door slam somewhere below, the sound dull and distant and somehow ominous. He thought it would be Atkins, back from chatting up the neighbour housemaids. He went to the top of the stairs, looked down in time to see Janet looking up at him.

'The police are questioning Bernat,' she said.

'What about Mankey?'

'Mankey? Who do you think's questioning him!'

He went down, taking his time, trying to think of calming things to say. Standing a step above her, he said, 'Are they at the surgery?'

'His wife came to tell me. She's funked.' She wrapped her arms around herself. 'So am I.'

'Does she know about the—operation?'

'Denton, what will they do?' Loose hairs that had escaped from a coil were trembling; he could see the tremor in her entire head.

He led her down the long room. 'It depends on what they find.'

'Will they arrest us?'

'If they know what he did—I don't know.'

'And then they'll come for me!'

'Janet, they won't.' He put her in his armchair.

Her face looked thinner, ill. 'I won't let them arrest me!' She scrambled out of the chair and threw open the box from which he'd taken the derringer. 'Give me a gun!'

He shook his head. 'You'd hurt yourself.'

'I'd *kill* myself, you fool!'

He stared at her, shook his head. She looked away, put her hands at her temples as if trying to push something back into her head, then put her face in her hands and sat again. She whispered, 'You don't know what it's like.'

'We have to wait. Will you eat something?'

The Second Woman

She gave him a disgusted look and again got out of the chair and began to walk up and down. He could hear her breathing, a coarse rasping like the sound the dog made when it laboured up the stairs. Her face was pale and the tremor in her head and neck had become shudders that shook her whole body, her hands visibly shaking like an old woman's. Denton caught her as she came towards him and hugged her to him. She pushed him away and, weeping, rushed back up the room to stand at the window with her face in her hands.

After another half an hour, during which she lay almost comatose in a chair, still trembling, neither speaking, the downstairs bell rang. Atkins, looking grave, came up and muttered that the doctor was coming. Janet lay very still, facing the door as if a monstrosity waited behind it. They heard Bernat's breathing as he came up the stairs, a soft man with too much weight.

But when the door opened, he was smiling.

'Well?'

'I am such a skilled liar.' He seemed to be exhausted but exhilarated. 'I told them that woman they described to me was the one who had come to my surgery.' He looked down at his shoes, then, his eyes amused, at Janet. 'Because it was *not* the same woman they described. They described a different woman—older, more plump. I thought, if this is a different woman, then there is no sign of an aborted pregnancy on her. So I said, this sounds like the same woman. Then we went over it and over it, and they asked what procedure, and I said what you told me to say. And they went away. And you have no worry.'

Denton said, 'What name did you have for the woman in your book?'

'Rebecca Shermitz. The name she gave me.'

Janet pressed her face into the green plush of the chair.

Later, while Janet slept in the chair after a brief, almost hysterical frenzy of relief, Denton sat alone and thought, *It's all right for now. For now.*

She was tottering with exhaustion when she woke and insisted on going home alone. Denton let her go and slumped in his armchair. Atkins reported on the morning with the housemaids, apparently spent almost entirely in his answering their questions rather than the other way round; only one of them, and she not the most trustworthy, thought she had seen 'two ladies crossing the garden', but she was vague about the time, and, pressured by Atkins, was not entirely sure whether they were going from Janet's house to Denton's or the reverse.

'Worse than nothing at all,' Denton groaned.

'Be a disaster in the witness box, that girl. I asked her how she knew they were ladies, and she said that they both wore hats—she thought.' Atkins made a rude sound. 'Then I asked her something else and it was plain to me she'd had the whole tale from Annie in the first place—hadn't seen a thing with her own two mince pies.'

'Meaning that Annie saw Mrs Striker and the woman crossing the gardens to her house, although she didn't tell the police. But Mrs Striker has already told them, so there's no harm done.'

Denton ate a supper brought by Atkins from the Lamb—sprouts, mashed turnips, mutton masquerading as lamb—and lay back again, his coccyx almost on the front edge of the cushion, only his head and shoulders against the green velour chairback. He had his lips pushed out like a pouting child's, the tip of his huge nose caught between the knuckles of his first and middle fingers. From time to time, he sighed.

When he had been lying that way for more than an hour, he heard the bell ring downstairs, then Atkins's footsteps and then the clatter of the door lock. Seconds later, Atkins's footsteps clumped up the stairs and the door opposite the fireplace opened.

'You interested in having a look at a dark person looks like he was run over by a steamroller and has a suit looks like it was made in Buda-Pesht for somebody long since dead?'

'What's he want?'

'You. Name of Shermitz.'

Denton started to tell him to send the man away, then knew that the name Shermitz meant something, rooted around in the still-drowsy clutter of his brain, came up with the name that Dr Bernat had given the police: Rebecca Shermitz. He pushed himself upright. 'I'll see him.'

Atkins sighed and went down again. Denton smoothed his hair, parted his moustache with his fingers, straightened his somewhat stained corduroy jacket—frogged, sold as for genteel smoking and dressing—and carried the supper tray up to the pantry beyond the huge, never-used porcelain stove. As he came back towards the chair, the door opened and Atkins, standing back against it, motioned in a compact young man with a puffy, discoloured eye and yellowing bruises on his jaw and cheeks. Nowhere near as tall as Denton, he nonetheless gave a distinct sense of self-confidence despite his injuries. He had a straight, black moustache and terrific eyebrows; his suit, indeed, was oddly cut and shabby.

'Mr Shermitz,' Atkins said. He closed the door, put a wide black hat on a side chair, passed behind the visitor and opened the dumb-waiter doors as he headed for his own stairs.

Denton and the visitor sized each other up. Denton said, 'I believe I know your name.'

'Shermitz!' The voice was surprisingly deep, unnecessarily loud. 'I am husband of woman dead here two days.' The accent was Middle-European, perhaps further east than that.

Denton muttered something about being sorry for his loss, mumbled words about sitting down, and again took to his armchair. 'What can I do for you, Mr Shermitz?'

'Of my wife, I am seeking informations.'

'I'm afraid you have to get that from the police.'

The visitor waved a hand.

'You've been to the police?'

'Most certainly.'

'Forgive me if this offends you—did the police have you identify your wife's body?'

'I identify, yes.'

'Then they got her name from you.'

'Yes, Rebecca Shermitz.'

'Why did you go to the police? Had she been missing?'

'Missing, yes. I missing her.'

'How long?'

'Ah—' Shermitz looked around the room, his eyes moving quickly; he might have been a would-be robber, sizing the place up. 'Long time.'

'How long?'

Again, Shermitz waved his hand as if he couldn't be bothered. Impatience in his voice, he said, 'I am seeking the informations, not you! I want to know what you know!' He pointed a finger at Denton, who flicked his eyes to the box that usually held the derringer, wondered now if he had put it back or if it was in a pocket somewhere.

'I don't know much of anything, I'm afraid.'

'You find her!'

'No, I didn't find her. A workman putting in some heating found her.' Idiotically, he pointed at the hole in the floor, as if it would prove the existence of the workman.

'In garden!'

'Yes, the rear garden.' Denton cocked his head that way.

Shermitz jumped out of his chair and strode down the room to the window and pushed the curtains apart so hard the rings clattered. 'Is darkness!' he cried, as if Denton had played a trick on him.

'Sit down, please, Mr Shermitz. Come back—there's nothing to see.' He didn't like having the man down in the gloom of the unlighted end of the room. 'Shermitz—!'

He came back but didn't sit, his right hand shoved halfway into his jacket pocket in a way that Denton thought probably Middle European, perhaps affected. 'So?' Shermitz bellowed, 'What you know?'

'Nothing, I'm afraid. Look, Shermitz, I know you're—'

'In your garden! Woman is dead! How can you know nothing? I am reading newspapers: you are famous killer, why not you should be killer of her?'

Denton stood and slid his hand towards the box. 'I think you'd better go, Mr Shermitz.'

'I want knowing how she died! Who does this thing to me?' He struck his chest a theatrical blow. 'I am suffering!'

'I'm sure you are.' The derringer was not in the box. He remembered that it was still in the pocket of the old tweed suit he had worn for the shooting party. 'I'm very sorry for your loss, but I can't tell you anything.'

'Where is her dress? Is very good dress. A hat cost two shillings!' Shermitz came towards him, both hands balled into fists, his eyes hot. 'Where is her handbag, I am asking? Where is this handbag that had money inside? I need that money!'

'Go back to the police. What policeman did you deal with— was it Detective Mankey? Talk to him again. Mankey—was it Mankey?'

'Mankey.' Shermitz shrugged and, suddenly deflated, gave a short version of the waving-away gesture. 'You are no good to me.' He turned about and grabbed his hat and went rapidly downstairs, the steps light and almost pattering.

Denton went to the front window as he and Atkins had two days before and watched Shermitz, now with the hat on his head, come through the front door. Within seconds, he was striding up the pavement past the Lamb, an admirably fast walker.

'Did he come in a cab?' he said when he realized Atkins had come into the room.

'Could have come in an ascension balloon, for all I know. First I heard of him was the doorbell.' He went down to the lower hall, slammed the outer door and locked it and came back up. 'Bloody Polack, doesn't know enough to wait for me to show him out.'

'Pole, you think? I thought more like the types we saw in Transylvania.' Denton and Atkins had made a now-famous motor car trip there the year before; Denton had written a successful book about it.

'Polack, Russky, bubble-and-squeak, who knows?'

'And poor. Wouldn't you think?'

'Oh, no—shoes with the sole half off are all the fashion in Buda-Pesht these days.'

Denton was thinking of the expensive underwear that the dead woman had worn. That and her age: she had certainly been older than this man.

'Oh, well.' He fell into his armchair again and sank down on his spine. 'I'll let Mankey work all that out.' He stayed that way for half a dozen ticks of the mantel clock and stirred. 'Mankey never showed up at Mrs Striker's.'

'Busy quizzing Bernat.'

He thought about that. 'Maybe.' He sank down again on his spine, sat up again. 'Cohan must be off at his boxing club's opening. His wife's in a state.'

'She's got Mrs Striker.'

'Yes, but—' *Yes, but Janet's in as bad a way as she is.* But there was nothing he dared do about it. If he went over to check on her, she'd be outraged.

With a groan, he sank down yet again.

CHAPTER

6

The Kestrel was one of a large group of men's clubs that seemed to take up most of St James's Street: it rubbed shoulders with the Royal Societies and the New University, faced Brooks's and the Devonshire, and had for near neighbours the Conservative, Boodle's and the Cocoa Tree, and was neither the best nor the worst of its kind. Denton entered it carrying a small Gladstone bag with his boxing clothes in it (his knee-length flannel rowing trousers and rubber-soled rowing shoes) for his meeting later with Cohan at the boxing club. The porter took it without even a lifted eyebrow.

Hector Hench-Rose had come late to clubbability because of his comparative indigence; in his early days, he had belonged only to the Junior Naval and Military, about which he had written to Denton with some bitterness. Of the many grievances he had had against his older brother, the baronet, club membership ranked high. Hector had been genuinely delighted when his brother had died suddenly and made him a baronet and a wealthy man. The Kestrel was one result.

Another was the suit that Hench-Rose was wearing when he greeted Denton. The overall effect was rather purplish, also rather hairy. In one lapel, a V-shaped something glinted; Denton's memory was tickled—recently?—but he couldn't quite catch it. 'Do you like my tweed?' Hench-Rose was saying. 'Isn't it superb? Isn't it tasteful? I had it woven specially for me. The colours are from my grouse moor—lavender for the heather; grey for the rocks; grey-blue for the more distant hills; white for the water falling from the tops of the crags; green for, of course, grass and gorse and so on. It makes me practically invisible against the landscape!'

'You could never be invisible, Hector.'

Hench-Rose laughed, greatly pleased. He seemed excited, even agitated. On their way to a table in the dining room, he introduced Denton to half a dozen other members. 'Want you to meet people,' Hench-Rose muttered. 'Important you meet some members.'

'I can't think why.'

'Because you're a *famous man*, Denton! And you should belong to a club.'

'Aw, Hector—'

'Enough, enough! Not another word.' Hench-Rose had been making noises about Denton's joining a club ever since he'd come to London. Denton always shied away.

As they sat down, Denton jumped to the subject he thought had got him there. 'I suppose the important matter you want to see me about is last weekend. Hector, I apologize for leaving the butt. It wasn't my idea of sport, but—I was rude, I know—I apologize—'

Hector looked blank, then: 'Oh—the shoot.' He was studying the menu.

'I let you down.'

'The Fennimans were beside themselves, it's true.'

'I behaved badly.'

'At first. Then Held, the financier, said he saw you make two of the finest shots he'd ever seen, and the under-keeper who was loading for you told Fenniman that you could have taken five hundred birds if you'd been put in the centre.' Hench-Rose leaned forward. 'They want you back!' He grinned.

'There's no understanding the English.'

'It would give them credibility, Denton. To have a first-class shot come and make a big bag shows that they have worthwhile shooting. That makes them something more than Johnny Jump-ups, eh?' He put on a suddenly serious face. 'Though I do think a letter of apology is in order.'

'I'll write one as soon as I get home. So—that takes care of the vitally important matter you had to talk to me about.' Denton was relieved that it was done with so easily.

'What—the shoot? No, no, no.'

Denton felt vaguely irritated. 'Then what's all the fuss and feathers about? Joining your club?'

'Of course not. Although it's important, of course it is. Clubs very important. Arguably one of the pillars of life as we know it. But no—something else. Hmm. Not ready to talk about it yet. The turtle soup is *not* good; I don't know what they do with it. Did I say that the food isn't the great attraction here?'

'What, then—the excitement?' Denton looked around at one of the more depressing dining rooms in the West End.

'Mmm. I think Dover Sole. What in the world do you suppose brains in brown sauce are like? I think I should stay away from those, if I were you.'

Denton ordered something called a biftek and a potage, which Hench-Rose said would be a soup made from yesterday's vegetables, ground up.

'So if it isn't the food or the constant thrills, what are we here for?'

'I think I'll let the suspense build.'

'Hector, what's the important matter?'

'Well, mmm, well—Oh, if we must. I don't want this conversation to be bruited about. All right?'

'I won't put adverts in the newspapers, then?'

'Well, speaking of newspapers, I saw your name—I warned you about the potage; those are the very carrots I was served yesterday.'

'Not the *very* ones, I hope.'

'What? Oh—ha-ha. Where was I? Conversation is so difficult with you. Ah, confidentiality. Agreed?'

'Sure.'

'Don't be light, Denton. It detracts from your gravitas. All right, confidentiality taken as read. Now. Hmm. What was I saying? Ah, the newspaper—yes, in fact quite relevant.' He lowered his voice and said with a solemnity that indicated that they had now come to the Important Subject, 'What happened at your house on Saturday?'

'A woman's body turned up. Behind the garden shed. In her underclothes.'

'Yes, yes, I know all that. Then what?'

Denton cocked a mental eyebrow: the information about being in her underclothes hadn't been in the newspaper. 'Is this prurient curiosity?'

'Certainly not! What else happened on Saturday?'

'Police wouldn't let me in my own house.'

'Of course not. But I don't mean that sort of thing.'

Denton realized that the corpse in his back garden was the important thing that Hector wanted to talk about. It was very unlike him: Hector was fascinated by gossip about his class and what he called 'our betters', presumably those who had higher titles and even more money, but murders hadn't much interested him even when he had had a sinecure at the Police Annexe. Toying now with his biftek, which was tougher than a cow he'd once bought right from the trail, Denton said, 'What *do* you mean, Hector?'

'One hears of some sort of brouhaha.'

'One hears?' This was unlike Hench-Rose's usual sort of talk, too; he was a 'hearty', his persona that of a bluff-but-honest soldier (and, now, baronet). '*One hears*? What's got into you, Hector?'

'Office talk.'

'Office? You left the police.'

'Oh, I've been asked to take on something else. Didn't I tell you? Military—more my line, of course. Whitehall-ish.'

'You said last year you wanted to get into Special Branch.'

'Anarchists and the Irish? Not what Special Branch is, I mean; what they're warranted to protect us from. Yes, well, mmm, I haven't fallen too far from that tree.' He smiled, clearly pleased with himself. 'That's not to be spread about. Strictest confidence. Mum's the word.' He barked one note of a laugh. '"Mumm's the word." Sell champagne with that—rather good, eh? "Mumm's the word?" Eh?'

'You're fighting anarchists and Irishmen?'

'Mum, mum, Denton! Really! No, not those specifically, something else, but I can't talk about it.'

'Is this connected with your prying into the corpse in my garden?'

'Did I suggest such a thing? Now, why would you think that?' Hench-Rose, who was a dreadful liar—one of the things Denton liked most about him—was suddenly giving all his attention to his plate, which was empty except for three peas that he was pursuing as if his career depended on them.

'What is it you want to know? About the brouhaha? "One hears about a brouhaha."'

'Oh—did I say something like that? Oh, well, I suppose I did. Was there a brouhaha?'

'The Metropolitan Police were interfered with by two dodgy types who had some sort of paper that they claimed was from the Home Office and gave them the power to do everything this side of child molestation.'

'How you authors exaggerate.' Hector looked disapproving. 'Why do you say "dodgy"? I'm sure that if the Home Office commissioned them, they were fine young men.'

'The one I saw looked as if he'd rape a sparrow if he liked its feathers.' Denton was mulling over Hector's use of 'young'. The two bullyraggers had looked youngish, but how could Hector know that?

'Rape a—? You'd be a dreadful witness in the box, Denton—all this metaphor. What did the police do?'

'Apparently they let themselves be flummoxed. Lot of arguing, but instead of throwing the pair of them out on their arses, they stood around and palavered and let a crime scene get turned into a pigsty.'

'Yes, but how did the two from the Home Office behave? Honourably? Politely?' Hector's entire attention was now on Denton's answer.

'I didn't say they were *from* the Home Office.' Denton stared into Hector's eyes. Hench-Rose frowned and looked away. 'I doubt that they were honourable and I certainly don't believe they were polite. But you know, Hector—' Denton was using a piece of slightly stale bread to sop up a puddle where the biftek had stood. 'You haven't asked how I know about it, when the police had barred me from my house.'

'Mmm? Oh, I assumed you'd know.'

'Hector, you're the worst liar I've ever known. You *knew* I was in my house, didn't you? How did you know?'

'Oh—must have been in the papers. Quite a lot about you in the papers. Penchant for violence—rather a magnet for it, in fact. That's the line they took. Must have picked it up there.'

'Hector, Hector—what are you up to? What are you doing?'

Hench-Rose pushed himself away from the table, muttered the word *coffee* several times and said they could have their coffee in the writing room.

'We haven't had dessert yet. Hector, I've never known you to leave a table without dessert. I'll have the jam tart and custard.'

'Oh.' Hector sat down as quickly as he had got up. He refused from then on to talk about Saturday or what he did and didn't know or the two dodgy types and the police. It was as if he'd never introduced the subject; when Denton tried to go back to it, Hench-Rose looked blank and talked fast about something else. He babbled about cricket; Teddy Roosevelt (and was displeased when Denton called him Teddy, the Tiffany Cowboy);

some damned young MP named Churchill, with whom he was disgusted; the rest of the shooting weekend; and golf.

'The custard tastes a little as if they made it with plaster,' Denton said when Hench-Rose ran down.

'I told you, one doesn't come here for the food.'

Hench-Rose led him to the writing room and picked a corner away from the few other members, three of whom were sleeping. Coffee was brought in; they were silent until the waiter had gone. Then Hench-Rose said, 'You *must* let me put you up for membership, Denton. It's why I got you here.'

'It isn't. You got me here to pump me about Saturday.'

'Nothing of the kind! I want you to be seen! I want to introduce you!'

'You said it was important.'

'Club membership *is* important! Nothing more so!'

Denton, chuckling, shook his head. '"Tell that to a sailor on a horse," as we used to say. Hector—'

'Mum's the word.' Hench-Rose put his finger on his lips. 'Forget what we talked about.' The finger crooked and tapped his nose. 'A word to the wise.' With elaborate casualness, he changed the subject. 'You haven't noticed my buttonhole.' He put a thumb under one revers and pushed the buttonhole forward. The light glinted on the golden badge, V-shaped, now seen as two forearms joined in a hand-clasp.

Denton had remembered where he had seen something like it when he had started telling Hench-Rose about the bullyraggers: one of them had had something similar in a buttonhole. Instead of saying as much to Hench-Rose, however, he now said, 'What is it?'

Hector beamed. 'The Brotherhood of Britons. Like-minded fellows who know what's good for this country.'

Denton didn't see how Hench-Rose and the bullyraggers could be like-minded fellows. 'What *is* good for this country?'

'Being British. That's what it's all about. Ridding ourselves of degenerates, keeping out people who don't belong. You can never make outsiders British. "The lesser breeds without the law."'

Denton could tell that Hector was quoting but didn't know what, so he said only, 'I'm not British.'

'But you're from the same Nordic stock as us.'

'Hector, you disappoint me.'

'Europe is being overrun by racial degenerates. Italians, Mongols, Jews, they're going to pollute our racial stock if we don't act. This is proven, Denton. You don't read up-to-date stuff, so you don't know. *I'm* on the qui vive.'

Denton thought that Hector's usual level of reading matter was *Boy's Own*, but he guessed that somebody had probably pressed a couple of pamphlets on him. 'Slavs, too, I suppose.'

'Slavs, of course—though the danger is the Russian Jews. The Russian Bear is driving the Jews out, not that I say he's doing so properly or humanely, but he is doing it! The result is that the world is going to have to take what the Bear won't tolerate. Your USA is getting shiploads of them. Wait and see what that leads to.' Hector tapped the little table that stood between them. 'It mustn't happen here. Already there are more than a hundred thousand of them in East London. Enough! *Baas!* No more! And the ones who are here must leave.'

'Including your friend Held?'

'Held the millionaire? Of course not! Where do you get these ideas?'

'He's not "Jewy"?'

'Of course he isn't.'

'But the Jews in East London are.'

'Precisely—you've got it! That's the problem with them. We Britons have been very good about the Jews—oh, a few unfortunate incidents long ago, but times were different—we've let them marry into our aristocracy, make fortunes, mix with the best people. That's entirely proper. But Denton, we can't have a hundred thousand *poor* Jews bringing racial pollution to our shores. We won't allow it.'

'Back to Russia?'

'Certainly not! The Russians treat them horribly. No, no—we must be humane—they must have their own country somewhere. I am involved in a project with that very end, in fact—in confidence, mum's the word—but this is why I wear this little gold pin. The aim of the Brotherhood is to encourage the Jews to emigrate to their own land. As soon as possible.'

'Palestine?'

'The Porte closed Jerusalem to further immigration. Not very helpful, the Turk—sick man of Europe, and so on. No, another place shall be found. We have ideas.' He leaned forward, voice lowered. 'We have friends in high places. *Members* in high places. Schemes are in train.' He touched a finger to his lips. 'Confidential.'

'Hector, this isn't like you.'

Hench-Rose smiled. 'You think I don't deal in serious matters, but now—you'll see!'

Denton nodded. 'I don't know what I'll see, but I'll see.'

When they parted at the door of the Kestrel, Hench-Rose made Denton agree to have his name entered for the club. (Denton supposed he could withdraw it later.) Hench-Rose said 'mum' several times, not specifying what Denton was to be mum about. He repeated a few of his best ideas about poor Jews. He told Denton to go on to wherever he was going, as he had to get to the office.

'I'm heading for the East End.'

'Ah. I'll let you go, then.' And Hector signalled for a cab.

Which was odd, Denton thought as he strode away, because if Hench-Rose's office was in Whitehall, he was within a comfortable after-lunch walk. On the other hand, he might have offered to share the cab.

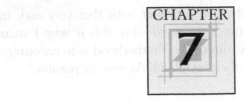

CHAPTER
7

He walked to Westminster Bridge station and took the Metropolitan Railway to Aldgate, then walked east and north up Whitechapel High Street and Whitechapel Road, then north to Old Montague and the alleys above Finch Street. This was Jewish East London—kosher shops, tailors by the dozen, beggars, little factories owned by 'sweaters'. Cohan's Masada Club was up one of these narrow ways, an otherwise typical building of a couple of storeys now painted a dazzling white, so that it leaped from the surrounding grime as if it were being pushed forward by an express train.

Although both Denton and Janet Striker had put a little money into Cohan's club, neither had yet seen it. Denton now stood across from it, trying to take it in from the few feet that the pavement allowed him. A couple of passing men, certainly Jews, eyed him and looked away, closing themselves to strangers.

Cohan's building had been a warehouse. Pushing open the small, man-sized door in a pair of wooden gates that had been made for loaded wagons, Denton passed into a stone-floored space that filled most of the ground floor. Four beams that had perhaps come out of ships supported the floor above. In the centre was a boxing ring at floor level, around it on the walls smaller spaces marked out where two men might spar, another with a heavy bag hanging from the ceiling. It was spare, even ascetic; it smelled of paint and old wood and perhaps rats.

'Wot you think?'

Cohan had appeared from a door at the back. Before Denton could answer, he said, 'I know it ain't no Crystal Palace. Not meant to be.'

'It looks like you mean business.'

'That's exactly wot I want it to look like. I want the casuals to take one look and walk away. Serious boys only.' He was leading Denton back towards the rear door.

'How was the opening?'

'Did wot it was supposed to do. Had the *rebbe*, said a few words. Jews here are poor, lot of them not been here long, don't know our ways—can't even ask their way to the WC. I kept it short and said in good English wot I was about and wot I meant to do, and the *rebbe* said it for them in Yid, and me and Flash Moscowitz boxed a couple of rounds to show how it's done, and that was that. Signed a few kids on, laid down the law to them. They'll be back tonight with tuppence each—they *say*.' He opened the door. 'Change in here. Should of told you to bring your own lock.' He waved at a row of wooden cupboards along the far wall. 'Be all right today, just lock the door when you come out and bring the key. When we're done, you pour a bucket of cold water over yourself in there—' he waved at a closet-sized space with a grating in the floor—'and that's that. No fancy baths or massewsees here.' Cohan tossed a Turkish towel, already worn rather thin from another life somewhere else, on a bench.

They boxed for half an hour, stopping often for Cohan to explain some fine point. Denton would have been the better in a street brawl, but in a ring with rules, Cohan, although shorter and without Denton's reach, was the master.

'I hear you knocked some copper on his arse,' Cohan said when they stopped, both winded.

'Wasn't a copper. But, yes, I used that straight left you like.'

'Broke his nose, I hear.'

'Stories do get around.'

Denton went to the changing room, leaving the key in the lock, and stared into the doorless space where he was supposed to pour water over his head. He thought a hot bath at home would be more welcome. He pulled off his wet singlet and then the flannel rowing trousers and tossed them into the Gladstone. He was settling on the rough bench to remove the rubber-soled shoes when he heard a sound at the door, metallic, mechanical, and he knew that the key had been turned in the lock. It occurred to him that Cohan might be playing a joke, some sort of rite of initiation; he suppressed righteous anger. He waited, poised with a shoelace in his fingers. Would Cohan relent and open the door and ask him if he had been frightened? Or would he be expected to break out?

Then there were voices in the big room beyond the door, a shout from a voice he thought was Cohan's, the words unintelligible, and then muffled sounds and a scream. Denton jumped to the door and tried to open it. It was, indeed, locked.

'Cohan! Cohan!'

He leaned against the door, one ear against the panel. Low sounds repeated, and then one scream that tailed into a groan. Denton tried to wrench the door towards him, but it stayed closed. He leaned on the door again, his nose close to the crack between the door and the jamb, and he drew his head back from an acrid smell.

Not the smell of sweat or old wood or rats, but the smell of fire.

'Cohan!'

He kicked the door, but it still held. Picking up the bench, he rammed it into the door, backed off and rammed it again; an upper panel burst outwards and the smell poured in. He ran at the door a third time and knocked the centre rail loose, then kicked until there was a space large enough for him to force his way through. Wrapping his overcoat around his bare body (irrelevantly concerned about going nearly naked), he pushed against the shattered wood and half fell into the larger room beyond.

Flame was roaring up the far wall; between Denton and the boxing ring, a tongue of it was darting over the stones. The air reeked now of smoke and coal oil, and as Denton watched, another flame began to race towards him from the far wall, licking up a long, deliberate splash of oil.

Cohan lay in the ring with his head and one arm resting on the lowest rope, the arm outside.

'Cohan!'

The man didn't move.

Denton ran to him. The flames were hot on his skin now. Cohan's face was pulp, blood oozing from a dozen places; welts on his bare torso were bleeding, too. At the far corner of the ring was a bucket of water; Denton grabbed it and threw it over the boxer, then dragged him over the rope and out on the stone floor. Behind him, the tongue of flame had almost closed with flames coming at right angles, nearly surrounding the ring; Denton pulled off his overcoat and beat at the line of fire that burned between him and the outer door. He looked for more water, saw none and slammed the overcoat down into the puddle in the ring where he had soaked Cohan. He pushed it across the wet surface, then threw it over Cohan and picked the old boxer's body up and put it on his shoulder, his abdomen stabbing with the weight. He grunted, then surged forward, eyes closed, into and through the flames, aware of fire on his naked legs and under his feet; one of his shoes was unaccountably sticky.

Then he was outside. He stumbled over the sill, went down to one knee, with Cohan, still wrapped in the wet overcoat, sliding forward almost to the pavement. Denton tried to get up, felt his lungs hot with pain, and then people were around him, hands under his arms, somebody beating at his head. He tried to fight the man off, saw faces he didn't know, fear on them, a hand holding his own. A voice: 'Hair—your hair—'

His hair was on fire.

People shouting in a foreign language. Somebody wrapping something around him. Men and women carrying Cohan away from the burning building. Then his own body being lowered to the pavement, his back against the wonderfully cool brick of a tenement. A bell ringing; horses' hooves. Somebody holding a cup to his mouth.

'I'm all right. All right.'

'No, no.' A woman was looking at the side of his head. She pointed at the side of her own head. 'No.'

A horse and wagon appeared and Denton, protesting, was lifted into it. Cohan, no longer wrapped in the overcoat, lay next to him. A couple of men got in with them, one lifting Cohan's head to cradle it. 'Jew hospital,' the man said, the voice heavily accented. 'We—go Jew hospital.'

Denton became aware of pain.

He said no to morphine and then later asked for it. Two nurses hovered near him as one doctor and then a second studied his burns, paid a great deal of attention to his right eye and sutured a gash he hadn't even noticed in his right arm, high up near the shoulder. Denton said several times that he was really quite all right and they all but told him to shut his gob.

He was in the London Hospital on Whitechapel Road, better known as the Jewish Infirmary because of the unit within devoted to the care of poor Jews. One of the doctors had an accent thicker than Bernat's and a face that Hench-Rose might have called Jewy, perhaps the model for *The Command*'s comment about a hook-nosed Rothschild. Denton found after a time— hours had passed, he was sure, but his sense of time was off, particularly after the morphine—that he was himself a partic- ular focus of attention, both men and women passing the door of the examining room to look in, study him, exchange a word with one of the doctors or a nurse.

'You are a cynosure,' the Jewy doctor said as he swabbed Denton's back with a red-brown fluid.

'Not my looks, I suspect.'

The doctor chuckled.

They wouldn't let him walk but insisted that he lie face down on a stretcher and be carried to a ward. Long rows of beds stretched down the room with an aisle between them. The beds were iron, the paint chipped, the covers showing here and there a hole or a patch. Mostly, the men there lay still, three or four coughing, one steadily; somebody breathed like a whale and said 'Mama' over and over in a soft voice.

Denton found it oddly peaceful. The hard bed felt soft, the cold air warm; he floated. He slept.

'You are losing some hair,' Dr Bernat said. 'I have woken you, I know; it is deliberate. I want to look at you.'

'Everybody does,' Denton said, surprised at the hoarseness of his voice. He coughed.

'Smoke. The lungs are affected, but only for a day or two. You will heal all over; you will be the same again.'

'They were worried about my eye.'

'The fire was mostly on your right side. The eye is inflamed, maybe had too much smoke. You have singed your—what is the word—lashes on that eye. Also the eyebrow.'

'No hair over there, I hear.'

'Some, but quite short. Not to mind, Mr Denton; you will be beautiful again.'

Bernat was lifting compresses, adjusting his glasses to peer over them; Denton, lying on his front, couldn't quite see what he was up to. He said, 'How is Cohan?'

'Worse than you.' Bernat straightened. 'Roll on your good side, can you do that? Like thus, yes. I am examining your shoulder.' He was silent for some seconds; Denton could hear his breathing close by. 'Cohan is not so good.'

'He was beaten up.'

'He was almost murdered.'

'How bad?'

Bernat touched his shoulder. 'You can lie again on your front side. Does it hurt to lie? We can put you on your back, but I don't like your burns that way. The shoulder is being burned mostly on the top, not the back, but still—you lie so all right, we leave it so.' He sat on the bed without touching Denton's legs. 'Cohan has lost one eye. Who beat him, they were using devices—there is a word—a metal that goes around the hand to hurt—'

'Brass knuckles?'

'Aha, you know them! This is what a policeman tells me. Some people say three men, some people say two; somebody sees them running down the street. Anyway, Cohan has been done murderously with these knuckles.'

'How bad?'

'The cheekbone under the eye crushed. The nose broken—worse than broken. Teeth broken. Four ribs, one piercing the lung. Both hands. The hands are broken like you would make meat tender—many blows. The police think a hammer. Maybe they can be made well, maybe not. A broken leg—maybe somebody jumps on it when he is lying down. They mean him to be dead.'

Through the fog of morphine and returning pain, Denton thought how fast they must have worked. At least three men, to do so much damage so quickly. Then pouring the coal oil on the wall and the floor, tossing a match.

'I didn't see them.'

'The police will talk to you, no matter. Not tonight, I think. Tomorrow.'

'Is it night already?'

'After nine.'

'I thought I would go home.'

'Maybe tomorrow. You will have pain. Burns give pain. You are better here.'

Bernat leaned close, his face seeming huge above Denton. 'Mrs Striker was here. She comes again tomorrow.'

'They didn't wake me.'

The huge face smiled. 'This is an hospital, not an hotel.'

The pain was worse. They changed his dressings, said how well he was doing and swabbed the burns with something that smelled like creosote. The side of his face and his legs felt merely hot, but the shoulder was bad. They offered him more morphine but he refused, and they gave him aspirin and something else and promised chloral hydrate. He asked for the newspapers, but he was still lying on his belly and couldn't read them.

A constable came and 'took his statement'. He told Denton that a policeman had been stationed outside Cohan's boxing school. Denton thought this was a fine example of locking the barn after the horse was gone, but he supposed the police wanted to be seen to be treating serious crime in the Jewish neighbourhoods seriously.

Atkins came with Janet in the middle of the morning; Atkins hung back while she came to him. She told him he looked absurd with only half a moustache. They hadn't told him about that. She hunted for a part of his face to kiss without hurting him, then gave a very light touch of her lips to his left cheekbone.

'Cohan's bad,' he said.

'I thought Leah would despair, but she actually seems to have come out of her funk a little. She was here all night and she says she's going to stay; she's found somewhere to room in the next street. I saw her just now; she was full of—I think it's hate. It's given her strength, a look like—she looks heroic.'

'Who's taking care of you?'

She shook her head. 'Don't be absurd.'

'Anything new about—the other business?'

'Silent as the grave. Mankey was supposed to come back, but he hasn't. Let sleeping dogs lie, I say.' She moved off to see about Cohan.

Atkins had brought clothes and opined that Denton would be better off at home. 'Rum lot of mates they've given you.'

'The care's good.'

'They're all Jews.'

'That's why they call it the Jewish Infirmary.'

'What you need is Army and Navy Coca Wine. "Best Port and Peruvian Coca Leaves." Looked it up in the catalogue last night. Hurts a bit, I daresay.'

'A little like being burned.'

'Fosdick's Burn-No's the thing. Lay in a supply on the way home. The missus moving in with us?'

'It wasn't discussed.'

'Might be the best thing. You'll need caring for. *Again*.' Less than a year before, Denton had been shot. 'No offence, General. My little joke.'

'Forgive me for not laughing.'

Atkins had brought the mail. Denton gave him most of it back unopened but asked Atkins to read him a few pieces that looked promising. He laughed outright at one of them: his motor car, on order for three months, was expected to reach the Royal Albert Dock within two weeks.

He stayed another night in the Infirmary and went home the day after with what looked like an explorer's chest of bottles and tins. In fact, Atkins's coca wine did more for the pain than the hospital's anodynes, although it left him with bizarre dreams and a feeling of weightlessness. With him, too, came the remains of his overcoat, burned and blackened; Atkins pronounced it past saving but found in the pocket the derringer Denton had forgotten. 'Came through the fire better than you did, General.'

Denton made his own way up from the ground floor of his house to his sitting room, complaining at every step, but the chafing of even light clothing made his burns hurt. Janet slept that first night in his bedroom on the next floor, Cohan was still in the hospital and Leah with him. Annie, told to spend the night alone in Janet's house, had got hysterical; Janet had brought her to Denton's and tried to put her in the extra room on Atkins's floor, but Annie, faced with sleeping in a room next to the one in which she was sure the woman had been murdered, not to mention that there was now a man in it, got hysterical again. She wound up in a small room on the same floor as Janet. Denton, no happier than Annie about the sleeping arrangements, slept in an extra and mostly unused room next to his sitting room. He had to lie on his front still, could manage on his back only if his feet and ankles stuck out beyond the bottom of the bed and his right side was on a pillow to keep the shoulder from touching. It wasn't a satisfactory night.

'I hate this room,' he said the next day. Even to himself, his voice sounded like a whine. 'I associate it with being an invalid.' He had spent six weeks in it after being shot.

'Well?' Janet was amused.

'I'm not an invalid. I'm just a little under the weather.'

'And rather hairless.'

'Only on one side. You could sit on my left and pretend I'm right as rain.'

'I've saved all the newspapers. Do you want to read about being a hero?'

'I'd blush, but I suppose you couldn't tell because I'm red to start with. What else do they say—that my love of violence led me to start the fire myself?'

'Only that you're heroic. The *Daily Graphic* referred to you as "the heroic novelist"; the *Telegraph* said you "demonstrated Anglo-Saxon heroism to the residents of east London".'

'What did *The Times* say—"Heroic Novelist Injured"?'

She laughed. '*The Times* didn't say "heroic".'

'I'll cancel my subscription. Oh, God, it hurts to laugh.' He made himself stop laughing and said, 'What about the woman who was murdered?'

She shook her head. 'Nothing. A deafening silence. Maybe it never happened.'

'Oh, it happened! Hell! If I could get about, talk to people—Janet, something's going on. It makes no sense that nothing's been said. There should be an inquest—'

She pushed his face gently into the pillow. 'There's nothing to be done until you're well. You need to take your mind off it. Do you suppose you hurt in too many places to make love?'

'Maybe if I lay on my left side.'

'That sounds possible.'

And it was. But they hadn't resolved whatever had happened between them several days before. He wondered if she was finding his injuries a useful distraction. She seemed, he thought, too ready to skate quickly over any thin ice.

She had a class at University College; afterwards, she told him, she would have to take Annie back to her house and stay there with her. 'I'll be in and out all the time,' she promised. 'But Annie's hopeless.'

'So am I.'

'You're about as hopeless as the Monument. Don't be selfish, Denton; the only other thing I'll be doing is afternoons in the Isle of Dogs; the rest of the day until Annie's bedtime is yours.' She kissed him. 'Don't be cross.'

But he was cross. He wondered if it was the coca wine, told Atkins to bring him some as a means of finding out.

Atkins had found what he called 'a rum old Dutchy', who turned out to be a German immigrant named Gratch who went about the streets on a bicycle with an elbow of stovepipe over each handlebar. He could 'fix the furnace mess', or so he said; and indeed, he proved to be a skilled carpenter and a knowledgeable stove man who laughed at the holes in the floors, repaired the damage and loved the Dresden stove that had sat unused in the long room for as long as Denton had owned the place. 'Dot,' he said, 'iss a heater!' He became a mostly silent presence, going up and down with a tool or a length of pipe, passing through a room like a ghost while Denton read or talked with Janet or stared at a wall.

'He's so easy to become used to,' she said. 'I passed him on the stairs just now and it was like meeting somebody who lives here. He's only been in the house a day. You'd think he was a lodger.'

'Or a ghost. Don't let Annie see him.'

'What exactly is he doing?'

'Yesterday he closed up the holes, which wasn't so quiet; this morning he varnished the new wood; this afternoon he's pulling out the pipe that other lot had run up and setting the dumb waiter to rights. Tomorrow, he promises he's going to finish a pipe to carry heat from the furnace—which stays in the cellar— to Atkins's part of the house and the lower hall. Then he "hass a plan" for repairing the porcelain stove to heat the upstairs. And I just sit here and wish I could go walk in Regent's Park.'

'Don't be cross.'

'I *am* cross. It's no good telling me not to be—it makes me crosser. More cross. Hell!'

Mornings and evenings, Atkins changed his dressings and smeared on more tarry goo.

'Disgusting,' Denton said.

'Could be a lot worse. Could be the Crimea, you could have gangrene and I could be Florence Nightingale.'

People called and left cards; people wrote him notes expressing shock and hopes for a swift recovery: Henry James, who included his latest book, *The Wings of the Dove*, which Denton had already read; Arthur Morrison, who also sent his new book, *The Hole in the Wall*, which Denton had also read; Conan Doyle, who sent his latest, *The Hound of the Baskervilles*, which Denton hadn't read and had no intention of reading, although another on spiritualism in the package (not by Conan Doyle) called *The Scientific Séance and Eusapia Palladino* rather intrigued him; the irascible editor Frank Harris; people like Shaw, who never remembered him when they met face-to-face; and, surprisingly, Henry Held, the financier he'd met while relieving himself at the Fennimans'. Held's note was entirely conventional but ended with 'hoping to see you quite soon to discuss an important matter', which seemed odd but not worrisome. Still cross, Denton didn't want anything worrisome.

Next, Denton had a visit from his friend Detective Inspector
Munro of the CID. Apparently Munro had intended only to leave
a card, but Atkins was alert enough to tell Denton he was there,
and Denton, delighted, barked to send him up.

'My God, I'm glad to see you!' he shouted while Munro was
still climbing the stairs. 'I'm desperate!'

Munro stopped in the doorway and looked him over. 'What
the hell have you got yourself into now?'

Munro was a big man with a big head and a huge lower jaw
that made his face seem to slope outwards from the hairline. He
walked with a slight limp (from falling off his own roof), had
a tenacious mind that chewed slowly and missed very little. He
held out a hand. 'Been a while. Don't get up.'

'Do I look that bad?'

'Worse.' Munro looked for a chair. 'I meant only to leave a
card—up to my arse in work.' He pulled a chair over and sank
into it as if he intended to stay. 'But—I can't get any farther
behind than I already am. How's Mrs Striker?'

'I telephoned you from her house on Saturday.'

Munro grunted, grinned. 'Heard you didn't take my advice
and crossed a police line.'

'Into my own house.'

'You know better than that. How'd you do it, anyway?'

'Heating men had cut a hole in my front hall, the stupid
bastards. Went up that from the cellar. How'd you hear?'

'Coppers' gossip. It's all over the Yard. Although since
Sunday, nothing—deafening silence, as they say.' Munro shook
his head, chuckled. 'Heard it was all widdershins, anyway, what
you found when you got inside. The griffin is that somebody
went over E Division's head and took the case away from them.
You know anything about that?'

'Widdershins, indeed.' Denton told him about the two
bullyraggers and Mankey.

'Mankey's got pudding for brains.'

'The pigeon who let them get pushed around was somebody
named Steff, not Mankey.'

'Steff's always got his lips in a pucker, hoping to kiss somebody's bum. Ambitious, but always goes about it wrong. He's got his pego in the mangle over this one.' He lowered his voice as if eavesdroppers might be close by. 'The truth is, Mankey and Steff were pulled out of E Div Monday morning. They're reassigned to two empty desks at Whitechapel Road, where the big men can keep an eye on them.'

'What happened to the body?'

Munro shrugged. 'The edict's come down from Caesar Augustus that all's well at E Division and shut your mouths. "Normal procedures were followed." What d'you make of it?'

'That's what I'm asking you.'

'The blind leading the blind. Tell me again about these two roughs who pushed Steff and Mankey about.'

Denton described the little he'd seen, the falsely posh accent on one of them, the clothes. 'One of them had a gold thing in his lapel—like a V. Something called the Brotherhood of Britons.'

'Oh, cripes, we've got them at the Yard, too. Anti-immigration, foreigners out, Britain for the British, make you weep. Not that they don't have a point—too many immigrants, not enough work. Lot more of them around the docks—do some pretty vicious stuff in the East End, as I expect you know better than me. How's that Jew boxer you pulled out of the fire?'

'Hanging on. They meant him to die, Munro.' After a moment's wry thought, he said, 'They meant *me* to die.'

'Mmm. CID got the case. Ugly business. We can't find the tykes that did it. Everybody's being see-no-evil.'

'You think it's some of the Brotherhood people?'

'Doubt it—not their style. Brotherhood's all talk.'

'I'd been with one of them just before I went to the East End. Talk, indeed—he lectured me about the Jews. In fact, you know him—Hector Hench-Rose.'

Hench-Rose had introduced Denton to Munro when he'd been with the police, pre-baronetcy. Munro shrugged. 'So what's *Sir* Hector up to?'

'I thought you might know. He was being kind of mysterious with me.'

'Haven't laid eyes on him since he got his title and flew the coop. Not that I wouldn't do the same in his shoes. He went up the road.' He meant towards the upper end of Whitehall. 'Between you and me and the gatepost, some of the bigwigs thought having a baronet in the Met was coming it too fancy. I think that Melville used his connections to move Hench-Rose back to the military.'

'Who's Melville?'

'Who's Melville! Did you just get off the boat? Melville's the darling of the Special Branch, a fine tec, saved England from the bomb-throwers and the Irish gunmen. Brilliant copper, actually.' Munro shifted his bulk in the chair. 'Little bird said Hench-Rose wanted to be the new Melville.'

This was a side of Hector that Denton didn't know. A little defensively, he said, 'You never liked him.'

'Never disliked him, either. I did police business with him. It was chalk and cheese—he's all country sports and clubs, and I'm football and roses in the back garden.'

'He seemed to know a lot about what went on at my house with the dead woman. As if he had police information.'

'Keeps up on the gossip, probably. Always liked gossip, Hench-Rose did.'

Denton wondered if he should tell Munro about Hench-Rose's perhaps odd behaviour, thought he wouldn't, then changed his mind. 'Hench-Rose kept saying "Mum's the word" and making a great to-do about the dead woman and the two inter-lopers and then denying he was interested in any of it. When we separated, he said he was going to "the office" but went off to find a cab—to get from St James's Street to Whitehall, supposedly.'

'Ate too much lunch, probably.'

'So he'd get a cab for himself and not invite me to get in?'

'What're you suggesting?'

'I don't know.'

'He's your friend—ask him.'

Denton grunted. Something held him back from doing that, probably a sense that Hench-Rose might be hiding something that could hurt their friendship. 'It's coincidence, I suppose, that Hench-Rose and one of the pushy types at my house wore the same lapel pin.'

Munro shrugged again. 'You get any sense who those two are?' His manner said he had a real interest.

Denton made a bad-smell face. 'I told you, Mankey said they had a piece of paper from the Home Office, whatever that means. One of the two, the one I nailed, said something about Bart's. "Let's go back to Bart's," something like that.'

'Bart's is the hospital. St Bartholomew's.'

'I know that! God Almighty, Munro, *I* didn't get off the boat this morning.'

'Well, it makes no sense, somebody like that saying he's from Bart's. Fella who waves some sort of warrant from the HO is hardly from the hospital.'

'They wanted the body. Maybe they were taking it for a PM.'

'Mmm.' Munro scribbled on an envelope he took from a pocket. 'Unlikely, but might be something.' He looked up at Denton through his thick eyebrows. 'You didn't see me do that. We're keeping our hands strictly off the whole business, just like we've been told to do.'

'He also mentioned going to "M". You know anybody they'd call "M"?'

'Special Branch officers used to call Melville that to show they were in the know, but these boys don't sound like Special Branch. And Melville would never interfere in a division's business like this.'

'And somebody named Gorman? He talked about "Gorman".'

Munro shook his head.

'He called Gorman an idiot.'

Munro grinned. 'Couldn't be anybody in the Home Office, then.'

'Did I tell you that they brought in that pompous old smoothie Freethorne, who said he was the Home Secretary's lawyer?'

Frowning, Munro made another scribble on his envelope. 'Meaning maybe the HO document is legitimate.'

'You're just like Hench-Rose—you're more interested in the two bullyraggers than you are in the dead woman. There was murder done here, Munro!'

'That's E Div's business.'

'And *my* business. Look here—the dead woman was called "an immigrant" in the newspaper. Could be there's some sort of anti-immigrant connection?'

'And therefore what? It's the Brotherhood of Britons with their little gold kickshaws? It's a long way from joining some sort of jaw shop to killing people, Denton. The few nuts out there who'll actually kill a perfect stranger don't kill women, unless it's sex. This wasn't sex—was it?'

'Ask the medicos. Any idea where the corpse is, by the way?'

'Your two laddies took it somewhere—and how Steff could have been stupid enough not to have them followed, I don't know!' He leaned forward. 'Look, Denton, try seeing it from our perspective. The crime is E Division's. But the two "bullyraggers", as you call them; taking away the body; yanking Mankey and Steff—that's a different kettle of fish. We—CID—are taking this pretty seriously, even though we're not supposed to. When people start suppressing cases in the divisions, it doesn't matter who they are, it's like getting all our bollocks cut off.' He lowered his voice to a rumble. 'Anything you know about it, I'd like to hear. You hear something from Hench-Rose or anybody, sling it over to me.' Munro stood and put out his hand. 'Shall we meet for a pint in a few days? Just to chat.' He hung his overcoat over his arm. 'Wife always expects me home for tea at seven, so we might meet at six. You know the Princess Louise? Each of us come halfway, and it puts me close to the underground. Monday at six?'

'If I'm out and about by then.' Denton let a half-grin form. 'Even if I'm not.'

Later that same evening, Atkins again answered the door and came up looking grim. 'Now there's *another* copper down there,'

he said. 'Name of Guillam. Haven't we had a run-in with him?' Atkins knew better than that: Guillam had been thrown out of CID and reduced to Detective Sergeant because he had given somebody confidential police information about Denton.

'Guillam!' Denton had had some of the coca wine and was feeling muzzy. 'Good God, Guillam's the one who got me shot last year. Or as good as caused it—trying to please the upper crust. Throw him out.' Atkins looked a little startled (Guillam was four inches taller and five stone heavier) but put on a serious face. As he braced himself to go downstairs and tell Guillam that Mr Denton was indisposed (the nearest he could come to throwing him out), Denton shook himself awake and said, 'No, show him up.' He sounded to himself like a cranky old man who felt much put upon. Pulling himself upright in the armchair and trying to sound alert, he said, 'He's got some bee in his bonnet or he wouldn't be here. Let's get it over with.' As Atkins made a face, he called after him, 'And bring me some coffee.'

Denton was wearing the ancient smoking-cum-dressing jacket, whose right sleeve Atkins had slit to allow for the compresses on his arm. His feet were in carpet slippers but without stockings because of the burns on his calves, now healing but red and itchy; above them, he wore another of his pairs of knee-length rowing trousers. 'Do I look all right?'

'No offence, Major, but you look a bit like a below-stairs concert party.'

Denton had looked at himself once in a mirror, one look enough. He would have said he had no vanity, but that in itself is always a vain illusion. What hurt him was that he had lost what Hench-Rose had called his gravitas, which he now saw had consisted almost entirely in the long moustache that had hung down both sides of his mouth and now hung down only one. As well, his right ear, burned on the rear face, had swollen enormously, causing it to stick out almost at right angles.

'Just show him up.'

Guillam moved into the room ahead of Atkins, who came behind with his hat and overcoat, both wet. Guillam stood inside the door and studied Denton, who studied him back. Guillam was heavy, fat layered over a powerful body; his face, rather brutal, was fleshy, the skin marked with deep pores and pits; he was losing his hair but wore what he still had very short.

'Don't miss anything,' Denton said. The coca wine, when its anodyne effect had worn off, made him irritable. So did Janet's absence at her own house.

Guillam watched Atkins go down the room to his stairs, opening the dumb waiter as he passed; when he was gone, Guillam strode to the dumb waiter and closed the doors again. 'I've seen him pull that trick before,' he said. 'This is just between us.' He looked at Denton's head and legs. 'I'm sorry you've been hurt.' He said it like a bad actor who has memorized the line but not got himself around it.

'That your idea of a joke?'

Guillam made an impatient sound in his throat. 'Look, Denton: you've no reason to think well of me, I know. Nor me of you: we got off on the wrong foot, we did.' He grew very red. 'I've come to apologize.'

'Been attending a revival meeting?'

'All right, all right, rub it in! I've spent a bloody year in bloody Siberia because of you!'

'That sounds more like the real Guillam. And it hasn't been a year; it's ten months, I think. Ten months is a little short to work up a full head of contrition.'

'I said I apologize!'

'I know what you said.' He held Guillam's eyes, watching the face seem to swell with anger. *Same old Guillam.* 'Let's forget apologies. You hate my guts and I'm not really in love with yours. What do you want?'

'You're a right bastard, you are.' Guillam laughed, shook his head. He dragged a carved, curved-back side chair closer to the coal fire and sat. 'I'm a right bastard, too, I am. We'll leave it at that.' He pulled out a box of cheap cigarettes and took one, as an after-thought offered it to Denton; he refused, then thought better of it. Guillam said, 'Though I've learned more than you think these last months. Not contrition, not on your life. Maybe something about playing between the lines.' He shrugged and lit their cigarettes. 'Right. Forget the personal stuff. I want to talk to you about this body was found at your place.' His eyes moved and Denton swivelled to follow them. Atkins was coming down the room with a tray. 'Port or whisky, sir?'

Guillam refused both. Denton took his coffee, waited while Atkins set up a small table and a plate of cheese and biscuits between them. He watched Guillam's face as Atkins went away: Guillam's mouth twisted into a disgusted grimace, and he shook his head. Denton laughed and turned around: Atkins had opened the dumb-waiter doors again.

'Thinks I'm stupid, don't he?' Guillam said. He hitched his chair closer and lowered his voice. 'All right, I'll do it this way.'

'You wanted to talk about the body. Why?'

Guillam looked down the room and then said, almost in a whisper, 'I've been transferred to E Division. Mankey and Steff are out.'

Denton had decided not to tell Guillam that Munro had been there. 'Out of the police?'

'Sent to Whitechapel Road, where the bigwigs can keep an eye on them.'

'Why you?'

'Because I've had a request for transfer in since I landed out there in West Ham, that's why. It could have been anybody. Now look—' He pulled the chair still closer. 'I'm going to be on the straight with you.' He looked up to see how Denton had taken this, found no encouragement in his face. 'All right, all right! Let me have my say, anyway. I *am* on the straight, dammit!' He lowered his voice again. 'I get to E Div this morning, Mankey and Steff are already long gone. They've given me Mankey's cases, which don't amount to tuppence except for this thing at your house. The others I could do in my sleep, but this one looks something else. But there's no file and no detective's notes— *nothing.*' He seemed to wait for some reaction. 'You follow what I'm saying?'

Indeed, Denton did feel slow and rather muffled. 'I can just manage to keep up.'

'Agh—' Guillam made a face. 'Who do you think they gave me for a partner?'

Denton shook his head.

'Only on this case. Eh? Who? One of the two tykes that came and wangled the body away from Steff, that's who. My partner! And he isn't even from the Met!'

That did impress Denton. He managed to say, 'Which one?'

'How do I know which one? He's the only one I've seen, isn't he? Oh, I see, though—I hear you laid one of them on the floor, put a fist up his conk. Well, *not* that one.'

'Who told you that?'

'A PC who was supposed to be watching the body but saw you through a window.' Now he came to his real reason for being there: 'Denton—I'm being straight—what am I getting myself into?'

Denton had been reaching for his coffee, but he hesitated, raised his head to look down his nose at Guillam's crouched head. He tried to sweep the fog out of his brain, worked out what Guillam was telling him only slowly. 'You're worried that maybe they didn't just happen to pick you because you had a request for a transfer in. You think maybe the powers that be said to themselves, "Guillam will do anything to get out of West Ham."'

'Something like that.'

'Why come to me?'

'Because it happened here and because you were here and because you're nosey.'

'I've nothing to do with it.'

Guillam gave him a strange look and sat back, then lunged forward and poured himself a small whisky and brushed cigarette ash from his waistcoat. 'Freddie—Freddie's my new partner's name—says there's nothing more to investigate.'

'Be careful, Guillam.'

'You take me wrong. This is Freddie's idea, not mine. There's no inquest. The super at E Div is putting it about that this is one we'll never solve—random violence, object was theft because no handbag was found. Looks to me like he's dancing to somebody's tune. Maybe Freddie's.'

'Freddie's Home Office, for sure?'

'He's not saying. Nobody's saying. Look, Denton, I'm keeping both hands and my hat over my arse on this one, because it stinks. There's been no investigation and there's to be no investigation; whatever Mankey and Steff may have seen here, there's no notes and no record. The Met put out the official story on what happened, including the deceased's name, but it's my name will be on the paperwork. They've given the dead woman a name, but I'm supposed to take it on faith from Freddie that it's the right one. And he won't tell me where he got it.'

'He got it from her husband.'

'Husband! What husband?'

'Rebecca Shermitz's.'

'That's green goose shite. Nobody's mentioned a husband; where'd you hear such a thing?'

'He was here two, no three nights ago. He'd been to the police already.' Denton heard himself say that and added, 'He *said.*'

'Aye, saying it's cheap. What the hell did he come here for?'

'I'm not very clear about that. He got all agitated about her handbag, then said it had money in it and he could use the money.'

'What'd this "husband" look like?'

'Like somebody'd taken a hammer to his face.' He thought of Cohan, the cruel marks of the brass knuckles. 'Small, young, maybe Austro-Hungarian, something like that. On his uppers, I'd think.'

'Been laid into? Bad? Could the dead woman have done it—maybe fighting him off?'

'I thought the bruises were older than that—turning yellow. He was on the mend. And this didn't look like woman's work.'

'You'd be surprised.' Guillam stared at his whisky. 'A husband. And he said he'd been to the cops? How are we supposed to have found him, us?'

Denton shook his head. It was a good question.

'And of course he left you no address, and of course he gave no proof that he was her husband. It's havers, is what it is.'

'Then who made the identification?'

Guillam shrugged. 'You work it out. One, nobody's mentioned a husband till now. Two, if Freddie knew about a husband, he'd be in a state. Don't you think that if we had a husband, the Met would be in the papers with him as the top-of-the-list suspect? It's always the bloody husband did it!'

Denton tried to think about it. He poured himself more coffee. Of course, a husband would have been a gift to the police. But if Shermitz hadn't been to the police…perhaps he wasn't really Shermitz? He said, 'Maybe you shouldn't tell Freddie about the "husband".'

'Good Christ, you think I want him to even know I was here? You're poison with him.' Guillam laughed. 'It's a bit of a joke—the "husband" may be somebody who got the name from the papers, and then he fed it back to you.'

'And the papers got the name from the police?'

'I've told you, I don't know anything, I don't.'

'So the Met could have made it up, or they could have real information.' Denton's muddled brain produced an idea. 'Maybe she had her name sewed into her dress. Or her hat.'

'Do you know for a fact there *was* a dress or a hat? Somebody at E whispered to me that there'd been a dress and a hat, but there's no box of evidence and no dress and no hat. It's all a sell.'

'So the Met, for reasons of its own, has decided there'll be no investigation. And it's put you in charge.' He drained his coffee and poured more, the bottom of the pot. 'Freddie strike you as a cop?'

'He's cute on some things, but he doesn't know how many beans make five when it comes to procedure or investigation.'

'I thought his pal might be military.'

'Could be.'

'Mankey called them "little tin gods". Freddie seem upper class to you?'

'Nothing like. Freddie's got a semi-posh accent that comes and goes. He dresses better than a copper but everything's new, like he just cracked out of the egg. He's a twister.' Guillam scowled. 'And I'm the mug.' He drank down his whisky, got out another cigarette and tossed one to Denton. 'I don't like stumbling about in the dark.'

'Maybe you should back out of it.'

'Can't do that; I'd never get out of West Ham.'

'Have you talked to Munro?'

'Donnie's down on me.'

'You have an answer for everything.'

'And for nothing.'

'Well, obviously you're supposed to write up some paperwork and do no investigating and let the whole thing just fade away. Is that so hard?'

'It gravels me.'

The two of them smoked in silence. Guillam was not the kind to go over the same territory twice: he was smart, and a good cop when he didn't try too hard to advance his own career. He sat until his cigarette was done, then stood and asked for his hat and coat. When he had the coat on and the hat was in his hands, he said from the door, 'I meant what I said—I apologize. I don't expect gratitude to run out of your nose because of it, but I think you might take it as sincerely meant. If you learn anything, I'd like to hear of it.' He turned to go, then looked at Atkins, who had helped him on with his coat. 'And if you try to play that dumb-waiter trick on me one more time, I'll have you up on a charge.' He went heavily down the stairs.

CHAPTER

8

The next morning, Janet stopped by with half a dozen newspapers for him, perhaps an offering because she was on her way to the Isle of Dogs and he wouldn't see her all day. She was wearing one of the old black dresses from the days when she had worked for the Society for the Improvement of Wayward Women and she had had so little money that she had bought her clothes in Petticoat Lane. She looked plain and poor.

'I've gone off the coca wine,' he said. 'Munro was here last night. Guillam, too.'

She knew about Guillam. Her eyebrows arched. 'The two things are connected?'

'I had hell's own time trying to concentrate.' He told her about what looked like the Met's intention to suppress the case and use Guillam as its face. Without explaining the link, he said, 'When you used to buy your clothes off the barrows, did they ever have the former owner's name in them?'

'Now and then. Why?'

'What did you do with the names?'

'Left them, I suppose, if they were sewn in. What are you after?'

'Guillam doesn't know how the Shermitz name got into the papers so quickly. Bernat gave Mankey the name the next day, but the papers already had it.'

'Women usually give false names when getting an abortion, anyway.'

'You mean she might have given Bernat the name Shermitz because that was what was in her dress, which she'd bought from the old-clothes man? Well, that might explain things. Even though the woman Bernat saw wasn't the woman who turned up dead. Or so he said.' He took her hand. 'How's the Isle of Dogs?'

'Not so bad as you'd think. Except for the lice and the fleas. Some of them accept me—some of the women, anyway. The men are mostly out looking for work or lollygagging in the boozer. I knew some of the women from the Society; they're taking me around.'

'You getting what you want from them?'

'It isn't easy to ask a woman who says she made seven shillings last week to tell you how much she spent on food, how much on the burial society, how much on clothes, and the rest of it. What you're really asking is how much more she made in the dark—stealing off the docks or nicking things off a barrow. One woman was honest enough to tell me she sent her kids out begging and made eleven shillings that way. Her husband sweeps, but he drinks up most of it.' She took her hand back. 'He walks from the Isle of Dogs to the nice part of Whitechapel Road and sweeps the manure out of the way of likely-looking ladies and gents, and tips his hat and holds out his hand, and now and then they give him a penny.' She shook her head. 'My God, what a country!'

She went off.

The newspapers told him little that interested him: the king was to process through south and east London, supposedly a boon to his 'poorer subjects'; Mr Andrew Carnegie was to be installed as Rector of St Andrews University; the birthplace of John the Baptist may or may not have been found; the leader of the Irish contingent in the House of Commons was in the United States raising money, and in his absence the other Irish parliamentarians 'have entered upon a campaign of disorder'. Everything he read seemed to be utterly meaningless stuff that suggested a world devoted to theatricals. There was still nothing at all about the murdered woman or the changes at E Division.

'Or maybe that's theatricals, too,' he said aloud.

'Sir?' Atkins was behind him, holding medications for the morning treatment.

'Don't creep up on me like that!'

'Thought I was being discreet.' Atkins pulled a hassock near and put Denton's heels on it. As he started to unwind the bandage on the right calf he said, 'What d'you know about Marconi?'

'Italian food, isn't it?'

'Oh, ha-ha. You know very well what I mean. The wireless bloke.'

'So?'

'Friend of mine has a scheme for winding wire on a paper core with some sort of thing like you dry a fishing line on. To make the what-d'you-call-it that sends the Marconi signal.'

'Antenna.'

'There, you see, you know more about it than I do.'

'This friend looking for you to put some money in?'

'Thought there might be something in it.'

'And how is he to get money out? So far as I know, Marconi has his equipment made and keeps a tight leash on it, plus I don't see much market for something that sends dots and dashes through the ether.'

'Navy loves it.'

'Yes, enough to have one per ship some day. How much does your pal think he'll make per antenna?'

Atkins was patting the back of Denton's right calf. 'I see your point,' Atkins said. 'Not a big enough market.' He began to apply ointment. 'He says there'll be one in every house one day, though.'

'Receiving dots and dashes? Put your money in something sensible.'

'Your pardon, General, but "sensible" don't bring big profits. And it's big profits I'm after.'

He reached for a fresh compress, and Denton said, 'Let's leave it bare. Good for it. You can bandage it tonight to save the sheets.'

Atkins started on the other leg. Denton said, 'What did you make of Guillam's visit?'

'Torn between being a decent copper and doing what he's told, i'n't he? Sounds like he sprouted a conscience in West Ham.'

'Stranger things have happened.'

'Very tempting, though, to earn a pat on the back for doing nothing. What I think is, he's waxy because they're not telling him what they're about, and that makes him want to poke his nose around and find out. He's trouble, Colonel.'

'I don't intend to help him.'

'The lady still in danger?'

'That seems to be over.'

Atkins gave him a sharp look and started on his right arm. He began to hum, some repetitive, bouncy tune that Denton didn't recognize. Atkins had a pleasant voice, fancied himself something of a performer—had in fact been in demand in the non-com clubs of India. He had got to the point where the wrappings were off Denton's right forearm, and he had the can of salve in his hands, when a loud thump sounded from the front wall of the house. Atkins spun around to look that way; another came, softer, and then there was a smash of glass, and a pane of the front window exploded inwards and a hard object struck Atkins in the left hip and bounced towards the side wall.

'What the H?'

Denton was out of his chair and limping towards the window.

'Watch the bloody broken glass!' Atkins shouted.

Denton hopped over several shards and lurched to the side of the window and looked down. He was just in time to see a small figure, face still turned up, who apparently saw him, ducked and began to sprint away.

'You little devil!' Atkins bellowed through the broken pane. 'I recognize you, Alfie Meeker!' He raised his volume as the figure disappeared. 'I'll tell your mother!' He turned an angry face towards Denton. 'It's that Meeker brat! I'll bloody kill him. Look at this floor, and Mrs Char here only yesterday!' He swung back to the window. 'Cost one and six to get that fixed. I'll have it out of his rotten little hide!'

Denton put a hand on his shoulder. 'It's all right, Atkins— it's only a pane of glass—' But his own heart was racing: the surprise of the thing, and the feeling of invasion.

'Strike while the iron is hot, I say!' Atkins, who had removed his jacket to minister to Denton, was rolling down his shirtsleeves. 'No time like the present.'

'Might better wait, Atkins—anger not the best thing to use as fuel—'

Atkins turned from the door. He pointed a finger at Denton. 'She pays for the window, or it's the police.'

He raced down and the front door banged. Denton subsided into his chair and began to apply the ointment to his arm. The skin felt hard, wrinkled stuff all over the burned surface. But the actual extent of it was small; beyond the scabbing, much of the forearm was red, but he saw no blisters, no open sores. Sworn off the coca wine, he was more aware of pain, but he thought it was bearable now, much of it turning to itch. He hobbled down the room and took three aspirin, hobbled back and applied salve to his right ear and then put drops into his right eye. When Atkins came back, he was making himself tea in the pantry.

'You're up and about, Colonel!'

'What happened up the street?'

Atkins opened a fist and showed three sixpences. '"My boy was put up to it and it isn't his fault." Very conscious of her middle-class dignity, Mrs Meeker. However, she paid up and was sure you're too much of a gentleman to call in the police.' Atkins opened a news-sheet that he had been carrying in a pocket. 'Look familiar? Appears her boy was told by his dad to pass these out to the neighbours.' He held it up. 'Along the way, he decided to throw mudballs at the front of the house.'

It was another issue of *The Command*. The headline blared, 'IS FAMOUS NOVELIST A SECRET JEW?'

'That would be me, I suppose.'

Atkins whipped the newspaper around and adopted a theatrical pose to read it aloud:

This correspondent has learned from a confidential source that the American novelist who styles himself *Denton*, a guest in this country who has been granted all the privileges of our very best people, may well be a *Secret Jew*! Unknown to fame until uncovered by *The Command*, one of the initials that the cosseted *Denton* has long hidden is 'H'.

For what does H stand? Is it Harold? Is it Henry? OR IS IT HYMIE?

On Tuesday last, said Denton descended from his mansion to the Oriental streets of the Judaic community and there gave help and support to a Jew rabble-rouser who had the intention to stir up the Chosen People to violence. This wretch, one Cohan, had the temerity to start a school of pugilism—for Jews! Typical of the closeness and the inwardness and the pride of his people, this school was to have been only for Hymie and Ikey and Abie, Jew-boys like himself—for such he once styled himself, 'The Jew-Boy', when, some years ago, he was known in local pugilistic circles for his Jew tactics in the ring. What was it he intended to teach Ikey—the thumb in the eye? What instruction would he have given Abie—the knee in the groin? For it is only by such underhandedness that THE JEW can succeed.

Providentially for all those beyond the boundaries of the ghetto, the Jew-Boy's *schul* burned to the ground on Tuesday. The source of the fire is yet to be determined, but our advice to the brigade is to look for signs of divine intervention, perhaps a lightning bolt launched by a Christian God weary of falsehood, treachery and usury by the tribes of Israel!

Suffice it to say that H. Denton was a friend of the Jew-Boy's, and that it was H (*is* it for Hymie, Mr Denton?) who carried the comatose Jew-Boy from the building. Bystanders who saw the pair when they emerged say that both were unmarked, but by the time they could be seen by this correspondent at the Jewish Infirmary, they had been so wrapped in lint and swathed with tinctures, that even a trained eye would have thought them the victims of a collision between two speeding locomotives, at the very least.

Denton has Jew friends. Denton goes to the Jew-Boy's school. Denton rescues the Jew-Boy from the flames.

IS HE A SECRET JEW?

CONFESS, HYMIE! THE COMMANDO IS WAITING!

Atkins lowered the paper. 'That's a threat, I think.' He bobbed his head towards the broken window. 'Somebody already taking it seriously, looks like.'

'Only a kid.'

'Who was put up to it, and by who, I would ask. By his sweet papa, you can lay a tanner to it.' Atkins stomped off to a cupboard for a broom and dustpan.

'Now, now.' Denton took the sheet of newsprint and read it over again. He felt no anger, but a great discouragement seemed to fold itself around him. 'It's such rot,' he said.

'But the kind of rot people believe. Because they want to believe!' Atkins hesitated. '*Is* your initial H?'

Denton thought of denying it, then saw how pointless a denial was. 'One of them. How the hell did they find out?' He exhaled noisily. 'I feel like I've been poleaxed. What the hell!' He looked at the broken glass as Atkins swept it into the pan. 'Get somebody to repair the window.'

'The Dutchy's upstairs. He can fix anything, he says.'

'Get him, get him.' As Atkins was going down the room with the now full dustpan, Denton said, 'Can you fix a suit so I can wear it?'

'You're not going *out*!'

'I need to see my solicitor.'

'I ain't going to slit the trousers of your good suits so you can do a walkaround on burned legs that should be in hospital, not cruising the streets!' Atkins, not yet finished, came back towards him. 'And I'll not have you going out in public looking like some-body in panto!'

Rather than being annoyed, Denton was cheered; he even laughed. He put a hand on Atkins's shoulder. 'I'll clean myself up, Ma. Let's get moving on fixing this window.' Limping towards his temporary bedroom, Denton raised his voice. 'And move my things into my room upstairs!'

'You'll tear your scabs off, prancing about!'

Denton turned back to him. 'Sergeant, did you ever have to stand guard or fight or work for an officer while you were sick?'

'Did I! My hat!'

'My point.'

Denton went into the downstairs lavatory behind the Dresden stove, remembered there was no hot water there and bellowed at Atkins to bring down his travelling kit. When that was grudgingly done, Denton unpacked his shaving kit, assembled the one-cup alcohol stove ('The Silver Shaving Etna') and, back in the lavatory, heated the water. He became aware of a trickle on his right ankle, saw a ribbon of watery blood; he swore, blotted it with sanitary tissue, and ignored the pain in his burned shoulder.

He stropped the razor on the portable strop, whipped soap and hot water to a foam in the now very hot cup, and lathered his face with the brush. He hadn't shaved since the fire; now he winced but went forward. The face that emerged looked more uniformly red, certainly more closely shaven, but the half-mast moustache was a poser. Finding his scissors in his kit, he ruth-lessly trimmed the long side of the moustache to match the burned one, then trimmed both and the growth between. The result was something he had never seen: a businessman's brush, his huge nose looming above as if it meant to devour it.

Like I was carrying a clothes brush under my nose.

He tried brushing his hair so as to hide the protruding ear, but it was no good. The ear was out there in the world, and it would have taken a woman's wig to hide it.

The hell with it.

Atkins had spread two suits on the makeshift bed in the room he so hated. Seeing Denton, he straightened, studied the face, shrugged. 'Be it on your head,' he said. He pointed at the suits. 'The brown lounge has slightly wider trousers, might go over the compresses if we can pull a silk stocking over them. The blue double-breasted will look better if you're going to a man of law.'

'Looks ain't in it, I'm afraid.'

'You're just being contrary—like a kiddie putting beans up his nose—can't wait three or four days to heal—' Atkins was muttering as loud as he dared.

Denton was winding a torn strip of cloth over the right calf. 'I had a wash in the can. Let's try these stockings.'

Atkins sucked in his breath when he saw the trickle of fluid on Denton's right leg, but he presented the stockings; Denton worked first one and then the other up, wincing despite himself. 'Capital.'

'My hat. Hurts like billy-o, is my guess.' He held out the trousers. Denton got those on pretty well, had some trouble with the shirt, far more with the collar.

'Ready to give it up?' Atkins said.

'Shut it.' He finally settled for a collar that he never wore because it was too big; now, lined with a linen handkerchief, it was bearable against the burns around his ear. Tying a necktie, he said, 'Looks as if I'm wearing Dad's clothes, I suppose.'

'I didn't say a word.'

He inserted himself into the jacket. It chafed. 'So long as I don't move, I'll be fine.' He grinned at Atkins. Atkins curled a lip. It was impossible for him to walk without limping, and he tended to favour the right shoulder by curling a little into himself from the left. Still, he could manage—for a few paces.

'I shan't be running to catch a bus,' he said.

'You're really going through with this.'

'I'll need a cab. Chop-chop.'

When Atkins came back with the cab, Denton was sitting in his armchair, watching the elderly German remove the remains of the pane from the front window. Denton had fortified himself with painkillers but still felt every fibre of his clothes on the burned skin. 'I'll need my overcoat,' he said.

''Course you will.' Atkins came back with a hat and the coat and held it for him to get into. Patting the pocket from habit, Denton said, 'No point in the gun. I couldn't put this hand in there to get it even if I had to. But considering what's been happening, I'd like to take it.' Atkins had sewn a cloth holster into his overcoat pockets to hold his new Smith & Wesson .32. 'If I could carry a holster over my waistcoat, I could get at it.'

'You'd look fetching at your solicitor's in a gunbelt.'

Denton limped downstairs. Atkins raced ahead of him to the door, but stood as if barring it and said, 'Hat!'

'No hat. Burns won't stand it.'

'No hat!' Atkins was scandalized. 'I'd rather you went out without trousers.'

'I'll try that next time.'

He went out to the cab. When he trotted away, he looked back to see Atkins standing there shaking his head.

Sir Francis Brudenell had chambers in the Temple. Denton told the driver to get there by way of Wych Street, which was in fact out of the way but for which he had an affection, the more so as Wych Street was about to disappear—absolutely disappear as if it had never been—to make room for a grandiose scheme to be called the Aldwych and Kingsway.

'Not going to be any Wych Street soon,' the driver said as

they jogged over the bricks. He had opened the hatch above Denton's head when he had found his passenger was willing to chat. In fact, Denton was eager to chat; despite his pains and itches, he was delighted to be out. 'Going to be what they call a modern imperial thoroughfare instead, the which I says will be nothing but a madhouse of traffic because of Waterloo Bridge.'

Wych was a street of small shops and questionable dwellings, the houses built right after the Great Fire, many with gable ends projecting a foot or two over the street to provide shelter for pedestrians. The shops had the small-mullioned windows of the eighteenth century; here and there, a half-timbered front remained. It was a Dickensian street, a picturesque street, for that reason one that Denton had thought of as 'the real London' when he had first arrived, and it was going into history's dustbin with one sweep of the broom.

'I shall miss it,' Denton said.

'Not half. Wait till you see what they gives us instead.'

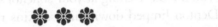

Sir Francis Brudenell was very tall and very rich and had come Denton's way when he had needed defence against criminal prosecution. A devoted fisherman (self-described as 'a real dry-fly man', meaningless to Denton) he was known to leave his chambers at noon on Friday for lunch at the New Reform and then take the train so as to be on the Houghton Club waters for the evening rise. He looked somewhat equine, therefore aristocratic, and he was the man to go to in London if you were in trouble— and if you had the money.

'Aha, aha, aha,' he said as he shook Denton's hand. 'Not the police trying to charge you improperly again, I hope.'

Denton sketched for him the ravings of *The Command* and the smashing of his window. Sir Francis smiled. 'I don't know if I have ever been retained over a broken window.'

'You said to me once that my life is fascinating and anything that happened to it would interest you.'

Sir Francis smiled and nodded like one of those toys whose head is mounted on a pivot. Sitting with one slender leg over another in a rather delicate armchair, he held a knee between his clasped hands. 'The woman with the disrespectful child is hardly worth our time. One can sue such people, but costs always exceed the potential return. Judges can be quite vexing in such cases. However—' He shifted an inch to the right; sunlight, striking silver through low clouds, shone on his grey, metallic hair. He fingered *The Command*. 'The matter in this wretched sheet is perhaps libellous, and it interests me, although my speciality as you know is criminal and not civil law.' He raised his thin eyebrows. 'I could recommend someone to you, if you like.'

'You want to pass me on?'

'Not at all, but I want you to have the best.'

'You're the best.'

'Not at civil litigation. However, as we seem to suit each other, I could, if you'll have me, advise you until such time as litigation seemed wise, and then perhaps we might bring in somebody else.'

At my expense, Denton thought. 'What do you advise?'

'Nothing.' Brudenell unclasped the knee and sat straighter. 'Whoever wrote this is clever and sailed along the coast of the litigious but never quite went into port. I suggest we wait and see how far he will go.' He tilted his head back an inch and looked at Denton down his long nose. '*Are* you a Jew, by the way?'

'Of course not.'

'Do you mind being called a Jew?'

'Of—' Denton caught himself. Did he mind? 'I don't think so.'

'Because if you do, then a lawsuit would have more force; that is, we would show how the denomination of "Jew" is pejorative, has negative social consequences and so on. However, to say all that is perhaps to play into the hands of the author of the screed—I mean by that, that if you say you are harmed by being called a Jew, then you agree that a Jew is a bad thing.'

'But I don't agree.'

'Then, you see, you cannot go into the box and under oath aver that you have been harmed. A good barrister would perhaps bring a jury to understand that you could be harmed even without thinking that to be a Jew is itself no good thing, but it would be tricky—tricky. I should myself rather wait to see if the writer will berth his little boat snugly in the port of libel.'

'Can I answer him?'

'Mmm.' Sir Francis looked out of the window into the wintry green of the Temple; the clouds had closed over the moment of sun and the light was diffuse, slightly misty. 'Y-e-e-s, if you will yourself stay well away from libel and slander. I could of course be useful there.' He turned back to Denton. 'But in what venue? A letter to *The Times*? To do what—deny the allegation? A waste of time. And not having a scandalous rag at your immediate disposal, you can hardly otherwise get something into print in time to have an effect. As is so often the case, the villain has the advantage here: having neither truth nor honour, he lays about at will while you, having both truth and honour, are constrained. Therefore, wait! Let him make his mistake—and we will have him.'

'And what will we have? Suppose it turns out to be somebody like the broken window, with nothing to win?'

'Ah, money would not be the object. You would win the scandalous rag, for one thing, and you would win an apology.'

'At my expense.'

Sir Francis smiled. 'Some things, reputation among them, are beyond price.' He didn't need to say that, nonetheless, he would be able to put a price on his own services. 'Meanwhile, you will be patient.'

Unsatisfied but accepting the wisdom of patience (easier when one has no alternative), Denton prepared to go. As he put his hands on the arms of his chair to push himself up, Sir Francis said, 'Forgive my noticing, but you've been injured. This was the rescue that I read of in *The Times*?'

'And the immediate cause of the screed in the scandalous rag.'

'How is the man you saved?'

'He's lost an eye.'

Sir Francis said he was so very sorry, and Denton must be in pain, and could he have him run home in his motor car? Denton put it all aside with a grunt, but he did say when he was on his feet, 'I ran into a lawyer named Freethorne the other day.'

'Ah, William. Not on the wrong end of his stick, I hope.'

'Maybe.' Denton told him about the two 'little tin gods' and Freethorne's appearance. 'He said he was lawyer to the Home Secretary.'

Sir Francis allowed a tiny smile. 'That is not *quite* right. William likes to make himself greater than he in fact is. Though he can be a rather dangerous fellow. And you struck somebody? Is this going to law?'

Denton shook his head. 'But a woman's dead and nobody's doing anything.'

Sir Francis's eyebrows made a small comment. 'Brother William's darker side rather intrigues me.' He pulled himself very straight and stared at nothing over Denton's shoulder. 'So does a crime that no one will investigate.'

A moment later, when he saw Denton wince again as he tried to get into his overcoat, Sir Francis insisted on the chauffeured motor car. Denton, admitting to himself that he was exhausted, more by discomfort than activity, accepted with a good grace.

Janet was home ahead of him. She was reassuringly angry.

'You fool! You absolute fool! What were you thinking of?'

'I had to see Brudenell—'

'You had to do nothing! Look at you—you're about to fall over. Oh, get those clothes off—'

She began to pull the overcoat off his back—they were still in his downstairs hall—and he groaned aloud and she said it served him right. Yet he took her anger for an expression of affection, and he was pleased.

She gave him a small shove in a part of his back she knew was healthy. 'Go on upstairs, you fool.'

'Where's Atkins?'

'He's cowering in the back because I told him I'd take care of you myself, or else. Go on, now.'

Upstairs, she piloted him into the despised invalid's room and began to undress him.

'This promises well,' he said as she unbuttoned his collar.

'It doesn't. I could smack you, Denton!'

'Does it help if I say I meant well?'

'Does it ever?' She was pulling off his shirt. 'Look at this sleeve—it's covered with stains! It's ruined, I'm sure. Dear God!' She flung the shirt on the floor. 'You might have thought of Atkins, who has to clean up after you. And don't tell me he gets paid enough—he doesn't! And you might have thought of me!'

'I think of you all the time.'

'Oh, don't talk nonsense.' She was unbuttoning his flies, ignoring his quite evident erection. 'Sit down.'

She began to pull off his trousers. When she peeled down his right stocking, she sucked in her breath at the sight. 'Have you no nerves to feel with?' she said angrily.

'Janet, Janet—' He was lying on his back; he held out his arms. 'Come.'

She threw the stocking aside. 'I'm not to be made up to that way, Denton. I'm not your doxie. When I want you, I'll have you, but right now I don't want you.' She peeled off the other stocking. 'I'll send Atkins up to change your dressings. Is it really fair to him that he has to do it again, and will have to do it *again* tonight? You're as thoughtless as a timber baulk.'

'I take it that the Isle of Dogs bit you today.'

She made an impatient sound. 'One drunken husband who blackguarded me, and two women who told me to go about my bloody business. *The Command*'s everywhere down there. Somehow it's got about that I've a connection to you.'

'How, in the name of God?'

'Gossip. They're right by the West India Dock; the trade union's rabid with anti-Semitism. One of the women called me "dirty Jew bitch" and said I was kept by a Jew, wasn't I? Great lot of good to deny it.'

'I'm so sorry, Janet.'

'I don't care, except it makes my work so much harder. It's all ridiculous.' She stared at him. 'But I'm going back! And don't you try to stop me!'

And with that, she left him. And stayed away. He sank back on the bed, meaning to feel sorry for himself, but he was asleep almost at once.

'I've been thinking,' Atkins said. He had woken Denton to change his dressings.

'Always a good start.'

'The missus was on the rampage about you being gone.'

'Don't call her the missus.'

'Well, she is a missus. All right, Mrs Striker.' He started to apply salve. 'She's worried about you.'

'That's reassuring.' And in fact it was.

'If I might suggest, a little consideration of her might be in order, Colonel.'

'She said I should have more consideration for you.'

'Very nice of her, I'm sure. The point is—' Atkins got the cotton bandage. 'You're not fit yet.'

'I found that out.'

'Well, then, I've had my say. How was the man of law?'

'Expensive. Wants to sniff around the lawyer, Freethorne.'

'Why?'

'Something personal, maybe. But he was interested in the fact that the cops have given up on the dead woman. Which raises a question—' Denton propped himself on his left elbow and held his right arm up. 'Who *did* kill that woman?'

'I wondered when you'd get to that.'

'Oh, did you?'

'Easy to see your concern's been for Mrs Striker, who you said's involved but you won't tell me how; oh, dear, I just have to muddle along in ignorance. But I knew you couldn't stay away from the smell of a murder for long. You're like a dog at a lamp-post, bound to get to the real piddle before you finish with it.'

'Well—who killed her?'

Atkins finished his arm and gave him a light shove to put him on his face. He peeled a compress off Denton's shoulder and said, 'This one's healing, at least. Lint's clean. A bit of ointment and we're done here.' He reached for the box. 'Who killed her? One of the workmen? Be a bit of a trick, to leave the job, murder a woman, carry her out behind the old privy, wrap her up and leave her. Somebody who wandered in the front door, which I'd wager was open because the furnace wallahs was going in and out? But how does he know she's there? He don't. But we'll say he came in to rob the house. Daring chap—hears the hammering and sawing upstairs, ducks through my door, looks about for something to steal, finds a woman, kills her, carries her out behind the privy, gets a tarpaulin he doesn't know the existence of from the old privy, wraps her, dumps her. Why?'

'Not only why, but what woman?'

'The woman in my bed, the woman that hung her black dress and hat on my hook.'

'What's a woman doing in your bed? Nothing personal, Sergeant—I meant, when you aren't in it.'

'Well, the missus says she brought some woman through the house on the way to hers.'

'But put her in her own house.'

'But she could've come back.'

'Why?'

'You always want to know why!' Atkins sounded irritable. 'I say you'd know why if you knew who she was.'

'She was a patient who was feeling tired and ill.'

'That's no reason to take her dress off and get into my bed.'

Denton was frowning. 'I kind of lost all this. The coca wine, maybe. Now that I can think about it again—yes, why did she take her dress off?'

'To get into bed.'

'But Mrs Striker says the woman lay down on a bed in the Cohans' quarters—nothing about taking off her dress. So if she came back here to lie down, why strip to her knickers and corset?'

'And stockings.'

'But not shoes. And no handbag, which her "husband" was particularly interested in.'

'You're thinking now he isn't her husband.'

'Guillam made a pretty good case for it. Which suggests something going on outside this little ring of heating men and strangers we've set up. For example—she's carrying a handbag, and it's the handbag not the woman herself that's important. The "husband" comes in the open front door, kills her, takes the handbag.'

'Cute, Major, but he come to see you because he *wanted* the handbag.'

'All right, he came in the open front door and she didn't have the handbag, and he killed her out of anger.'

Atkins was rolling the dirty compresses in a piece of newspaper to go in the rubbish. 'Not even I think that's very good.' He mashed the bundle together against his chest. 'Look here, let's be honest—we're leaving out at least two possibilities, but they ought to be considered: Annie and Mrs Cohan. All they had to do was walk across the gardens, kill the woman, dump her. They prob'ly knew about the tarp—seen Cohan and me use it in the garden.'

'Annie couldn't break somebody's neck. Nor Mrs Cohan, I'd think.'

'Nor either of them carry a dead body about. Take two, at least.'

'Annie and the "husband". It's a love triangle.'

'Now, you be serious, Colonel! I'm trying to put this thing together, and you're being jocular.'

'Mrs Cohan and the "husband".'

'I give up.' Atkins stamped off to the lavatory. Denton heard the sound of fairly extended hand-washing. When he came back, Atkins wore a look of hurt dignity; he went around the room, straightening the furniture, folding Denton's clothes, picking up his shirt and stockings. When the room was again immaculate, he said, 'Will there be anything else, sir?'

Denton laughed. Atkins tried to hold on to his dignity, made a face and sat down on the edge of a velvet-covered chair with his arms full of dirty clothes and medical supplies. 'You going to be serious or not?' he said.

'Serious, absolutely. Here's a serious question: why did they or he—or she—put the body behind the privy?'

'To hide it, what else?'

'From whom?'

'Them central-heating wallahs, I suppose; they were the only ones about.'

'But why not leave it in the bed? They're upstairs; you've just killed her; all you need do is walk out that open front door. Once you're gone, what does it matter if she's found?'

'You're her husband—the first one the coppers will look at.'

'So, behind the privy, she'll never be found?'

'Well, not for a bit. Time to get away. Somewhere.' He sounded unsure. Rallying, he said in a stronger voice, 'Crime of passion, you don't think them things through.'

'Granted. So it's a crime of passion?' Denton pulled on a clean pair of the rowing trousers. 'If I had an old privy handy and I wanted to hide a body, I'd put it *in* the privy, not behind it.'

'Full of garden tools.'

'Not that part of the privy—down below.'

'Never get a body through the holes were meant to sit on. Anyway, we turned that part into shelves.'

'In the back, where the body was found, there's a hatch. Isn't there? Where the dustman shovelled out the night soil?'

Atkins rocked back and forth, lips pushed forward, his brow in a frown. 'Then why didn't they?'

'We nailed it shut when we turned the privy into a garden shed. But the killer didn't know that. So he or she or they carried the body out and put it behind the shed, meaning to dump it in, and there's the hatch nailed shut. So he or she or they looked for tools to open it in the shed but saw the tarp and settled for wrapping her up. And skedaddled.'

'Yes, but—' Atkins looked unhappy. 'That's as bad as leaving her in the bed.'

'Not as bad, no—if one of the heating men hadn't reverted to his origins and gone out to piss behind the privy, she wouldn't have been found until Monday, at least, when we came home. And maybe longer.'

'Rupert'd have found her.' At the mention of his name, the huge dog wagged his little tail but did not seem to wake up.

'All right, Rupert would have found her. The killer doesn't know that.'

Atkins looked canny. 'Does he know that we're away?'

Denton lifted his chin. He had been buttoning himself into a long-sleeved wool undershirt; he stopped the buttoning where greying chest hairs sprang out between the wool edges. 'Ah. Damned good question. Hmmm.' He went back to his buttoning more slowly. 'If he does, then it's somebody who knows us, isn't it. Like Annie or Mrs Cohan.'

'Or Cohan. Don't take it personal, General, I know you like the Jew-Boy and so do I, but all we know is he was supposed to be at his boxing school getting ready for the opening, but he could've walked around the street and come in the door and killed half a dozen women and nobody the wiser. And he's got the strength to break a neck.'

Denton puffed out his cheeks, blew a long breath. 'And to carry her out to the privy. But why?'

'Love triangle. Crime of passion.'

'He knows the woman whom Mrs Striker took to her house?'

'Maybe not. Mrs Striker brings her in, makes her comfortable. Mrs Cohan's out; Cohan gets a letch for the woman, tries to march on her, she runs out and through the gardens to your house, and he comes behind and kills her.'

'There was no rape, no bruises that I could see. Cohan didn't have any scratches or marks when I saw him that afternoon.'

'He come up behind her and broke her neck. She'd already refused him and he was in a rage.'

'And the dress? He undresses her and then carries her out to the old privy? Which, by the way, Cohan knows has been nailed shut.'

'She took her dress off in the Cohans' quarters, and that's what's made him lecherous, seeing her lying there all akimbo. To cover himself, after he's killed her, he goes back and gets the dress and carries it to my room and hangs it up.'

Denton thought about it. 'It doesn't sound like Cohan.'

'I know that. I'm just talking.'

Denton didn't want to say too much to Atkins about what had happened at Bernat's surgery; still, he wanted help in thinking. He said, 'What if Bernat was wrong about the dead woman being his patient?'

'I don't follow you, General.'

'I don't either. But it's a possibility.' He couldn't tell Atkins that it was a certainty, that in fact the dead woman was not the same as the one who had come to Bernat's surgery, that there had been two women—one of whom was alive somewhere and perhaps knew a great deal. 'Suppose—just suppose—the doctor was wrong and the woman in the garden wasn't the same as the woman he'd treated that morning. He never saw the body, after all.'

'You mean, what if there was *two* women? My hat!'

CHAPTER

9

Atkins's voice came from a distance, but clearly. It inserted itself into his dream—horse, smoke, fear—and woke him, the pleasant baritone a relief after the dream:

> *I'm a knut! I'm a knut!*
> *Oh, I'm the knuttiest one of them all!*
> *I put in my eyeglass, I tip my t-topper over my no-ho-ho-hose*
> *And I'm off to the knuts' fancy-dress ball!*

'Morning, General.'

'Music-hall mood this morning?'

'I'm composing.'

Denton rolled himself over on his good shoulder. 'That song?'

Atkins put a tea tray down on a carved, hideous table. 'My virgin effort. You want your wounds done before or after the tea?'

'Tea and wounds together.' As Atkins poured, Denton thought of Janet's anger of yesterday. 'Do I ask too much of you, Sergeant?'

'What—in the work department?' Atkins laughed. 'Had an officer once had me digging a hole for a lily pond. You're a lark by comparison.'

'You want some tea?'

'Brought only the one cup and already had mine. Your ear's made a fair mess of the pillow, I see.'

'Still bleeding?'

'Looks more like it pissed on it, from the colour. Shoulder's better, though, nice growth of scabs you got. Legs very good. Still, you stay close to home today, like the missus says—I'd rather not have any more shirts and collars coming back like yesterday's.' He finished the bandaging and picked up the tea tray. 'Got a couple of eggs, if you like. Coddled or fried, no gammon. Toast by the pound.'

'Fried. Jam. Coffee.'

Atkins stopped in the doorway with the tray on one hand, the bundle of compresses in the other. 'You like that ditty I was singing?' He said it too casually, so Denton knew he was nervous about the answer.

'Catchy, I thought. Pleasant to be woken to.'

Atkins came back in a step. 'Funny the way things happen. Met a chap at the Jewish Hospital when I was visiting you and O'Cohen; he's the comedian at a theatre down that way. He said—well, it's a long story that I won't go into. But him and me have an idea. Might be something big in it.'

Denton groaned inwardly but said only, 'Remember the vacuum cleaner.' Atkins had tried peddling a friend's invention, a hand-pumped sweeper that would have exhausted Hercules.

'Ahead of its time, was the trouble there.'

'And the Marconi apparatus.'

'Colonel, you have to face it—I'm a visionary.'

After his breakfast, Denton went up to his bedroom. He managed the stairs by bending his legs as little as he could; once up there, he sank into the desk chair, then leaned forward and felt through the litter for a pencil. He scribbled 'The Secret Jew' on a clean sheet of paper. Something he had thought about in a waking hour in the middle of the night—something he had dreamed about first? He was never sure. He would wake with an idea seemingly whole, at least in silhouette. Now this.

He scribbled, 'Religion—passion to believe. Seeking the lost tribe of Israel?' He tossed the pencil away and stared at what he had written. 'The Secret Jew', which was a working title, did not mean at all what *The Command* had meant by it: not somebody hiding his Judaism, but somebody discovering Judaism in himself. He took the pencil up again and wrote, 'But not a *real* Jew. No Jewish parents, looks, culture etc.' He stared at that for a while and then rooted out some old trousers and an ancient shirt and dressed himself so that he looked at least a little less like a tramp who'd been run over by a dray. Then he went back to the sheet of paper and wrote 'guilt' and underlined it twice.

He apologized to Janet for overdoing it the day before and persuaded her that evening that he was fit enough to go to the Domino Room of the Café Royal. She was rarely willing to go there—because, he thought, she saw it as his preserve, some sort of masculine retreat. He had once told her it was as close as he'd ever come to having a club; perhaps that was it. That she would go now was a sign of special effort. He should have been pleased, but he thought again that she was trying too hard to make the atmosphere around them normal, thus was behaving abnormally.

Or perhaps he was simply making too much of things.

The Domino Room was a high-ceilinged, noisy place with acoustics that sent voices and the clatter of plates and glasses ricocheting everywhere. Columns, gold and green, rose up into caryatids and abundant leaves. The clientele was varied: many men, most of these 'Bohemians', kept their hats on, as if it were a public house; the women with them, often models or artists themselves, were colourful in gypsy wear or sometimes daring dresses. Tobacco smoke was thick. Custom divided the huge room along invisible boundaries into duchies and principalities and squabbling states, the end near the Glasshouse Street entrance owned by critics and magazine people, that near the Regent Street end largely artistic; the banquettes along the wall at right angles were a haunt of bookmakers and, late at night, tarts.

Denton took a table near Regent Street. Janet, looking at the two or three tarts having something to eat before they went out, said, 'They'll be French. Regent Street's the French whores' pitch.' She laughed. When she had been young and green and destitute, she'd known no better than to make her first try at prostitution on Regent Street because it was one of the 'nice' streets she knew. The French whores had slapped her about and threatened to cut her nose off.

Denton smiled around him at the noise and the colour. 'I love this place.'

'It's what Ruth Castle would call "louche". One of her favourite words.' Mrs Castle, the 'Mrs' perhaps honorary, had been her first (and only) madam, was still a close friend. 'I think one of the louches is trying to get your attention.' She pointed with her chin.

Along the bookmakers' wall, a middle-aged fat man in checks big enough to play chess on was waving at Denton; now, seeing that he had been noticed, he ambled over.

'I heard you'd been hurt—the Jew-Boy, too. Made a packet on the Jew-Boy once. I've something nice I'd recommend at Newmarket tomorrow.'

'Hello, Daggett.' Horace Daggett was a bookie, better known as the Downy Bird, but Denton preferred his real—supposedly real, anyway—name. Denton introduced Janet and said, 'Sure thing?'

'If there was sure things, Mr Denton, I'd be hauling dust-bins. A *good* thing is the best I can do.' Daggett was rumoured to be the man—or the brother of the man, or a friend of the man—who fixed the Prix de Longchamps in 1896. His air of affable fat man hid a good deal.

Denton pushed a chair with a foot and said, 'Have a seat.'

'Mrs Daggett's a bit impatient—' Daggett muttered, bobbing his head towards the wall; his bowler hat, already perched far back, wobbled, and he gave it a rap as if to discipline it.

Janet said, 'Ask her to join us.'

The Bird glanced towards a formidable-looking, scowling woman with a remarkable nose under what seemed to be twice as much black hair as was needed to support her hat. He waved her towards them. She jerked in her chair as if she'd been touched. The Bird leaned over Denton. 'Mrs Daggett's eager to be off home. Wonderful woman.' He laughed, like a horse yawning, then leaned closer. 'That flying machine had better take to the air pretty smartly, or you're down ten pounds, Mr Denton!' He bellowed out a laugh. The Downy Bird was running a pool on the date of the first true aerial flight, and Denton had money in it, now lost because the date he had picked was only two weeks off and nobody had flown. They both laughed. Daggett waggled his fingers and headed towards the door, where Mrs Daggett was already tapping the tip of her umbrella on the floor.

Janet giggled. 'Flying machines! You're worse than Atkins, trying to make money off every new thing.'

'Atkins told me today he's dreamed up some scheme with somebody he met at the Infirmary.'

She was studying the menu. She nodded. 'Shmuel Broder. He's a comedian at Dilke's.' She looked up. 'It's a pub with the music hall upstairs.'

'You've been there.'

'Often and often! That was my night out when I lived in the East End. I'm trying to persuade Leah to go, to take her mind off Hyam, but Leah's dour. All she can think of is getting him home to make him well, and of course Bernat insists he has to stay in hospital for weeks more.' She put down the menu. 'I think I'll have the French dinner. Can you afford five shillings?'

'I was going to let you pay. I'll scrimp by having the chicken pot pie.'

'You always do.' They smiled at each other: they had reestablished normality.

Halfway through their eating, a shabby figure came through the Regent Street doors and stood looking about. He wore a huge overcoat with the remains of a fur collar; his pockets bulged with papers and what appeared to be at least one thick book. Janet said, 'The *roi des louches?*'

'Oh, cripes, that's Crosland.' Crosland was a fixture, known to cadge the odd shilling and then stand the donor a drink with it; he was a professional journalist of an odd and independent sort who had once told Denton that he 'gave new meaning to the term "hackney writer",' Denton waved.

Crosland saw him and made signs of recognition with his eyebrows, but instead of coming over, he headed for somebody else he seemed to know on the other side of the room.

'Well, that's a first.'

'Maybe he *schnorred* somebody outside. The French girls, perhaps—they can be generous, whores.'

'What's "schnorred"?'

'Oh—Yiddish, to cadge—you know, beg.'

Denton watched Crosland disappear behind a pillar. Janet wanted a pudding; Denton ordered coffee, refused brandy—she shook her head at him when the waiter suggested it—and sat with his head back, smiling, watching the spectacle. As she was finishing her pudding, there was a disturbance at the Glasshouse Street end, and a rough cheer went up, then some catcalls.

Denton laughed. 'Frank Harris has arrived.'

'The notorious one?' She licked her spoon. 'One hears bad things about him.'

'One hears bad things about me.' He waved at Harris and shouted. 'You should meet him, then you can judge for yourself.'

She turned in her chair and looked for him.

Denton said, 'In the soft hat—coming towards us—'

Frank Harris was an editor and writer, rather peripatetic, usually in the process of leaving one magazine and going with another. He knew everybody, said he knew everything, had a reputation as a sexual opportunist, about which he was so outspoken that even upper-class London, usually broad-minded so long as you were quiet ('Don't scare the horses'), refused to have him inside its houses. His eyes always looked angry, often bloodshot (alcohol); his smile was sharkish. He seemed actually to respect, even like Denton, perhaps because he had lived in America and claimed he had even been a cowboy.

'Ha-ha!' he was shouting over the Café's clamour. 'Ha-ha, Denton!' He came close, stepping around so that he could have a frank look at Janet, then immediately taking off his hat and even bowing. 'Mrs Striker, I am Frank Harris. I am *delighted* to meet you.'

'You know my name.' She didn't seem to like it that he did.

'I know everything.' He handed his coat and hat to a waiter. He was wearing a dinner suit, the jacket cut quite short in the bum-freezer style. He had been drinking, but then he had always been drinking. He sat, still turned towards her. 'Denton so often comes here alone, and it isn't good for him.' He turned to look at Denton. 'You don't look as bad as I'd heard.' He signalled to a waiter and ordered brandy.

'I'm healing.'

Harris made an effort to please Janet. He was wise enough not to use the techniques that apparently worked on 'his' women, often suburban wives, nor to flatter her; rather, he began to talk about the East End and socialism and the push now on, led by the MP for Stepney, Evans-Gordon, to limit immigration. '"Britain for the Brutish", as the saying goes.'

She remained rather prickly, but she couldn't resist the subject. 'You're for unlimited immigration?'

'I'm for more art and more intellect and more culture, none of which will come from people like Evans-Gordon. Let's throw out some English blockheads and get more Jews and Italians. Perhaps we could trade Evans-Gordon for a decent mathematician. I'd even throw in Mr Balfour.' He gave her a restrained, unsharkish smile. 'I'm Irish, myself.'

'It's a matter of class, not nationality, isn't it?'

'Of course; what isn't? We have millions of native-born slackers and criminals I'd happily exchange for something foreign. Come to think of it, I'd exchange our entire middle class for one good composer—get rid of propriety and narrow-mindedness and moral dishonesty and bring in somebody with some moral backbone.'

'You'd be the first to be stoned,' Denton said.

'Well, of course, but look at the good I'd have done.' He leaned in towards Denton, his eyes hot. 'Your name isn't really Hyman, is it?'

'Oh, for God's sake—! If I ever find who wrote that, I'll wring his neck.'

Harris made a barking sound, his version of laughter. 'You don't know who wrote it?'

'Do you?'

'Of course I do!' Harris barked some more. 'Three guesses.'

'I don't do guesses! Don't play with me, Harris—do you know, or don't you?'

'Of course.' He leaned in again. 'It was Crosland.'

Denton simply stared at him.

'Crosland boasts that he can write anything on any subject. It's his notion of true professionalism. Somebody paid him to write a diatribe against Jews. Fine. Pay him to write an encomium to them, that would be fine, as well. It's just all words to him—it's all "art".'

'You're sure it's Crosland?'

Harris looked pained. Of course he was sure.

Denton scrambled to his feet and looked around the room. Crosland was far up towards Glasshouse Street, hunched over a table with a couple of other people. Denton started for him.

Janet said, 'Denton—!' but he paid no attention.

One of the men with Crosland saw him coming and looked panicked. *He knows, then. Everybody knows.* For an instant, dodging around tables and avoiding staring eyes, he hated London and the British, all these complacent faces, all these sharers in a secret against him; and then he was at Crosland's table. The panicked man was halfway on his feet; Crosland had turned around and was raising an arm as if he could ward off Denton's charge.

'Crosland!'

The noise at that end of the Domino Room dropped. People looked expectantly at each other. He saw a woman lick her lips, eyes wide. He grabbed Crosland's greasy necktie and pulled him up by it, Crosland helping by trying to get to his feet at the same time. Denton swung him on the necktie, pushing a shoulder to spin him so Crosland's back was against a pillar, then shoving him hard against it. Three waiters began to converge on them: fights were far from unknown in the Domino Room, frowned on by the management, to be cut off as soon as possible.

'You slimy hack!'

Crosland, who had been sinking down the pillar as if his legs were melting, came abruptly upright. 'I resent that! I am a professional writer!'

'Did you write that crap in *The Command* about me?'

'Of course I did! But it wasn't *personal*!'

'I should flatten you!'

Denton felt a waiter's hand fall on his right shoulder; he winced when the burn was touched. 'Oh, leave us be!' he growled. 'I'm not going to hit him.' He turned back to Crosland. 'But I should! I should flatten you!'

'Sir—sir—sir—' The waiter had an Italian accent, was perhaps two-thirds Denton's size; even though he was backed up by two other waiters, one fat and one ancient, he didn't seem to want to use force. 'Please, sir—'

Denton pulled his face back from Crosland's; they had been close enough for him to know that Crosland had been drinking port. 'You and I are going to talk,' he said.

Crosland pulled his disastrous overcoat around him and then tried to straighten his necktie, which Denton was still holding. Brushing the hands aside, Denton pulled Crosland down the room towards his own table but veered off when he saw Janet, one finger pointed at Harris, saying, 'You don't know what you're talking about! I *do* know what I'm talking about! I've been on the street and I've lived in the slums, so don't you dare patronize me with your—'

Denton found an empty table nearby and dropped Crosland into a chair. He pulled up one for himself facing him, called 'Two brandies!' to the three waiters, who had followed him. Putting his forearms on the table, he loomed towards Crosland. 'How could you do such a thing?'

'It's my profession.' Crosland was panting.

'Have I done something to you? Have I ever harmed you? For God's sake, I buy you drinks!'

Crosland waved a hairy hand. 'Oh, everybody buys me drinks. Denton, it's just a job to me. I'll write anything for anybody—and it will be *good*!'

'You call that tripe good? That shithouseful of lies?'

'They aren't lies. Not quite. Read it carefully and you'll find those are not lies. They are—artfully contrived implications.'

'Who's paying you?'

Crosland laid a hand on the bulging overcoat more or less where his heart lay under it. 'I can't say. Matter of professional ethics.'

Denton started to roar the word *ethics* back at him, and then saw what he must look like—the lopped moustache, the swollen ear, the missing eyebrow—and he knew that he looked absurd. He laughed. And laughed. He pushed himself back and, with both palms flat on the table, laughed so loud and long that other diners stared at him. With tears in his eyes, he leaned towards Crosland again and said, 'Crosland, you have the innocence of a new-born babe. But—' He pointed a finger, thumb up like a cocked hammer. 'If you ever try this on me again, I'll tear off that overcoat and burn every paper in it.'

Crosland flinched. 'It wasn't directed at you. I *like* you.'

'Well, thank God you don't love me; no knowing what you'd say. Look, Crosland—' He explained about his broken window, the mud thrown at his house, the attack on Cohan, Janet's trouble in the Isle of Dogs. 'Whoever you're working for moves from words to acts very easily. For them, Crosland, it *is* personal.'

'I have nothing to do with that.'

'But words aren't harmless. Or innocent.'

The brandies had appeared. Crosland sipped from his, eyes still on Denton's, lips pursed to drink again, eyebrows raised. Denton said, 'How much of that rag do you write?'

'Everything.' Crosland wiped his mouth with finger and thumb, pinching the lips forward. 'I'm the editor and writer.' He cleaned his fingers on his overcoat. 'I'm a professional, Denton, a *consummate* professional—I do what I do for money, and I do it well. You must admit, the piece about you was masterful in its way: skirting libel, never quite lying, implying matters so as to enrage certain readers. Really one of my best. Of course, as a professional, I could as well have written from the opposite point of view. For money, I mean.'

'You're not an anti-Semite?'

'Are you suggesting that I write out of *interest*?'

'What do they pay you?'

'Guinea an issue, and I'm a bargain at such a figure. Regrettably, *The Command* is sporadic. Very sporadic. Hardly reliable work.' Crosland looked at him. Their eyes held each other's for several seconds; Crosland's eyebrows moved, as if at a discovery. 'For the right offer, I'd jump ship.'

'For two guineas? Three? Five?'

Crosland made a rumbling sound that could have been laughter. 'For five guineas, I'd leave my mother.' He frowned at the brandy. 'I still live with her, poor old thing. Of course, I wouldn't leave her for the wealth of the Indies.'

'And a consummate professional might jump at a chance to write a *pro*-Semitic piece. To show his ability to take both sides.' Denton smiled at him. 'For—five guineas?'

'Five guineas.' Crosland looked into his empty glass, licked his lips. 'Attractive as a demonstration of my skills.'

Denton signalled to a waiter. 'Five guineas to write a pro-Jewish pamphlet of, let's say, twenty-five thousand words. Making it clear that my name isn't Hymie. Plus you keep the income from any sales. And you drop *The Command*. For good.'

Crosland's eyes darted back and forth. 'They mightn't much like it.'

'"Nothing worthwhile comes without pain."'

Crosland made a face. 'I'd best lie low for a bit.' He looked around as if expecting spies, lowered his voice. 'I'm your man.

Purely as a professional matter. Michelangelo did the *Pietà* and *David*. Mozart wrote masses and *Die Zauberflöte*. Art is not a matter of *attitude.*'

Denton held out a hand. Crosland barely touched Denton's fingers. 'When do I start?'

'Now. Find us a printer and all that.' He pushed a coin across. 'Advance on future earnings. I don't want to hear you're doing anything for *The Command*, you understand—no working both of us at the same time, however much that might tempt your professionalism.' As Crosland pocketed the coin, Denton said, 'Ever run across something called the Brotherhood of Britons?'

'Lot of them around the docks, not a few in the police. Some swells, as well—a glaze on the cake, aimed at the political side to push the anti-immigration bill.'

'Is the Brotherhood behind *The Command*?'

Crosland made a point of picking up his again-empty glass and looking through it as if searching for brandy. Denton signalled for a waiter.

'Common interest, nothing more.'

'Ben Tillett?'

'I shouldn't think. Tillett's in fairly bad odour since he took the union out two years ago and fell on his arse. Some of Tillett's underlings, well—' Crosland made a rocking motion with the hand that was not clutching the brandy glass. 'I'm telling the truth when I tell you I don't know who's behind *The Command*. It's an answer to a need, is what it is—a lot of people hate Jews.'

They sat together for another few minutes. Denton glanced several times towards Janet and saw her always deep in talk with Harris, both a little red-faced. When Denton joined them and slumped into his old chair, they were still arguing, both so intense that neither so much as looked at him.

'Hating everything is an easy box to stand on, Mr Harris!' Janet was saying. 'Try instead having a programme and an idea!'

'I do have a programme; it's called misanthropy. The human race is hopeless.'

'How easy to say so! And how useless. What's the point, then, in talking? Or in my discussing anything with you? If nothing's worthwhile, the only reason to say anything at all is to call attention to yourself, which I suppose is your motive.'

At this point, Harris decided to notice Denton and gave him a huge grin. 'I haven't been so disrespected since I left school,' he said. 'Do change the subject and save me.'

'Nothing can save you, Harris.'

'Did you beat the living daylights out of Crosland?'

'I bought him off.'

Harris was delighted with that.

He spent the next day at his house, now staring out of the bedroom window, now changing his own dressings and feeling over the scabs on his shoulder to find where the salve was to go. He would wander to his desk and stare down at the paper on which he'd written 'The Secret Jew', sometimes adding a few words—*haunted, murder, hallucinations.* Then *North Pole.* Then he crossed out *murder* and wrote *wife and children murdered? Search for justice? The just god? Sense?*

In the afternoon, he dressed himself in his oldest, loosest clothes and went through the garden to Janet's. He went in the back door, startling Annie in the kitchen. She stared at him as if he were carrying a bloody axe.

'Annie's seen the ghost again,' Janet said. She was working at a desk in her music room, papers spread around her and on the floor, an unsteady pile of books rising next to her.

'You're working. I'll go away.'

'No, stay a bit; I need a change. I'm tired of economics.' She rang for Annie and asked for tea.

He said, 'Where did Annie see her ghost this time?'

'On the attic stairs, she says.' Annie slept in the attic. 'She was coming down to the WC and the ghost was looking up at her.'

'A beautiful lady in an old-fashioned dress?'

'More like a dark one in a nightgown. She didn't make much sense.'

'I suppose she saw her own reflection in a window.'

'Could be.'

'Did she fuss?'

'There was rather a lot of screaming. She says it's the woman who was murdered in your garden. I shall really have to get rid of her, I suppose. I miss Leah—she's moody, but she doesn't scream and she doesn't see things, and she takes Annie off my hands.'

The tea came. He wanted to talk about the dead woman, go over more or less the same ground he'd covered with Atkins, but he was afraid that he would upset whatever knife-edge balance they seemed to have reached. He was surprised, therefore, when she said, 'I've been thinking about your corpse.'

'Oh? Me, too.'

'There were *two* women, weren't there? The body you saw wasn't the one Bernat treated; your description is too different. I brought the one through your house to this house, and then the *other* one was murdered. But the two have to be connected.'

'There's nothing to connect them.'

'It makes sense though, doesn't it?'

'Melodrama sense, maybe. Not logical sense.'

She was quiet for a little. 'I think the woman I brought here killed the other one.'

'Good God.'

'Because she's the oddity. It makes far more sense than somebody coming in off the street to rape or rob.'

'I guess I don't see that it makes any more sense at all. What's the logical difference between somebody in off the street and a woman we know nothing about? I suppose that if you say that the dead woman knew the woman Bernat treated, then there's a connection, but we don't know that. And why should one woman have murdered the other? It's like one of those plays in which everybody turns out to be everybody else's long-lost child. It'll all come right in the last act, but there won't be any last act here.'

Janet stared into her teacup, swirled the dregs and then turned the cup one way and then the other, studying the leaves. 'Leah said the woman I brought here went away during the morning. I never asked her what "went away" meant. Maybe she went away the same route I'd brought her, through the garden and your house, and met the other woman and they had a set-to and one murdered the other.' She turned her cup again. 'I seem to be about to make an ocean voyage.'

'Not without me, I hope.'

'There's a bit of something just under the sail that might be you.' She smiled. 'I had a good time last night.'

'I thought you and Harris might kill each other, but you got along like fire and wood.'

'He'd drive me mad if I were around him much.' She put her cup down. 'I have to work.'

Denton stood. 'My question is, who is the woman Bernat treated that morning? I think if we knew that, we might know everything.'

'So you do think the two women are connected!'

'Not necessarily, but—' Did he think that? The truth was, he didn't know what he thought. 'Even if we knew who the *dead* woman was, it would help.'

'Well, *we* may ask that, but I don't want the police to do so. They think there was only the one woman, and she didn't have an illegal operation. Let sleeping dogs lie.' She made shooing gestures with her hands. 'Let me work now.'

When he was at the door, she said, 'Come back later, if you like.'

'Shall we go out?'

'I'll do some eggs.' She made the gesture again. He went through the bright, small rooms, was relieved to find Annie gone from the kitchen. In his own house, Atkins was just looking into the sitting room when he limped upstairs.

'You going out?'

'Only the house behind. You want the evening off? Take it.'

'Dutchy's coming in the morning to fix the stove; then he's going to fire up the furnace, give me heat. I expect coal smoke everywhere. Right mess it'll be, so tomorrow night I'll be cleaning the lot, best make hay tonight with nothing to do. I'm off at six, then.'

'Where to?'

Atkins hesitated. 'Pal of mine has a recording machine. Asked me to make a wax cylinder of my comic song. You know—*I'm a knut, I'm a knut*—that one.'

'Shmuel Broder again? Is he selling recording machines?' Denton slitted his eyes. 'Is this the money-making scheme you two have cooked up?'

'Oh, ha-ha. You mean, am I being led down the garden path of the newfangled *again*? Nothing like. We do have a notion of selling recordings, however. Make you a copy for a bob, if you want one.'

Denton groaned. 'I don't own a machine, thank God.'

On Monday, Denton slipped out at barely daybreak, feeling suddenly impatient with his own house, his body eager to be active despite the now healing burns. He had meant only to walk as far as Bernat's corner, perhaps into Coram Fields, but, seeing a cab emerging from the morning mist like a spiritualist's trick, he clambered into it and ordered it to Regent's Park.

The morning was almost springlike, all wrong for the date. The air felt moist yet fresh, distant buildings graced by the faintest mist. The city, not yet awake, was nearly silent, a low, almost subliminal humming the only sound. In the park, Denton could hear birds as he made his way up the Broad Walk towards the zoo, a favourite when the weather was wrong for rowing. He could have been on the river now, he thought, the unseasonal day fine for it, but the shoulder wouldn't yet put up with rowing. His legs, on the other hand, felt sound except for the chafing of his trousers.

He went on, seeing at first nobody, then a man with two dogs, probably a servant. In the middle of the park, the birdsong increased, almost that chorus that poets were supposed to hear at break of day, although mostly crows and blackbirds. At the same time, he was sure that the city's growl was already rising towards its daytime roar: he heard distinctly the hooves of a horse on Albany Street, then the flatulent cough of a motor car.

At the kiosk, he bore left on a gravelled path because now he wanted the public toilets that he knew lay along it. He moved into a band of oaks, the sound of birds now loud; a flock of crows went up, cawing, as he approached. A hundred feet from the small building, he became aware of something darker than the trees among them; a few feet more told him that it was a man in a black overcoat. Nonetheless, he walked confidently on; if somebody wanted to lean against a tree (hangover? urination?), that was his business; but as he came opposite, the man beckoned, the gesture oddly languid and yet strange in this setting—the almost rural trees and birds, mist blurring but never obscuring things—and odder for suggesting something personal, perhaps sexual. Denton stopped. The man beckoned again and took off his bowler hat. Denton saw that it was Guillam.

He walked through the dew-wet grass; when he was close, Guillam put his finger to his lips. 'Headed for the pisser?' Guillam said.

'Caught short.'

'Rather you didn't.' Guillam, to Denton's surprise, pulled him by the sleeve until he was next to him and behind the tree. 'Keeping an eye on somebody,' Guillam said. 'Should be out soon. Hold it, can you?'

'There's a name for people who spy on public conveniences, Guillam.'

'Aye, there's a name, too, for fellas that get off in public toilets, which my chap is doing, he is. One way to start your day, isn't it—right in the smell of other people's piss and shit?' He glanced sideways at Denton, most of his attention on the toilets. 'What're you doing out at sparrow-fart?'

'Taking a walk. You're on a case?'

'Mmm. Receiving stolen goods. What he's doing in the pisser's nothing to do with it, but I'm trying to see where he goes next.'

'Maybe he's receiving stolen goods in there and not getting off.'

'Well, he's picked one of London's prime spots for getting his Johnson kissed if he is. Opposite the Horse Guards is another— better class of military; those from the cavalry barracks up the way are a bit of a come-down, I suppose. No, he's in there getting licked; he receives the goods at his place of business.'

'Likely to get caught, isn't he?'

'The morals squad doesn't leave Bow Street until eight. Bankers' hours.' Guillam still had his hat off; his large face looked puffy, as if he'd just got out of bed. 'I was coming to see you later.'

Denton started to say *What now?* but caught himself and said, 'Oh?'

'I thought we might pick up something on the dead woman from Missing Persons. I used to have that office in my parish, you remember—before I was exiled to West Ham—so I was able to see some things without letting it be known everywhere.'

'I thought you were going to let it go.'

'Maybe I am and maybe I'm not. But Freddie's sloped off, so I'll make a bit of hay while that sun shines.' Guillam looked around the tree. 'He's taking long enough at it. Trouble getting it up, I suppose. Hard times, as the saying is.' He gave up looking and put his back against the tree. 'Bloody hot it's going to be.' He fanned himself with the hat. 'You'd be surprised how many women went missing the day your body was found. A lot of them look possible. I'm going to make some home calls, and then if I find a likely one and I can get a photo, I want you to take a look. All right?'

Cautious because of Janet, Denton said, 'I didn't see the dead woman very well.'

'My arse.' Guillam gave a wooden smile. 'You've a good eye, and you're honest. That's the one thing I know I can depend on with you—you're honest. A Jew doctor, I'm not so sure.' He saw Denton's expression and he smiled. 'Mankey's notes are gone, but somebody at Bow Street told me Mankey interviewed the doctor before he got turfed out. They thought he'd said he *thought* it was the Shermitz woman. That the way you remember it?' He heaved himself up and looked around the tree. 'Ah, there's my man. A smile on his face and a lilt in his walk.' He put his hat on. 'I'm off. You'll look at a photo, yes?'

'I suppose I have to.'

Guillam pointed a finger, thumb up, like a gun. 'Right you are.'

Denton watched him stride down among the trees, keeping parallel to the path but well behind his quarry, now a small figure hurrying towards the Broad Walk. Denton turned away and went into the toilets, glad to find physical relief at last but aware of gnawing anxiety over what Guillam had said. He ignored the no-longer-young man who smiled at him from near the stalls. The urinal was a long zinc trough with water running down it; some splashed on his trousers. 'Looks worse than it is,' the man said. He laughed. He looked tough, perhaps uncouth, maybe from the cavalry barracks.

Denton left.

He was back in his house in time to meet Atkins with his breakfast and the mail as he came into the long room.

'Where've you been? I thought you'd got yourself snatched.'

'Walked in Regent's Park. I met that copper, Guillam, up there. Like a bad penny.'

'What's he doing in the park at this hour?'

'Watching a gent's pisser. Odd scene.'

'Bleeding odd tastes, I'd say.'

'He was on a case.'

Guillam's interest worried him. He remembered that he was supposed to meet Munro at a pub later; maybe he could get Munro to call Guillam off. He didn't want Guillam poking around Bernat and the abortion and Janet. He also wanted to see Cohan today because he felt guilty about not having visited earlier.

When he went out he looked for his derringer in the box where it was supposed to be kept but didn't find it. Atkins, sounding long-suffering, said he'd look for it, but it wasn't his fault if the owner couldn't keep track of his own possessions.

Cohan was in a ward much like the one where Denton had spent two days. There were the same uneasy sounds, the same smell of carbolic and bodies, the same spare look of poverty.

Leah was sitting in an iron chair by Cohan's bed. He was still sedated, in and out of consciousness; his head was almost all bandage, one eye and the nose alone visible. His hands were in what looked like giant mittens; his left foot hung from a contraption rather like a dockyard crane, the leg in a thick cast. Denton spoke to Leah, who moved her head and lifted a hand a few inches, but she seemed to be in one of her non-English days and didn't speak. He tried to talk to Cohan but got no response.

'Atkins sends his best.' Atkins hadn't, but Denton decided that he would have if the subject had come up.

He wondered if he should go out and buy flowers from a street-seller, but there was no vase and no table to put one on.

'You get well, Cohan. I miss our boxing. We'll be doing it again soon—you'll see.'

He had been bending over the injured man; now he straightened and took up his hat, which he'd set on the bed. He felt a pull on his left sleeve and found Leah plucking at it, her other hand making jerky, back-and-forth motions towards Cohan. Denton bent again, bent lower, and from somewhere in the gauze and the lint came a whispered 'Ta.'

He walked away up the narrow aisle between the beds, wondering if it didn't do the sick more harm than good—forcing them to rally, to feel, to speak, perhaps to be depressed by comparing themselves with their visitors. Certainly, visiting was depressing for him. He'd rather, as Cohan might say, go three rounds with Bob Habbijam.

From the hospital, he walked up to the boxing club, first losing his way, then suddenly finding himself across from it. A constable stood in front of it, profoundly bored. Nothing had changed that Denton could see. Smoke had blackened the whitewash around the door, and the roof had partly collapsed.

'Closed, sir, sorry,' the constable said. 'Fire.'

'How bad is it inside?'

'No idea, sir. Best move along, if you don't mind. People here get excited if they think anybody's looking crosswise at it. If you don't mind, sir.'

Denton did mind, but he supposed the man was right. He moved along.

Munro was waiting at the Princess Louise, even though Denton was a few minutes early. 'Thought you might forget,' Munro said. 'Or be under the weather.' He already had a pint and had found them a nook to themselves. 'You look better.'

'Better than Cohan, at any rate. I visited him today.' Denton shook his head 'Poor bastard. His boxing days are over.' He dropped his overcoat on the banquette. The day was still warm, the morning mist now gentle rain, but rumblings from the west suggested that worse was coming. Denton got himself a half of best bitter and sat down. 'So?'

'So, indeed. How is it, being up and about?'

'Itchy. If I had a shilling for every time I've had to stop and scratch today, I'd be well off.'

Munro snorted. Clearly he thought that Denton was well off as it was. 'Not much progress been made on whoever tried to kill your pal Cohan. Not that the Jews aren't trying—they want to help us because he's one of their own, but you know what witnesses are. Three men it was, that's pretty clear, and not men anybody knew. Not Jews, they're sure of that. They all say it was dockers, but they don't know; it's just what they believe.'

'And they're probably right.'

'That's as may be, but I can't take it to court. Faces and names, faces and names. What's this about your house having stones thrown at it?'

'A kid. Neighbour. His pa read that rag that said I'm named Hymie. Anyway, that's not CID business. Catching the ones who beat up Cohan is.'

'Thank you for telling me what our business is.' Munro drank. He stretched his back and tipped his head back to stretch his neck. 'Long day.' After another drink, he pushed his arms forward on the little table so as to be closer to Denton. 'Now, about this other brouhaha: the dead woman and the boys who left with her body. Which isn't supposed to be CID business.' He pushed his hat back, revealing a red line across his forehead. 'This is confidential. Absolutely not to be talked about to anybody. You promise me? Promise? All right. My deputy super called me in and told me we're not going to let your dead woman just disappear. If E Division won't move on it, then CID will. *Sub rosa*, as they say.'

'Guillam's got it now; did you know that?' He sketched for Munro what Guillam had told him about 'Freddie' and the aborted investigation. 'I thought he was going to let it slide, but I saw him this morning and he was talking about trying to find who the woman was through Missing Persons.'

'Yeah, I know about that. You tell him, if you see him again, to be damned careful.'

'He thought nobody would know.'

'He thought wrong. Anyway, he's not to know CID are interested, you understand that? And he's not to know I'm involved.'

'How involved are you?'

Munro grunted. 'I've been put in charge of finding out what the hell went on that day at your house. It's just me and another detective so far.' He made a face. 'I was volunteered. Because of you.'

'What have I got to do with it?'

'You're the source. I told the deputy super I was looking into the attack on Cohan, and he says, "Good, then you've a reason to be seeing this man Denton. Use that as cover for the other." So I got put in charge of both, Cohan *and* the two that made off with the woman's body. So, here we are conspiring, and we just look like two pals having a drink in the boozer. What do you think of Guillam's idea about missing women?'

'Not much of an idea, is it? A lot of work for no very likely outcome.' He wanted to steer Munro away from it because of Janet.

Munro said, 'I'm going to let Guillam pursue it, see what he finds. We can't be seen to do it ourselves, but it's good police work.'

'I think it's a waste of time.'

Munro shrugged. 'It's Guillam's time, not mine. Maybe he'll lead us to the body, or at least to an identification. If we knew who the woman was, we might get an idea why she was important enough to pull Mankey and Steff off and close the case.'

'And Guillam's not supposed to be continuing with it. He's going to get caught. You want that?'

'You and Guillam are chums now, are you?'

'I told you—he came to see me the same night you did. Wanted to apologize, he said. Chums, hell. I think he wanted to pump me. He's determined to get out of West Ham, that's for sure. He knows they're using him.'

'He came to see you today, too?'

'No, I met him in Regent's Park. He was trailing somebody.'

'Guillam? My God, maybe he has reformed! Well, keep in touch with him. This is good: you can let me know if he turns up anything.'

'I told you, I don't like it!'

'Don't get your dander up. I'm telling you what's going on my end; I expect a little in return. Fact, I've bleeding little to tell

you, but it's early days. I'll see if there's anything on this "Freddie";
that's a help. Oh, I asked about Hench-Rose; nobody my end
knows anything. Last anybody knew, he'd gone to Whitehall to
something called army-navy liaison. Can't help you there.'

'He wasn't going to Whitehall when I had lunch with him.'

'You didn't know that, in fact, when we last talked. Still
your guess, or you have new facts? Give it up: Sir Hector is about
as mysterious as the smell of fish. If you're in doubt about something, ask him.'

'What about "Freddie" and the one I clouted?'

'I told you, we're working on it.'

'What d'you think it means that "Freddie's" disappeared?
Last week, he was going to be Guillam's partner; now, Guillam
says he's gone.'

'Nothing. Taking a day off to do his paperwork—who
knows? If he hasn't appeared in three or four days, it might mean
that they—whoever *they* are—believe they're done with your
dead woman and E Division and the investigation, and Guillam
can write a report and it's over.'

'And the body?'

Munro tightened his lips and accordioned his nose as if at a
bad smell. 'The LCC coroner doesn't have it. Officially, therefore,
there is no body. Coroner's jury can't sit on a body until it's there
before them, and a coroner can't convene a jury until he knows
that the body is in his jurisdiction. So, with nobody knowing
where this body is, no coroner is claiming it and no jury's been
called.'

'No body, no crime?'

'No body, no inquest. You can have a crime without a body
if the circumstances are suspicious enough, and these circumstances are full-bore suspicious, but we're supposed to shut up and
not lean on the coroner—if we knew which coroner. If the lack
of a body kept the police from investigating, we'd have only half
the murder cases we get. And wouldn't that be nice!'

They left shortly afterwards. Munro wanted to meet again
in a few days. He named the Old Red Lion, nearby. Laughing,

he said, 'If anybody asks, I'm showing an American the sort of pictur-ess-cue pubs they think are reely, reely English. If there's a change of plan, I'll send you a wire or something.'

Denton pulled himself up in a parody of hauteur. 'My good man, as of tomorrow, I shall be on the telephone.'

Munro raised his extravagant eyebrows. 'Well, I can give you a shout then.' He shook his head. 'The way the world's going, we'll get so we never need to look another human being in the face.'

CHAPTER

11

'First post's come.' Atkins dropped a pile of envelopes on Denton's chairside table. It was morning; the weather threatened by the thunder had come, pouring rain and a wind that was turning umbrellas inside out.

'Short spring,' Denton said.

'Wind coming through the letter box'd about blow your brains out your earholes.' Atkins poured Denton more tea, then poured himself half a cup and took a piece of toast from the rack. 'You still ambulant, as they say, after yesterday?'

'Sound as a dollar.' His legs and shoulder itched ferociously; he had some suppurating from his ear but didn't say so.

'Dutchy says he'll finish today. *He'll* have to be paid.' Atkins looked severe. 'How's our new book coming?'

'Still in the pencil. Don't worry, Sergeant, it'll all work out. Don't chivvy me.' Denton was opening the mail—more sympathetic notes telling him how shocked the sender was, 'outrage' a favourite word; but three were the opposite, calling him various things, 'dirty Jew' the mildest—and he paused over another note from Henry Held the financier. 'I suppose that if a millionaire's sending his carriage for me, I can't refuse.'

'Coming it a bit strong, sending the carriage. Who?'

Denton held up the note. 'A man named Held. "Very important." I wish people wouldn't be mysterious. I met the man once and now he wants me to appear at his house. No offer of supper. Millionaires are like that, I suppose.'

Atkins, slightly near-sighted, was holding the envelope at arm's length and trying to read it. 'Held the big insurance man?'

'Pots of money, but I don't know how he made it. Seemed nice enough, although I've never noticed that niceness and pots of money go together.' He sounded exasperated. 'I don't want to go!'

'Don't. He can come here if it's so important. You're injured.'

'He says that, in fact, but pretty clearly doesn't want to.'

'Better him than you.'

'No, because if I go to him, I can leave when I want to.' They talked about clothes in which to visit a millionaire. Denton, who had hoped to lure Janet to the Café Royal again, saw that notion vanishing. 'Hell,' he growled. As he went upstairs, he said, 'And don't forget the telephone's coming today. Be here so they can get in.'

'Wouldn't miss it for two and a kick in ready money.'

Yet, once out on the wet streets in Held's carriage that night, Denton was almost glad he was going. The wind had fallen to a brisk breeze; the air was colder; the stars, rarely seen above London, were bright when scudding clouds did not obscure them. He had passed the day at his desk, staring at the words he had scribbled on the piece of paper, then spending hours on a new story about somebody he had seen at a formal dinner once, trying to seduce the woman next to him.

He had eaten supper at Janet's, food sent in from the Lamb and served by Atkins and Annie. Janet had been mostly monosyllabic; her work on the Isle of Dogs was going poorly, and he knew she was thinking of it and not whatever he was saying. Finally, he had stopped talking and let the silence envelop them. It was rather comfortable. When she came to after fifteen minutes, she gave him a surprised and guilty smile. Yet he thought that instead of increasing his sense that something was wrong between them, this very ordinary evening had lessened it. Dullness as resolution. Or at least as balm.

The derringer was still not to be found. Denton shrugged and went out.

His mood of patient tolerance stayed with him through uninteresting streets, ugly streets, drab streets, his interest increasing as they climbed above the rest of London. Held lived beyond Maitland Park, a region Denton hardly knew. The sky cleared as they came to the height; the moon appeared. Held's house was huge, as expected, and hideous, as he supposed he should have known it would be. He was set down in a porte cochère that seemed to swallow them, pulling them into the house's darkness and hiding the brilliant sky.

Yet inside was a Germanic comfort, over-heated, over-carved, over-furnished, nonetheless welcoming after the cold. Held, in dinner clothes, received him in a room presumably a study, large enough to have played some active ball game in. Up high were ornate mouldings varnished dark brown; dark-brown pilasters pretended to hold them up; the walls were covered with books where they were not covered with tapestries. Denton wondered if the books had been bought by the pound; he knew nothing about tapestries but questioned that they were old. What would it matter if they were? Or weren't? Of what was he suspecting Held to be guilty—decorating his house as he wanted? He realized that he resented being there instead of at home.

Held came forward, smiling. They shook hands. 'You'll forgive me, I hope, for not having asked you for dinner; in fact, I suspected you'd rather not. There were only the three of us. We're very dull for someone like yourself.' He added that his wife had already gone to bed. It was just nine.

Held offered cigarettes, cigars, brandy. He seemed not nervous, but wary. He was nowhere near as tall as Denton, clean-shaven, rather fair, his skin sleek and looking polished, rather handsome. He did not at all 'look Jewish', but to Denton more like one of the Nordics Hench-Rose talked about. To Denton's ear, too, he had no accent, meaning that he had an accent but it was neither aristocrat's drawl nor 'Cockney'.

'I'm sure you're wondering why I've asked you here.' Held was standing in front of an enormous fireplace with a carved stone mantel, his right hand in his jacket pocket, looking as if he was about to tell the board of directors what they were to do next. Denton was sure he was a practised speaker (maybe too practised), and that he would have his points memorized and in order: the flow would be smooth and assured. However, Held said without preface, 'What do you know about Zionism?'

Surprised, Denton had to think; he said, 'A homeland for East European Jews.'

'For *all* Jews. Do you know the World Zionist Congress?'

'Didn't they meet in London a couple of years ago?'

'Very good, yes. You've surprised me. I meant to make a little speech.' Held smiled one of those smiles that lift only the corners of the mouth, but some of his air of the too-pat and the too-prepared vanished. 'The man you saved was a Jew.'

'Cohan? I know that.'

'In fact, the name means—You know about the *Kohanim*? One surprise after another. Well! I shall have to start again.' Held gave him the smile again and walked a step towards him. 'Have you known many Jews, Mr Denton? No? You can take us or leave us?'

'I guess I can take or leave most people.'

'You don't know many Jews, but you have no feelings about us?'

'I suppose I take people one at a time.'

Held went to a bookcase and extracted a book. It was a real book, and, unless he had planted it ahead of time among the decorative backs, they were all real books and were there as books, not as décor. As if to make the matter clear, Held said, 'I collect books. First editions, that sort of thing. I confess to a pro-Jewish interest.' He handed the small book to Denton. 'Know it?'

Denton looked at the spine. *The King of Schnorrers*. Israel Zangwill. He shook his head.

'Do you know Zangwill?'

'I think we've met.'

'But he's not a friend? And you don't read his books.'

'There are a lot of books I don't read.'

'But I'm sure you read books by German writers, French writers—Zola, Huysmans?—and have probably seen a Norwegian play—Ibsen?—so you read foreign writers. Why not Zangwill? Because he's a Jew, Mr Denton?'

Denton winced as that truth came home. Feeling himself redden, he said, 'I suppose. I thought—he wrote in Yiddish—or something...'

'You must read him.' Held pointed at *The King of Schnorrers*. 'Keep that. I have another.' He walked a few feet up the room, turned back, not looking at Denton. The chairman-of-the-board manner was entirely gone; he seemed now introspective, rather uncertain, perhaps embarrassed. He might have been talking to himself or to the room. 'I wanted to make a point about being a Jew. About never belonging. Zangwill was born here; that book is about London. But he isn't an English writer to you, is he? He's a Jewish writer. More foreign than Zola or Ibsen or...' Held shrugged. He took a few uncertain steps, stopped, turned as if to say something more, then turned back and took a cigarette from a box, belatedly offered it to Denton. 'My native language is German. I was born in Berlin. My father came to London when I was one year old, but we spoke German at home. I knew nothing of Yiddish or Hebrew. Yiddish was low and vulgar, Hebrew was the language of an old-fashioned and un-German religion.' He took a bit of tobacco from his lower lip and rubbed his fingers together to rid himself of it. 'My father was a convert to Christianity.' He blew smoke out in a thin stream. He smiled. 'There is a story about a woman and a boy on an omnibus in Berlin. The boy is studying Hebrew, and the mother keeps talking to him in Yiddish. A man on the bus says to her in German, "Woman, why do you speak this wretched Yiddish to the boy when he reads wonderful Hebrew?" The woman says, "Because I don't want he should forget he is a Jew."' Held looked at his cigarette, then stubbed it out. 'We have many jokes. You know what a *schnorrer* is?'

'A beggar.'

'Yes, but worse than that—a leech. There are lots of jokes about *schnorrers*—usually these days, the *schnorrer* and Rothschild. It used to be the *schnorrer* and the Rich Man; now it's Rothschild. Or Held. It's the duty of the rich Jew to help the poor.' He got himself another cigarette. 'A *schnorrer* goes to Held but can't get past the gate. He stands outside the gate and makes a huge noise, so Held tells his servants to let the man in. Held gives the *schnorrer* a shilling and says, "If you hadn't made all that racket, I might have given you half a crown." The *schnorrer* says, "Held, do I tell you how to sell insurance? Don't you tell me how to be a *schnorrer.*"'

Denton smiled. He didn't understand where Held was going: maybe he wasn't going anywhere, and Denton could leave soon.

'Jews have many jokes. If anybody else told them, they'd be anti-Semitic. Maybe we tell them so other people won't. Or maybe we want to laugh at ourselves. Or something worse.' He sat down in a chair near Denton and, after inhaling the cigarette, said, 'Jews must have a land of their own, Mr Denton. Wherever they—we—go, we are outsiders. Perhaps we make ourselves outsiders, although I tell you, no man could have worked harder than my father to be a German. He was, as they said then, "emancipated"—freed from being a Jew, it meant. He spoke only German; he had served in a German army, he revered German culture, he loved Berlin. But...' He cocked his head. 'You understand that "but"? *But* he was a Jew.' He ground out the new cigarette. 'The world is one of nations now. Not religions and communities and principalities, but nations. The Jews must become a nation—for which they must have land.' He stood up and walked quickly towards a door beyond the fireplace. 'I want you to meet someone.'

Denton had been about ready to start making moves towards leaving. The visit had become bewildering, and he wondered if he had been got there only to listen to the musings of a very rich man. He didn't doubt that Held was sincere, but if he had been another writer talking about a book, Denton might have said, *What's the plot? Just tell me the story and get on with it!* But he couldn't say that to a man like Held, not because he was rich, but because he wouldn't have known what Denton was talking about. Taking advantage of Held's absence, Denton stood; he could more easily move to a departure from a standing than a sitting start.

The door opened again and a tall man came through, at first silhouetted against light, then filling in his outline as he moved into the room. He was long-bearded, younger than Denton, rather sharp of eye. Held, coming along behind, said, 'This is Dr Theodor Herzl, President of the World Zionist Congress.'

Denton had in fact heard of Herzl—but that was all. The same superficial, newspaper-born knowledge that had given him his three-word sense of Zionism gave him the scantest awareness of Herzl. They shook hands. Herzl barely smiled, stepped back and put on a patriarchal frown.

They sat down. Held said something to Herzl in what Denton supposed was German. Then Held said to Denton in English, 'Dr Herzl is here for what we hope will be a great step forward for Zionism. This is in strictest confidence, Denton: he is to negotiate with the British government for a Jewish homeland. Within the Empire.'

Denton remembered his conversation with Hench-Rose. 'I thought the Turks had closed Palestine.'

Herzl said something in German. Held said, 'Not in Palestine. Palestine is the ultimate goal, but it can't realistically be hoped for yet.' He glanced at Herzl, muttered something, and Herzl nodded. Held looked back at Denton. 'You must keep this confidential until there is a public announcement. Perhaps two weeks.' Again, Denton was reminded of Hench-Rose: mum was the word. Held was going on. 'The British government are receptive to the idea of making part of their African protectorate of Uganda available as a temporary Jewish homeland—"temporary" meaning for several decades, perhaps.'

Denton had only a hazy idea of where or what Uganda was, although there had been a lot about an Uganda Railway in the papers. He remembered only that Uganda was in Africa, somewhere in the interior, hence the importance of the railway to reach it. He said what came first to his mind, not the most politic words he might have spoken: 'Doesn't somebody already live in Uganda?'

'Not enough to matter. Nomads—savages.' Held spoke in an undertone to Herzl, who answered vigorously, his hands moving as if he were doing some sort of athletic exercise. 'Dr Herzl says the government have assured him that there is no problem of evictions or of moving people out. If there are people there, an influx of Europeans could only do them good. We would bring modern agriculture, medicine, knowledge. We would live in peace with everyone.' As an afterthought, he said, 'They would make a ready labour supply, too, and we would give them jobs.'

Herzl began speaking again before Held had finished. The two men talked together; Denton watched Herzl, thought he saw the passion and the excitement of a man dominated by a single idea. Herzl's eyes were bright and wide; his vigorous hand gestures were like assaults on the air around him. His voice rose, fell to a dramatic whisper, rose again: he was lecturing Held. He began lecturing Denton, as well, still in German.

Held summed up some, perhaps all, of what Herzl had said, although he got through it much more quickly: Eastern European Jews *must* have a place to emigrate to. The pogroms were terrible. Walls were rising against Jewish immigration everywhere. Uganda would offer rich land, the railway to move goods and products, the protection of Britain. Wealthy people in Europe and the United States would underwrite the costs. Held waved a hand when he had finished; perhaps he had heard it all too often. He said, 'You are wondering why you have been told all this.'

'Well, I guess maybe I am.'

Held gave him the corners-only smile. He muttered yet again with Herzl and then said, 'Three weeks ago, a woman and a man left Russia separately and, we believe, came to London. The man is, or was, named Gowarczyk. The woman was then calling herself Tania Simonova. Our sources tell us that their goal is to kill Dr Herzl and the British negotiators in the Uganda matter.'

The word *sources* stuck in Denton's consciousness, but he said, 'Why?'

Held sat back and folded his hands over his crossed legs. 'In Russia, there is an organization called the Bund. It is Jewish but anti-Zionist. *Strongly* anti-Zionist. We think that they have made an alliance with Jewish anarchists to stop Dr Herzl's project, perhaps to stop the Zionist Congress altogether.' He leaned towards Denton and said in a low voice, as if he didn't want Herzl to hear him, 'Herzl is the heart of the Congress—the heart of Zionism. If he goes—' He shook his head.

'Anarchists?' Denton had heard about anarchists but viewed them rather the way a grown-up views the bogeys of childhood. The press was always in a dither about anarchists somewhere, but the actuality seemed to Denton to be meagre (although, as he knew, an anarchist had killed the American president only a year before).

'You sound doubtful. Anarchism is very real, Mr Denton. It has no realistic programme, but those who believe in it are often violent, even suicidal people. A few of them might change the history of a nation. Or a people.'

'Why in the world would the anarchists care about Uganda?'

'Because it would give the Jews a nation—and a government, and anarchism is opposed above all to governments. Some Jews are anarchists, Mr Denton, and they most definitely don't want a Jewish government!'

Herzl said something. Held looked at Denton. 'Dr Herzl is tired and wishes to retire, but he must know first if you will help us.'

Denton was now thoroughly confused. 'To do what?'

'Protect this Zionist effort. Protect Dr Herzl.'

'Held, with all respect, you want the police.'

'Oh—!' Held made an angry gesture. 'We *have* the police! The British government are taking every precaution, or so they tell us. They have set up some sort of office dedicated to the matter. And I, on my own initiative, have hired private detectives to protect Herzl. The driver who brought you here is one of them, for example. But—The police haven't caught Gowarczyk or Simonova. That's the crux. So—I'll go into details with you later—will you help us?'

Denton thought that his reputation as a Wild West law man was coming back to haunt him. He said, reluctance and caution very clear in his voice, 'I'll do whatever I think it's appropriate for me to do, I guess.'

As if he knew what Denton had been thinking, Held smiled. 'We don't want you to shoot anyone, Denton.' He spoke in German to Herzl. Moments later, Herzl grasped Denton's hand, squeezed it, said '*Danke*' several times, and, after another outburst of German at both Held and Denton, left the room.

Held watched him go. 'A wonderful man. An indispensable man at this point in our history. But—' He smiled and sat down. 'Rather trying.' He sat quite still; then, like a man who has pulled his thoughts back together and is ready, he said, 'I think the woman who visited your Dr Bernat and who was then taken to your friend's house was Tania Simonova, the female anarchist.'

Denton digested this. Two things struck him—that Held seemed to know a good deal about his private life, and that a woman who was an anarchist might find it easy to be a murderess. What he said, however, was simply, 'So you know Dr Bernat?'

'I have had a conversation with him, yes.'

'What did he say?'

'You must understand, Mr Denton, nobody knows what this Simonova looks like. She is merely a name. So I didn't expect Bernat to identify her, as of course he did not. But he was helpful.'

'What took you to Bernat? How did you make a connection with this Simonova?'

Held frowned: Denton was asking the wrong questions. 'Dr Bernat is a talkative man. He said things that...interested us.'

'Said them where? How do you know?' Denton stood. 'Look, Held, I respect your cause; I'm all for a Jewish homeland if it's going to stop people treating them badly. But you're telling me that you've—what?—had spies on Bernat? Or on me? What the hell's going on?'

'They are not spies!' Steel sounded in Held's voice; Denton got a hint of how he had become rich. 'Bernat talks at the Jewish Infirmary. People there, Zionists, talk to me. That is not spying!'

'All right, it's gossip. Tale-bearing. What tale did somebody bear?'

Held threw up his hands, let them fall back on his knees with a slap. 'Bernat said he had treated a woman who was the daughter of a woman he had known in France years ago. The woman was a socialist and an anarchist, back when it was possible to be both at the same time. This story—a French mother who was a socialist-anarchist—was one that Simonova used, gave as her own history.'

'You said nobody knew her.'

'They know *of* her! She is a name, a reputation, but not a face. She has killed two people, they think—the Principessa Margarita in the Boboli Gardens three years ago, with a knife; the minister of finance in St Petersburg last year, with a pistol. Maybe she and Gowarczyk were also behind the plan to dynamite Marconi's laboratory; nobody's sure. Anyway, that one failed.'

'Is she invisible?'

'Don't mock. We think the German intelligence police know who she is, but we can't crack them.'

'"We"?'

Held massaged the skin between his eyebrows. 'Friends of Zionism, all right? Don't push this, Denton. If I'd known you were going to be this hard-headed, I'd not have invited you.' He threw the hand down and said, 'We need help, not cynicism!'

'I'd better go.'

'No!' Both men were on their feet. 'Something happened at your house after Bernat saw the woman. That is where you can help us. It's all I ask. Bernat says the woman whose body was found in your garden was the same as the woman he had seen in the morning. If that is true, then maybe Simonova is dead, and a great part of our worries are eased. But dead how? And why? Because if she was Simonova, then somebody killed her *because* she was Simonova. There are no accidents, Mr Denton. And if somebody killed her because she was Simonova, then there are things going on that we don't know about. And that is very, very troubling.'

So Bernat had not told Held the truth: he had stayed with his lie that the dead woman was the woman he had treated, to protect himself and to protect Janet Striker. Denton said, 'Well, the doctor says it was the same woman, so your Simonova's dead. I'd say that who killed her is a minor affair, as far as you're concerned. Tell the police and let them sort it out.'

Held shook his head. 'Something happened, as you well know—some outside authority took her body away. As if they wanted to *prevent* a positive identification. That's worrisome. It suggests that perhaps the dead woman *wasn't* Simonova.'

'You question Bernat's identification?'

'He could be wrong. He never saw the body—he saw only a woman that *other* people say was the same. If he was wrong... Why couldn't it be equally the case that the killer was Simonova and the body is that of somebody there to—' He raised his hands in a huge shrug. 'I don't know to do what; it's all through a glass darkly! But the body was there, and it looks as if Simonova was there, and she is a killer! I *must* know which of them was which!'

'Well, I own the house where it happened, is all. That doesn't make me an expert.'

'But you have insight. And you know Bernat. And others. And you have friends in the police. *Do* you know anything?'

Now we've come to it, Denton thought. It was very simple, now they were there: after all the prologue, what Held wanted was to know what Denton knew.

The Second Woman

Which he couldn't tell him.

A few minutes later, Denton said goodnight. He promised Held to tell him anything that turned up. Held promised to give any help, any information, that Denton might need. They were equally insincere, Denton thought. And equally unsatisfied.

The clouds had closed over the sky, and the ride home was cold and dark.

I'm a knut, I'm a knut,
Oh, I'm the knuttiest one of them all...

The voice faded as Atkins finished climbing the stairs and came into the room. Denton, his now-daily walk to the zoo and back already completed, heard him come towards his chair, the voice still humming. A morning newspaper was dropped into his lap, and Atkins began to set up the folding table.

'So how was the millionaire, Major?'

'Puzzling. I'm thinking.'

He heard Atkins pour tea; the cup and saucer, then an arm appeared in front of him; he took the tea. A plate of Peek Frean's breakfast biscuits followed. Denton was lost in the mental squirrel cage of the night before. He remained indifferent to a silence that usually meant that Atkins wanted to talk; he hardly heard several throat-clearings and a cough. Eventually, Atkins moved where Denton could see him. 'You going out today?'

'Not sure.'

'Doctor's coming to see you noonish.'

'I may go out after that, then.'

'Want to give a hint as to clothes?'

'The millionaire thinks that the dead woman was an anarchist, here to blow somebody up.'

'My hat! In our house?'

'I think the blowing up was to happen someplace else. He told me a lot of muddle about her not blowing people up if she got herself murdered here. Didn't make a lot of sense.'

'I should think not! Ruining my swedes in the process. I'm replanting, by the way—found Russian seed at the Army and Navy, guaranteed as a winter crop. Or so they say. World is full of cheats and liars.' Atkins took a biscuit. 'You like these?'

'They're all right. Hardly a breakfast.'

'Did I say they were? You can have kippers, toast, jam—gooseberry, plum, also Frank Cooper's Oxford—and an egg, boiled or poached. What's wrong with the biscuits?'

'Nothing. Where'd you get them?'

'On the sales table. Dented tin. Saved you a packet. Who'd this female anarchist plan to kill?'

'Nobody we know. The real question is, who was the other woman?'

'I don't see that.'

'There's two women. One's the anarchist, the other isn't. One dies. Which, and who is she?'

'Anarchists throw bombs and kill kings and politicians and that type.' Atkins took another biscuit. 'O' course, anarchists must have private lives, too, just like the rest of us. Jilted boyfriend, for example, might kill an anarchist. Surely anarchists have boyfriends.'

'Let's keep to the two women.'

'Jilted girlfriend.'

'Not strangers, anyway.' He finished his tea and banged the cup down on the saucer. 'It's beyond me.'

'Well, don't go breaking the china. Them cups don't grow on trees. Twelve and nine a dozen, you paid for those. Are you going out or aren't you?'

'I'll see.'

On the way to his bedroom, he passed the new telephone. He had seen it the night before when he had come in, and he had winced then as he did now. The thing was huge. The part to shout into stuck out into the room like the head of some big bird with its mouth open; its neck led back to a wooden box as big as a case of ammunition. He knew he was going to walk into it a dozen times before he got used to its being there.

'One of us is going to kill himself on that thing,' he said to Atkins, who was still the length of the room away, putting dishes back on the tray.

'That's the price of progress, Major.'

The King of Schnorrers was lying where he had dropped it when he had come in. He opened it and started to read. The stories were illustrated; quickly he came to believe the illustrations were themselves anti-Semitic—hooked noses were common—but he read in the preface about Zangwill's enthusiasm for them. He read a couple of the stories and thought that they were anti-Semitic, too, the picture of the poor Jew mocking and sometimes cruel. He was, in fact, the Jew of Christian jokes, even to the accent—'Ve vind up de night glorious,' a *schnorrer* says upon being taken to a theatre. The rich men, on the other hand, speak good English and are 'one of us', as Hench-Rose had said of Held: they are 'emancipated', a word that shocked Denton because of its association for him with American slavery.

Held had said that the jokes were told to keep others from telling them. Now Denton wondered if the Jews told them, if Zangwill wrote them, out of self-hatred. Did Herzl want to lead them out of self-hatred into the pride of nationhood?

What, then, of the anarchist who wanted to stop Herzl? Held had said that some of the anarchists were themselves Jews: had they pushed self-disgust so far that they couldn't bear the idea of their own nationhood? Or was anarchism as Held had said—a political idea so passionately held as to be deadly to anyone who would try to organize and govern?

Can you kill for an idea? he thought, but he knew the answer to that: he had survived three years of a war for an idea.

The idea of somebody's killing Herzl was abstract to him; so was the idea of blowing up the government's representatives. He didn't know Herzl; he didn't know the government men; but he knew the dead woman because she had been found in his garden. His thinking was petty, but it was the way he was, bound to the immediate.

He found himself thinking about Zangwill and *schnorrers*. Maybe the *schnorrer* was simply a human type. Or a human condition—we have to beg and scheme for anything worthwhile. He was a *schnorrer* with Janet, perhaps. A writer going to his publisher had certain affinities, too.

Bernat came later. He examined Denton's burns and said that he was a strong man, also a fairly foolish one. 'What is wrong with a few days in bed?' he said.

'I saw Cohan.'

Bernat was pulling at one of Denton's scabs with a fingernail. 'Sick in his spirit. That is not what you say, is it?'

'Sick at heart?'

Bernat nodded. 'They do more surgery today on his hands, but he has too many bones broken to fix them all. His hands will be—' He made a claw of his right hand. 'Maybe he never holds anything again. He must have surgery on his face—the cheekbone under the eye.'

'When will he come home?'

Bernat shook his head.

The doctor finished his examination. Denton rolled on his good side and, his head propped on a hand, said, 'I went to see Henry Held.'

'Oh, yes? A very fine man. Very generous.'

'He said he'd talked to you.'

'Oh? Well, he did.' Bernat was making himself busy with packing his medical bag.

'He said you'd put out the story that the woman who came to your surgery was the daughter of a Frenchwoman.'

'I told only one or two colleagues at the Infirmary.' He made a business of getting out his watch. 'I am always late.'

'Held thinks the woman was an anarchist.'

'Oh—maybe...'

'Don't go yet, doctor. You know, I've been wondering ever since it happened why you performed an abortion on that woman.'

Bernat laughed. 'She was pregnant.'

'But you didn't know her. You put yourself in jeopardy because she was a stranger. Didn't you?'

'It is something I do.'

'For strangers? Don't you ask for some sort of bona fides—a reference, a recommendation? You don't usually do abortions on strangers, doctor. Do you?'

'She had a recommendation.' Bernat's voice sounded starved for breath.

'What?'

'Please—this is painful—'

Denton sat up. 'What recommendation?'

Bernat sat in a hard chair near the bed. 'This is private. It is confidential. I cannot.'

'Did you tell the police?'

Bernat shook his head.

'But you can tell me. Doctor? You have to trust me. You know that the dead woman wasn't the woman you did the abortion on. In fact, the "daughter of a Frenchwoman" may have murdered the woman whose body was here. *Who was she?*'

Bernat sighed. 'She said she is my daughter.' He had been holding his medical bag on his lap; now, he put it on the floor beside him. 'When the German army went into France in 1870, I was a medical officer. I was barely out of medical school, but I was very patriotic.' He smiled a little. 'During the siege of Paris, I was with a field hospital. We set up in the town. I was quartered with a family. The family had a daughter.' He pressed his lips tight together and pulled down the corners of his mouth; he shrugged. 'The inevitable. "Love." Then the hospital moved closer to Paris; Paris fell... I didn't see her again.' He looked quickly at Denton. 'You are not to tell this to my wife, yes?'

'Of course.'

'That was the end of it for me. We withdrew, we went back to Germany; soon, the Germans showed that whether I had been in the army or not, I was still a Jew. I came to England. Then that woman appears one morning with a letter from—the woman in France. "Here is your daughter, please take care of her."' He looked at Denton, raised his eyebrows as if asking a question, then tilted his head back and slitted his eyes. The look was challenging. 'What would you have done?'

'You believed the letter.'

'I—Yes. I could have not believed it and sent her away. What would I have gained?'

'Safety.'

'But—*what if?* Better to be wrong for a good reason. The past—the past has a long arm and a hard grip.'

'You *wanted* to believe.'

'Yes.'

Denton pushed himself up and stretched his legs and his neck. They were in the room he disliked; he moved around it, touching the furniture, wondering if he would like the room more if he got rid of it. 'How many people did you tell at the Infirmary?'

'I told nobody!'

'Not about her being your daughter. About the woman whose mother was a French socialist and anarchist. Was she a socialist and anarchist when you knew her?'

'No, no, but the woman said she had become those things after. People grow, they change.'

'But you told people this at the Infirmary.'

'I thought it was *interesting.* It was talk, only talk. I am a talkative man!'

Denton came opposite him and leaned on the back of a chair. 'What you said was enough to alert Held. Did he tell you that? He has spies in the Infirmary.' Now that the doctor and his tale and the Infirmary were real to Denton, he could see something else. 'And, if Held, why not other people?'

'The police?' Bernat's voice was hoarse.

'I suppose the police have informers all over the place. But I was thinking that maybe somebody else heard what Held's spies heard and made the same conclusion—that the woman was an anarchist named Tania Simonova.'

'That is not the name she gave me.'

'No. If she was the daughter of you and the French girl, she'd have your name or hers, wouldn't she? Did she tell you she was an anarchist?'

'She said she was a Zionist. I, too, am a Zionist. I was sympathetic. She said also that she shared some of her mother's ideas.'

'Did she say she was here to kill somebody?'

'Of course not! She was *frightened*. She said if her husband found she has an abortion, he will kill her. She *was* frightened. I know terror, Denton—I have seen enough of it! She wanted me to hide her in my house.' Bernat spread his hands, his round face shocked. 'My wife was coming back. I couldn't have this woman who says she is my not-by-marriage daughter there with my wife! So Mrs Striker brought her to her house. That is all I know!' He stood. 'I am very late.'

Denton came around the chair to him. 'Doctor—in her condition after the abortion, could she have killed the other woman?'

Bernat stared away from him. After some seconds, he said, 'The surgery is not that debilitating if there is no haemorrhage. This was a woman of great conviction, of passion. If moved sufficiently—yes, she could kill.'

'With her hands? She was strong enough?'

'We do amazing things in desperate times. You and the fire—if I asked you now to put Cohan on your shoulder and carry him away, you couldn't do it. But *then*, in that extreme moment, you did it.'

He picked up his bag and started out. Denton put his hand on his arm. 'Now that you've had time to think about it—is she your daughter?'

Bernat stared at the closed door. 'I don't know.'

He went out. Denton sat on, staring at the door. Bernat had talked at the Jewish Infirmary; that talk had reached Held. Had it reached others, as well? Someone with an interest in a woman with Simonova's story—perhaps somebody also interested in Zionism? Somebody else had talked to him about finding a homeland outside of Britain for the Jews: Hench-Rose. Why?

Footloose and aimless after lunch, afraid of falling into the inertia that took him whenever he wasn't writing, Denton went to his new telephone and stared at it as if it were an animal he was trying to master. *Hench-Rose.* He picked up the earpiece and put it to his burned ear, then moved it to the other side. When he leaned close to the mouthpiece, the cord was in his way. He swore, stood sideways and looked for the crank he had seen people use on other telephones.

'Where's the goddam crank?' he shouted down the stairs.

'Central Exchange ready,' a crackly voice said in his left ear.

'There is no crank!' Atkins shouted. 'We're on the new machine!' He raised his voice to a bellow. 'We have our own battery!'

'Central Exchange,' the crackly male voice said again. 'Ready. The number you wish to call, please?'

'Hello?' Denton said.

'Speak louder, please.'

'HELLO!'

'I can hear you now, thank you. What number, please?'

'Who is this?'

'This is Central Exchange, sir. Did you wish to call a number?'

'I don't have a number.'

'You must have a number, sir.'

'My book is only for Central Exchange, and I want to call someplace else!'

'Perhaps I can help you.'

'Good!'

'How can I help you?'

'Find me the number!'

'You haven't told me what for, sir. For what?'

'For—for—' He didn't want to telephone Hench-Rose at home. He wasn't even sure that Hench-Rose had a telephone at home. But he wouldn't be home in the middle of the work day, anyway. What had Munro said Hench-Rose had gone into? 'Army-Navy Liaison,' he shouted.

'I'm sorry, sir, I didn't understand that.'

'ARMY-NAVY LIAISON!'

'Is that army and navy lesion, sir?'

'Army dash Navy L-i-a-i-s-o-n!'

'Where would that be, sir? Do you know the exchange?'

'It's at Whitehall somewhere.'

'Whitehall is not a Post Office exchange, sir. It is a National Telephone Company exchange. Would you like me to switch you over?'

'Ah. Oh. Yes. Please. Switch me over.'

He had much the same conversation with the National Telephone Company's Whitehall operator, but he did agree to connect Denton with the central army number, where, the operator assured him, they would be able to help him. The central army operator, however, said that there was no telephone for a Hench-Rose, and there was no office called Army-Navy Liaison. However, there was an Army Personnel office number. The Army Personnel office connection was a very poor one, with a great deal of the kind of noise that crisp paper makes when it is crumpled up in the hand. Before the line went dead, Denton learned only that they knew nothing about the navy and he had the wrong number.

When he put the earpiece back on its hook, Atkins was standing beside him. Denton said, 'I think this machine is a mistake.'

'Takes some getting used to.'

'I guess I'll go back to letters.'

'Now, now, General—progress is the god of our age. I read that in the *Graphic*.' Atkins took the earpiece and rang the operator, asked briskly for the Whitehall operator, rapped a number and within less than a minute said, 'Hallo, Jimmy! Atkins here! Ho, Jimmy?' Atkins laughed, bent closer to Denton and whispered, 'Old pal of mine,' and put his mouth to the contraption again. 'Jimmy, I need a favour. Name of Hench-Rose, initial H—find if he's on the telephone, will you? Yes, in your book, of course in your book, you think I think you keep it in your head? What? Oh ha-ha.' Atkins leaned against the wall. He winked at Denton. 'Whitehall what? Two-one-three? You're a prince, Jimmy. See you Thursday. Right. No, don't bring Mavis. No. Don't bring Ruby, either. No! No!'

He put the earpiece back on its hook and grinned at Denton. 'Old chum from India. Useful.'

'I could have walked to Whitehall and seen Hench-Rose in the time I've wasted.'

'Progress, General, progress—!' Atkins gave the operator the number he'd got from his pal and handed the earpiece to Denton, who found that Hench-Rose hadn't been there for more than a year—had Denton tried the central army operator? Denton mentioned Army-Navy Liaison and was given another Whitehall number, which proved to be the Admiralty; it had no Hench-Rose and knew nothing about liaison with the army but suggested he try the Post Office.

'I think I'll send this damned thing back,' Denton said when he had hung up.

'You'd regret it. Find yourself behind the times, neglected and forgotten. Mocked, even.'

'Or I may just tear it off the wall. Or shoot it.'

Atkins opened his mouth to say something, and the telephone rang.

Atkins grabbed the earpiece, put his mouth to the speaking part and shouted, 'Central 437, ready!' He listened. 'One moment, please!' He handed Denton the earpiece. 'For you.'

Mystified, Denton moved in, put the piece to his ear and said, 'Hello? Ready. Oh, hell—!'

He heard laughter. It was quite clear. He even recognized Munro's voice. 'If you swear over Post Office equipment, you'll be charged with endangering public morals. And stop shouting. It's Munro.'

'This thing baffles me.'

'Couple of days, you won't be able to live without it. Can you meet me tonight instead of Thursday? Same place we talked about. Have a chat. All right?'

'A chat?'

'Something's—come—up.' Munro made the words very distinct, and he spoke them very slowly. It was his way of saying *Stop being stupid*.

'Oh. I get it. Seven?'

'That's right. Thanks. Say hello to Ronald.' As Denton didn't know a Ronald, he supposed that Munro was talking for somebody else's benefit. Another of the advantages of the telephone—people could overhear your bellowing.

'See?' Atkins said.

'See what?'

'He got through. You understood him. The machine works. It ain't all Whitehall, General.'

Denton growled, partly because he had hoped to spend the evening with Janet. Later, when he struck the burned part of his shoulder on the mouthpiece as he went by, he swore and shouted again that he'd shoot it.

'Guillam's getting too close to something.' Munro had been at the pub ahead of Denton again; he had glanced at his watch when Denton had come in, and he had started without any preliminaries. 'He's going down his list of missing women like lard through a goose. I don't want him getting ahead of me—for his own good and for mine.'

'What's the harm? He said he wanted me to identify the woman if he found a likely one. I'd tell you once that happened.'

'The harm is that I wouldn't be in on it from the beginning. If he actually finds that the dead woman was somebody's wife who hasn't run off with the postman after all, but instead got her neck broken in your garden, he isn't going to let it lie. He's going to investigate and he's going to pull down a mountain of trouble for himself. I've got my super's backing to do it. So here's what we're going to do.'

'We?'

'Yeah, we.' Munro's huge lower jaw manoeuvred itself into a grin. 'Guillam's being sent to N Division for a couple of days. *We* are going to talk to the people he's found who're missing a female family member, aged twenty-five to forty-five, dark hair, maybe a few strands of grey, height five foot to five foot six. Right?'

'In expensive underclothes.'

'Not in my description. Anyhow, that's what we're doing. Tomorrow.'

'I'm getting my new motor car tomorrow.' He had just had a letter from the agency.

'What's got into you? Time was, you were dying to help me out; now some bleeding new mechanical toy is more important. Denton, you're the one who can identify her! Don't give me aggravation about this. You're going.'

'Where?'

'One in Brixton, one north of Victoria Park and one in Primrose Hill.'

'Good God, it'll take the whole day!'

'You know how to drive this motor car of yours? You drove all across Europe for that book you wrote, didn't you? To Checko-Slovakia or some such place. If you won't get me killed, you can drive us and save a lot of time.'

'I don't get the car until the p.m.' When, Denton thought bitterly, he had been planning to drive Janet on a tour of London.

'Tell 'em you want it at eight tomorrow morning, no tears.'

'It has to be polished. It's been on a ship.'

'Polish my arse! What do I care about polish?' Munro leaned over his beer. 'Denton—get it or be prepared to spend the day on the bus!' He sat back. 'And the trolley and the underground and waiting for cabs.' He smiled. 'Quite nice, though, having my own motor car.'

'*My* own motor car.' Denton let his bitterness show in his voice.

'A manner of speaking.' Munro hefted his glass, said, 'Cheers,' and got up. 'I'm for home. The wife's having Yorkshire pudding. Murder if I'm late and it falls.' He heaved himself into his overcoat and plucked his bowler from a hook. 'Pick me up at the Yard at nine. The Parliament Street side.' He put his hat on his head, slapped it into place and gave Denton a parting wink as he strode out.

The New Century Motor Car Import Company were appalled at the idea that Denton wanted his car unpolished and immediately. He began trying to telephone them at seven in the morning, finally raised somebody at ten minutes to eight, and bullied his way up through the hierarchy until, at twelve minutes past eight, he had reached the Head of Sales. The man sounded stern, in fact censorious, and made it clear that he should not have been there at all so early in the morning.

'I want my motor car,' Denton said.

'It hasn't been polished.'

'Damn the polish. I'll be there in less than half an hour.'

'The framing reciprocal transverse gear hasn't been adjusted yet.'

Denton laughed nastily. For the Transylvania book, he had spent two months at the Panhard factory learning to repair an automobile. 'There's no such thing as a framing reciprocal transverse gear. Don't give me any sauce. Is my car going to be ready, or do you want to find another buyer for it?'

They went on like that for a bit, but Denton was shrugging himself into his coat while they wrangled, and the salesman's heart wasn't really in it. Five minutes later, Denton was in a hansom; three minutes after that, he was trotting down Gray's Inn Road, and twelve minutes after that he was in the Strand. The motor car agency was mostly an office in a part of the Strand that, with Wych Street, was about to be demolished, but in a carriage house behind it had space for three motor cars and benches for two mechanics.

'I hate to have it said that we let a motor leave our premises with the grime of sea travel on it,' the man who had sold him the car months before told him.

'After a day in London, who'll know?' The car, a Barré, had been pushed out into a patch of pale sunlight, where a desperate-looking man—one of London's casuals glad for a day's work—was trying to make it gleam with a chamois and a bucket of water. The surface, Denton thought, was already beautiful enough—a lustrous maroon that was almost brown; touches of brass on the lamps and the doors, perhaps less glittering than they might have been, but bright; leather upholstery the colour of shagreen.

Denton looked into the open interior. 'Gears, brake, spark. Foot throttle down there. That pedal's the clutch device. All set.'

'I haven't shown you the removable top,' the salesman said.

'I promise to bring it back tonight. You can show me then.' He gave the desperate man a shilling. 'And you can give it a real polish. Who's cranking?'

The salesman bent over the front of the car. 'Advance the spark.'

Denton did so.

'Contact!'

The salesman turned the crank and grunted; the engine coughed and caught; the car shook, and the cylinder began to bang along. 'I'm off!' Denton shouted. He hadn't been behind the wheel of a motor car for more than a year, but he was able to wave with one hand while steering his way around the corner of a building into a large yard, and out of the double wooden doors being held open by the desperate man. On Wych Street, for that was where he was, he almost ran into a barrow, but dodging it was nothing to a man who had come bonnet-to-nose with a bear in a mountain pass, and soon he was tooling happily along the Strand and making the turn into Whitehall. Soon—too soon, in fact, because he was enjoying himself, for all that he felt as exposed in the open car as if he were going down the roadway on nothing but a couple of wheels attached to his buttocks—he pulled up at Scotland Yard, fitting the tiny car neatly between a Metropolitan Police horse-drawn van and some bigwig's carriage.

Munro was waiting. He said, 'I expected to find you in goggles and a bunnet. Instead, you look like a stockbroker without a hat.'

'And you look like a cop. *In* a hat.' He put the car into gear and pulled out into the traffic, earning a stream of curses from an omnibus driver. Munro, after trying to settle his big bulk in the leather seat, said, 'Bit small.' Indeed, he looked as if he were sitting on some kind of toy. He looked behind at the backward-facing third seat. 'That's for those what want to see where they've been, is it?'

'Atkins insisted we had to have room for the dog. He doesn't care what he looks at. Where are we going?'

'Brixton first, I think.'

Denton, trying to concentrate on the vehicle, quickly lost track of where he was; he was reassured when Munro shouted at him to slow down because he couldn't pick his route this fast. Both men were walkers; in cabs, they let the drivers find the way.

'Maybe we should take the underground,' Munro growled.

'After you got me to badger people into giving me this thing this morning? Not a chance, Munro!'

He managed at last to get across the river and then, stopping twice while Munro thought it over, found Kennington Park Road and moved with a swarm of horse-drawn vehicles through south London. Lost again, they moved aimlessly through quiet streets and were about to stop and ask their way when Munro declared that they were on the one they wanted, Bramah Road. Minutes later, they were talking to a sad, middle-aged woman whose daughter had gone missing. By then, Denton already knew she wasn't the one: the photographs on the walls were all of the same five people, the woman and her husband and her three children.

'Very sorry, madam,' Munro said. 'Not to offer you false hope, but it's good news that she isn't the one we're looking for. Eh?' He gave her his card. 'If I can be of any help.'

Denton showed Munro how to crank the engine, then got in and advanced the spark and shouted, 'Contact!' Munro cranked and gave a sudden howl. 'Mind the compression,' Denton said. Munro got in, rubbing his wrist, and said it might be bloody well broken; then they sat in the car and wondered how to get back to Kennington Park Road. Denton had a vague idea and turned the car around and poked left and right until Munro shouted at a man who was walking a dog. The man seemed astonished. 'Right there!' he shouted back. At the end of the street, traffic was roaring by.

By the time they reached Primrose Hill, a fine rain had started to fall. 'There's supposed to be something called a removable top,' Denton said.

'Where?'

'They didn't tell me that.' He grinned at the now wet Munro. 'If I'd been able to wait until this afternoon, I'd have had time to find out.' Hatless, he was getting wetter than Munro.

The view over London from the hilltop was obscured now by the drizzle, St Paul's only a grey mass against the grey, but the sense of the city's looming shapes and its sheer size were still there. On a clear day, this was a magnificent panorama; now, it was a magnificent hint, perhaps more compelling for that reason.

The house they wanted had been a fine one, was now cut into rooms that were not quite flats. A harried-looking man met them at a door on the second floor. Three children, the oldest perhaps nine, stared at them from the floor. There was very little furniture.

'I got to be back on the job p.d.q. They dock me for every minute.' He was a confectioner's cook, meaning that by comparison with most working people, he made good money—a couple of pounds a week, at least. He showed them the only picture he had of his wife, something a sketch artist had done on a day's outing in Brighton. Even allowing for bad art and a desire to flatter, the sketch couldn't have been the woman in Denton's garden: this one was snub-nosed, blue-eyed, rather chinless.

'Any reason she might have gone off?' Munro said, perhaps to cushion what he thought would be disappointment. The man looked sullen. 'She's on the booze. I can't keep her off it.'

'She's gone off before?'

The man shrugged, then nodded. He ruffled the hair of one of the children. 'Thanks for trying,' he said.

Back in the Barré, Denton said, 'I'd have as soon missed that one.'

'Yeah, poor bastard. If he's telling the truth.' Munro tried to sink down. His knees hit the dash. 'There any more room in that back seat?'

'Less.'

'All right, driver, Victoria Park. Third time lucky.'

Denton took them through Camden Town. Cooking smells drifted in the wet air. 'You hungry?' Munro said.

'Later.'

'Somebody's cooking cabbage back there. I could tuck into some cabbage right now.' Munro sighed. 'Coppers learn to eat when they have a chance.'

'So do soldiers.' He glanced at Munro. 'I'd rather not right now, unless you're hurting for it.'

Munro shrugged and pulled his bowler down.

The north side of Victoria Park had been a place of rather elegant houses once; although some streets had come down, most still had the swagger of the City money that had built them—the trim painted, the brass nameplates and door-knockers polished. It was in front of one such house on Rutland Road that Denton parked the Barré, then sat looking the place over as Munro got out his notebook.

'Some money there,' Denton said.

'Lieutenant Colonel Alken, Royal Marines. I suppose his wife's run off with a subaltern.'

The door was opened by a sandy-haired man in his fifties, coatless and with a rag in his hand as if he had been polishing silver. He heard Munro's spiel, held the door open wider for them. 'Missus still gone,' he said as he closed the door. 'Hell of a thing.' The odour of gin lingered in the enclosed entry.

He led them into an unheated parlour and through it to a small room behind, by contrast stuffily hot. A fire burned cherry-red in a coal grate; at the other side of the room, a patent coal-oil heater was going. Between them, a large man sat slumped in a wooden wheelchair, a dark-red blanket over his lap and a plaid shawl around his shoulders. His thin silver hair stuck up in unwashed spikes.

'Gentlemen from the police, Colonel,' the servant said. 'About the missus. You warm enough?'

The seated man flicked a hand to send him away. The servant shrugged and, without looking at Munro or Denton, went out of a door at the rear of the room.

'Lieutenant Colonel Alken? I'm Detective Inspector Munro of the Metropolitan Police. Mr Denton.'

The room, although rather small, held a somewhat truncated grand piano of the 'boudoir' sort; Denton noted that double doors at the parlour end could be opened to make a single large room, presumably big enough for musical evenings. The piano was closed; a big paisley shawl hung over it, blood-red and purple, the shawl itself covered, except for where it hung down the sides, with photographs, most in tarnished silver frames. Three that he could see closest to him were of the woman who had been found in his back garden.

'You have news of my wife?' the man in the wheelchair asked. His voice shook, not with emotion but with age and perhaps illness; 'news' came out as 'newsh'. His eyes were too wide. A glazed line of dried spittle ran down from the left corner of his mouth, the mouth itself always open and slightly slack on that side.

Stroke, Denton thought.

Munro was explaining that Denton had seen a so far unidentified corpse and that they needed to look at a photograph of Mrs Alken, if he had one—this said in a voice of surprising gentleness.

The Second Woman

Alken waved his right arm towards the piano, his quivering voice saying the obvious: many of the pictures were of his wife. Munro relayed this to Denton, but he had already given Munro a little nod. Munro went on with the charade, picking up each photo and taking it to the old man for confirmation that it was of his wife, then showing it to Denton as if he hadn't already seen it.

'You're sure?' Munro held the third of the photos in front of Denton, his back to Alken. 'Quite sure?' His voice was almost inaudible.

'Yes, quite sure.' He was thinking, *Old man, young wife.* Denton hung back as Munro gave Alken the news. He showed no reaction, although he said, 'I was afraid of the worst. But are you sure? You could be mistaken. With the best of intentions...' His voice trailed off. 'Everybody makes mistakes.'

Munro began to ask questions. Denton was standing by the piano. He looked over the collection of photographs standing like headstones on the paisley field. Some of them were of Alken himself, several in uniform, like the photos of the woman, all done in a studio. Other pictures of the woman were there, as well, some recognizably younger. Denton picked up one in which she looked adolescent, the pose demure, the dress with a large bustle. He guessed that it had been taken about 1880, but he was no expert on fashion. In the corner of the photograph it said *Vishinsky, Cracowa.*

Munro was saying something about the telephone: she had received a telephone call. Yes, it was a Saturday. Alken had no idea who had called her; he never used the telephone himself. Yes, his wife had used the telephone. Yes, she often went out. He had used to go out himself until he had had an unfortunate incident of a medical nature.

When Munro was finished with his questions, Denton said, 'Was Mrs Alken Polish, Colonel Alken?'

'Polish, yes. From one of the best families.' He slurred his s's again. 'I met her in Warszawa—serving with the, with the—delegation—diplomatic—legation. I was, not she. Related to the Hohenzollerns.'

'What year was that, sir?'

'What? Year.' The wide eyes tried to squint; the lower lids, permanently rolled down to show the red-yellow lining, twitched. 'Eighty-four. Yes, it was eighty-four. People thought I was mad—penniless foreign girl. But—she was my bright star. She was my...' The eyes teared up.

'We must be going now,' Munro said. 'I'll have a word with your servant on the way out, if I may, sir.'

'Barton? Useless fellow. I brought my batman with me when I left the Royal Marines, but—he died!' He sounded astonished and deeply affronted. 'Dead on the pantry floor one morning. Shit his trousers when he died. Terrible thing.' His head went down still farther. 'Now I have this lout.'

Denton and Munro both said how sorry they were several times and in several ways. Denton was not sure, when they left, that Alken entirely understood that his wife was dead: he understood what had happened—one of his visitors had identified his wife as a dead body he had seen—but the meaning of the identification may not have reached him yet.

At the parlour door, waiting for Barton to let them out, Denton said, 'Did you tell him you don't have her body?'

Munro shook his head. 'Sufficient unto the day. He hasn't got it yet, anyway.'

Barton came from the back of the house, pulling on a black alpaca jacket. Munro said to him, 'Mrs Alken got a telephone call the last morning she was here.'

'She did?'

Munro's eyes narrowed. He was holding his hat by the brim; now, he tapped Barton's chest with it. 'Don't take a tone with me. That understood, Barton? I'm a policeman. I don't like tones.'

Barton said he hadn't meant anything.

'You answered the telephone, did you, Barton?'

'I did, sir.'

'Who was calling?'

'They didn't say.'

'Man or woman?'

'I think a man, sir.'

'Mrs Alken get many calls from this man?'

'I couldn't say, sir. The house don't get that many calls—you see what it's like here.'

'You know what I'm getting at, Barton. Mrs Alken was donkey's years younger than the colonel. Anything going on with her?'

'I'm sure I wouldn't know, sir.'

Munro tapped Barton's chest with his hat again. 'We'll meet again. Next time, I don't want tone and I do want answers.' Munro turned and opened the door into the entry, went on through and grasped the handle of the front door as if he expected Denton to follow. Instead, Denton took out a half-crown he had been holding in his jacket pocket. He held it out. 'Thank you, Barton.' As the other man's fingers closed around the coin, Denton said, 'Did Mrs Alken speak with an accent, Barton?'

'She did, sir, yes.'

'Did the man who called her on the telephone?'

'Oh, no, sir—very proper voice.'

'You'd heard it before, then.'

'Well, not so as to say for certain. I *might* have heard it, I might. But voices on the telephone—'

'What name did she give him? Didn't she say anything like, "Hello, Charles or Fred or Alec or—"?'

'Don't know, I'm sure.'

Denton held Barton's eyes. When they shifted away, he took another coin from his pocket. 'What name?'

Barton took the coin, shrugged. 'I might have heard Michael. Or might not. Maybe some other day, I might have heard a name to put to that voice.'

Seeing Munro signalling from the entry, Denton started away. Still, he turned back to say, 'Was Mrs Alken good to work for?'

'Not so bad. For a foreigner, if you follow me.' They looked at each other. Barton's little smile stayed in place: he was back to his 'tone'. *Britain for the British.*

Outside, the crank in his hand, Munro said, 'What was that all about?'

'He thought he "might have" heard the caller's voice before.'

'Man friend? Crime of passion? Old husband, still-young wife. My thought, too.' He twirled the iron crank in his hand. 'If this thing slams me in the wrist again, *you're* going to do the cranking and I'll be the one sitting on his jacksie and singing "Contact" when I advance the bloody magneto or whatever it is you do.'

A few seconds later, he shouted in pain and swore.

'So the servant thought maybe the caller's name was Michael— "posh" accent, maybe he'd heard the voice before.'

'Let sleeping dogs lie, Denton.' Janet sounded listless. He had told her about the morning's visits, the old man who had had a stroke. Beyond an irritation that he had let himself be dragged into it again, she said nothing.

It was raining, her windows covered with rivulets of water. She hadn't gone to the Isle of Dogs, didn't say why when he asked her, only that it was raining.

'You feeling all right, Janet?'

'Of course.' She was staring out of or at the window. She traced a descending drop with a finger. Denton said, 'Anyway, Mrs Alken may have had a lover. That's as good as nothing, isn't it? Plenty of pictures of her—the husband's besotted. One that says "Cracowa".'

'Cracowa's in Poland,' she said. 'What we call Cracow.'

'He married her in Poland. She looked young in the photo. He implied he was infatuated—"people" didn't approve.'

She didn't say anything. After some minutes, she went to a sofa and sat, then reclined, one arm over her eyes.

'You sure you're all right?'

She said nothing, then murmured—clearly a non sequitur— 'I miss Leah.' She moved her body as if it were uncomfortable. 'Annie's no help. I'm tired of being my own servant.' She arranged a small pillow next to her head and turned her face into it. 'You go away now. I'm sorry, Denton. I'm simply feeling lazy.'

He kissed the side of her face and went off. Passing the windows that looked down into the gardens, he stopped. He wondered how much Annie could actually have seen from here, if this was where she had stood when the woman was killed. She had, according to Atkins, told another housemaid she had seen 'two ladies', but they almost certainly had been Janet and 'Tania Simonova', or just possibly Simonova and the dead woman. Could she actually have seen anybody at all?

He headed down to the kitchen, then detoured back to look for her and found her, at last, in a second-floor sewing room, looking out at the street. Hearing him, she must have hurried back to the sewing table, but she spilled a box of pins and was red and flustered.

'Annie,' he said.

'Something knocked over the pins; I'm sure as sure it was a mouse. The house is teeming with mice—'

'Annie, I don't care about the pins. I want to talk to you.'

She looked terrified.

'Annie, when you saw the two ladies in the garden—'

'I never said I saw no ladies in no garden!'

'I think you told people that you saw two ladies.'

'I never told the polis nothing!'

'Not the police, Annie. It doesn't matter who you told. Don't cry. Annie—the two ladies—'

'They wasn't there!'

'They were wearing hats, you said.'

'Well, they was.' She had been sewing the hem on a handkerchief, now used it on her nose.

'What colour?'

'Black.'

'Both hats?'

'Did I say both hats was black? Oh, I don't know, I don't know—' She started to wail.

'Annie—please—' He got out a coin. 'Annie, don't be upset.' He put the coin down in front of her. 'I'm not scolding you. I just want information, Annie. There, there's a sixpence. Would I give you a sixpence if I was scolding you?' He waited until she had picked up the coin and the wailing had subsided, and then he said, 'Annie, the woman who was killed—'

'I never seen her!'

'I'm sure you didn't, unless she was one of the two ladies you saw.'

'She wasn't!'

'Annie, how would you know?'

Annie's narrow, chinless face took on a feral look. 'She wasn't.'

'Then one of the two ladies you saw was the other one.'

'Yes. That's it.'

'So you knew her. Annie? The other one was downstairs in Leah's rooms.'

'I never go down there. Them and I don't get along—ask anybody.'

'But did you see her?'

'See who? Ye're mixing things all up in my head—I don't know what I seen—'

'But if you knew she was one of the two ladies, then you must have seen her.'

'I oney went to the top of the stairs there; I oney talked to Leah to tell her—' The feral look gave way to panic. Eyes wide, she stared at Denton. 'I didn't.'

'I didn't know that Leah was home while the woman was there. Annie?'

'Leave me be—please leave me be—' She clutched her head.

'You said that you went to the stairs to talk to Leah.'

'Maybe I did.' Her eyes were still wide, her mouth open. Her slow brain was trying to catch up with him.

Suddenly, he knew she was trying to find a way to lie. He said, 'Why did you want to talk to Leah if you and she don't get along?'

'Oh, it was just—we was talking about—' Her face was anguished. A wail burst from her mouth and she stood, holding on to her head. 'It was the woman said I must ask had I seen nobody!'

'What woman?'

'The woman—the woman—' She wept. 'I don't know, oh, please, don't tell the polis, don't tell the missus, they just got me so mixed up I couldn't remember! It ain't my business, mister! Leave me be, leave me be!' Her voice had fallen to a groan.

'Annie.' He made his voice gentle. 'Annie, come, there's no harm in what you're saying. I don't care about the police. But when you say "the woman" told you to ask if Leah had seen anybody—what woman? What woman, Annie?'

Annie fell into the chair again. Now she covered her eyes with her hands. 'The woman what come to the door. That woman. She wanted the missus and the missus wasn't here, so she said I must ask downstairs if there was anybody. She made me do it, she was that bossy.' She raised her head, showed him swollen eyes. 'I didn't want to! I didn't know the missus had brought no woman down there! How am I supposed to know things?' She went back to weeping.

'What did Leah say?'

'She tole me to mind my own business, the Jew slut!'

Her eyes challenged him; he looked away and tried to maintain the gentle voice. 'So, the woman who came, Annie. The one who told you to ask downstairs. What was she like?'

'She was another cut from the same cloth. She spoke foreign, and she was hoity-toity with me. Like it was her house. "My girl, do this! My girl, do that!" I didn't know which way my head was screwed on.' She began to weep again. 'I didn't know no better, mister.'

'So she had an accent—yes? And her clothes, were they good clothes, Annie? Nice clothes? And her hat, was it black? Ah, green like her dress. And was she old? Not so old.' Whatever that meant to Annie at seventeen.

Denton thought he had got everything from her he would get right then. He put another coin on the table. 'I'm sorry that I upset you, Annie. I swear I won't tell the police or anybody. This will be our secret. All right, Annie? Annie?'

Her face was in her hands. Her head nodded, two short jerks; that was all he would get. He said again that he was sorry and, feeling helpless and somewhat guilty, he left her.

He went down through the house. Janet was asleep on the sofa where he had left her. He let himself out into the garden and went through into his own, then stood there in the rain staring at the place where the dead woman had lain. He thought that the woman whom Annie had talked to was the woman in the photographs at the house north of Victoria Park—Lydia Alken, who had received a telephone call earlier from a man who spoke well and who might have been named Michael. Then she had come here, apparently fairly directly, because she had been found behind the old privy before mid-morning.

There must, he thought, be a way to find where the telephone call had come from.

He went into his own house and upstairs, passing Atkins, who was standing by a window doing nothing. Seeing Denton, he said, 'Writing a new song. In my head.'

'Think it's possible to trace a telephone call back to the person who made it?'

'Cripes, I hope not.'

He went upstairs and retrieved the slip with the telephone number that Held had given him. There were two numbers on the paper, one for 'Highgate' and one for 'private office'. He got on the telephone and shouted at the Central operator that he wanted City 243. To his surprise, it worked. A male secretary told him that Held was in conference but he would take a message. Disappointed—if people had telephones, surely they ought to sit by them to take calls—he asked that Held call him on the confidential matter that they had discussed.

But Held didn't call. To Denton's surprise, he showed up at the front door a couple of hours later, leaving his chauffeured Benz purring at the kerb.

Held was brisk and rather steely. He didn't take his coat off, stood in Denton's sitting room with his hat in his hands. 'I have a meeting in twenty-five minutes. I hope this is important.'

'I think I've found something, and I think it's important, but I need you to do something for me or I can't proceed.'

'What's happened?'

'I can't tell you yet. I *will* tell you, but not yet.'

'You want something for nothing, Mr Denton!'

'A promissory note.' Denton thought of the Zangwill book. 'I want to *schnorr* you for a shilling and give you back a pound. Maybe.'

'What is it you want?'

Denton gave him the date that the woman had been found dead in his back garden, and the telephone exchange and number for Lieutenant Colonel Alken. 'Somebody telephoned that number that morning. I want to know where they called from.'

'Mr Denton, I am neither the Post Office nor the National Telephone!'

'But you know people who are.'

Held said that this was, indeed, a *schnorrer's* sort of request, and did Mr Denton understand the concept of *chutzpah*? He went on without waiting for an answer, tried a question or two to find if the request was related to the woman he called Tania Simonova, said after these that he would try. He promised nothing, but he would try.

'You ask a great deal. Is this truly *important*?'

'Held, you got in touch with me. You asked for my help. Now, to try to give that help, I need something from you.'

Held stared at him, then put his hat on and clattered down the stairs. Seconds later, the Benz roared and moved off.

Denton sat in his green armchair and tried to think backwards from what Annie had told him. What did it mean if it really was Lydia Alken who had come to Janet's house that morning? It meant, for one thing, that she knew the precise house she wanted; and it seemed to mean that she knew that 'Simonova', or at least a woman, was there. She could have learned both things from Bernat or from Bernat's blabbing at the Infirmary.

But why? Why send somebody to Janet's house to seek 'Simonova'?

To help her? That would make the caller another anarchist. *To harm her?* That would make the caller—who, 'Simonova's' husband? But in either case, why hadn't the caller simply come himself?

Because he didn't want to be seen as part of it. Maybe.

So maybe Lydia Alken had come to Janet's house and asked to see 'Simonova', although it wasn't likely she had known that name (or that 'Simonova' would admit it if she had), and poor Annie had made some sort of effort to talk to Leah and apparently been snapped at. And had the woman gone away then? Probably she had, to turn up next as a corpse behind a privy-cum-tool shed.

And in between? And where, come to that, were her clothes?

And 'Simonova'? If she was the woman who had had the abortion, then she had told Bernat she was a socialist and a Zionist, but it looked as if she was an anarchist, as well. A practised liar was what Denton thought she was.

Held didn't call him until after ten that night. He sounded far away, his voice without resonance; perhaps it was the telephone, but Denton thought that the man sounded angry. Denton said, 'I've put you to great trouble.'

'Not such great trouble. But there was great resistance. Such favours don't come without an expectation of repayment in future. And they don't come cheap.' His voice grew, if possible, even thinner. 'Are you involved in party politics?'

'Of course not.'

'One of my Liberal friends refused outright, and he's a director of National Telephone. I had to go to a Tory.'

'I'm very sorry.'

'A good *schnorrer* is never sorry, Mr Denton; he makes all difficulty the giver's fault. You might tell me that overcoming difficulty builds character, so I owe you ten shillings for educational services.' The voice, although tinny and marred by crackles, was sarcastic. 'Look here: getting the information you want is actionable and probably illegal. I think I've dodged that, but I want you to know that the only reason I was able to get the information is that the call was made from a telephone that has a mandated tracking of all calls made to or from it. I'm told that this is unique. Normally, the calls are made and no record is kept unless they go beyond the boundaries of the area. In this case, a slip of paper has to be made out for each call; when a transfer has to be made to another exchange or to a national exchange, another slip of paper is filled out. Needless to say, these slips are private and confidential. '

'I'm sorry. I didn't realize—'

'Perhaps it will interest you also to learn that the Metropolitan Police are asking the same question. In fact, it's because of their interest that the slips were already being sorted when my source went looking for them.'

Munro, Denton thought. He said, 'But you did manage to get to them?'

Held's voice sounded metallic and disapproving. 'The exchange number is 34. The telephone is 568. The subscriber is the Essential Oils Import Company, Limited. The telephone is located at 22 Charrington Street, Camden Town.'

Denton said that he was grateful, very grateful, very, very grateful. He felt shamed without quite understanding why. Held did not sound at all pleased with Denton's apologies, and certainly not convinced by Denton's assurance that the information might be important. His last words were, '"Might be", Mr Denton, is hardly worth saying.'

Denton went to bed wondering what essential oils were and what they had to do with the dead woman in his garden.

CHAPTER

14

He was awake before the late-autumn sun rose, his bedroom barely visible in the first grey light. It was still too early to go poking into 22 Charrington Street. He dressed quickly in walking clothes and let himself out of the front door, turned right towards Coram's and picked his way north and west to Regent's Park. It was full light by the time he was striding up the Broad Walk, the air cold and his breath visible in small puffs. A damp breeze was blowing from the west and he wished he could wear a hat. He pulled his collar tighter. Passing the gravel path that led back to where he had seen Guillam that morning, he thought he would turn aside and use the public toilets but didn't want to because he was enjoying the physical pleasure of walking, the returned feel of strength in his legs and back. He would wait until he walked back.

He went up to the zoo and along its periphery, turning west up the path that led behind the wolves and foxes, the smell intense in the damp air; then past the sheep pen, wondering how the wolves could stand to be so close to the sheep and not able to get to them; past the ponds and then the pigs, odours of rot and excrement, an overall sweetness; and turned at the Outer Circle to go south, his strides fast and long now, his shoulders rolling with the pace. When he could get to this rhythm, it was almost like rowing though never as strenuous, but there was the same satisfactory sense of propelling the body, almost of flying. He turned again before he reached the suspension bridge and headed into the trees, making for the kiosk and the toilets that lay this side of it. The need was urgent now, the earlier decision to postpone a mistake.

He glimpsed the toilet building ahead, moved to the grassy verge to be on that side. A smaller path led to the building. He cut across to save time. From the corner of his left eye, he sensed anomaly, turned his head. Fifty feet away in the shadow of the trees was a figure, little more than a dark overcoat. Then Denton saw it all at once: the standing man, another, partly concealed by the coat, kneeling. Denton threw himself forward to get away before he was seen, but it was too late.

Two things happened at once: the standing man turned his head towards Denton, and the kneeling one turned his away and pushed off like a sprinter from the start to run into the trees.

The standing man was Guillam.

For the instant that Denton couldn't entirely look away, their eyes met. Guillam's head was lowered, his posture bearish, threatening. His erection was visible through his unbuttoned flies.

Denton raced past the toilets and into the trees on the other side. He was as embarrassed and humiliated as if he had been in Guillam's place; the horror of seeing it—not of what was happening, but of having seen it happen—made him sick. His bladder felt as if it would burst, but he couldn't stop, didn't until he was at the park entrance, where he blundered into another lavatory and relieved himself, gasping, sweating, staring around him in fear that he'd see Guillam.

At home, his horror and embarrassment changed into sadness and a kind of guilt. It was as if he had willed to be there, a peeping Tom. It was no good telling himself it had been an accident, a coincidence. Guillam's accusing look stayed with him, an open, animal hatred.

He rushed through breakfast, monosyllabic in answering Atkins's patter. Guillam rode on his shoulders like a great weight. Janet had said once, when he had said he loved her, 'Rather weighty, being loved'; she had said it lightly, but it had hurt him. Yet he had known what she meant: other people piled the weight of their feelings on you, he his love, Guillam his secret life. Like Atlas and the world.

As soon as he was done eating, he said, 'I'm going out.' Atkins waited for an explanation, got none, shrugged. Denton changed into fresh clothes, a double-breasted suit, then went through the gardens to see Janet. To his surprise, the back door was unlocked and there was no fire in the kitchen. Going through the cold downstairs rooms, he looked for Annie; on the floor above, he looked into Janet's bedroom, saw her still sleeping, her breathing heavy, and no fire in her grate, either. He went on up another flight, then called up the stairs to the attic where Annie slept.

When there was no answer, he went silently up. Guillam's weight was still on his shoulders; it combined somehow with Annie's tales of ghosts to make him jumpy. Yet the attic was as cold as the rest of the house and as silent. The door to Annie's little room was open, and the room itself was empty—the narrow bed stripped and the mattress rolled down, the pegs on the wall empty. A little space had been curtained off for clothes. That space was empty, too.

Denton searched the rest of the house for her, checked the kitchen and the pantry again and saw that the clothes hooks by the back entrance held neither her coat, which usually hung there, nor the apron she sometimes wore. A pair of men's rubber boots that she had worn over her shoes in foul weather were gone.

He went up to Janet's room and sat on her bed. After several seconds, she opened her eyes and looked at him as if she couldn't remember who he was. He said, stupidly, 'Are you awake?'

'I am now.'

'Annie's gone.'

She stared at him, then gave a quick sigh and turned her head. 'Oh, well.'

'Are you all right, Janet?'

'Why wouldn't I be?'

'You never sleep late.'

'Well, today I did. What of it?'

She put the back of her hand on her forehead, shielding her eyes. Perhaps she didn't want to look at him. He wanted to tell her about Guillam but couldn't. He said, 'I'll start some fires. The house is freezing.'

'Don't bother.'

'Janet—'

'It doesn't matter, Denton!'

He stood. 'I'm going out for a little. I'll send Atkins over.'

'I don't need looking after. I want to sleep. I shall see you when you come back.'

'You're not going to the Isle of Dogs.'

'Perhaps later.

He made the mistake of trying again. 'Can I get you anything?'

'Oh, let me be!'

Back in his own house, he told Atkins to go over in half an hour and make sure she was all right. 'Don't wake her if she's sleeping. But the house is like an ice cave; start a fire in the kitchen range and one in her sitting room. If she's awake, offer her tea. You know the sort of thing.'

'You need the new black overcoat with that suit.'

'If you say so.'

'And with the black overcoat you need a hat.'

'And with a hat I need a head that won't hurt. No hat.'

He went upstairs and felt in the box for the derringer and remembered that he'd left it in a suit at some point; Atkins must have gone through his suits by now; where the hell was his derringer? He thought of taking the revolver, but the black overcoat was tight-fitting and it had no holster sewn into the pocket like his other coats. *And why do I want a revolver to go to Camden Town?* The British authorities would have answered, 'You don't!' They were about to institute a licence for handguns. Denton thought it meant the end of individual responsibility, but he would apply for one.

He decided not to take the motor car: Charrington Street was close to a bus route. He walked to Oxford Street and caught the 34 bus up to Camden High Street. His mood was grim— Janet and Annie piled on Guillam, his reason for going to Camden Town reduced to a mere scratching at his attention. He got down almost automatically and looked around as if he had no idea where he was. He found his way to Charrington Street with the help of a constable, having to go so far south that he suspected he was really in Somers Town, wondering if the number that Held had given him was a Camden Town exchange only through some anomaly of the early telephone companies.

Number 22 Charrington Street was a greengrocer's.

No sign of essential oils. No sign, really, of the sort of people and the sort of offices that he associated with 'import company', which surely smacked more of the City.

He approached the greengrocer's on the same side of the street, getting increasingly doubtful as he got closer. He saw the awning and the stands of fruits and vegetables, and he thought that they looked quite wrong. Or he looked quite wrong, and the essential oils import business was wrong. But there was Number 22, right enough. Boxes of pippins filled one of the elevated bins; another had purple-and-white turnips and mounds of brown, knobby potatoes. Beyond them were green and yellow things, the lacy fronds and bright orange of carrots. Certain that he was on a wild goose chase, Denton went inside.

A fat man in waistcoat and shirtsleeves, a bowler jammed on his head, was tearing the wilted outer leaves from a lettuce. 'Help you, sir?' he said, his tone sounding as if help was the last thing he wanted to give.

'I'm looking for number twenty-two.'

'This is twenty-two.' He was throwing torn and blackened leaves into a barrel. He dropped the newly re-greened head into a pile and started on another.

'I'm looking for the Essential Oils Import Company.'

'And who'd they be when they're at home?'

'They're an import company.'

'Don't know nothing about that. No import company *here*, for certain. This is my shop, not a company. What's essential oils?'

'Could they be upstairs?'

'Maybe they could, but they ain't. Rooms and flats upstairs. Nothing to do with me what's up there, most of them gone all day and me gone all night. I'm not the landlord, if that's what you're asking.'

'Is there an entrance?'

The grocer jerked a thumb. 'Down the passage.'

Denton went out and followed the thumb's direction and found next to the shop on the far side a narrow passage between it and the next building, the walls sooty, the sky all but hidden overhead. Bits of paper and some carrot topping lay smashed flat where the concrete underfoot met the blackened brick of the walls. He moved into the passage and found a locked door without signs or bells. Nothing suggested that an import company might be found on the other side.

He walked as far as the passage would let him, found a high wooden fence, a few dead and dry weeds that had somehow managed to grow there. There were no other doors. Denton returned to Charrington Street. He walked farther along, past the next two buildings, then came back and looked at the building on the other side of the greengrocer's. Finding nothing, he crossed the street, dodging a wagon and two piles of horse dung, and turned on the opposite kerb to study the buildings again. He had thought he might see a sign of some sort in the storeys above the greengrocer's. Instead, he saw only a painted name, once white, now somewhat sooty: GORMAN'S GREENGROCERS.

Gorman. The recognition was instantaneous: *Gorban's a bloody duffer. Him and his rules of war.* The blond man whose nose he'd bloodied, the bullyragger in his house the day the woman's body was found, saying 'Gorban' for 'Gorman' because of his nose.

But if Gorman was the greengrocer—? Rules of war? That didn't sound like the greengrocers Denton dealt with. He thought of crossing back over to talk to the greengrocer again but felt suddenly cautious: something was very wrong. It made no sense that a greengrocer—and he was a greengrocer, or he was giving a superb imitation of one—was somehow connected with two men who could bully the police and have the legal protection of somebody like William Freethorne.

He looked up at the building above the level of the greengrocer's. The windows were mullioned, three bays across the façade, most curtained. No hint of life within. *Rooms and flats.*

A man in a lounge suit had come out of the greengrocer's and was looking across the street at Denton. When Denton looked back at him, the man turned and began to pick among the pippins. The eye contact made Denton uneasy, but nothing further happened. Nonetheless, he moved up the street. His thoughts of Guillam and Janet were banished now; his mind was fixed on this place, Gorman, the 'rules of war'. And the missing essential oils importing company.

He turned at the corner and crossed Charrington Street again and walked to the next corner. He thought it might help to have a look at the back of Number 22; however, the little street back there, Penryn, was filled solidly with three- and four-storey buildings that stood shoulder to shoulder like a wall. Denton crossed to the far side and made his way along, moving almost sideways. He stopped when he thought he was about opposite where the back of Number 22 Charrington Street should be.

But he couldn't see the back of Number 22. What he could see was a blackened stucco façade whose windows had been bricked in long ago. A flight of stone steps led up to a doorway that had once had some style, now needed paint. Between the second and third storeys, old white letters were barely visible. He stared at them until they made words for him: BARTH'S BEST

BATHS. Smaller letters had once said something about cleanliness and vigour.

Barth's.

The bullyragger's voice: *I say we go back to Bard's.* But the blood-clogged nose had made Barth's into Bard's. But if it had, it didn't mean to go back for a bath; Barth's Baths had obviously been up the spout for years. So the name was simply a way of designating the place, in fact could have been a private code for a place—the building that has the almost illegible Barth's on it.

As, perhaps, Gorman stood for the building that had 'Gorman's Greengrocers' painted on it?

But the bullyragger had spoken of Gorman as if it was not a place but a person—*Gorman's a duffer.* Yet there was the British convention of letting places stand for things, sometimes for people—Number 10, the Court of St James's. Could Gorman stand for somebody *inside* Number 22, maybe somebody who lived upstairs in one of the rooms or flats? And if Barth's Baths actually backed on Number 22—

He crossed the street and counted the paces from the corner of the building to the cross street, then walked around to Charrington Street again and counted the paces from the corner down to the greengrocer's. The two buildings seemed to be offset from each other by only about five feet. He was aware that he might be imposing his own situation on this one, but couldn't Barth's and Gorman's, backing on each other, be connected as his house and Janet's were? That way, somebody might talk about Barth's and Gorman's in the same breath: *Let's go back to Barth's and talk to Gorman about it.* That suggested a degree of organization, true, and the spending of some money. Was it like saying, *Let's go back to my house and talk to Janet?*

But where did the export company come into it?

He backed to the kerb so as to see over the greengrocer's awning. He looked up.

'Beg pardon, sir?'

Startled, Denton stepped back and stumbled as he went off the kerb. A hansom, about to discharge a passenger, was heading

in towards the pavement; he heard the driver cry, 'Here, now!'
He jumped back on the kerb and turned to see who had spoken
to him: a middle-aged constable with a grey moustache and a
look of liking his pint.

'Sorry, Constable. I didn't see you.'

'Not at all, sir. You the gentleman is looking for the Essential
Oils Import Company, are you?'

'Yes!' He sounded eager, even to himself.

The constable chuckled. 'Bit hard to find, i'n't it. And *he's*
no help.' He tipped his head sideways towards the greengrocer's.
'I can show you the way, sir. Follow me.'

They were going, as it turned out, only the half-dozen steps
to the passage. Denton was aware of the hansom's moving next
to him, its passenger not yet let down. At the entrance to the
passage, the man he had seen come out of the greengrocer's was
standing as if he were waiting to take the cab that was pulling
up. He looked to be in his late thirties, had a fringe of beard;
seeing Denton, he smiled, as if, having looked at each other across
Charrington Street, they were acquaintances.

'There's a doorway down the passage, sir. The bell's actually in the doorjamb, high up, right up in the corner, it is. Daft
place to put a bell. And they call theirselves businessmen!' The
constable laughed and led the way down the passage.

Denton turned in behind him; then he was aware of movement at his back and he started to turn, but he was grabbed from
behind around the neck and swung against the brick wall to his
left; at the same time, the policeman whirled and stepped back
to him and swung his truncheon against Denton's right kidney.
Denton groaned and struggled, trying to push away from the
wall and stamp on the foot of the man who had hold of him. He
kept both his hands curled around the arm that gripped him, and
he thought he had the purchase and the strength to pull it away,
when the chemical odour of chloroform reached him and a cold
cloth was pulled against his nose and mouth. He tore at it, pushed
against the wall, flailed at the man behind him, and began to sink
into unconsciousness. He tried to shout, and then it was too late.

The Second Woman

He remembered nothing of the dreams he had as the chloroform took hold, and he probably could have made nothing of them if he had. They involved his taking off, again and again, a strange garment that was somehow Guillam's but was also, when he got it off and held it up, the underclothing of the dead woman in his back garden. The thing frightened him and repelled him, but Guillam kept making him put it on, and he took it off, and it was pink elastic, something of hers, and he had to put it back on, and...

He was lying on his side on a stone floor. He could smell the chloroform on his moustache and taste it like hot metal, the taste mixed with vomit. He was naked. The stones were grey and shiny, and his vomit had gathered in the cracks between the stones. He tried to move and found that his hands and feet were shackled.

'He's coming round.'

Denton rolled his head. A horrible deadness smothered his senses. He blinked.

A face appeared above him, small, male, wire eyeglasses magnifying the muddy eyes. A thumb raised his right eyelid, then his left. The man's breath was foul with decay. He put fingers on Denton's throat and left them there for what seemed a long time.

'All right. He's all right.'

Denton heard footsteps on the stones. He tried to roll on his back to see who was coming; the shackles pressed into his back and stopped him. Hands reached into his armpits and pushed him until he was sitting on the stones, then lifted him until he was standing.

'Stand up.' It was an order. 'Is he going to fall down again?'

'He's all right.'

The hands let him go, then took him by the shoulders and turned him a quarter-turn to his right. 'Walk.'

When he didn't start at once, he was given a push on his right shoulder where the burn was. He stumbled forward and almost fell, and another pair of hands caught him. 'Stand up!'

The small man with the foul breath was standing near the only door. He was wearing a dark suit, buttoned up very high, and a high collar. Near him was a wooden desk, nothing on it. Denton moved his head to look around him; the movement felt slow, his head ponderous. He saw rough stone walls, two wooden barrels, clothes that he thought were his own in a corner. The room was about twenty feet on a side. Overhead were old beams, thick boards crosswise showing between them, three electric bulbs with new, thick, cloth-covered wires. The room was cold.

'I didn't say you could have a look round. Walk.' He moved forward. He had to shuffle because of the shackles. 'Stop.'

Denton knew the voice. Semi-posh. It was the other of the bullyraggers—not the one whose nose he'd broken. 'Freddie.' The man was behind him; so was a third person. He had heard the feet moving on the stones. *The other one. The one I punched.* Denton said, 'What the hell is going on?' although he knew what was going on. There was no answer. He looked at the little man against the wall, who he thought was probably a doctor, and said, 'What the hell is going on?' The little man's face twitched and he looked away.

A large man moved from behind him to his left side and then around to the front. He was wearing a kind of boiler suit, dark blue, apparently with nothing under it because Denton could see skin as far down as it was unbuttoned. The man wore a balaclava over his face. He carried a rattan cane. 'We want you to answer some questions,' he said. It was Freddie again.

'What the hell is going on?'

The man moved to Denton's right. After standing there a moment, he suddenly whipped the rattan cane against Denton's shins. It was acutely painful, catching some of the burned skin; Denton gasped. Before he could recover, the man hit him backhanded on his hamstring muscles, the blow not careless but calculated to paralyze. Denton lost control of his legs and pitched forward, rolling to the side to protect his head; even so, he fell with a bruising force, and his head struck the stone floor sideways.

'Stand up.'

Denton rolled to his knees and found he couldn't stand. He bent forward. The cane flashed and his buttocks stung. 'Stand up.'

The shackles kept him from getting his feet under himself. He inched his left foot forward as far the shackles would allow and then forced himself up, twisting to put his other leg under him as he rose. Although he came to a standing position facing a different part of the room, the man with the cane had moved, too, so as to be still behind him. Denton's back was now to the doctor, and, presumably, to the third man.

'State your name.'

'Tell me what the hell is going—'

The cane gave him three lightning strokes, the man incredibly fast: calves, right shoulder, buttocks. Hating himself for cowering, Denton nonetheless curled into himself.

'Name?'

'You know my name, you bas—'

The blow came right across both Achilles tendons, and he went down again. He tasted blood in his mouth, felt blood run down his forehead.

'Stand up.'

The same procedure, slower than the first time.

'Name?'

'Denton.'

'Full name?'

He never used his full name, except on legal things that demanded it. He feared the cane now, however. There was some kind of Oriental torture with a bamboo stick, he thought, that broke the bones one by one. This man knew how to do that, he thought. What he had done so far was bad, but he could do much worse. Denton told them his full name.

'Residence?'

He told them. He knew they had been there, because they were the bullyraggers.

'What were you doing on Charrington Street?'

'Walking.'

The cane flashed across the fronts of his thighs. 'What were you doing on Charrington Street?'

'Looking for something.'

'What?'

'An import company.'

'What company?'

'The Essential Oils Import Company.'

'Why?'

He hesitated too long; the cane fell on his left shoulder. 'Why?'

He knew he was going to have to make things up. Telling the truth would lead only to more questions, and more questions; everything would come out—the abortion and Janet's part in it. He didn't want to mention Held. He thought he owed the man that. He said, 'I thought the woman whose body you took away from my house worked for the import company.'

He thought the part about their taking the body away would bring another blow, and he cringed in preparation, but none came.

'Why did you think that?'

'I found her handbag in my house. It had the company's name and the address in it.'

The other man said, 'He's bloody lying.' The one whose nose he'd broken.

Then the first man: 'Where did you find the handbag?'

'In my bookcase. Behind the books.'

'He's lying!'

Freddie came around so that Denton could see him. He put the cane against Denton's larynx. 'Don't lie. The next time I hit you, it's going to be right there. I can kill you by hitting you there, but I'll just break it this time. Don't lie. Mm?' He stepped back. 'Now. What was the woman's name?'

'There was a letter in the handbag addressed to Lydia Alken. I think that was her name.'

Their silence was astonishing. It was as if they'd stopped breathing, their hearts had stopped beating. Then the one who had said that Gorman was a duffer said, 'He's lying. Let's get to it.'

But the other one said, 'Then you had an address for her, too. On the letter. What was it?'

He realized he was about to implicate the old man in the wheelchair, Lieutenant Colonel Alken. He tried to get out of it. 'It was in Hackney somewhere. I don't remember.'

The man with the cane tapped it on Denton's larynx hard enough to hurt. 'You don't remember it. You came *here*, but you don't remember her address? You went to her address, didn't you? Eh?'

Denton turned away from the cane and took the light blows on his shoulder. 'I gave it to somebody else to do.'

'Who?' The taps became a hard cut.

'The police! I gave it to the police!' He cringed and tried to scream. 'Please don't hit me again—I'm telling the truth—'

'He's lying.'

'You're lying.' The man grabbed what was left of Denton's hair in his left hand and pulled his head back. 'Who are you working for? Who sent you to Charrington Street?'

'Nobody—I swear—'

'He's fucking lying!'

'You're lying.' The man let his hair go with a push that almost knocked Denton over. 'All right, get the sack.'

Denton turned to see what they were going to do, but he couldn't turn fast enough. The one whose nose he'd broken was already behind him somewhere; he tried to turn, but he got a cut with the cane, and then something was put over his head from behind, white, translucent. He tried to struggle out of it, but his head was pulled backwards and he was hit another blow in the kidneys. Something was pulled tight around his throat.

He found he could breathe. The sack was clean enough that he could see the lamps' spots of light through it. There was a smell of something dry and nutty. *Rice*, he thought. A common rice sack.

'Walk forward two steps. Now—' Hands on his shoulders turned him at an angle. 'Now walk forward. Keep going. Another step. Stop!'

He couldn't tell where he was in the room. The two men were slightly behind him, one on each side. Abruptly, his knees were pushed forward by light blows in the back: he knew the trick, putting your own knee behind another's to bend his leg, part of a technique for controlling prisoners. He tried to step forward but felt pressure under his arms. A voice said, 'Hup!' and he was being lifted, their arms across his belly, then one sliding down into his groin and clutching his thigh. His chest hit something hard and rough, and then he was tipping forward, his head going down now, pressure on the back of his head, the two men gasping with the effort, and he pitched ahead and water rose over his head and shoulders, and he was upside down in one of the barrels.

He feared water. He didn't swim. Panic clutched him as he saw himself upside down in a barrel, shackled, no way to push himself out. He had had his moments of courage.

seven of them standing down there and only me but I had the shotgun and they had

He tried to lever himself out with his torso but did nothing but scrape his back, the barrel too constricted to allow him to bend and reverse his position. They still held his legs; he tried to kick them, drowning.

*only pistols, black powder, only luck if they hit me at that
distance and I had the ten-gauge, all buckshot*

He tried to relax, to conserve the air in his lungs. He went limp
in their arms. Would they think he was unconscious? Of course
not. He could even hear their voices, the words unintelligible
through the water, but they were shouting at each other. The
voices sounded excited, even happy.

*like shooting fish in a barrel, killed two and reloaded and
put down two more, like shooting fish in a barrel, that
isn't courage*

Then the air began to fail him. He let a bubble escape, even heard
it as it went upwards. He fought the desire to breathe, forcing it
back, back, back, and then he had no more air and his lungs were
starved and his discipline cracked. He tried to breathe.

*they said I was brave standing there letting them shoot at
me but that isn't*

They pulled him out when water had flowed into his lungs and
he was twisting like a fish. Only half conscious now, Denton tried
to breathe, felt the wet sack pulled against his nose and mouth.
A great cough came from his gut; water flowed out of his nose.
He was shaking so hard his shackles were rattling on the floor.

Then he was on something hard and round. Somebody was
pounding on his back. The thing under him moved up his chest
and back again and down his legs. Water poured out of him
into the sack and choked him. Somebody was shouting, 'Christ!
Christ!'

Then the sack was being pulled off him and the doctor was
shouting, 'You've gone too far! No more! No more today!' and
Denton was vomiting up water and trying to breathe, choking
on the water in his nose and throat. He was turned on his back,
falling to the floor, aware that they had been rolling him back and

forth over the second barrel to get the water out of him. He rose on his hands and knees and coughed up a great splash of water.

'Put that sack back on him,' the one he'd hit said.

'No!' The doctor sounded hysterical. 'No more!'

'Get out of it, doctor. You don't fucking tell us what to do.'

'I have my orders. I'm supposed to tell you when you go too far.'

'All right, you've told us; now go play with your Johnson someplace.'

Denton's eyes were swimming with tears, the scene around him distorted and unreal. He was shaking all over. He kept trying to suck air into his lungs and getting more water and coughing it up. His breathing was like a saw.

One of the balaclavas pushed the doctor away; he backed a step, holding up his hands. The much bigger man pushed him again, then turned him around and frogmarched him to the door, wrenched it open and shoved him through it.

On his knees, Denton coughed and bent until his forehead touched the stones. And coughed. And tried to breathe. When he breathed in, he heard a sound like water sucking in a drain. He coughed.

'All right.' The one with the cane pushed on Denton's spine and forced him down until he was lying flat. Then the foot moved up to his back and pushed. Water came out through Denton's nose. 'Now, you can go into the barrel again. Or you can tell us the truth. If we get the truth, we won't put you in the barrel. If you lie, we put you in the barrel. Get it?' He poked Denton in the side. 'Get it? I like answers to my questions!'

'Yes.' Denton's voice was barely audible, strangled by his raw throat and the cough that came with it.

'You're ours. You understand? Nobody knows you're here. We've got you for as long as we want. So it's us and the barrel. And if we decide you're lying and will go on lying, then we just may put you in the barrel and go out for our tea. You understand me?'

'Yes.'

'Good.' He had been kneeling next to Denton's head; now, he stood and put a foot on Denton's back and put pressure there. Denton tried to breathe in, gagged. 'Now—who are you working for?'

Denton had been thinking about that. Not clearly, not even in any kind of sequence, but in flashes. He knew he mustn't implicate anybody close to him, therefore he must lie. He must implicate people who were abstract to him, better yet people who could take care of themselves. He had thought of Guillam, but Guillam had become close to him by accident, and he couldn't do it. He said, 'Melville.'

'What name was that?'

'Melville. William Melville.' Hench-Rose had used the name. Munro, too. Head of Special Branch.

'He's lying! That's shite!'

'I'm not lying,' Denton rasped. 'Please don't put me in the water again—' It was easy to put on the sound of terror. He *was* terrified. 'William Melville. Special Branch.'

'Never heard of him. Some sort of policeman, you mean?'

This didn't sound right, even to Denton: these two had claimed police powers when they took the body away. They should know who Melville was. 'Head of Special Branch. Anarchists and, and—the like.'

'You're a bloody American. Why would British police send you to Charrington Street?'

'To look around.'

The foot pressed heavily; Denton groaned, spat up more water. 'He's a friend! He asked me—because nobody knows me. *Because* I'm American. See?'

The other man swam into Denton's vision. 'Let's have that sack on his head again.'

Denton screamed. 'No—no—please, I'm telling the truth—please—!'

There was a thud and bang from the side of the room, and then a huge, parade-ground voice bellowed, 'WHAT THE BLOODY HELL DO YOU THINK YOU'RE DOING?'

The foot came off his back and the man with the cane stepped away from Denton; the other one, stooping to put the sack over Denton's head, stood but kept himself close to him. Denton pushed himself up on his elbow and rolled so that he could see the door; his arm gave way but he stayed on his side.

Hector Hench-Rose and Munro were standing there. Behind them, the little doctor cringed in the doorway as if afraid to put a foot inside the room.

The two balaclavas moved past Denton as if he were a piece of fallen furniture, and the one with the cane said, 'This is no place for you, sir.'

The parade-ground voice belonged to Hench-Rose, it seemed, for now he shouted, 'DON'T YOU BLOODY WELL TELL ME WHERE MY PLACE IS! DO YOU UNDERSTAND ME?'

'Sir, this place is——'

'DO YOU UNDERSTAND ME?'

There was movement near the door, and the man who had looked at Denton across Charrington Street, and who had smiled at him just before he went into the passage, came into the room. The doctor cringed away from him. He had been the one with the chloroform, Denton thought.

'I'll handle this, H-R.'

'Like hell you will.' Hench-Rose put out a hand and prevented the man from coming in any farther. He turned on the man with the cane and said, 'DO YOU UNDERSTAND ME?'

'This is our business—you're interfering——'

Hench-Rose seemed to inflate to twice his normal size. Stepping forward, he grabbed the top of the man's balaclava and pulled. Denton saw the man's fist come up as if for one moment he actually thought of striking Hench-Rose. At the same time, Denton was aware of somebody behind him, pulling him gently backwards, arms around his chest, and squeezing him: Munro.

Hench-Rose snatched the balaclava off. Denton had never seen the military side of his old friend before; now, he saw the face that had terrified even veteran sergeants, and he heard the voice that had shouted down sergeant majors. 'GO TO MY OFFICE AND WAIT THERE UNTIL I APPEAR. IS THAT UNDERSTOOD, YOU BLOODY SORRY SUBSTITUTE FOR A TARTED-UP APE?'

Again, the newcomer tried to step into it. 'H-R, let me.' To the man with the cane he said, in a voice that suggested that nothing that Hench-Rose said was to be taken seriously, 'You two, come along to my office. We'll sort this out.'

Hench-Rose acted as if an other-ranks had interrupted his tongue-lashing of a subaltern. 'KEEP THE BLOODY HELL OUT OF THIS, MICHAEL! I'LL TELL YOU WHEN I WANT YOUR INTERFERENCE!' He turned back to Freddie, now revealed with the balaclava off, and dropped his voice to a hard-edged near-whisper. 'Get your arse to my office *now* and wait there until I come or I'll have you up before M with your balls between your teeth! And take this chimpanzee with you!' He showed whom he meant by snatching the balaclava off the other man—the once-bloodied nose. 'And you won't be needing this!' He grabbed the cane. When neither of the two moved within the next fraction of a second, Hench-Rose swung the cane over his head and brought it down on the wooden table with a thunderous clout. 'GO!'

They went. The man he had called Michael went after them, dark as a thundercloud.

Denton was lying on his right side from hip to foot, his torso off the floor and supported against Munro's chest, shaking. Hench-Rose flung the cane away and walked to them, squatted down on his haunches to look at Denton. 'Oh, my God— Denton—it's you!' Denton realized that he hadn't known until then who he was. Tears came to Hench-Rose's eyes. He pushed himself away and began to shout in an angry voice, 'Where's that bloody doctor? Doctor Angevine, goddamn it to hell—!'

CHAPTER

16

Janet was sick.

That was the first thing that Atkins said to him. The second was, 'Cripes, General, what hit you?'

Munro had brought him home in a cab. Denton had first spent an hour with the frightened, apologetic doctor, being examined and anointed and pilled, and when he had refused absolutely to go into a hospital, the doctor had advised him to go home. His last words to Denton were, 'I hope you realize that my role here is only advisory. I have no power. I'm only here to prevent worse things happening.' And saying again that it was he, after all, who had run to Hench-Rose.

Denton had wanted to say that he was a disgrace to his profession, but he was too hoarse to speak, and still shaking so badly that he had to concentrate on his overcoat buttons and not on the man.

He had red welts across his buttocks and the backs of his legs and exquisitely painful bruises across his shins. Most of the water was out of his lungs—he had lain across a leather armchair for far too long, getting it out—and the doctor had sprayed his throat with something that was supposed to be soothing and that tasted like tar. Denton told nobody that the physical damage was mostly negligible to him, but the psychic damage of his own terror—his cowardice, as he saw it—while in the barrel was searing. He had been frightened in war as all soldiers are frightened; he had been frightened of the pain of being wounded, and, when he had been wounded, of death; but he had known nothing like the helplessness, and then the terror, and then the physical anguish, of the barrel. He wondered now if he would have let them put him in the barrel a second time, or if he would have shouted out the truth. He was ashamed.

So, in answer to Atkins's question, he rasped, 'I got my comeuppance, Sergeant. How bad is Mrs Striker?'

Bad enough that Atkins had tried to telephone Dr Bernat at the Jewish Infirmary. That hospital had a telephone, but Bernat was nowhere near it, and there seemed no way to call him. The best Atkins could do was run down to Bernat's surgery and tell his wife that the doctor must come at once to Mrs Striker's when he appeared. Then Atkins had got 'the wife of a pal, she does some nursing' to come in and sit with Janet. The level of nursing would not be very high, Denton knew—emptying a chamber pot and trying to stay awake would be about the extent of it—but having her there allowed Atkins to return to their own house to greet Denton.

'I think myself it's the typhus,' Atkins said. He was helping Denton up the stairs. 'She's a headache would kill a cow, and she's started on a fever.'

Denton had to stop to cough. 'It could be anything, Sergeant.'

'No, because it ain't a broken leg and it ain't leprosy, but you're right, I'm no doctor and it could be other things. But I've nursed officers through some right horrors, so I've seen typhus.'

Denton had to clear his throat, which rattled as if he were coming off pneumonia. 'How could she have got it?'

'Bad water, some people say. Some say fleas. Down there in the Isle of Dogs, you could get anything.' Atkins had been helping Denton off with his overcoat—his clothes had been returned to him—and had seen each of his winces. 'All right, now, General, just *what* happened to you?'

Denton tried to sit in his armchair, had to settle for perching on the edge of the seat. 'I'm not supposed to tell anybody until after tomorrow. It's what you might call a right bollocks. I fell afoul of the two nice fellows we overheard in the dumb waiter.' His voice wasn't his own, rather some rough basso who'd been shouting and smoking all his life.

'Them two bullyraggers? What—they waylaid you for revenge for breaking one of them's nose?'

Denton groaned. 'I think that revenge just gave it a little spice for them. This was more like an official act.'

'Official! You don't mean they're legit?'

'I think they're official but *not* legit.' He held up a hand. 'Don't ask me any more. Help me down the stairs, will you?' He had found that he had trouble with stairs when Hench-Rose had half-carried him out of the room where he had been questioned. He had been able to limp along a brick-and-concrete corridor that was as plain as something on an industrial site, gas pipes and fabric-covered electrical wires overhead, electric bulbs in porcelain sockets every twenty feet. He had had to go up half a dozen stone steps at the end, and this was where he had found he had trouble; beyond them had been a small office where the doctor had 'cared for' him. Denton had had the sense of being the centre of a swarm of bees, in this case acutely anxious bees: faces kept appearing at the door, looking in, vanishing; footsteps pounded overhead; voices and footfalls sounded in the corridors, coming and going, going and coming.

Munro had waited while the doctor worked, leaning against the wall with the rattan cane in his hand. When the doctor was done, he had pulled a bell and the man Hench-Rose had called Michael had come in, with him another of the bullyragger type. Michael had tried to tie a blindfold around Denton's eyes.

'That won't do!' Munro had bellowed.

'He can't be allowed to see where he is.'

'Good Christ, you think he's stupid? Stuff that thing back in your pocket.'

Michael had pulled himself up and become the military person he certainly was. 'You be quiet and stay out of it, my man, or I'll have your number.'

Munro had pushed himself away from the wall and expanded into his complete, large self. 'You threaten me again, cock, and I'll have you up on a charge. Denton, let's go!'

The bullyragger had put himself between Munro and Denton. Munro moved forward, clouted the man with a forearm, then kneed him in the groin and stepped over him as he sank to his knees, yelping. Munro handed the cane to Denton. 'Lean on this. It's got a steel centre, like a heavy fishing rod. Right, then—off we go.'

Another half-flight of stairs had stood in their way, then a door; beyond that was a lobby with a floor of small, octagonal tiles in black and white, the tiles missing in patches and the floor wavy. Daylight came from the panes and fanlight that surrounded a heavy door. Through that, Denton was confronted with more steps down to the street. At the bottom, leaning on the iron rail after coughing, he had looked up and seen the faded paint that said Barth's Baths.

'I was in there the whole time,' he had whispered.

'Yes, and I'll want to know why.' Munro had been angry. 'I'll give you twenty-four hours to come up with an answer I can live with.' He had waved at a waiting cab, two constables beside it, and he had ridden all the way back to Denton's house without saying another word.

Now, Denton said to Atkins, 'I want to see Mrs Striker.'

'You're a glutton for punishment, you are!'

'Gently, Sergeant, gently. I've been spoken to harshly enough for one day. Come on, help me down the stairs.'

He crossed through the gardens to her house and went up to her bedroom. She was asleep, her hands on the bedcovers moving as if she were trying to pluck hairs from them. Her face was only slightly flushed, her breathing a little fast but not, he thought, frightening.

The nurse began to try to dribble water into Janet's lips from a wet cloth as Denton came into the room. She made rather a show of pouring a dark liquid from a bottle and lifting Janet's head to pour the stuff in.

'What's that?' Denton said.

'That's Parrish's Syrup.'

'Has the doctor been?'

'I don't need a doctor to tell me she needs Parrish's Syrup!'

'I'd rather you'd wait until the doctor's here. We'll ask.'

She called herself Mrs Holroyd, added, 'Mrs *Pusser* Holroyd,' but Denton thought that Pusser was a first name and not a naval rank, so he wasn't as impressed as she seemed to think he should be. She said, 'I've been using Parrish's in the sickroom for all my born days.'

'Yes. Well, the doctor will be here any minute now.'

'It's liquid food, it is. Given to the sick and *infants*.'

'Let's see what the doctor says.'

She sat down with her hands folded in her lap. She sniffed. She turned her head to look at him and said, 'I brought that bottle of Parrish's *personally*.'

Janet stirred. Her hands stopped moving on the bedclothes and her knees came up. She threw the covers off and lay under only the sheet, her eyes open. 'You're here,' she said.

Denton bent to kiss her; she held him off with a hand. 'I'm a bit ill,' she said. 'I don't want to give it to you.' She raised her head, then let it fall back. 'What awful dreams you have when you're sick. May I have some water?'

The nurse hurried to fill a glass and held Janet's head up, trickling water into her mouth and glancing at Denton as if she expected him to snatch the head away. Janet said to the woman, 'Where's Annie?'

'Annie's flown the coop,' Denton said.

'Oh, the fool.' Janet dropped back on the pillow. 'I shall have to look for her.' She looked at Denton. 'I'll be better tomorrow.'

'Of course you will.'

'It's the Isle of Dogs. It sounds like an artillery ground, all the coughing. I've picked up something there.' He was holding her hand; her fingers moved over it as if she might be playing an instrument. 'I'll be better tomorrow.'

A minute or two later, she was asleep again.

The doctor came through the gardens to Denton's house a little after seven. He looked tired, seemed impatient. 'She has a small fever,' he said. He looked at Denton's face and watched him cough and began to examine him. 'You need me more than Mrs Striker does.' He held Denton's hands out and watched the shaking.

'No, no—'

'Sit back—no talking—' Bernat put his ear to Denton's chest, then took a bone tongue-depressor from his bag and put it in Denton's mouth and twisted his head until the light from the lamp shone in. He opened his bag and took out two glass phials of pills, then wrote on two slips of paper and wrapped the pills in them. 'You have been shouting?'

'I got into some water.'

'The river? It's almost winter.'

'No, some water—in my lungs.'

'I know, I hear it.' He put the two folded papers on Denton's table. 'Painkiller, two now and two each four hours; the other is for the chest, to make you spit. One tonight, one in the morning.' He snapped his bag shut. 'I come back in the morning.'

'Are you going to see Mrs Striker then?'

Bernat spoke his words clearly and slowly to make his annoyance plain. 'Yes, I am!'

'Atkins thinks she has typhus.'

'Atkins, with such medical abilities, will be appointed, I am sure, to HRM. Me, I have to wait for symptoms.' He put on his hat. He evidently saw that Denton had more doubts; he said, 'The nurse is with her. The nurse is quite competent, Already, she is giving Parrish's Syrup, which is liquid food and does no harm, sometimes good. Maybe tomorrow we give quinine and iron tonic. There is nothing other to be done, Mr Denton—I don't do magical spells; we don't do surgery for low fever; she is a strong, healthy woman. You stop listening to your servant and listen to me: I am saying go to bed and stop worrying about Mrs Striker!'

Denton coughed and cleared his throat and said, 'I'm sorry,' but only to the closing door.

He let Atkins make up the bed again in the room that he hated so that he wouldn't have to climb the stairs to his bedroom. He was exhausted; he thought he would sleep, but his mind tumbled with images and memories, Janet, Guillam, the dead woman, the barrel. The shame of remembered fear. He stayed awake, eyes open, seeing on the ceiling light that he never saw in his bedroom in the back, hearing outside voices and horse hooves that were inaudible up there.

The woman. Mrs Alken. Was the Michael of Charrington Street the Michael whom Barton, Lieutenant Colonel Alken's servant, thought—maybe—that he remembered? Had he called her to ask her or tell her to go to Janet's house that morning, where Annie remembered—maybe—letting her in? But why? Because, perhaps, he too had heard of Bernat's gossip about a woman patient who might be 'Tania Simonova'?

Or was there some other connection among Michael and Mrs Alken and 'Simonova'? Maybe, as Atkins had suggested at the very beginning, a love triangle? Something passionate enough to lead to murder? But why, even so, in Denton's house or his garden?

The thread between Michael and 'Simonova' seemed frail until he thought of his astonishment at seeing Hench-Rose in the room where he had been tortured. Not so with seeing Munro, who had undoubtedly found his way to Charrington Street the same way Denton had, through the telephone call. Munro must have persevered in the greengrocer's as he had not, showing his police bona fides, not taking no for an answer. But Hench-Rose?

He remembered Hench-Rose's talk of a couple of weeks before of being in a new post. 'Mum's the word.' Well, mum was certainly the word at Charrington Street: a mysterious activity disguised as a greengrocer's and a deserted bath-house. Gorman's and Barth's. The bullyragger whose nose he'd broken had said that 'Gorman was a duffer', that he had 'rules of war'. Well, that could be Hench-Rose. So Gorman's was a place, all right, but it was also a person. Was Hench-Rose in charge at Charrington Street, hence 'Gorman'? And the other bullyragger was 'Freddie', who had been ordering Guillam about and then had disappeared—back to Charrington Street.

And the bullyraggers had mentioned 'M'. Something about going over Gorman's head to M. Hench-Rose had threatened the two who had tortured him with going to M. They had reacted when he had lied and said he'd been sent to Charrington Street by Melville. Munro had told him that M was Melville's nickname. Was that the pecking order, then—Melville, then Hench-Rose, then, perhaps, Michael?

To do what?

If Michael had sent Mrs Alken to Janet's house because of 'Tania Simonova', and the connection was not personal, then what would Michael have wanted Mrs Alken to do? Identify 'Simonova'? How? Held had said that nobody knew what she looked like. Follow her? Confront her? Kill her?

Ah, that was an idea to play with. But far-fetched, surely, the wife of a retired British officer as killer. As *official* killer, as it were.

He had reached this point by many twists and turns, digressions to Janet, Guillam, his torture, his shame. He rolled over, determined then to sleep.

'Sir? You asleep?'

The door had opened far enough for Atkins to put his head through. 'That copper Guillam's insisting on coming up.'

'Wh—' Denton could hardly make a sound. He coughed. 'Get rid of him. It's—my God, it's almost midnight!'

'Yes, sir, well, he was very—'

'Denton!' Guillam's bellow sounded like an enraged animal's. It also sounded drunk. 'Goddamnit, Denton—' The voice was coming closer. Atkins's head abruptly left the doorway as Guillam shouted, 'Get the hell out of here!'

'Here now—sir—!'

Denton struggled out of bed, felt his weight come on his shins like a blow. 'Guillam! For God's sake—'

Denton hobbled to the door in time to see Guillam turn towards him, having pushed Atkins towards his own stairs. Atkins, small and thin but feisty, was reaching into the pantry, came out with a bottle of beer held by the neck.

Guillam put a hand on Denton's chest to push him back into the bedroom. Denton shouted at Atkins; Guillam pushed; Denton went backwards, fell over his bed and landed on his back on the floor. Guillam came forward and seemed about to do something more when Atkins hit the back of his head with the bottle, a sound like two pieces of wood striking together, and Guillam went to his knees almost on top of Denton, moaning, 'Jesus.'

Astonishingly, the bottle hadn't broken. Atkins was ready to use it again, but Denton squirmed away from Guillam and shouted. 'That's enough, Sergeant! No—no more! Back off, man—'

He bent over Guillam. 'Let me see your head.' Guillam's hands were clutched over the place where he'd been hit. 'Light a lamp and then skedaddle for some ice.' This to Atkins; to Guillam, he said, 'Take your hands away, for God's sake.'

Guillam put his hands on the floor. Denton parted the thick black hair and, as a light came on, saw blood. 'Well, you've had a whack. Can you stand up?'

Guillam put a hand on the bed and pushed himself up. His hands came to his head again. 'That's assault,' he growled.

'So was what you did.' Denton pulled a chair over. 'Sit down.' As Guillam dropped himself clumsily into the chair, he said, 'Christ, you're drunk.'

'I'm fucking bleeding.'

'Of course you are. You'll have a lump, too.' He raised the lamp high and looked at the back of Guillam's head. Blood was flowing fairly freely. The lump was already there.

'Could have concussion,' Guillam muttered. The last word came out a little oddly, strained through whatever he'd been drinking.

Denton picked up a stone paperweight he'd always disliked, a bad copy of Rodin's *Kiss*, and put it against the lump. 'Hold that there. It's cold.' He went to the toilet opposite the room's door and got a towel; by the time he was back, Atkins was there with a bowl of ragged shards of ice from the ice cave. Without a word, he took the towel from Denton and wrapped it around the ice and handed it back. 'I'll make some tea.' He vanished after a contemptuous glance at Guillam's bowed and bloody head.

Denton took the paperweight away and replaced it with the ice. 'You've got blood on your collar.'

Guillam sat back far enough to look up at Denton. He was holding the ice against his head and so looked somewhat ridiculous; he was sober enough to be aware of it, apparently, because he stood clumsily and swayed over Denton. 'I want to talk to you!' he bellowed.

'Judas Priest, it's the middle of the night, Guillam! Let it go until tomorrow.' Denton was wondering if he should send Atkins for the doctor.

'Like hell will I let it go! You know what I want.'

'No, I don't. For God's sake, sit down.' Alcohol plus bleeding plus possible concussion: that sounded like something a doctor should look at. 'You're pie-eyed.'

Guillam muttered something about giving Denton a round if he wanted it.

Denton pulled on an ankle-length robe and shoved his feet into slippers. Surprisingly, he felt better than he had since he'd woken in the stone room with the two bullyraggers. Then when he thought about it, his legs and back started to hurt again; he coughed. He said, 'I've had a tough day.'

'*You* have! Oh, ha-ha.' Guillam was still holding the towel, whose ends had fallen over the sides of his head, giving vaguely the impression of a turban. Whatever had carried him to Denton's door and driven him to shove Atkins, however, had vanished. He sank down in the chair and stuck his legs out. 'I want to talk to you.'

'You said.'

Atkins appeared in the doorway and announced tea in five minutes. Denton asked him to fetch Dr Bernat, at which Atkins groaned and said the doctor might as bleeding well move in with them, but he spun about and headed down the stairs.

'Don't need a doctor,' Guillam growled.

'Let's hope not.' Denton sat on the bed. 'How do you feel?'

'Like I've been hit from behind with a hard object—what do you think? Christ, what a lump.' He sprawled lower in the chair, took away the towel and looked at it, now pink with blood and melted ice, then put it back. 'I want to know what you're going to do.'

'About what?'

'About what you saw this morning! What d'you think I mean, "about what"? You think I came here because I want to talk bloody literature with you?' He switched hands holding the towel to his head and leaned forward, his face grim. 'Who are you going to tell and when?'

'I'm not going to tell anybody.'

'I've got a wife and kids—at least you owe it me to tell me when. What d'you think news like that will do to them, eh? Fat lot you'll care, am I right? You hated me on sight, you did— you've had a down on me since you first set eyes on me.'

'I think it was the other way around.'

'Now's your chance, right! Vengeance is mine, saith the great Denton! Where do you think I've been all day, waiting for the axe to fall, eh? In a boozer, yes, that's where I've bloody well been, I have! Because of you, you pokeful of shite!'

Denton stared at him. 'You came to call me names?'

'When? When the hell are you going to rat me out?'

'I'm not.'

'Oh, fuck!' Guillam jumped to his feet, lurched towards the cold fireplace and came back, the towel still held against his head. He gestured with the free hand, finger pointing at Denton, 'I know you! You're a bleeding self-righteous holier-than-thou, you are. You can't stand to have somebody get away with something. I know you—I've seen it! You can't stand for somebody to slide!' He made his voice sarcastic and growled, his eyes red and his head pushed forward, 'You have to see *justice* is done. God's little judge here on earth.'

Denton knew there was enough truth in that to hurt. 'God doesn't give a crap about justice. We have to make our own.' What was he arguing with a drunk for? He said again, the tone almost hopeless, 'I'm not going to tell anybody, Guillam.'

'Like hell. You can't wait.'

'I'm not going to tell anybody.'

'What—hide the truth? You? Tell me another! You mean if they put you in the witness box and asked you, you wouldn't tell? You? I know you, Denton—you can't lie! Mr Denton—' Guillam stopped pointing at him and flung his arm out as if he were a barrister performing for a jury. 'Did you see the accused, the said wretch Guillam, standing behind the public conveniences in Regent's Park? Oh, I did, sir; I cannot tell a lie. And was he standing? Oh, yes he was. And was there another person, a *man*, Mr Denton, kneeling in front of him? Oh, yes, for I'm a truthful man, there was. And did the wretched Guillam have his flies unbuttoned? He did. And did he have his pego sticking out? Oh, yes, he did. And was his pego in the other man's *mouth*, Mr Denton?'

Guillam was shouting; Denton was sure he could be heard on the street. He said, 'Shut up, Guillam.'

'You wouldn't lie, you bastard. You wouldn't lie if your mother was in the dock.' Guillam threw himself into his chair.

Denton felt exhausted again. He said, 'I'm not going to tell anybody, Guillam.'

'But you wouldn't lie, either.'

'No, not for you, I wouldn't.' Denton got up. 'Look here—I don't care what the hell you did. What I saw was meaningless. It's your business; it's not my business! I don't *care*, can't you get that through your thick skull?'

Guillam stared at him as if the drink had come back and made him stupid all over again. He said, 'It can get me turfed out of the Met. It can get me a spell in quod. You think that's meaningless?' He was suddenly limp in the chair. 'I've a family, man.'

'Then don't do it again where somebody can see you.'

'Easy for you to say.' Guillam sighed. 'Easy for you to say...' He looked around the room. He took the towel off his head and put it, still in his hand, on his lap. 'It's like drink. I can go without for ever so long—two years once—and then—' He raised a hand and let it fall. 'I have to have it. Have to have it.' He pulled himself up and scowled at Denton. 'But I'm not one of *them*! I don't, don't—dress up in women's clothes or Mary-Ann around or—you know! I don't! It's just a disease, something that comes on me.' He stared at Denton. 'You don't believe me.' His voice sank and he seemed to say to himself, like a dog who has to give one more muffled bark after it's been scolded, 'It's an illness...'

'It doesn't matter, don't you hear me? I don't care! Judas, man, if you want to be got off in somebody's mouth, find yourself some tart! Nobody'd so much as say boo to that.'

Guillam shook his head. 'It isn't the same. I've tried, Denton. I just have this—disease...' He was sliding into drunken self-pity, tears in his eyes now. 'I'm dirty. I'm foul.'

Denton astonished himself by feeling sorry for the man. He put a hand on Guillam's shoulder. 'Guillam, you and I've never liked each other, probably never will. But you have to believe me, what I saw this morning, I'll never tell to anybody. In a court of law, yes, I'd tell the truth, but you're a long way from a law court.' He patted the shoulder. 'My God, man, be more careful.'

Guillam sat quite still. After some seconds, he said, 'It would kill my wife. I love her. That's bloody laughable, right? *But I can't stop.*' He looked down at the stained towel in his lap and suddenly threw it aside. Then there were footsteps on the stairs and Atkins and Dr Bernat came in, Bernat looking weary and long-suffering; yet he waved aside Denton's apologies and muttered something about duty. He was wearing a nightshirt, tucked into trousers, and an overcoat and slippers.

'This is a real bump,' he said when he had looked at Guillam's head. 'Ice was good.' He applied a red-orange anti-septic from his bag and dressed the wound. He turned Guillam's face to the light, looked into his eyes, parting the lids with thumb and fingers (Denton was reminded of the doctor's doing that before he had been tortured) and said, 'I think no concussion yet. But we know better tomorrow.' He stood and looked down at Guillam. 'You have had much spirits, yes?'

Guillam nodded without looking at him.

'You are friend of Mr Denton's? Then I suggest you stay here tonight, sleep. I come first thing in the morning and look at all my patients in this house and the one behind.' He closed his bag. 'My hospital.'

'He has a house of his own—his wife's waiting for him—'

Guillam shook his head. 'Sent her a wire—working all night.'

'Then no problem with staying here. Good.' Bernat patted Guillam's shoulder, as Denton had done. 'Drink less. It is worse than concussion.' He looked at Denton. 'This happened how?'

'I thought he was a burglar and I hit him with that ugly paperweight over there.'

'Mmm. Maybe it should be reported to the police.'

'I *am* the police,' Guillam growled.

'Ah. In that case, I go back to bed.' And Bernat pattered off, his slippers sliding down his heels with each step to make a sound like a lick.

'Wasn't necessary to lie for me, General,' Atkins murmured.

'Wasn't necessary for you to save me from a drunk, either. Let's put him upstairs in my bed.'

Atkins rolled his eyes but did it. Guillam went without a murmur, not even looking back at Denton as he left the room. Alone, Denton tried to sleep, thought now about Guillam's 'disease', then about his own shame, then Janet, around and around, and at last slept, only to entertain chaotic dreams of which he had no memory when he woke.

Oddly, what was fresh and clear in his mind upon waking was a memory, long unvisited: he was a tiny kid, three or four. His father had put four kittens in a sack and dropped them in the rain barrel that stood at the corner of the farmhouse. The tiny Denton had got a chicken crate and clambered up on it and looked down into the water, seeing his own reflection and, through it, the pulsing sack. He had tried to reach down to save them but could barely reach the water. Bubbles rose. Weeping, he had been sure he could hear their tiny cries rising in the bubbles.

Winter was coming on. Overhead, low clouds lay in regular ranks like folds in a heavy fabric, line after line, dark on the bottom and brighter until each disappeared behind the next one. The noise on Parliament Street was terrific, iron-shod wheels and hooves, hurrying feet, voices, and from the Embankment the grim rumble of traffic crossing Westminster Bridge with a sound like millwheels grinding pebbles into dust.

Denton got down from his cab at the corner and walked a little shakily towards New Scotland Yard. The rattan cane tapped on the pavement. He could see Munro waiting for him outside the Parliament Street entrance, huge in an ulster that ballooned in the wind. His face was dour, then angry when he saw Denton.

'Got your explanation ready yet?' He was standing in the middle of the steps as if to block Denton's way.

'For yesterday?'

'No, for the nature of the bloody universe. You got your arse whipped yesterday, and I'm almost ready to say you had it coming! What the hell were you doing in that place?'

'The same thing you were, I suppose.'

'I told you to stay out of it!'

'I don't do everything I'm told.'

'Bloody hell!' Munro came down to his level and put his face close to Denton's. 'You found it through the telephone, didn't you!'

'I don't think the police are supposed to go into telephone records without a warrant.'

'I had a warrant! You're too smart for your own good sometimes, Denton. How did you find that place?'

'I called in a favour. What difference does it make? As you say, I got what I deserved.' Denton was watching a large motor car pull towards them, slowing and angling at the kerb. 'This is for me, I think.'

The vehicle pulled to a stop. A chauffeur drove in the front; a grey-haired man rode alone in the back, the car open, no rain imminent. The chauffeur scrambled down and stood on the pavement as the passenger got down, said something to him and then strolled towards Denton and Munro, smiling. It was Denton's solicitor, Sir Francis Brudenell. He came quite close and said, 'Well, well, you look better than the last time I saw you.' He turned his smile on Munro. 'You're DI Munro, aren't you— we met at another of Mr Denton's scrapes.' Without waiting for an answer, he turned back to Denton. 'I got your wire. Are you being arrested?'

Denton glanced at Munro. 'I don't know.'

'He certainly ought to be!' Munro growled.

'Are we heading to police court at this early hour?'

'No, no—not yet, anyway. There's some sort of meeting.' Denton looked again at Munro. 'Munro knows more about it than I do.'

'I do not! Sir Francis—you'll want some time with your client. The meeting's here at the Yard; more than that, I don't know. I can find an office.' Pointedly, he said, 'You have fifteen minutes.' He turned and went up the steps.

Apparently in no hurry, Sir Francis turned towards his car. The chauffeur had just finished polishing some speck of dust from a lamp and was climbing back in. Sir Francis said, 'You like my Parsifal? I just got it. It's a Benz, of course. They call it the Parsifal. I think it's more a Brünnhilde, myself, but then I'm not German.' He took Denton's arm. He smiled. 'What have you got into now?'

Munro led them to a vacant office on the first floor, cleared a stack of accordion folders off the desk and fetched a chair from some other room. Leaving, he said, 'Ten minutes. I'll come for you.'

Sir Francis stood by a grimy window while Denton talked, his view not of Parliament Street but of a sooty air shaft, equally sooty windows twenty feet away, through which little was to be seen. When Denton had gone over all of it—Gorman's and Barth's, the abduction, the beating, the barrel—Sir Francis said, 'Let's see the damage.' He insisted that Denton strip to his underclothes, then peeled his shirt upwards and his pants down. He made little ticking sounds with his tongue when he saw the welts, murmured, 'We shall want photos of those.' He pulled the underclothes back where they belonged and said, 'Go ahead and dress. Could you say truthfully in court that you suffered mental as well as physical anguish?'

'I was terrified, to my shame.'

'Truly? You understand the meaning of the word—of course you do, been a soldier. Worse than battle?'

'I was sure I was drowning.'

'As to your presence in this place, you made no attempt to enter under your own volition?'

'I went into the greengrocer's.'

'Irrelevant. Anybody can go into a greengrocer's. But the private, or perhaps official part of the buildings—we shall see which in a few minutes, I think—you entered them only as the result of coercion?'

'I was carried as the result of being chloroformed.'

'Good! Very good.' The solicitor rubbed his hands together. 'Well, I think we're ready for the fray.' His eyebrows went up. 'This Hench-Rose—I knew his late brother, not too attractive a type—he's a friend?'

'For many years. A good friend.'

'Good. I shall just stop at a convenience along the way; I suggest you do the same. My legal mentor had a dictum: never cross a hostile threshold with a full bladder. Ah, there's Munro. Also a friend, I think? A bit dour this morning? Ah, I see—dour in his official capacity, but a friend. Well, that's all right, then. Lead on, Inspector!'

They made their way up broad staircases and along broad corridors, stopping as Sir Francis needed, and through a suite of connected offices to a room that could have served an Oxbridge college for a common room: big stone fireplace, much carved; three arched windows, very large, with a view towards Whitehall; chairs, some leather, some tapestry, both soft and hard; a cabriole table that might usually have stood in an alcove (the alcove was empty) but now served as a desk for a grey-haired, oldish man in a dark frock coat. He was listening to a younger man, rather Bank-of-England in a Prince Albert and striped trousers, who was muttering too low to be heard from even a few feet away. Some of the room's chairs had been set in a rough semi-circle facing the table.

Sir Francis murmured, 'I think we are about to be lectured to.' He chuckled. 'We shall see.'

Three other men were standing around the room. Denton saw Hench-Rose, nodded; he recognized the man named Michael and pointed him out to Sir Francis. Freethorne, the lawyer who had come to his house to advise the bullyraggers, was talking to Michael.

'Brother William,' Sir Francis murmured. 'They'll have to do better than that before this is over.' Denton tried to clear his throat, coughed. When he was done, Sir Francis said, 'Do feel free to do that all you like during this "meeting" or whatever it is. Rather makes a good point.' He nodded towards the table. 'The older chap is William Melville, the "M" you told me of. Or perhaps you know him? No. The man he's talking to is Evelyn Bledsoe, the Home Secretary's hatchet man. Don't underestimate him. Ah—is this Hench-Rose heading our way? A bit of the brother in the forehead, I think.'

Hench-Rose gripped Denton's hand, said how awful yesterday had been and how sorry, truly, *awfully* sorry he was. He shook the solicitor's hand. He said this would all be over quite soon. He had been heartbroken that such a thing had happened under his very nose.

'Indeed, I'm sure you were,' Sir Francis said with his cheerful smile. 'We shall need that under oath, perhaps.'

Hench-Rose put a hand on his heart. 'I'd say it under oath right this minute if it would help anything. It was horrible— horrible! It isn't the way the game is played.'

Denton saw Bledsoe, the hatchet man, winding among the chairs towards them. Bledsoe ignored Denton and Hench-Rose and went straight to Sir Francis and said, 'I'm astonished to see you here, Frank. Surely you weren't invited.'

'Mr Denton thought he might have need of my services.'

'Good heavens, Frank, what a thought! Nobody needs legal representation at a thing like this.'

'Odd, I see Willie Freethorne not thirty feet away. Is he here to hand round the teacups?'

Bledsoe laughed. It wasn't a good laugh, more like something a machine might have pumped out. 'We don't want this to become adversarial.'

'No one ever does. But you'd best skip along, Bledsoe: Melville's looking meaningfully at your back.'

When Bledsoe had hurried back towards the table, Brudenell said, 'He was at school with me, a year or two younger. One of those boys who always seem to have water drops condensing on them. Rather like a cellar wall.' He moved Denton forward. 'Let's get the armchairs before the rest do and be comfortable.' Denton signalled to Munro, who had been hanging back but now came forward, apparently reluctant, his limp more evident than usual—perhaps a comment on what seemed to be going on.

The others drifted to chairs, too. When they all were seated, Bledsoe taking a hard chair at the end of the table, a scattering of papers in front of him as if he were the recording secretary,

Melville stayed on his feet and said, 'It's Detective Inspector Munro, isn't it? You're not supposed to be here.'

'I was there yesterday, sir. I believe that as I was there, I belong here.'

Melville looked at Bledsoe and seemed to give up on that point. 'This is a purely informational gathering.' He looked at each of them. 'We do not intend to engage in quibbles or wrangles.' His eyes rested on Sir Francis Brudenell. 'No record will be kept.'

When this had sunk in, he went on in his raspy voice, 'Mr Bledsoe will read to you the Official Secrets Act of 1889, as amended. I take it as read that you all accept that whatever happened yesterday, it falls under the Act and must be so considered.'

'Oh dear, oh dear,' Denton heard Brudenell say. 'Forgive me for interrupting, Melville, but I am already rather confused. The Act of 1889 applies only to employees of His Majesty's government, and as amended it applies only to those same and journalists. As Mr Freethorne and Mr Denton and I are neither government employees nor journalists, surely the reading of the Act, even by so eminent a man as Mr Bledsoe, is gratuitous.'

Bledsoe looked at Melville and said, 'Mr Denton is a journalist.'

'Oh, no,' Sir Francis laughed, 'he's nothing of the kind. You, busy man that you are, Evelyn, can't be expected to know such things, but Mr Denton is a literary man, and quite an eminent one. I don't wish to take up your time with a dispute over the difference between journalism and art, but let me say, with all the good will of which I'm capable, if some turn of events should cause the government to try to apply the act to Mr Denton, I should write a brief that could be argued with all the vigour of the best legal minds in London. I think, quite honestly, that by the time testimony had been taken from such people as Mr Henry James, Mr Conrad, Mr Shaw and others on the definition of literature, and such folk as the editor of *The Times* on the subject of journalism, you would not—well, forgive me, but you wouldn't have a leg to stand on.'

Bledsoe went to Melville and whispered in his ear; Melville whispered something back and then said, 'The Act applies to *certain* people in this room who are employees of the Metropolitan Police and the British military establishment.'

'I shouldn't dream of arguing the point.' Before Melville could go on, Brudenell said, 'However, as I take it that you accept that it doesn't apply to Mr Denton or to me, I'm sure you will acknowledge that our proceeding to a civil action over the way in which Mr Denton was mistreated yesterday is entirely within our right—passionately as I pray that such a thing does not happen.'

'I don't acknowledge anything of the kind!'

'Well, well, we can argue that if and when we come to it. For now, let me merely emphasize that it is our right.'

To Denton's surprise, Munro's voice came from just behind his left shoulder. 'And, sir, I have to say that CID believe there's a matter of criminal behaviour here—Official Secrets Act or no Official Secrets Act.'

'Absolutely not!' Bledsoe snapped. Melville held up a hand; suddenly Denton realized, seeing something—a sadness, a guilt—in Melville's face, that perhaps he disagreed with Munro less than might have been thought. Melville was a cop, after all.

Still standing, Melville said, 'You're subject to the Act, Inspector Munro.'

'With all respect, sir, I think that that should be judged by the legal folk at the time that we'd proceed to charges.'

'You cannot proceed to charges!' Bledsoe cried. 'That would violate the Act of 1889 by making official secrets public!'

Melville was shaking his head. 'Munro, you're out of order; this isn't what this meeting is about.'

'Then what is it about, sir? It seems to me it's about shutting some of us up, but as we don't know what hornet's nest we put our thumb into yesterday, how do we know that we're to shut up? And about what?'

'You are to remain silent about everything you saw or heard at 22 Charrington Street!' Bledsoe shouted.

'I saw the results of a criminal act, sir. As a policeman, I can't remain silent about that.'

Brudenell intervened. 'Am I to understand that HM's government are claiming that the protection of "state secrets" surrounds what happened yesterday?'

'The Home Office are, yes.' Melville stared at Brudenell unhappily. 'It isn't an ideal situation, I grant you.'

Munro was still on his feet, now standing next to Denton. 'A policeman who witnesses a criminal act must report it, as you well know, Mr Melville. Yesterday, I saw this man seconds after he'd been abused by two men in the employ of—'

'Objection!' William Freethorne, the other lawyer, shouted, also on his feet. 'The officer didn't see any abuses.'

'I saw a man with red welts on his body who'd been almost drowned, gasping for his life! If I came across that on Shaftesbury Avenue, I'd lay charges of assault with intent to kill!'

'You had only a latecomer's view, and probably of injuries he suffered at the fire in the Jewish—'

Melville was pounding on the table with his fist. Bledsoe was standing now, too, rapping a heavy finger ring against the mahogany top. Both of them were shouting 'Sit down!' and 'Order!' And then, in a near-silence, Hench-Rose stood and said, 'Melville, I was with Detective Munro when he saw it. I wish to say to all of you, I am ashamed of what I saw and what I know had happened. *This is not the way that English gentlemen behave!*' He started to sit back down, then straightened again and said, 'And although I believed in our project when we got into it, Melville, I'd have chucked it *instanter* if I'd known that my good friend, or any gentleman, was to be so abused by men working for the Crown.'

'Enough, enough—' Bledsoe shouted.

'If this is what secrecy brings, then secrecy comes at too high a price! It isn't *British*!' He turned and looked at Denton. Tears glinted in his eyes. The gold V of the Brotherhood of Britons glinted in his lapel.

Bledsoe grasped the papers that lay in front of him and said very loudly, 'I will now read the Official Secrets Act of 1889 as amended!'

Melville, however, waved a hand. 'Don't bother.' Bledsoe looked stunned, then enraged. Melville paid no attention. He looked at Sir Francis, then at Denton, then at Freethorne. He let a mordant chuckle into the room. 'You lot are like trying to shut a snake into a shoebox. Look here: we have a genuine problem. You, Sir Francis, have a genuine point. Detective Inspector Munro has a point, too; nobody knows that better than an old copper like me. But, gentlemen, I tell you as surely as I stand here—and my apologies to you, Sir Hector, for what I'm going to say—I tell you that a modern government must have secrets, and it must apply an official secrets act. A modern police department must have secrets, too—*you* know that, Munro! I learned that in the early days of the Special Branch: we couldn't have accomplished half of what we did if we hadn't been able to keep our plans secret from the Irish and the anarchists. We're talking about protecting *Britain*, gentlemen. The MPs will tell you that we're not at war, we just finished a war, but I'll tell you that we in fact *are* at war with certain elements and certain beliefs, and in war you must sometimes move secretly!' He looked at Hench-Rose. 'And, I'm sorry to say, brutally.'

Sir Francis raised his head. 'But only if you do not your-self commit a crime, Mr Melville. Crimes were committed yesterday. I agree with Inspector Munro: if those crimes had been committed in the daylight, we would have been in police court last night. And instead, where are the perpetrators?'

He looked around. The question and the gesture were rhetorical, but Hench-Rose took them seriously and said, 'I hope they're somewhere sitting on a block of ice, because I certainly flayed their backsides for them! Awaiting punishment parade now, I hope.'

'Actually,' Michael said languidly, 'they've been reassigned.'

Hench-Rose spun around. 'What's that?'

'I believe to the Irish constabulary.'

'I expressly forbade that Simms and Gratton should leave London! They were to consider themselves under house arrest!'

Michael concentrated on the crease in his trousers. 'They've been reassigned. Ask Mr Bledsoe.' He smiled.

Munro got up again. 'This is interfering with the police—you know that.'

Bledsoe murmured, 'We *are* the police,' and Melville waved him quiet. 'Munro,' Melville said, 'we don't always get what we want.'

'But we have to try!'

'Sit *down*, sit down—please—'

But when he did, Denton stood up. 'Mr Melville.' Melville met his look, his ageing face pained. 'Or "M", as you're called. As I heard you called by those two bullies you sent to my house to steal the body of the woman who was murdered there.'

'He didn't send them,' Freethorne interrupted, 'Hench-Rose—'

Denton paid no attention. 'Let me tell you what happened yesterday.'

'I know what happened yesterday, Mr Denton.'

'Have you ever been held upside down in a barrel of water, sir? No? Then you don't know what happened.'

Bledsoe groaned theatrically and slapped his papers. Melville studied Denton, then looked at Munro, then Hench-Rose. Then he walked slowly to the end of the table and bent over Bledsoe. Their exchange, made in fierce whispers, was watched by everybody else in the room. It seemed to come to some sort of conclusion, Melville standing straight and looking down at Bledsoe, Bledsoe looking up with an anger-swollen face. Denton, who was still standing, thought that Melville had probably said something like, 'I told you it wouldn't work,' for, after some seconds, Bledsoe stood and, turning his back on the rest of them, started another scolding whisper. Brudenell reached up and pulled on Denton's sleeve, drawing him down again into his chair. Sir Francis leaned close and murmured, 'Old Melville knows when to cut his losses. Bledsoe doesn't. But I think we're about to see a change of tactic.'

Bledsoe gathered his papers and marched out through a door in the wall behind Melville. When he was gone and the door had closed again, Melville came around to the front of the table and, leaning his backside against its edge, folded his arms. 'I'd like to meet privately with Mr Denton and Sir Hector. Before you interrupt me, Sir Francis, I assume that you will insist on being there as well. So be it.' He looked at Michael. 'Major House, it'd be best if you would go down to CID with Munro and let him question you. Mr Freethorne, you can go along to prevent any violation of the Act.' He looked back at Munro. 'Major House is not a suspect, I hope, Munro?'

'I make him a material witness in a murder investigation, anyway. And a witness in the matter of Mr Denton.'

'To which no charges will be laid because they would violate the Act and subject you, Munro, to prosecution. That is a promise, Major House.' He looked again at Munro. 'I'll see about the two who've been shipped off to Ireland. I didn't know that had happened. You might ask Major House about it when you're in the interrogation room.'

'This is very high-handed!' Freethorne said.

Melville shrugged. 'It's nothing to what happened yesterday, is it? But you may object all you like when the examination begins. Get it on the record.'

'I will not allow this to go to the prosecutor!'

'Nor will I. I'm going along a little way with Detective Inspector Munro's insistence on police procedure. We'll follow that procedure and then see what we have. And see what the Act of 1889 has to say.' Melville swept his glance over all of them. 'I don't want to see a word of this in the press, is that clear? Nor hear a word of it in gossip, police or otherwise. One word, and the Home Secretary will come down very heavily. Sir Hector, Mr Denton—if you'll follow me...'

CHAPTER
18

Melville went out through the same door that Bledsoe had used and walked down a narrow corridor, never looking back, a Pied Piper who believed utterly in his ability to lead rats or children or high-priced solicitors. He turned in at a door, crossed an ornate, rather formal anteroom, passed a male secretary and went into a large office, where he sat behind the desk as if it were his own—as it was. Denton had time to notice a couple of portraits in oil, several framed pieces of calligraphy that must have been citations, and a glass case against a wall with hand weapons, mostly pistols and knives, on display.

'Sit wherever you like,' Melville said. 'Anybody want tea? Or something stronger?' He pulled a bell. 'That was rather a total balls, wasn't it? I feared it would be.' He seemed about to say something impolitic, thought better of it. 'Tea all round, please, Grace,' this to the male secretary, who had appeared in the doorway. 'All right, Mr Denton, tell me what I don't know about yesterday's events. You have five minutes.' Melville laid a thick gold repeater on the desk.

Denton told it as it had happened, beginning with his abduction from the passage alongside the greengrocer's. He stopped at the point when Munro had brought him home. Melville picked up the watch, snapped the cover shut and put it in into a waistcoat pocket, never looking at Denton. He sighed. Finally, he said in a weary voice, 'You're right, Denton; I wasn't told everything that happened. I'm so dreadfully sorry.' He looked up. 'But we can't let you make the thing public.'

'That remains to be seen,' Sir Francis said. 'Forgive me, but I don't believe you're the one with whom I should be discussing compensation.'

Melville shook his head, his mouth forming the word *no*. 'Why did you go to Charrington Street?'

'The dead woman had been telephoned from Number 22.' Denton watched Melville digest this. 'By Major House, I think.'

'Is that a guess?'

'N-n-n-o.'

Melville looked at Hench-Rose, exchanged something with him that was meaningless to Denton. Melville said, 'You were able to follow the telephone call back from the woman to the major.'

'To Number 22, anyway. Somebody had made it easy by having a record kept of all calls in and out. Major House, in fact, I suspect.' He looked at Hench-Rose. 'It doesn't sound like you, Hector. Was it Major House? He doesn't seem to have trusted anybody who worked with him very much. Or anybody he worked *for*.'

Hench-Rose twisted his legs and body in a slow-moving squirm. 'I had no idea.'

Melville gave him a sharp look and said that they'd talk about that privately. To Denton he said, 'You know you violated the law about telephonic records.'

Sir Francis swung a leg over a knee. 'Oh, pish, toosh, Melville. Anyway, you can't prosecute because of the Official Secrets Act. If the Home Sec wants to use the threat to bargain with me about compensation, I shall be able to bear up under the strain.'

Melville looked disgusted, might have said something, but the secretary came in with tea. The tea was merely tea, the biscuits hard objects that could have passed for ship's rations on a long voyage. Melville, he supposed, was one of those people who lived for the play of power and didn't care what they ate. Cups and saucers were passed around. Melville went to Hench-Rose and bent over him with his back to Denton and Brudenell, who murmured to Denton, 'Don't eat the biscuits,' he said. 'I think the Home Office bought a warehouseful of them back in the seventies.'

When Melville went back to his place, he was looking grim and Hench-Rose was red-faced. Melville said to Denton, 'Did you have any idea that your friend Sir Hector Hench-Rose was to be found at Charrington Street?'

'None.'

'Did you know that those two—Simms and Gratton—were there?'

'Not until I woke up in shackles.'

'Nor Major House?'

'Never saw him before. I knew his first name. Or thought I did.'

Melville smiled feebly. 'Perhaps you should be working for us. You seem to have talents in that direction.' He took the watch out and opened the case and stared into it, then shut it, the snap the only sound in the big room. 'I'm allowing Sir Hector to tell you what Charrington Street is all about. He insists he'll tell you no matter what. As one gentleman to another.' His voice was bitter. 'I apparently didn't explain to Sir Hector when I appointed him that this isn't an activity where the gentlemanly virtues are of much use.' He leaned his forehead on the fingertips of his right hand, the position exposing age spots high on his skull and into his thin hair. 'The operation that is under way at Charrington Street is important. If you compromise it, Denton, or you, Sir Francis, you'll ruin something that is good and necessary. I apologize to you for the mistakes that were made, but I won't apologize for Charrington Street itself. These things are much bigger than one novelist who gets caught up in the machinery.' He put the watch away in his waistcoat. 'Please go now. I have other work to do.'

Brudenell gave Denton a look and stood. 'You understand, Melville, that I shan't let this rest.'

Melville nodded gloomily.

'Well—we're off, then. Sir Hector, can I drop you some-where? I have my motor. You first, Denton—' Brudenell shepherded Denton out, then pulled up in the corridor beyond the secretary's room. 'He's a decent man, old Melville, but they can't be allowed to get away with what they did to you. I'll just nip back to that secretary and get directions out of this warren—' He shot back into the secretary's office, almost colliding with Hench-Rose.

'That was awful,' Hench-Rose said when he came up to Denton. 'I had no idea, Denton—immoralists to a man.' He stared down into his hat. 'I owe you an explanation.'

'You don't owe me anything, Hector.'

'All right, I owe myself the satisfaction of giving you an explanation—how's that? Let's have lunch.'

'I should go home.' He was thinking of Janet; Hench-Rose took it otherwise, said something about his injuries, shock, unpleasantness. 'But you need good food. Build you up. Do you hurt like hell?'

'Only my throat. Screaming and puking.' He popped a cocaine pastille into his mouth. 'It was more mental than physical.'

'Just so. Come to lunch with me and I'll tell you all, and both the mental and the physical will find healing. Denton, I want to get this off my chest!'

Sir Francis appeared with a hastily drawn map and led them down through the building. At the same door through which they'd entered, the chauffeur was waiting; a word from Sir Francis, and he was off up Parliament Street for the Benz.

'I can't give either of you a ride in the new runabout? You disappoint me.' He tapped Denton on the chest. 'Not a word to anybody about this matter until I've sorted it out. I shall make an appointment with my medical man today, also a photographer.' He grinned at Hench-Rose. 'I hope we shan't have to sue *you*, Sir Hector. Difficult, lawsuits between friends.' The Benz pulled up and he climbed into it and waved. 'Don't despair! These things always work out for the best!' And off he went.

'For *his* best, anyway,' Hench-Rose said. 'Serve me right if you sued me, though, Denton.'

'Oh, chuck it, Hector; nobody's going to sue you.'

'You'll have lunch with me, then?'

'The Kestrel?' Denton was thinking of the awful food.

'I thought perhaps Kettner's.'

'Hector—you? Kettner's?'

'One can have too much of clubs. One needs to get out into the world, expand one's horizons.'

This sounded so unlike Hench-Rose that Denton thought he was joking. Then he had a terrible thought. 'Hector—is this because of me?'

'You like Kettner's, you've said so.'

'Hector, what's happened?' He watched Hench-Rose redden. 'It is me, isn't it? My God, is it that "secret Jew" business? Hector?'

Hench-Rose pulled himself up. '*I* knew there was nothing to it. But certain members—the wrong sort; I don't know how they got into a club I belonged to—some rather stupid remarks were made.'

'Because they thought I'm a Jew.' Denton slitted his eyes. 'I guess that ends your trying to get me into the Kestrel.'

'People behaved very badly. I had no choice but to—well—' Hector looked down Parliament Street. 'Why is it one can never find a cab when one really needs one.' He stood too far out in the street to talk, making a great show of signalling to cabs. Denton realized he was embarrassed about the Kestrel. At last a cab came; Hench-Rose pulled himself inside; the vehicle rocked. As it pulled away, he shouted back, 'Kettner's at half-twelve—don't forget!'

'No change' were Atkins's first words to him. He knew he meant Janet. He found her as Atkins had said, feverish but coherent, awake and feeling obscure pains and a bad headache. A different nurse was on duty, this one sent by Bernat.

'I feel like a sloth,' Janet said. She coughed.

'You need to rest.'

'What are you doing?'

He hadn't told her about yesterday. 'Meeting Hench-Rose for lunch.'

'Oh, go, go—I'm good for nothing and I'm sure I'm boring to be with.'

He told her about Hench-Rose and Kettner's. She seemed not to take it in, had no reaction. After sitting with her for half an hour, he kissed her cheek and went away.

'What happened to Guillam?' he said to Atkins in his own house. Denton had been up and off before the policeman had appeared.

'Did a certain amount of spewing and took himself off, looking like H. The doctor said he'd no concussion, only "a fine lump". Doctor thought you were a bad fellow for not being here.'

'He was late.'

'Doctors think the sun rises and sets on them. Ha, reminds me—heard a joke from Broder. What's the difference between God and a doctor?'

Denton didn't like jokes. 'Tell me.'

'God doesn't think he's a doctor. Eh? Takes a moment, doesn't it? Shmuel told me that one.'

'You and Broder seem pretty close.'

'We rub along, for a Jew and a *goy*.'

'A what?'

'What? Oh, *goy*? That's you and me. You planning on finding your luncheon here?'

Denton told him about Hench-Rose, was told if he was going he'd better go, as it was almost that time. He'd lost track. He rushed out, heading for the carriage shed he'd rented for his motor car three streets away, but he saw a cab and jumped into it because he feared he wouldn't find a place to leave the car in Soho while he ate. That set him to wondering just what the advantage of the motor was.

'I told Melville I had to make myself straight with you. Couldn't do otherwise and live with myself. He was quite unpleasant about it.' Hench-Rose spread butter on a piece of French bread, which he seemed not to like much. 'He's disappointed me.'

'You shouldn't get into trouble for my sake, Hector.'

'Not for your sake; for *my* sake. Damned conscience or whatever it is.' Hench-Rose looked around at Kettner's. 'This isn't so bad,' he muttered. Denton laughed. Hench-Rose had already pronounced the menu 'Frenchy', as it certainly was, and made it clear that he thought Soho was not up to a baronet's standard. Part of his now-abandoned attempt to get Denton into a club had been a hope of raising Denton's raffish tastes. 'You like the Café Royal, too,' he said accusingly.

'The Domino Room, yes.' Denton put his forearms on the table. 'All right, Hector, do your confessing and get it over with. What's the tale at Charrington Street?'

'Well—' Hector was staring down into the *soupe du jour*, which was something with beans in it. 'It's secret, for one thing.'

'I know *that*. Why?'

'Well—' Hector tried a minuscule sip of the soup, looked surprised that he liked it. 'Melville has a bee in his bonnet about having some sort of intelligence thingummy that nobody knows about but the people in it. I'd applied to come into Special Branch—of course I'd have had to come in at a high level; people like me can hardly be expected to start at the bottom—so it was made quite clear to me that Special Branch thought I was a right ass. However, Melville approached me on the sly and said he might have something for me.'

'Because of your good looks and your wardrobe.' Hench-Rose was wearing another of his post-baronetcy suits, rather extremely cut and tight-fitting.

'Because nobody would expect it. I'm not a *complete* fool, Denton. I knew he wanted a figurehead to deal with the Home Sec and the red tape specialists like Bledsoe. So I said yes. There was an implication that if it all worked out, I could come into Special Branch in a year or so.'

'But Melville was really in charge.'

'No. He surprised me there. I was in charge, but he put Michael House in as my deputy and "security officer", which I now know meant that House did things without telling me. The telephone records, for example. House also brought in types like Simms and Gratton, both of whom he'd known in South Africa.'

'Ah. I wondered what they had behind them.'

'Well, I didn't—I didn't ask enough questions; I see that now. House had run an army intelligence outfit in SA, and I learned as time went on that they'd done a lot of things on the q.t., particularly in the last year of the war.' Hench-Rose had moved from soup to *noix de veau*, which he may have mistranslated from the menu but pronounced good. 'They did some things that you and I wouldn't do. In their defence, I will say that the Boer bitter-enders had to be dealt with somehow or they were going to go on blowing things up and assassinating people and making an unholy mess.'

'"Dealt with". The way they dealt with me?'

'I feel terrifically bad about that, Denton. I didn't *know*.'

'I was the first one? They'd never done it before?'

'I'll get to that.' Hench-Rose was gesturing with his knife. 'First things first.' He chewed, swallowed. 'So we set up the unit, which had no name. I called it "the unit". The chaps started calling it "Barth's", after an old bath that—oh, you know? Good God, you're uncanny.'

'And you were "Gorman".'

'Well, we didn't want people using real names. House was "Barth". My offices were above Gorman's greengrocer's, you see, and Michael and some of his people were in Barth's. I thought it was deuced clever, finding two houses that were back-to-back. My idea. We could go in different entrances on different mornings and not be seen to be using the same entrance all the time. Plus we could go back and forth through the gardens and not be seen outside. Clever, eh? Never been done before.' Hench-Rose seemed not to know of Denton's and Janet's arrangement, although Denton suspected that he did and had in fact got the idea there.

'So there we were, and Melville wanted us to have a go at something. Not something big, but something we could do by way of trying things on. Learn by doing, eh? We wanted something a bit international and something a bit hush-hush, so guess what we settled on.'

'The Zionists' negotiations with the PM.'

Hench-Rose stared. 'How do you know about that?'

'Keep going.'

'Well. If you know everything, why am I bothering? There's an organization called the—'

'World Zionist Congress. Theodor Herzl.'

Hench-Rose put down his knife and fork. 'Melville was right: you ought to work for him. Or for us. Tell me what else you know, so I shan't feel I'm boring you.'

Denton was eating *omelette frites*, had in fact finished the omelette and was eating the potatoes with his fingers. 'Herzl's trying to get the government to let him settle half a million Russian Jews in Uganda. He's in London now. The negotiations will be announced soon. There's information going around that the Bund, which is an anti-Zionist group, wants to stop Herzl, maybe violently. That's all I know.'

'This was supposed to be secret! Who blew the gaff?'

'I didn't get this from your "set-up", Hector. It doesn't matter. You were saying?'

Hector was grumpy. 'I wasn't saying anything that seems to be news to you.' They exchanged a look. Denton shook his head.

Hench-Rose grinned. 'Being childish, ain't I. Wanting to be the first to tell Mummy. Very well. All right, you know all that: so we took on the Herzl negotiations as our charge. Nothing to do with the negotiation itself, not our manor; rather, we took the intelligence end—gathering information, frustrating the anarchists, all that.'

'Although at least some of you don't want Jews in England.'

'On the contrary, my boy, Herzl's goal is the same as ours: to find the poorer sort of Jew a home *outside of* England. I told you all this before. We're not "anti-Semitic", to use the fashionable neologism; we're pro-British. Quite different to hating Jews. No connection at all.'

Denton shrugged. 'Go on.'

'Before Herzl arrived on these shores, we already had information about people who wanted to stop him.'

'The Bund.'

'Perhaps. You mustn't over-simplify, Denton—it's a common mistake in people who themselves aren't intelligence professionals. Let's just say that we had information about "interested parties". We evaluated these, ranked them, et cetera, shovelled some off to New Scotland Yard and focused our attention on the most dangerous. At the top of the list was a Polish Jew named Gowarczyk. Bomb-maker. We had firm evidence that he was heading this way.'

'From Herzl?'

'I can't reveal our sources.'

'"Sources", plural?'

'One must confirm one source with another. It's one of the basic rules of intelligence.' Hector spread butter on another piece of bread and began to mop his plate with it. 'Gowarczyk reached these shores a month ago. My people picked him up at Dover and followed him to a lodging house in Bethnal Green. Rather laughably easy exercise for them. High marks for my people.'

'Only the man? No woman?'

'Aha, all in good time. Where was I? The lodging house in the East End. Rather a depot for anarchists and terrorists—place was full of them. Melville knew all about it, as it turned out:

Special Branch like it when they hang together—easier to keep an eye on them. At any rate, Gowarczyk began sniffing around building sites and such, asking about explosives. That seemed a bit rich for House—he explained this to me later—so he had Gowarczyk brought in to Barth's.'

'By Simms and Gratton?'

'As it happened, yes.'

'Who tortured him.'

'Nothing of the kind! They may have been a bit rough with him, but nothing like… One can't serve these anarchists weak tea with milk and ask if they'd like to chat about bombs, my boy.'

'And he told them everything.'

'He did, as a matter of fact.'

'Just like that.'

'No, no, of course not. But there was nothing *over the line*. I had Major House's word on that.'

'And you believed him.'

'Of course I believed him! Major House has a DSO!'

Denton ordered cheese and biscuits for both of them, asked for an apple as well for himself. When the waiter had gone, he said, 'All right, the honourable major and his merry men had a polite chat with Gowar-what's-his-name.'

'Gowarczyk. Polish Jew name. It wasn't easy, Denton; it took them several days! Gowarczyk didn't want to talk, naturally. They had to overcome resistance. You don't do this with kid gloves on. But they got results!'

'I'm sure they did.'

'Exactly. Thereafter, Gowarczyk was in our pocket. I had a personal interview with him. On behalf of the Crown, I offered him a new name and a pension, help with a new life. He was thrilled! He was frightened out of his wits, living in a strange country whose language he didn't speak at all well, skulking about planning to blow up Herzl and the Foreign Secretary. That was the plan—blow up the Foreign Secretary's country house when he and Herzl were there for talks. A bloodbath was what was wanted by his superiors.'

'Superiors?'

'Gowarczyk is part of an international conspiracy that's led from Moscow. Bigger than the Bund. Profound hatred of Jews—the eradication of Jews the goal. They *run* the Bund, and the Bund doesn't know it!'

'But Gowarczyk's Jewish, you said.'

'Bought off. Also pressure through family still in Galicia—a sister raped, an uncle beaten by the mob—not very subtle threats that if he didn't do as they wanted, worse would follow. I had to promise to bring his immediate family to England.'

'I thought you were trying to get the Jews *out* of England.'

'Well, it's only six or seven. At any rate, my goal had nothing to do with Jews; my goal was a successful anti-outrage operation.' The cheese arrived, along with a large plate of fruits. Denton selected an apple and began to cut it into quarters. Hector said, 'In short, we made Gowarczyk our agent.'

'Ah. The secret agent. Just like Conrad.'

'Don't mock what you don't understand. Gowarczyk told us the plan for his entire campaign, gave us the names of three associates already in London, warned us that four more were yet to arrive. The plan was intricate and infernal—dynamite in the Foreign Secretary's country house, men with guns lining the roads in case anyone escaped, a *second* bomb to savage the police and firemen who came to effect a rescue.'

Denton focused on the cheese before saying, in as neutral a voice as he could manage, 'I told them a pack of lies after I was in the barrel. It's the only thing you can do.'

'I'm sure you did. Smart fellow.'

Hector seemed to see no connection with Gowarczyk. Denton didn't press the idea. 'So you arrested everybody?'

'We did nothing of the kind!' Hector looked delighted with himself. 'We caused Gowarczyk to report to us on every move his associates made. We supplied him with explosives and detonators as his bona fides with the others.' He smiled, his voice condescending. 'The detonators don't work, Denton. Don't look so shocked. We're not children at Charrington Street.'

'And the woman?'

'Which woman?'

'The one with the French mother and the Jewish father. "Tania Simonova."'

Hench-Rose looked crestfallen that Denton knew this, too, but he brightened and said, 'Gowarczyk's wife, you mean.' He tried an experimental look of smugness, in case Denton didn't know about this. Denton pretended he didn't, and the smugness spread.

Denton was taking the cores out of the quarters of apple. 'What does this Gowarczyk look like? Small or large? Dark or fair?' When he had heard Hench-Rose's description, he said, 'Mr Shermitz, in fact. He showed up at my house and called himself Shermitz—the name that was in the newspapers for the dead woman.'

'Gowarczyk came to your house? I find that hard to believe.'

'He wanted her handbag. Said there was money in it.' He passed across a quarter of the apple.

'We were giving him plenty of money! It couldn't have been the same man. We watch him every second of the day.'

'Well, at least my visitor said he had a wife. What did Gowarczyk say about *his* wife?'

'We had a bit of a time with him over that. He finally admitted the wife was one of the gang, this same Tania Simonova you've mentioned.' Hector dropped his voice and put his face towards Denton. 'Shocking thing. She had an, mm, operation to, er, you know—get her out of the family way. He was in a rage about it!'

'An abortion, you mean?'

'Really, Denton! Hush. Yes, that sort of thing. He was in a terrible state, saying he was going to kill her. If he could find her—seems she'd done a flit. Afraid of him, I suppose. He was in a dreadful state. Threatened to use our explosive to blow them both up.'

'When was this? Before or after the dead woman was found at my house?'

'Mmm... After. Had to be after. House got the information about the bomb plot from Gowarczyk about a week before that damned woman was found dead. Then it was afterwards that he started the carry-on about the, mm, medical thing.'

Denton thought about 'Shermitz's bruises. A week made sense. 'How did he know?'

'She told him, I suppose. Then scampered, I expect. Knew what was good for her. Hell of a thing to do to a man.'

'And she's still gone.'

'He raves about it every time I see him. Can't keep quiet about it.'

Both men had finished their cheese. Hector said, 'D'you suppose I could get some sort of pudding here?'

'Just looking at their pastry cart should be all the pudding a body could need. However—' Denton waved to the waiter, pointed at the cart, just then parked by a distant table.

Hector said, 'Gowarczyk's wife must be an absolute hell-cat. I feel a good deal of sympathy for the poor chap. Try not to show it, of course—wouldn't be proper—but she's shown him a time. Not the most faithful bitch in the kennel, I take it. Certainly a murderess as well, eh? Killed the Alken woman?'

'It looks like it.' The pastry cart trundled up. Hench-Rose's greedy eyes swept over it. 'Yummy, yummy,' he murmured.

Walking later towards Oxford Street, Hench-Rose patted his waistcoat and said that they did one surprisingly well at that place, *louche* as the surroundings might be. Denton said, 'I suppose my secret Judaism has scuppered your getting me into the Kestrel. It's an ill wind that doesn't blow some good.'

'I don't want to talk about that. As a matter of fact...' Hector's voice trailed away. He shrugged.

Denton suddenly got it. 'Hector—have you given up the Kestrel?'

'Didn't suit me. Waste of money, as it turned out. Ha! There's Oxford Street—civilization—'

'Hector, you loved the Kestrel.'

A bus was just drawing up at the kerb. 'Not right, saying they'd blackball a fella because some socialist rag says he's a Jew.' Hench-Rose seemed to get even more militarily stiff-backed.

The Second Woman

'Clubs are easily come by. Matter of having the money and connections, nothing else. Bunch of old farts, mostly.' He paused at the bus stop. 'There's dozens of clubs. Friends come by ones.' He climbed into the bus, and the last Denton saw of him, he was sitting red-faced, looking straight ahead.

The Second Woman

CHAPTER
19

Denton found Atkins in the garden, pulling up weeds and jabbing along his rows of seeds with a tablespoon.

'We can't afford a trowel?'

'I'm airy-ating. Read about it in a book I got from a pal of mine. Spoon's perfect.'

'Not one of the silver ones, I hope.'

Atkins looked pained. He stood, stretched, put a hand in his own back. The air was cold, but he was in shirtsleeves and waistcoat. He sniffed. 'Swear I can smell that privy when the wind's right. Must be the neighbours.'

'We're all on the sewer. It's your swedes you smell.'

'Swedes, bloody hell—we'd be eating them by now if the coppers hadn't put their boots all over them. You going over to the missus's?'

'Yes, and how many times do I have to say it?'

'She isn't the missus, I know, I know. Well, get supper there or order in from the Lamb. Kitchen's empty.'

'Except for eggs, bacon, bread, kippers—'

'They're for breakfast. And I don't cook in the evening, as you well know.'

Denton passed through into Janet's garden and, crossing to the house, thought that he, too, got a whiff of something like a privy. *Damp air.* He went up to her room, found a nurse snoozing in an armchair and Janet asleep. She woke when he leaned over her and stared at him. Her skin was red and hot and she looked thinner.

'How are you?'

'I feel as if I've been beaten all over my body. I'm *never* sick.'

He offered her water; she sipped a little but refused the Parrish's and the iron tonic. 'Awful stuff. Anyway, I can't keep anything down.' She lay back, panting. 'I've come out in a rash.'

'I don't see it.'

'On my front. Ugly as sin.'

'I like your front.'

'Not now, you wouldn't.'

'Should I read to you? Would you like to sit up? Walk a bit?' She wanted none of it. A few minutes later, she was asleep again, her hot hand in his. When he had sat like that for fifteen minutes, he took his hand away and tiptoed out. In his own house again, he found Atkins and said, 'What's a rash on the chest mean?'

'It's a symptom of typhus, like I said before.'

'You'd better get the doctor again.'

Bernat showed up an hour later. After examining her, he said, 'Your man is the new Aesculapius. It is typhus.'

'That's serious!'

'Not always.'

'Can it be fatal?'

'Sometimes. Not so often. She's strong.' Bernat had insisted on examining Denton, whom he'd missed in the morning.

'She doesn't look strong! She hasn't eaten anything in three days. What should I do?'

'Wait.' Bernat patted his shoulder. 'We have no magic for the disease. The body is the magic. It fights, and it usually wins. She will have a high fever. Maybe delirium. Then—' He unbuttoned Denton's waistcoat and put his ear to Denton's chest.

'How long?'

Bernat was silent, listening. Then: 'Probably three or four days. Her body will use itself up, fighting. She will be very weak. But now she is strong.'

'You mean it's serious.'

'Yes, it is serious. But life is serious, as you know.' He looked at the welts, said they would heal. 'Your friend the policeman was unhappy this morning.'

'Hungover, you mean.'

'I told him to drink less. He was rude. He is not a happy man.'

'As you say, life is serious.'

While Denton was eating his lacklustre supper in Janet's kitchen, Atkins brought Munro over from Denton's house. Seeing the CID man, Denton said, 'You're out late. Eaten?'

Munro shook his head. 'Wife's holding my supper for me. Policeman's wife.'

'I thought she gave you a time if you were late.'

'She does.'

'I think there's a bottle or two of ale in the pantry. Not my house.'

Munro shook his head again. He sat and put his bowler on the table, away from the food. 'I just came by to say I was sorry for being so short with you this morning. Got a bit wound up about that meeting. Forgot what hell you'd been put through.'

Denton waved it away with his fork. 'You were right to be miffed over the telephone business. I shouldn't have interfered. But I got swatted for my doing it, right enough.'

'Swatted and almost drowned. Those bastards! And Hench-Rose and his arse-licker shot them off to bleeding Ireland.'

'Not Hench-Rose. That major—House—does what he wants. I think he's pulling the wool over Hench-Rose's eyes.'

'What have they got there, some sort of hush-hush special branch?'

'Not sure. Hench-Rose told me some of it, but I'm not supposed to pass it on. They seem to be a mix of police and military—well, you saw that this morning—with a pretty broad warrant.'

'Broad! Picking people up off the street and torturing them, that's broad, that is.' Munro was eating crumbs of cheddar from around a wedge that had come from the Lamb. 'What are they on about?'

Denton thought about holding information back, then thought that Munro's responsibility was more important than Melville's. 'They're concentrating right now on a plot to blow up some people, including the Foreign Secretary. Hench-Rose told me about somebody named Gowarczyk.'

'What's he—anarchist?' Munro had taken out a huge clasp knife and cut the pointed end off the wedge of cheese.

'Something like that. The same two that picked me up grabbed him. Hench-Rose said they didn't do to him what they did to me, but—This is between us, Munro, all right? I don't want it in a report yet, because it might get Hench-Rose in trouble.'

'Don't tell me, then.' Munro got up and went into the pantry.

'I want you to know.' Denton raised his voice. 'CID want to know what's going on with all this, don't they?'

Munro came out of the pantry with a dark-brown bottle, sat down and used a tool on the knife to open it. 'From the moment those bastards stole that woman's body.' He put the cheese on a slice of Denton's bread, bit, chewed. 'I didn't get a hooter from that major today, by the way. The lawyer sat there and said, "You need not answer" to every bloody question I put him. The major with an expression on his face like I was an interesting piece of some lower order of animal that had come his way. I wanted to conk him.' He made a bad-smell face and drank from the bottle.

'But didn't, I hope. Hench-Rose says the two bullyrag-gers—Simms and Gratton, the two who are supposed to be in Ireland—were "rough" with this Gowarczyk. The man who came to see me the night after the dead woman was found had a lot of bruises showing. As if somebody'd been "rough" with him.' He waited for some response. Munro simply looked at him. 'He said he was Mr Shermitz—husband of the dead woman.'

Munro sat back. He cut another slice of the cheese with his left hand, put it on a piece of bread that had the scalloped marks of his bite on it. 'The bad boys leather the man. The man shows up at your house, claiming to be the husband. Name, Shermitz. Now we know the dead woman wasn't Shermitz but Alken. What's the connection?'

'He said he wanted her things. As he wasn't her husband, he must have thought the body was his wife's—he was mistaken, I mean. You want some of these potatoes?'

Munro shook his head. 'Supper waiting at home.' He looked at a pocket watch. 'Judas Priest.' He drank more beer. 'So, this anarchist or whatever he is thinks his wife—does he have a wife, by the way? Do Hench-Rose and his hench-rose-men know?'

'Hector says they got "everything" out of the man when they were "rough" with him. One of the things was that he had a wife. But I'm not sure I believe everything he told them. Munro, when they put me upside down in that barrel, I was terrified. When they hauled me out, I'd have told any pack of lies I could think of to keep from being put back in.'

'Might have told the truth, too.'

'Maybe. But this fellow, he might have had a convenient set of lies ready. Hench-Rose told me that always having two sources was a rule of good intelligence, but the only source he has for what Gowarczyk told him is Gowarczyk. So maybe there's no wife and maybe there's no plot to blow people up. Maybe it's all about something else.'

'Well—' Munro finished the bread and then the beer. 'My interest is the Hench-Rose-men, not your Gorchuck or whatever his name is. Pole, is he? Sounds it. What I want to know is, where did your two bullies get the authority to come it over the police, to get Mankey and Steff moved out, and to take a body off? Which they did, by the way, to protect the skin on the major's arse, if you ask me. I think he was afraid the woman would be Mrs Alken, as in fact it was, and he wanted to hide the connection with him. Slimy bastard.' He tried to get another drop from the bottle by tilting it to vertical in his mouth. He banged the bottle on the table. 'Off I go.' He stood and picked up his hat. 'How's the lady?'

'Not good.'

'I'm sorry. Take care of her.'

Munro stood on the step of Janet's house, looking down into his hat for some seconds. His breath was visible in the night air. 'I've been told to appear at the chief super's office tomorrow. Going to get my hole scoured, I suppose. A policeman's lot, eh?' He put his hat on and went down the steps and out of sight in the darkness.

He woke sometime after midnight, aware that he was in her house. The night sounds were wrong, the light different. Had he heard her? He padded down the corridor in his nightshirt and bare feet and looked into her room: a single gas light was burning; the nurse was dozing in the chair; Janet was asleep, her breathing noisy. She made a sound like a whimper, and her legs moved under the bedclothes.

Denton watched her for more than a minute and then went back to the room he disliked. He sat on the bed, feeling the cold. He wanted to lie down, but he had been too hot. He would wait a minute more.

A sound reached him. Not her breathing or her whimper, but something less human. The nurse? Perhaps a snore? He heard it again, now definitely a scraping. *Ratwork.* He went to the doorway and listened. Again, a scraping and a *chink.* Not from her room but from the floor below.

The house was dark except for Janet's single light. The stairs, old painted wood now covered with carpet, were silent under his bare feet. He stopped halfway down and listened again. Somebody breaking in? He wondered if he should have a weapon. Maybe Annie had come back. He went down the rest of the way and stood in the small room with the piano. Nothing there. He moved to the doorway and, hearing the sound again, waited, then decided it had come from the drawing room. He moved to it silently, went in. On the opposite wall was a pier glass; he had often seen Janet check one of her bright costumes in it. Now, as he looked, something white passed across it. He thought, *Annie's ghost.* He whirled. Nothing was there.

But he heard soft sounds, half scuttle, half tiptoe. Three strides took him to an open door that led to the rear hallway. He looked down it. Nothing. But a sound: a closing door and the turning of a key.

A ghost who locks doors.

He put his hands out on each side of himself and felt his way down the dark corridor. There were three doors in the corridor, he knew; the first, which led to a closet under the stairs, was unlocked. He opened it, felt inside, thinking that he could be stabbed or sandbagged, that he was being stupid, but he didn't believe that anybody was in there. He had heard a key.

The second door led down to the Cohans' quarters.

It was locked.

He went on down to the third door, which stood across the end of the corridor and led to the kitchen and pantry. It was open, gloomy light coming from a rear window. This room was electrified; he found the switch and winced when the bright, clear-glass lamps sprang on. Tiled in white to shoulder height, the kitchen seemed shocking after the darkness. He looked around it with slitted eyes. Why would anybody have been in the kitchen? He found crumbs on the board in front of the bread bin, a dirty knife in the sink with a shred of some sort of meat on it. Had the nurses left it this way? Otherwise the place was clean.

The pantry was the same, except that in the icebox, part of a ham had been put back at a slant, looking untidy. Again, was that the nurses' work?

Annie's ghost.

Ghosts didn't, in Denton's scheme of things, eat bread and ham. Nurses, on the other hand, probably did.

262

He went into the dining room and slid open the drawer where he knew the silver was kept. He had to feel his way, the light from the kitchen inadequate here, but he found what he was looking for—a nut-pick with a slightly curved blade.

He turned off the kitchen lights and went upstairs again to put on his robe, his body now cold, then went to Janet's room. The nurse woke, looked startled. Denton put his finger to his lips and said, 'Did you eat some ham tonight?'

She was offended. She had brought her own supper, she said, and she didn't steal other people's food. He tried to mollify her, failed. He made the mistake of saying it was probably the day nurse. This offended her, too: the day nurse was a personal friend, and no finer human being walked the earth. Denton gave up and went into Janet's dressing room and got her keys from one of the hairboxes on her dresser. He had to pass through her room again on the way out; he smiled; the nurse turned her head away.

The key to the Cohans' door was a big one, heavy, with a head like an executioner's axe, much notched. He tried to ease it into the lock but was noisy; no matter. It stuck partway in: another key was on the other side. Unable to push it through, he withdrew the key from his side and fiddled with the nut-pick for almost twenty minutes before he was able to move the other key; after that, it took him minutes more to get it into the right position so he could push it through. It fell with a clank on the step below.

Denton unlocked the door. The stairway descended into blackness.

Not a sound below. But this was the door that had been locked, and this was where the ghost had gone.

He thought of going home for his flash-light and his pistol. By the time he got back, whoever—whatever—was below would be gone. He retreated to the kitchen, took the dirty knife from the sink and put it in the pocket of his robe, then went back to the Cohans' door.

And started down.

Even through his slippers, he could feel the breadcrumbs on the top step. He didn't know they were crumbs until he picked one up and rolled it in his fingers and thumb. He could picture the ghost, in the dark, putting bread and ham down on the stair, then locking the door, picking the food up again and going down. Where?

To the left from the bottom of the stairs was the old basement kitchen, now a large sitting room for the Cohans. It was at the back of the house; stone steps led up to the rear garden through what had been a slanted cellar door until Janet had had it removed. Denton went that way now, found the cord for the overhead electric lamp and gave himself light. The outer door was bolted from the inside, so his ghost hadn't gone out there. No broken windows. Nothing, in fact, except some dust on a table to suggest that Leah Cohan hadn't been there in a while.

Leaving the light on, he went back past the stairs, opening doors and looking in. The Cohans' bedroom, nothing. The box room, nothing. The vacant little room at the end, where Janet had put a narrow bed in case the Cohans needed it—

'Are you always visiting the women in the night?'

She had switched on a small lamp as he had stepped into the doorway. She was in the bed, wearing a long-sleeved nightgown that he thought was probably Leah's. Her black hair was down. She had an accent.

'Tania Simonova,' he said.

She made a disgusted face.

'Or Rebecca Shermitz.'

She shrugged. The nightgown went up and down, her breasts asserting themselves. She was a handsome woman, perhaps thirty; her look, partly amused, said she knew all about men and women and beds and nights.

What did Hench-Rose say? Not the most faithful bitch in the kennel?

The room was small. He glanced around it, saw a plate on the floor, empty except for crumbs; a yellow suitcase made of some kind of straw, rather large, something an actor might have carried in a play to suggest the rube come to the big city. Or the Pole come to London.

'Have you been here the whole time?' he said.

'How many questions you are asking! You give me wrong names; you ask questions. Who in the hell are you being?'

'If you aren't Mrs Shermitz or Simonova, who are you?'

'I am being Leah's niece! My dear auntie. I ask her, can I stay, I got no place, my husband is after me. He beats me. She says, stay. You are my sister's child, my house is your house. So I am staying.' She indicated the suitcase. 'See, I bring everything.'

'When did you say all this to Leah?'

'When I am coming here. Before, before her man, Kohn, Cohen, is being put in hospital. She says yes, yes, you are my family, you stay.'

'She didn't tell Mrs Striker. Upstairs.'

'So? Is not her business. This place, Leah's house. Down here. I am quiet, yes? I giving no trouble, yes?' She pouted. 'Nobody knows I am here. Now you ask me questions, like a police.'

'You visited Dr Bernat, and then Mrs Striker brought you here.'

'Doctor? What doctor? You think I have money for *doctor*? Nobody bring me here. I have this place, this—number on house—from my mother, she say when you get to England, look for your auntie. She is family. So I find this place; I walk and walk, carrying my baggages, I am exhausted, I find Auntie Leah, she say stay. So.'

'Where is your husband?'

'I come to London to get away from husband! He beat me and beat me. If he find me, he *kill* me. My blood be on your hands if you tell him!' She made herself more comfortable against a thin pillow, a smile of self-congratulation on her lips.

'You're a good liar.'

'I don't lie! *You* lie. You tell me some lies about a doctor, about her upstairs bringing me! Lies, lies!' The smile grew sly. 'Oho, I know what you mean by doctor! I hear her upstairs. "Oh, I am so afraid! Oh, I never go back to prison! I kill myself!"' She leaned towards him, her face cruel. 'Because she help some doctor do *aborting* and she so afraid! Yes, is a sin! She do sin; doctor does sin! Oho, police be very happy hearing this!' Her lips came forward, pouted, as if she were going to spit. 'So you remember, you do something to me, I tell police what I know about killing little baby. Ha!'

'You don't know anything.'

'I know what I hear.' She settled back. She smiled; with her left hand, she pushed the pillow behind her head. 'You think I am being stupid little Polish peasant, know nothing, hear nothing. But I knowing some things. And I hearing everything! So if you tell police lies about who I am, I tell them truth about things I am hearing.'

Denton looked at her. The threat unsettled him; worse, what she said made him less sure who she was. Leah was stolid enough to let a relative live in her basement and say nothing. But the coincidence, if she was not Simonova, was enormous. He said, 'You're Annie's ghost.'

She chuckled. It was real amusement; it made her human, briefly likeable. 'Poor little Annie. *Boo!*' She wriggled herself a little into the bed; the movement was provocative, meant to be seen. 'You are wanting to see me naked, yes? You are wanting me.' She smiled. 'Well—if you are being nice to me—ma-a-a-ybe...' She chuckled again.

'I see why your husband might want to knock you around.'

'Don't touch me!' She sat upright and pulled her right hand from under the bedcovers and pointed a tiny gun at him. It was his own derringer.

'*You* stole my Remington!'

'I not steal. Take for protection against husband! Against you, too!'

'You break into houses, too.'

'What "break"? House was open.'

'You mean you used Leah's keys.'

She shrugged. She frowned. 'I not like you. You not know how to be nice. Go away, else I shoot you.'

'At this distance, you wouldn't hit me. But I'll go away— until tomorrow. We'll talk some more.'

'You go up to her, eh? She, the lady, is sick. I know; I hear everything. She is dying?'

'No.'

'Maybe. She is being very sick.' She raised the derringer and extended her arm. 'You not forget what I say: you be nice to me or I tell police about *her*. Sick or healthy!' She let her arm swing down. 'Go away.'

He saw no reason to challenge her just then. She very well might pull the trigger if he tried to get close enough to take back his derringer; even if she missed, a gunshot would bring questions, maybe the police, and he didn't want to talk to the police so long as she was threatening Janet. He turned and went down the corridor and up the stairs, retrieving the key from the top step and using it to lock her down there. The thought of her moving through the house while they slept made him queasy: handsome she might be, sensual in her way, but there was something definitely creepy about her coming up the stairs, listening, perhaps watching. What had she seen? Despite the dark, he blushed, thinking about the nights he'd spent in Janet's bed.

He looked in on Janet. The nurse was awake, said only that the fever had broken, then gone up again. Janet was breathing quickly but was quiet.

He lay down again in the room he had taken for himself. When he woke, rain was hitting the window and grey light filled the room.

When, later, he went down to the Cohans' quarters, the woman and her yellow suitcase were gone. He could find no sign she had ever been there except that the abandoned privy at the back of Janet's garden had excrement in it. The ghost hadn't wanted to make noise flushing the WC.

Denton tried to convince himself that it was all for the best that she was gone, but he knew he should have had her arrested. Let the police sort it out.

But he hadn't.

Because of Janet.

CHAPTER

20

For five days, Janet lay in a fever. Waking, she seemed hardly conscious; sometimes, she was delirious. He heard her scream during the nights, heard her mumble 'Mother, mother' and babble disconnected bits of sentences. Her fever lessened twice but came back. The rash on her chest turned to purple spots. With the nurse, he stripped the bed each day, the sheets at first wet with her sweat and smelling of urine, then, as she failed to take in enough water, dry and smelling like dead flowers.

They dribbled water into her mouth from a sponge. She was rarely able to drink from a glass held to her mouth. She ate nothing; the syrups and tonics were vomited back.

Denton tried to work but threw down the pencil each time, sat with his head in his hands like somebody acting out a worried man. Sleeping badly, he was awake at night to wander the house, down into the Cohans' quarters, up to Annie's, finding nothing, meeting neither ghost nor human. Atkins brought him food; he would eat a little, then push it away and go to look at her. Twice, he left her house to visit Cohan at the Infirmary, only to turn around almost as soon as he got there and return to her, even though he could do nothing for her. The first time at the Infirmary, seeing Leah, he said softly to her, 'I saw your niece.'

She stared at him. She could be as obstinate as a mule when she wanted. After several seconds, she said, 'Yes, my niece.'

'I was down in your part of the house. I thought I'd heard a noise, a burglar.'

'My niece. By my sister.'

'She said she had your permission to stay down there.'

Leah hadn't understood 'permission', but when he explained, she said, 'Yes, my niece. My sister's.'

Denton had let it go at that.

By the third day, Janet looked gaunt, although he couldn't believe that she had lost so much weight in so short a time. Her lips, shiny with ointment, were nonetheless cracked. Her skin stayed hot to the touch. When he asked Bernat how long she could go on, all Bernat would say was, 'She is strong.'

Denton wondered if in fact she was strong enough. The scar down her face seemed to rise above the rest of the flesh now, as if the face were sinking away and leaving only it. The scar looked almost white against her red cheek. Purple shadows formed under her eyes; pustules formed on her forehead and down the sides of her nose.

On the fourth day, Bernat said, 'The fever is higher. The body is fighting. But only for so long. Then——the brain——'

'You said she is strong enough.'

'I thought it would be over in three days. Maybe today is the last.'

But Denton woke during that night to hear her moaning, and in the morning she was delirious. He sat with his head in his hands, trying not to hear her but unable to go far enough from her to lose the sound. Once, she said, 'What is that?' so clearly he thought she was talking to him, that it was over and she was awake. But then she said, 'I told you,' and 'Never, never——never.' And then, a couple of minutes later, 'I don't care.'

They sponged her with cold water, as they had been doing for days, and replaced the wet towel across her forehead. In the evening, Bernat came and said to him, 'This has to be the last day. I think tonight we have a crisis.'

'What does that mean?'

'It means the disease will either go away or it will win.'

'She won't die!'

Bernat looked helpless. He said, 'I am sorry if I have failed you.'

Sometime after midnight, he sent the nurse to his own room to sleep. She was trying to stay awake in the armchair, but her head kept dropping to the side, mouth open. Her snores irritated him. He told her he was sending her to bed because she was exhausted and needed sleep, but the truth was it made him angry to have her in the same room. After she had gone, he moved the armchair next to Janet's bed and took one of her hands and held it, hot, dry, spasming every few seconds as her legs moved and her voice groaned. He put his head on the back of her hand. 'Don't die,' he whispered. 'Please don't die.'

He had prayed as a child, but he couldn't pray any longer. He had prayed for the impossible once—that his mother would return, that his father would die—and the impossible of course hadn't happened. Now, even praying for the possible was closed to him.

'Don't leave me. *Don't leave me!*'

The wind came up and screeched at the corners of the house. He heard a shutter banging and wondered if he should go looking for it. His own eyes were swollen, his own exhaustion pulling him down towards sleep. Janet was making less sound, her breathing now shallow and fast, no vocalizing, her body still.

'Don't leave me,' he whispered again.

He didn't know when he slept. His dreams were not of her, but of his wife and the horse. They repeated and went nowhere.

When he woke, the room was cold. The wind had fallen. There was no sound.

He realized slowly that some sound should have reached him, not this dead silence.

'Janet!'

He threw himself halfway across the bed, his knees striking the floor. She was lying still. He touched her hand. It was cool.

'Janet—' Tears in his eyes and his voice.

Her eyes opened. A deep breath followed, a gulping intake of air that was almost convulsive. Her eyes searched the room and found him. She smiled.

'Janet—my God—'

She said, 'I dreamed—' She looked at the ceiling, where the pale light from a street lamp cast a distorted image of the window. Her voice was a dry whisper. 'I've been ill.'

'Yes. Very ill.'

'All day?'

'Several days.'

She frowned. Her lips moved as if shaping words, but she said nothing. Then, 'I stink.'

'You've been sick.' Indeed, her breath was foul. The room was foul.

'Well.' He felt her forehead, cool now. He brought her water and held her head while she drank. She took half of a second glass but then pushed it away, and in seconds she was asleep again.

He was afraid she would lapse into the fever. He sat with her for half an hour. Nothing changed: a measured, steady breathing; cool skin; the stillness of deep sleep.

He walked through the house. It was after four; first light would show soon. He went downstairs, walked through the rooms, went to the cellar and shovelled coal into the furnace and opened the grating to let more air in, then came up again and went to her, found her the same. He went along the upstairs hall and into a small room at the end and stood at its only window, as he had been standing at other windows for the last five nights, feeling how weary he was and now how much at peace. The elation of her first waking was gone; in its place, a settled contentment. He leaned against the window frame and looked out. He wished he could smoke, but he had nothing to hand. What could be seen out of the window was banal—the street itself, a patch of pavement, part of a tree whose bare branches were picked out by the light from the street lamp. Moments of happiness are inexplicable: he felt one now, thought he could have stayed there for ever, leaning on one shoulder, looking at an utterly ordinary scene. One could die at such a time, he thought, and life would have been worth it.

He went back and checked on her again. Nothing had changed, except that perhaps her colour was better. She was simply a woman asleep.

He went back to the little room and the window. The mood would not return: he was different, or the scene was. Then he realized that there was an intrusion—a sound. A low rumble was coming from below, slightly to his right. He cocked his head and pressed his cheek against the glass to look.

A coster's barrow was coming up the street, its iron-rimmed wheels grinding on the macadam. The cart itself looked strange; above the wheels, it appeared at a distance to be triangular, rising to a point. When it was closer, he thought that the upper part was like a tent, probably a tarpaulin; at the very top, something stuck up like a mast, a short cross-bar like a spar, where something fluttered. When it was close enough and passing a light, he saw that the fluttering was a Union Jack.

He had never seen a coster's barrow on these streets, but one seemed possible, even likely at this hour, somebody going up to the far side of Euston Road, maybe as far as a market in Camden Town. As the barrow came closer, he saw that two figures were pushing it: a man and a woman. They came on together, passing under the street light, their faces shadowed because each wore a hat. Then, to his surprise, they stopped just below his window. He drew back, as if he didn't want to be seen.

The woman detached herself from the cart, then swung around so that the light shone in under her hat. It was the woman who had been living downstairs. His contentment evaporated, replaced by something negative, even foul: first, a feeling of invasion, then the guilt he had felt when he had let the woman slip away.

The man grabbed her arm. There was nothing pleasant or affectionate in his grip. He must have said something to her; she pulled her arm away and came quickly towards the house, then disappeared, blocked from Denton's view by the window frame and the wall. He watched the man, who had turned to look after her and whose face was thus lighted. It was the man who had claimed to be Rebecca Shermitz's husband.

Gowarczyk.

Denton rushed to the back of the house. The woman had gone into the passage that ran alongside Janet's house to the back garden. She would, he thought, use a stolen key to get in through the back door to the Cohans'. He couldn't think of anywhere else she could be going. He could go down there, confront her—but not yet. What he wanted was to find what she and the man were doing.

He stationed himself by a window at the back. She must be at the door now, he thought; he would hear the lock, a footstep. But what he heard was not the sound of the key, but a gritty, scraping whisper. Like a grindstone. Then nothing. Then a metallic bump.

And silence.

He raced back to his original vantage point. The man was standing by the barrow, still looking where the woman had disappeared. One of his legs twitched. He took out a watch, put it back. He fidgeted.

The woman appeared, going towards him now. She was carrying the yellow suitcase.

What the hell! Where had she hidden it? He thought of the scraping sound, the metallic thump. *In the ash-house!* The little wooden lean-to, latticed, that jutted out from the back of the house, the inevitable result of central heating: a structure to hide the bins that hid the ashes.

She hoisted the suitcase in one hand, then swung it across her body and got her left hand under it and so pushed it up on the bed of the barrow. The man pulled the tarpaulin aside and then used one hand to help her push the suitcase in. He rearranged

the tarpaulin with some fussiness, and then, the Union Jack fluttering above them, they took their places and began to push it
again to Denton's left, towards the north.

Denton tried to follow them with his eyes but found the tree
in the way. Raising the sash without noise, he put his head out
in time to see them turn left into Guilford Street, meaning they
were headed towards Lamb's Conduit—his own street.

He was seeing, he thought, something mysterious and
perhaps dangerous. He should tell the police. Munro would be
unreachable at this hour. Who, then?

He dropped the sash and ran down the stairs, ripped open
the rear door and sprinted through the gardens. His own back
door was locked. He banged on it, hissed, 'Atkins! Goddamnit,
Atkins—' And where the hell were his own keys? On a bedside
table in Janet's house. Why didn't he have the sense to carry them?

Atkins opened the door. Denton's Smith & Wesson appeared
first, then Atkins's face. He was wearing an ancient army-issue
nightshirt and nightcap, his feet bare.

'Forgot your key, then, General?'

'Jump into your clothes and be quick about it! No time to
talk, no time—'

Snatching the revolver, Denton ran along the side of his own
house, hesitated long enough at his gate to see if the barrow was
in the street, then rushed through and began running towards
Guilford Street. At the corner by Bernat's surgery, opposite the
Foundling Hospital and Coram's, he looked left and right. No
barrow. Far away, a cab was moving; except for a cat, the street
was otherwise deserted. Denton turned left and ran to the next
corner and looked north up Lansdowne Place in time to see the
triangle of the barrow's tarpaulin, like a sail standing out against
the bushes of Brunswick Square, just taking the turn where
Lansdowne Place headed for Hunter Street.

He was wearing a nightshirt and a long robe and thin
slippers. He saw himself: a man standing on a dark street in
nightclothes with a gun in his hand. If he ran after them, he
would look foolish. Standing there, thinking that thought, he

felt self-disgust. Whatever they were doing, he was conniving with them by doing nothing. Because he felt foolish. And because of Janet.

By then he was on the run again for his own house. Cold daylight was showing in the sky.

'No time,' he panted when he was in Atkins's sitting room. Atkins was dressing, was at that moment pulling on his boots. 'You're going out,' Denton said. As Atkins got overcoat and bowler, Denton explained about the barrow and the pair trundling it up the street. 'They're headed north, on Hunter Street now. It's slow going with that thing, even with two of them.'

Atkins presented himself, fully dressed at last.

'I want you to follow them.'

'I knew it.'

'I'll be at Mrs Striker's. Use the telephone. Don't let them out of your sight, but call me whenever you can.'

'Oh, yes, with all the telephones that are lying about in the street for me to use. My hat!'

'You'll find something. Shops—businesses—there are thousands of telephones now!'

'Yes, well, I'll be lucky to find a pigeon that's heading this way, is what I think.' Atkins shook his head. 'I suppose you're keeping the pistol?'

'Get going, for God's sake!'

Atkins started out. 'You're a caution to work for, General.'

And he was gone.

Denton, a little weak in the legs from the running, trudged back to Janet's house. The nurse was up and cross, saying she'd been woken by 'a commotion like a burglar at a window'. However, she pronounced Janet 'over the worst', and said she could do with a bit of breakfast.

'There was a ham in the meat safe.' He thought with another pang of guilt of the woman who had hidden down there.

'Oh, *that's* gone, sir.' Not wanting to dwell on this, she asked him if he'd like a nice egg. Denton discovered that he was famished.

'I'll just have a look in the kitchen, then, if you'll mind the lady.'

Denton looked in on Janet, who was cool and breathing normally. He was afraid that Atkins might telephone, although of course it was too soon. He could hardly have reached the north end of Hunter Street yet. And if he telephoned, what would Denton do? What could he do without tipping the police to the woman who had threatened to tell about the abortion?

He put on the same clothes he'd been wearing all yesterday—probably the day before, as well. He'd brought the Smith & Wesson back from his house; now he tried to find a place to carry it. His trousers were too loose, worn with braces; the inside pocket of his jacket was too small. The pistol would go into one of the side pockets but rode heavily. He'd have to carry it in his overcoat. He put the pistol on the top of a bedside table and told himself to remember to get an overcoat from his own house.

He sat down, fully dressed. He must make a decision. He must act.

He was still sitting there when the telephone rang half an hour later.

'It's me,' Atkins's voice shouted.

'Yes, yes! What's going on?'

'We're up behind Euston station.' His voice began to disappear in the crackle of the line. '...Ampthill Square. Just...'

'What? Can't hear you!'

'*They're just standing about doing nothing!* Bloody hell, Colonel, I'm screaming me lungs out at you.'

'Where are you?'

'An ABC at Ampthill Square! I already told you! They let me use the telephone...breakfast here.'

'Stay there! Don't move unless they move! You understand me? Keep with them or stay there!'

'What?'

'Oh, hell!' Denton repeated it all again, and then again, and suddenly Atkins wasn't there any more. Denton hung up the earpiece, then thought of what to do next. He wanted his motor car, he thought, unused since he'd parked it in the carriage shed—when? a week ago? It seemed longer. And then? He could drive up to Ampthill Square and arrest the two of them. He had the pistol. Shoot them, if he had to. Kill the woman: kill the threat to Janet. Or he could call CID and talk to the duty officer, but there was too much to explain. Leave a message for Munro? Munro wouldn't be in until well after seven. Surely the pair with the barrow and the yellow suitcase would have done whatever they meant to do by then. Denton was trying to seem to have done the right thing, but at the same time keep the police away from that woman.

So he telephoned New Scotland Yard, simply telling the CID duty officer to leave a message that Munro should telephone him. But Munro, Denton feared, wouldn't be in for an hour.

And then he called Bow Street, the E Division headquarters, where Guillam was now stationed. He was usually leery of Guillam, the more so since his drunken visit, but, he admitted gloomily to himself, Guillam offered him one advantage that no other copper did: Denton had power over him. It made him sick to think it. Guillam was the one policeman he could call who would, if Denton leaned on him, do nothing to Janet.

And, as he well knew, Guillam was out and about early.

He left the same message for Guillam as he had for Munro: telephone me at Mrs Striker's.

Gowarczyk and the woman had gone north. Ampthill Square was not so far from Charrington Street. He should, he thought, try to reach Hench-Rose, maybe Melville as well. Hench-Rose lived in a draughty mansion in Surrey, no telephone. Gowarczyk was Hench-Rose's responsibility. The woman, too. He tried to justify himself by remembering that Hench-Rose believed his people knew what Gowarczyk was doing at all times. Maybe they were following him right now. But, of course, Hench-Rose hadn't known Gowarczyk had come to Denton's house that night. It was foolish and self-serving to hope that the Charrington Street people were following the pair and had some plan for them.

If Janet had died overnight—he could think of that now, rather coldly—he'd call in the police without a qualm. He'd risk looking like a fool if they found that the pair were simply trundling her suitcase to some hole north of Regent's Canal. If Janet had died, he could ask the police to put constables out to watch for the barrow and the pair. He could tell them where the pair were and what their connection to the murder of Mrs Alken was. He could, even now, get his motor and drive to Bow Street or New Scotland Yard and have it all finished in half an hour.

But Janet had lived; she would get well. He had told her he would lie for her, and, however much he hated it, he would do it now, not by commission but by omission.

Loving her, hating himself, he sat down by her bed again to wait.

His waiting lasted only fifteen minutes. He couldn't sit still. Guilt, learned at his father's fist, was too strong. Charrington Street was too close to where Gowarczyk and the woman were resting. Whatever they intended, he had to give better warning.

Cursing because he was afraid that Atkins or Guillam might telephone while he was calling, he told the operator to put him through to New Scotland Yard. There was a to-do about that, then a worse to-do when somebody picked up at the other end.

'What's that, sir? A warning?'

'A caution.'

'Are you threatening the police, sir?'

'No, no! I'm trying to warn you! There's a police unit—outfit—installation, whatever they call it, on Charrington Street!'

'Charrington Street, sir? In Camden Town? That's F Division. I'll find you their number.'

'No, look—just pass the word along, will you? Please! Pass the word to Charrington Street that Gowarczyk is headed their way. He could have—he could mean to do them harm.'

'I'm looking in the list, sir. There's no police installation on Charrington Street. That *is* Camden Town, sir? No, nothing there. Can't give you a telephone number, I'm afraid.'

'I don't want a telephone number! I want to warn them!'

'Warn who, sir? I don't have anybody on Charrington Street.'

'Look here—get the message to Special Branch. Mark it for Mr Melville. Mark it "urgent"! Tell him that Gowarczyk may be headed for Charrington Street. Give it to CID, too.'

'Could you spell that name, sir? Go-what?'

Denton spelled it. Twice. He had to repeat the message. He spoke Melville's name again. 'And get it to Sir Hector Hench-Rose. Urgent!'

'Hold on. What was that name? Hench what? Rose? Is Hench the first name? I don't have a Hench, sir. Neither as Hench nor as Hench Rose. No, sir, there's nobody in the police list of that name. Would you like to come in and report this, sir?'

'Just get my message to Melville and CID! Please!'

Denton hung up. As if he had triggered the bell himself, the telephone rang.

'Denton?' The voice was sullen, muted. It was Guillam. 'What d'you want with me now?'

'Can you come to Mrs Striker's house? Fast? Something's happening, Guillam—I think that the woman who killed Mrs Alken is nearby. I saw her. No, no, it's more complicated than that! I'll tell you when you get here. It's your case, man! You're still on it, right? All right. As fast as you can. It's *urgent*, Guillam—she'll get away! Yes!'

He hung the earpiece up and hesitated, as if it might ring again, and then ran up the stairs to Janet's room.

'I have to go out,' he whispered to the nurse, his eyes on Janet. 'Is she all right? I won't be long, only going to get a motor car. Now listen carefully—if a Mr Atkins telephones, ask him where he is and where he's going. Do you understand? Where he is and where he's going!'

The woman looked shocked. 'I never used the telephone in my life. I couldn't.'

'Yes, you can. You must. Look, all you do is pick up the earpiece and say "Ready". Then listen, and then talk into the tube that sticks out.'

'No, I couldn't. Machines frighten me.'

'You have to! This is an emergency. Come downstairs with me; I'll show you how to do it.'

She said she couldn't, she'd do it wrong, she'd break it, but he had her by the hand and was pulling her down the stairs. At the telephone, he explained it again and lifted the earpiece and mimed listening and talking, and then he made her do it. He might have been trying to kiss her or fondle her, given the fuss she made. Then when they had both turned away from the instrument, she to head to the stairs and he out of the door, it rang, and she tottered to it and shouted, 'Present! Present! What?'

Denton was back by then. He took the earpiece from her and said, 'Ready', and heard Atkins's voice.

'They're moving!'

'Oh, Chri—cripes! Where are you?'

'Ampthill Square ABC, where I been for hours!'

'Which way are they going?'

'Don't know! They aren't out of the square yet, and I can't see from here. But they headed on.'

'North?'

'Is that north?'

'Oh, Judas! Follow them, Sergeant. Just follow them! I'm getting the motor and I'll come after you. Can you hear me? I'm coming after you. Stay where I can see you. All right? Stay on the pavement! Left hand as you go on. All right?'

'You don't have to say everything twice, General. I'm on my way!'

Denton threw the earpiece at its hook and started out. The nurse, halfway up the stairs, sent him a scared look, as if she thought he might knock her down for not doing the telephone correctly.

The Barré was in its carriage shed, just as he had left it. He had to push it out to have enough room to crank it, then to hand-pump petrol to prime the engine. Until then, he'd had somebody else to crank while he advanced the spark; now he worked the spark, then jumped down and ran to the front to crank. It didn't start. He cranked again, getting a rap on the knuckles when the compression sent the crank backwards. He swore. He did the spark again and ran to the front and cranked and the engine barked and blew a cloud of black smoke, and the crank hit him another whack.

The engine died.

'Come on, come on—' He cranked, putting extra strength into it and saying, 'Ouf!'

That seemed to do it. The vehicle shook as the one-cylinder engine took up its noisy banging, loud in the morning quiet. The car began to roll backwards.

Oh, Christ, the brake—

He grabbed the bonnet, then the side of the driver's cowling, and stopped the rolling, scrambled in and grabbed the wheel and felt the car start to roll backwards again. He engaged the gear; the car shuddered and lurched forward, and he wrenched the wheel around and aimed the bonnet at the street. Coatless, he found he was shivering in the early-morning cold, despite the vigorous cranking.

Traffic was never heavy on the streets behind Lamb's Conduit, even less so now, but he was driving as fast as the little car would go; steering around a hansom and then around the other side of a wagon that took up the middle of the way was more risk than he liked. He raced across an intersection where he would have been wiser to stop, frightened a horse and turned down Janet's street with his narrow tyres skidding almost to the opposite kerb. A cab was pulling up in front of her house; as Denton braked, Guillam stepped down and looked around.

'Get in! Get in—they're on the move—!'

Guillam was paying the driver, hesitating over coins in his hand. Denton shouted, 'Give him the lot!' and squeezed the bulb of the horn. The cab jerked forward; Guillam chased it to hand up a coin, and Denton accelerated the moment that Guillam's foot was inside.

'What the bloody—?' The car had jumped forward, started to stall, then caught again. Guillam was thrown back in the seat, one foot still outside. 'Goddamnit, Denton!'

'We're in a hurry.'

'This had better mean something.'

'I told you—it's the woman!' He glanced at Guillam, swerved into Lansdowne Place and then swerved the other way into Hunter Street. 'The one who called herself Shermitz! Your murderess!'

Guillam was holding on to his hat with his right hand, his left trying to steady himself in the car. 'The one your Mrs Striker took to her house, you mean.'

Denton started to react to 'your Mrs Striker' and checked himself. He had troubles enough with Guillam as it was. He said, 'She's up ahead someplace with a man. Atkins is following them.'

'Why?'

'She's a witness, isn't she?'

'You said "the woman who killed Mrs Alken". You know that for a fact?'

'She's with a man that Special Branch say is an anarchist bombmaker.' This wasn't quite accurate, but close enough; Guillam knew nothing about Charrington Street and Gorman's and Barth's. 'They're pushing a barrow, and God knows what's in it. He's rigged a tarpaulin over it.'

'Heading where?'

'If I knew, we'd be there already.'

He came out of Judd Street into the post-dawn chaos of Euston Road. He had to stop, a seemingly endless train of empty buses clopping and rumbling by on their way to serving the hordes now waking in the city. When a gap appeared, he shot through it, squealed left and accelerated. 'What's the best way to Ampthill Square?' he shouted.

'Hampstead Road.'

'You sure?'

Guillam clutched his hat and stared ahead. He was offended.

Denton thought they were going too far west, but Guillam was of course right; it was a case of 'long way round, short way home', if only because Hampstead Road was wider and he could drive in the centre and pass the horse-drawn traffic.

Then Guillam was shouting, 'Here, here!' and gesturing, and Denton took a shallow right, and they were going along a row of shops on their left, the grassy half-oval of Ampthill Square on their right.

'An ABC!' Denton said. 'Atkins was in an ABC!' He reached the end of the row and turned a very hard right to take them on the curve around the plot of green, the ugly bulk of the rear end of the London and North Western station looming over them.

Guillam growled, 'I see it.' He pointed; Denton turned right again and started up the row of shops a second time. 'Here, here—stop.' Guillam jumped out and ran into the tea shop, was out again in thirty seconds. He climbed in, the car leaning to his weight. 'Not there.'

'He's following them.'

'Where?'

'North,' he said. He didn't add that Atkins hadn't been very convincing about the direction. 'North. You'll know Atkins when you see him? Of course you do. He's wearing a black bowler and a light grey coat.'

'Oh, that helps.'

Denton turned into Harrington Square and then they were in Hampstead Road again. Denton turned the car right into Crowndale Road.

'This isn't north!' Guillam bellowed. It was, in fact, east.

But Denton was thinking about Charrington Street. 'Keep an eye out for him.'

'You want to tell me why we're going the wrong way?'

Denton chewed what remained of his moustache. 'They might be going to Charrington Street. There's something there an anarchist might—' He shot across the mouth of Charrington, tried to look down it and, swearing at pedestrians in his way, cut hard down Goldington Crescent and back to Charrington Street, where he swung left and slowed. 'They may be along here.' He didn't feel confident of it. In fact, he was beginning to feel helpless, perhaps hopeless.

'I don't see your man.'

Nor did Denton. He passed Gorman's, the greengrocer's closed and shuttered, drove the short length of Charrington, turned left and left again and went up Goldington Street, thinking he would see Barth's, but he found that he was in fact a street too far east, the short street in which the former baths stood not visible to him. He had to hunt for it, losing more time, and then drove past it and saw nothing, not even anybody going in or out whom he could have warned. And why would they have believed him?

'North it is, then.'

He drove up College Street as far as the canal and then cut over and came back along Camden High Street. Shops were opening, the foot traffic getting heavier. When the High Street didn't produce Atkins, he began to search up and down the north-south streets east of it.

'Bitched,' he said as they came out of Camden Street to Crowndale Road again. He was shivering. He was thinking of what lay north beyond Regent's Canal, a maze of streets. Gowarczyk and the woman could be anywhere by now—

'There!' Guillam roared. 'There, there—!' He was pointing at the entrance to Charrington Street. Denton dared to take his eyes off the traffic in time to see Atkins, who seemed to be walking remarkably slowly, loitering southwards. He was one street north of the part of Charrington Street where Gorman's stood.

'Hold on!'

Denton pushed the one-lung engine to its limit and cut off a goods wagon, darted into the middle of Crowndale Road and brushed the kerb with his tyres as he swung across the west-bound traffic into Charrington Street. He braked; the tyres squealed; Guillam rocked forward and almost hit his nose on the cowling. 'Atkins! *Atkins!* Christ, is he deaf? ATKINS!'

'Oh, Crikey—it's the Royal Marines, come to save the day! Good Cripes, Colonel—' Atkins was climbing into the rear-facing third seat. 'I thought you wouldn't find me. Hello to you, Sergeant Guillam. D'you see them, sir? Up ahead. You can't miss that flag—'

Denton was almost standing, one hand on the wheel, letting the car shudder forward at a child's walking pace. Indeed, it would have been hard to miss the flag on Gowarczyk's barrow. It was waiting to cross Werrington Street; Gorman's lay seventy yards beyond. He saw the woman's shoulder and her little hat; Gowarczyk was only a black shape bent over the barrow. 'They're slow,' he said.

'Slow!' Atkins said. 'I thought they was crawling. But that barrow's heavy, General; I could tell from the trouble they was having with it. Moving gold bullion, are they?'

Denton tried to steer the car out a little to have a better view, but the street was narrow and the other drivers didn't care to give an inch to him. 'We've got to be able to see what they're doing. They'll be there in a couple of minutes.'

'What *are* they doing, then?' Guillam said. 'And be where?'

'I told you, there's a possible target in Charrington Street. Special Branch—some kind of hush-hush thing. They've taken over the building above a greengrocer's. I've got to get closer.'

Atkins keened, 'They'll see you! After all my work!'

'They've gone over the cross street,' Guillam said. He was craning to the left, halfway out of his seat. 'Oho! they're pulling in to the kerb.'

Denton tried to stand again. 'Where?'

'Get down, they're looking around.' Guillam had sat again, was peering ahead with his body leaned out the left side. 'Doing something to the barrow. There's some sort of covering—'

'It's a tarpaulin.'

'The woman's doing something—hold on. What the hell— she's getting out a bloody suitcase! Cripes, Denton, is this all about moving house and nothing more?'

Denton had reached a cross street. His way was blocked by a goods wagon and an omnibus. He stood and tried to see. 'A yellow suitcase?'

'Yes, looks like she just got off the boat. Now the fellow's pushing the barrow on down the street by himself. Now she's walking away—'

'Stop her!' Denton was squeezing the ball of the horn; its squeal was drowned by the noise around them. 'It could be a bomb. Oh, *shit!*'

Guillam was out of the car before he had stopped shouting; an instant later, Atkins followed. They dodged between the wagon and the bus and were lost to him. Denton tried to force a gap between the other vehicles; the driver of the bus wouldn't let him through and sat there, grinning at him over the rear end of his horses. Denton squeezed the horn. He tried to go backwards; his way was blocked by a beer dray. The goods wagon in front of him moved. He changed gear but was too slow for the omnibus, which came right across the front of his motor, the bright green sides only inches from the bonnet, and then moved with deliberate and murderous slowness until it was past him.

For an instant, Denton had a view of Charrington Street, caught for him in a sudden shaft of sunlight as if it were a photograph. Nothing seemed to move: people froze in the act of walking; birds hung in the air. Atkins and Guillam were statues on the left-hand pavement. And then, partway down, where the awning of a greengrocer's jutted out over the pavement, flame erupted and the entire front of the building's lower storey became dust and ballooned into the street, and above, the façade of the upper storeys crumbled and began to slide downwards, to disappear in a rising, billowing cloud of dust. The roar of the explosion came later like a huge hand. A horse hurtled up the street towards him, dragging a hansom blown on its side.

Denton accelerated across the intersection, meaning to go towards the explosion, but everything there seemed to be moving too fast: people were running; the horse with the fallen hansom was pounding for Crowndale Road; what he could see of Charrington Street was crowded with people and wagons and screaming, kicking horses. He turned left into Medburn Street but he was thinking about the people he had failed. *I killed them.* He hadn't got there in time. And he hadn't warned them. And he might have killed Guillam and Atkins, too.

For Janet.

Gowarczyk.

He powered the car right, shot past Barth's and turned left and then right again at the next corner, then right down Goldington and right again, tipping on two wheels as he screamed around the corners, now heading for Charrington Street at its lower end. The roar of the explosion seemed to go on and on, perhaps only something inside his head. He could hear screams now. Smoke was climbing with the dust, and when he stopped, because Charrington Street was blocked with panicked horses and running people, he could hear the crackle of flames. A woman was supporting a man with burned clothes, blood dripping from his left hand. A man without a jacket led a horse that had only three legs.

Gowarczyk and the barrow were on the opposite corner. He was staring up Charrington Street at what he had accomplished, his mouth open. His face looked astounded and ecstatic.

'Gowarczyk!' Denton was out of the car and running. He'd never have got the car across that terror-crowded street. He dodged, jumped aside, went between people, fending them off with his hands. Gowarczyk saw him coming when he was halfway across. He burrowed under the tarpaulin, came out again, his hands working at something. Denton dodged behind a running woman and was at the kerb.

Gowarczyk ran.

He was younger. They started only half a dozen feet apart; by the time he reached the next street, Gowarczyk was twenty feet ahead. He turned to the left. Denton pounded after him, cursing the gawkers now hurrying towards the column of smoke and the chaos of Charrington Street. When he turned the corner, Gowarczyk was looking back, slowing to do so, then turning. His right hand came forward. Denton saw a flash and a cloud of black smoke.

Black powder. My derringer! His own hand went to his side, where the Smith & Wesson should have been. But he had forgotten the overcoat. He had raced to get the car and had forgotten the coat. The revolver was still lying on the bedside table.

He had dodged instinctively when the derringer had gone off; Gowarczyk made up what he had lost and was moving away. He looked back again and then dived to his left into a passageway between two buildings.

Denton ran past the mouth of the passage but looked down its length. Gowarczyk was halfway down. A wooden fence rose behind him. *I've got to get him before he can reload. He has one shot left.*

Denton stopped, raced back, then burst into the passage with his suit jacket held open and flapping at his sides, making his silhouette four feet wide. Gowarczyk fired as soon as he was in the alley. The shot buzzed somewhere to Denton's left. As Gowarczyk tried to take more cartridges from a pocket, Denton ran straight at him, turning his momentum into a kick that caught the smaller man in the left side and drove him backwards, to fall so that Denton had to leap over him.

Denton caught himself against the board fence, turned and pulled Gowarczyk to his feet and spun him around and into one of the blackened brick walls of the passage. Gowarczyk squealed and started to fall again; Denton propped him up, put his arms behind his back and pushed his hands high against his spine.

'You piece of shit,' Denton growled. 'You're going to hang.' He forced Gowarczyk down again so he could pick up the derringer, which was lying in the angle of the stone paving and a wall. Dropping it into his pocket, he began to march Gowarczyk back to the street.

Gowarczyk surprised him by laughing. 'I do it! I trick them! They are such *intelligent* men!' But the laughter was false, faked. It stopped. He said, 'You are hurting me.'

'I mean to be hurting you.' At the mouth of the passage, Denton slammed him against the wall and searched him. He found a long-bladed flick knife. When a hurrying woman stopped and looked at them, Denton said, 'Police!' and she backed away. He began to march Gowarczyk back the way they had come.

A cluster of people had formed at the next corner. Several of the injured were there and had collected a crowd. Somebody was running towards it from a chemist's, bandages held against his chest. Denton looked for constables, saw none. He heard the bell of a fire engine, then another at a distance, then the hooves of the first one's horses.

He turned the corner. The outer fringe of the crowd watched him.

'What's this now?' a man said. He and another began to walk parallel to Denton.

'I'm taking him in. Don't come too close.'

'What's he done?'

'Committed an outrage.'

Ahead, three constables were trying to move the frightened mob out of Charrington Street. The fire engine was somewhere to Denton's right; one of the constables kept looking that way and holding up a hand. The other two were pushing people out of its path. Gawkers were staring off to Denton's left; above the houses, the pillar of smoke still went up. Then the constable waved, and the horse-drawn fire engine came through, pounding across the intersection with its bell clanging and heading up towards what had been Gorman's. Another came right behind it but stopped just beyond the corner; men jumped down and began to pull canvas hose off two huge reels.

Denton pushed Gowarczyk past the barrow, its flag still bright against the scene. Denton saw a piece of ash drift down. Another settled on Gowarczyk's hair like a snowflake.

'Constable! Constable!'

'Out of the way! Move out of the way—'

'Put this man under arrest.'

'No time for that now! You've got to go to the kerb. Sir—if you don't move—'

Denton forced Gowarczyk closer to the constable, a young man whose face was red from pushing people and whose temper was now short. 'Constable, this is the man who set off the bomb!'

'We haven't time for that! You'll have to get out of the way, there's more fire equipment coming! Now, I won't tell you again—'

'Constable, this man is the bomber!'

The young policeman looked at him and finally understood. He was already overcome by what was expected of him; now, he looked stunned. Then another fire bell sounded down Charrington Street and he turned away from Denton and began to wave at people to get out of the way of the galloping horses.

Gowarczyk was laughing again.

'Clear the way, there!' another voice shouted from behind Denton. He looked over his shoulder. Another constable was running towards him. 'Move, move, move—' He shouted. He grabbed Denton's left arm and tried to spin him around. Gowarczyk spun with the movement, hitting the policeman.

'Here!'

He swung his truncheon, which caught Denton high on his left arm. His grip on Gowarczyk loosened, and the man pulled free and butted the policeman with his shoulder, then sprinted towards his barrow, forty feet away.

'Stop him!' Denton had been determined until then to keep Gowarczyk alive, he knew now only that he had to stop him from doing whatever he was planning with the barrow. He believed that it was full of explosives and that Gowarczyk meant to blow himself up—and the crowd and the constables.

'Oh, no, you don't!' the policeman shouted. He tried to grab the back of Denton's collar. Denton put an elbow into his belly and pushed him away.

Gowarczyk was on the far side of the barrow now. The tarpaulin was moving. The barrow tipped.

Denton pushed a woman out of his way. She screamed. He rounded the barrow. The policeman shouted behind Denton.

Gowarczyk's body was extended in under the tarpaulin, his head just visible, his arms pushed out in front of him. Denton saw wires, the whiteness of Gowarczyk's hands in the dark space under the tarpaulin. He put his arms around the man's middle and raised his feet off the ground and pulled. Gowarczyk screamed, not in pain but in rage. Denton pulled him off the barrow; the wires came with them, behind them a heavy, wire-wound cylinder that crashed to the ground as Denton swung Gowarczyk up, got his shoulder under the man's abdomen and stumbled forward, pulling the wires and the cylinder until the wires broke, and then he spun his burden around and threw it to the pavement. Gowarczyk's head hit with force, but he scrambled up, blood on his face, and tried again to get to the cylinder. When he saw that the wires had broken, he screamed.

He screamed in a language Denton didn't understand. He gestured with the broken wires that were still in his hands. Then he threw himself at Denton. Denton hit him twice and would have hit him more, but the constable pulled him off. And a new voice roared, 'What's going on here?'

Guillam had lost his hat and overcoat and had a gash on his forehead. He was being supported by a fireman.

The constable shouted; Guillam shouted back and showed his card. Guillam put his face close to Denton's. 'What are you at now?'

'This is the bomber. I swear it, Guillam. For God's sake, don't let him go.'

'All right, Constable, hold that man. Find somewhere to put him.'

'What about Atkins? Did he make it?'

'He was behind me on the street, wasn't he?'

'And the woman?' Denton had hold of Guillam's arm. 'The woman with the suitcase?'

'She was in there when the explosion happened. She'd hardly got into the place, and hell broke loose. I saw it, Denton. Knocked me back on my arse, it did.'

Denton looked at Gowarczyk. He was bleeding, but he was still in a rage. 'She killed my son,' he said. 'She murdered my baby. Justice! I have had justice!' He began to rave again in the other language.

Guillam shook off the hand of the fireman who had been helping him. 'I'm all right. I'll get myself to the medico.' Guillam moved towards Gowarczyk.

Denton said, 'What about Atkins?'

Guillam, bending over Gowarczyk, said, 'Lost sight of him after the blast. I was out for a bit, in fact. He was behind me when the bomb went off, and he wasn't there when I could make sense of things.'

More police joined them, the street now dotted with their uniforms as a carriage-load of them arrived. Two of them listened to Denton's and Guillam's story and called a detective over. Melville came behind him, picking his way through the crowd until he saw Denton and then coming straight towards him.

'Well?' he said. He looked older, shaken. 'I only just got your message.'

'That's Gowarczyk. He used the woman to blow up Gorman's. And he's got more explosive somewhere along the street, because he was trying to wire up that device when I stopped him.'

Melville looked at the cylinder. 'That's a Marconi antenna. You mean he used that to set off a—' He looked around. 'My God.' He looked frightened. 'Don't talk to the press. We don't want them to get the wrong end of the stick.' Melville looked at Denton, then at the kneeling Guillam. 'It was a gas explosion.'

Moments later, a detective and the constable were marching Gowarczyk away, and Melville was walking slowly northwards, his eyes on the now-diminished column of smoke. Denton followed him.

The street was chaotic. Fire hoses curved underfoot; men with a body on a stretcher hurried past; closer to the explosion, Denton saw bloody clothing, pulped fruit, part of a shattered oak chair, glass and brick and mortar. Rubble. A human arm. When he was unable to penetrate any closer to what was left of Gorman's, he said to the policeman who held him back, 'I'm looking for somebody.'

'Try the hospitals, sir. Nobody left this side.'

'He may have tried to help people—if he was all right.'

'Try around the back, sir. Next street. They're still going in that way, bringing people out.'

Denton had to go back the way he had come. At the corner where he had left his motor car, still at an angle to the kerb where he had left it, Guillam was having his head bandaged. He pushed away the medic's hand and came towards Denton. 'I want to talk to you.'

'I'm trying to find Atkins. He may be in the next street.'

'I'll come along.' Guillam was tucking the loose end of bandage in as he walked. 'What's this about the bomber and his wife? Says he killed her on purpose? You heard him say that?'

'He's lying.'

'He says she got rid of a baby. You know anything about that?'

'How would I know anything about it?'

They were walking towards Barth's. The narrow street was blocked by ambulances and a police hearse. Two constables were keeping people from entering, wary eyes on a cluster of newspaper men at the bottom of the steps. As Denton watched, Atkins appeared in the doorway and handed mugs of tea to the PCs.

'Atkins!'

Atkins had lost his hat and had black smears on his face and hands. He trotted down the steps and pushed his way through the journalists. Denton put his arms around him. 'I was afraid I'd got you killed.'

Atkins, embarrassed, detached himself. 'Oh, I'm right as rain. I'm fine. Was even able to be a bit of a help. But—'

'What?'

'I gave a hand in bringing out the bodies, General. I...' Atkins chewed on his lower lip. 'I'm afraid that—I'm sorry, General—Sir Hector didn't make it.'

Denton couldn't speak. What had Hench-Rose said? *Friends come by ones.* And Denton hadn't warned him.

I killed him.

He shut his eyes against that truth. Tears trickled down. Only later did he realize that the big arm that went around his shoulders was Guillam's.

CHAPTER

21

St George's, Hanover Square was better than half filled for Sir Hector Hench-Rose's memorial service. The funeral had been private, on the family property in Sussex; the memorial service, therefore, was crowded. The family, his wife and children dry-eyed and stoic, had a front pew. Clubmen, including many from the Kestrel, took up several rows of the new pews. Policemen, a few recognizable to Denton despite their civilian clothes, took up many more. There was not, as might have been expected, a delegation from Mrs Castle's house on Westerley Street, where Sir Hector had been a popular client. The dress police uniforms that the dead man deserved were missing, too, undoubtedly by command from above. Indeed, little was made of Hench-Rose's police connections in either the reporting of the explosion or the service.

The newspapers had insisted that the Charrington Street blast had been a gas explosion, although the first two to cover it had called it in their early editions an anarchist outrage, then next day retracted the story. Denton had no idea what arms had been twisted or what editors had been visited by powerful men. By the time of the memorial service, the story was dead, anyway. Not in its place, but tucked into inside pages, was the muted announcement that 'Lord Lansdowne, Secretary of State for Foreign Affairs, has commenced talks with Dr Herzl of the World Zionist Congress on the subject of a temporary Jewish homeland within the confines of the Empire, with particular attention to the Uganda Protectorate.' It was, perhaps, gruesomely fitting that Hench-Rose's service was held the same day.

Weighed by his own guilt, Denton slumped at the back of St George's and stared at the great Tree of Jesse window. Prayers and eulogies meant nothing to him. The music, on the other hand, moved him and deepened his sense of self-inflicted loss. Eager to leave, he nonetheless had to wait until the family had slipped out. If Hector's wife's eyes met his for an instant, she gave no sign; he was, after all, that one of her husband's less respectable friends who as good as lived with a woman not his wife, and a woman of the streets, at that.

The crowd that surged out behind the family caught up with him before he was quite out of the door, and William Melville called to him before he ever reached the great columns of the church's portico.

'Denton! I say—'

Reluctantly, Denton turned.

'Denton, we must talk.'

'I think not.'

Melville led him away from the doors and into the shadow of one of the pillars. 'I feel that I owe you an explanation.'

'I don't give a damn for your explanations.'

Melville's head went back. 'We owe something to Sir Hector's memory.'

'You bastard!' Denton saw a couple of heads turn their way. He dropped his voice to a fierce whisper. 'Between us, you and I killed him. We're not going to bring him back by giving each other "explanations", and as for his "memory", I've my fill of that. I'll certainly not forget my part in his death, although I expect you will yours. You probably already have.'

'I feel no guilt, if that's what you mean.'

'Your hare-brained scheme made him a target!'

'He was a soldier; he knew that—'

'Hench-Rose was a good, brave man, but he had the brain of a child when it came to the kind of shenanigans you put him up to! He believed the crap that your two bullies screwed out of Gowarczyk! And you let him believe it!' Denton moved almost against Melville's chest, forcing the man backwards until he was against the column. 'Gowarczyk played Hector for a fool! Didn't it occur to you or Major House, in all your experience and your brilliance, that Gowarczyk let himself be caught? How do you think he found Charrington Street? By letting them take him there! And then he became their "agent", and Hector thought they had their own pet anarchist, just waiting to help them spring a trap and catch all the nasty people who were going to blow up Herzl and the Foreign Secretary. And all the time, Charrington Street was the target. *Always!*'

'You've no way of knowing that.'

'What the hell, do you really think anybody cares enough about some scheme to send Jews to Africa to go to all the trouble of setting up a bombing? This is supposed to be your speciality, Melville! You're supposed to be the great man when it comes to anarchist outrages!'

'I couldn't take a direct role in the operation.'

'No—or you'd be dead instead of Hector. You make me sick.'

'Britain must have a secret intelligence service!'

Denton hated Melville, he thought—hated what he stood for: ruthlessness, secrecy, evasion of the laws by which the world lived. 'You make me want to puke.' He turned away and, going around the column, found himself facing Guillam, who was looking up the steps at him and now started up. Denton went down at an angle, meaning to avoid him.

'I want a word,' he heard Guillam say.

'Not now.'

'Has to be now. I'm due at Bow Street. Unless you want me dropping in on you again.'

Denton stopped. The air was cold, both men in buttoned overcoats and black gloves. A thin sun cast faint shadows on the stones. A mourning bell began to ring.

'Had a chat with your anarchist before they took him away,' Guillam said. 'You know he murdered his wife, am I right? No avoiding it. Setting aside all this balls about leaking gas, he used Marconi antennas to set the bomb off, so he knew exactly when to do it. He didn't wait for her to get out of there, did he? No, he didn't. She wasn't in there three seconds before he blew the bomb. She must still have had the suitcase in her hand. It blew her into pieces, Denton—legs one way, torso another, head over there. I'm not supposed to know about that, but I've made friends all over the Met in my time. People tell me things.'

'I feel like hell, Guillam. This has hit me pretty hard.'

Guillam pulled him farther away from the groups clustering on the steps. At the kerb below them, carriages and motor cars were lined up to take the mourners; the family were already gone. Guillam dropped his voice to a barely audible rumble. 'He said he murdered her because she killed his baby. You heard him say it, you did. Eh? What'd he mean by that, d'you think? Did she drown a baby in the bath? I don't think so. Kill a kid with a carving knife? No. What she did was have a doctor cut it out of her. He told me that. That's an illegal act in this country. As you know. Eh?'

'Come to the point.'

'I talked with that Ikey doctor of yours. He told Mankey he'd "examined" a woman he called Rebecca Shermitz. Same name as in the dress found hanging in your house, Mankey says. Oh, yes, I've talked to Mankey, I have! Not the dead woman's dress—wouldn't have fitted her. I went to see the good doctor and asked him just what he examined about the woman. He wouldn't tell me. Patient's private information. But you see, Denton, as it's the same woman—Gowarczyk's wife and Rebecca Shermitz, I mean—then it's clear as glass to me that your Dr Bernat is the one that aborted Gowarczyk's kid. So your doctor is guilty of a serious crime.' He dropped his voice. 'And so is anybody who helped him.'

'There's no proof.'

Guillam looked out at the street. An elderly man was being helped into a carriage where several women were already sitting. 'I think I could bring a charge. I'd have you called as a witness.' He looked at Denton. 'You wouldn't lie on the stand, remember? Not in court. And oh, yes, I'd have charged your lady friend as an accessory.'

'You're the second person I've thought of punching out this morning, Guillam.'

'Wouldn't serve.' Guillam hunched his shoulders as if he were cold, his gloved hands pushed deep into his overcoat pockets. 'I'm just telling you what I *could* do. Just like you and I talked about what you could do about me.'

Denton saw that he was offering a quid pro quo. Guillam would never believe that Denton would keep quiet voluntarily about what he'd seen in Regent's Park, but now he thought he had something that would make Denton do so. The knowledge seemed to give Guillam quiet satisfaction. Denton said, 'If it makes you feel better to have it that way.' He was thinking of Guillam's arm around his shoulder when he had learned that Hector was dead: a moment of contact, a moment without overtones of threat or fear. 'I don't wish you harm, Guillam.'

Guillam nodded slowly. 'Nor I you,' he said very softly. The words seemed to surprise him. 'But I know now why it was me you called that morning and not some other copper. Let's leave it at that.' He went down the steps and crossed the street and disappeared along the curved railing of the garden.

Denton followed him more slowly but turned left and made his way through the people still waiting for their carriages. The crowd had got thinner and he had to go around only two or three. He was thinking that he would walk, clear his head of Guillam and Melville, try to clear it of his own guilt. His shadow, pale, compressed to a dwarf, went ahead of him, but as he passed the corner of St George's, a figure detached itself from a column and limped down the steps towards him.

'Guillam giving you grief?' It was Munro, huge and outlandish in mourning clothes.

'We were coming to a sort of understanding, actually.'

'I'm that sorry about your friend, Denton.'

Denton studied his shadow. 'I killed him. "Sorry" isn't in it.'

'Ah, you must stop saying that. Mind if I walk alongside of you? You were going to walk, weren't you? But you'd rather be alone, right?'

They set out towards Brook Street. Denton said, 'I feel like hell.' He kicked a pebble that had somehow found its way to the pavement. 'I could have stopped them. I saw them out the window. If I'd so much as shouted at them—I should have shot the both of them while I had the chance.'

'And been hanged for murder.'

'Three dead is better than eight. And one of them wouldn't be Hench-Rose.'

Munro groaned. 'That's havers, man! You can't go about shooting people. You did the right thing—you warned me, you warned Guillam. You warned Melville, too, didn't you? What else could you want, the bloody army?'

'You know what I mean.'

Munro walked several paces without speaking, then muttered, 'You have a way of doing things yourself, I s'pose you mean. Well, maybe, but given that, you did the best you could.'

'No, I didn't.'

They turned together towards Oxford Street. Munro said, 'How come you saw them? You said you saw them and could have shouted at them.'

'They came down Millman Street. I thought they might go around into Lamb's Conduit. I thought it might be me they were after.'

'Why? What were you to them?'

'Instead, they went north.'

At the corner of Oxford Street, Munro stopped and Denton stopped a stride later, had to turn to look at him. Munro said, 'There's something you aren't telling me, isn't there? Oh, it's all right. The investigation is stoppered, anyway. I was told yesterday that the two who beat you up have disappeared—not in Ireland, as it turns out. Maybe on their way to India or possibly SA. Major House has scarpered. Charrington Street never existed; eight people were killed in a gas explosion; Hench-Rose isn't a martyr but a fellow who happened to be in the wrong place at the wrong time. What you tell me or don't tell me is beside the point.'

Denton was staring into the headlong parade of Oxford Street and finding it disgusted him. 'It was a bollocks from the start. Melville's got a bee in his bonnet about having a secret intelligence force, so he set one up and put the wrong people in to run it. House brought in Simms and Gratton and God knows who else and made it worse. Somebody fed both them and a Zionist named Held the same information about Gowarczyk and "Simonova" and a plot to blow up Herzl, and each of them thought it was true because each of them confirmed the other. Hench-Rose's "outfit" thought they were playing with Gowarczyk, and all the time he was playing with them. Right from the beginning. And he had nothing to do with Jews or Zionism or the Bund.'

The busy street seemed to him to be populated by grotesques. A woman with a humped back went by, a maid with a sheep's face following her. He saw a fat woman with a face like a pig, a thin one who looked like a rat; a passing horse had a swollen hoof and fetlock as big as a man's head, and an ape who was lashing it to make it go. Nothing was pretty; nothing was good: it looked to him like a pageant on the subject of human ugliness. He said, 'Melville will work out who sent the bomber. My guess is he'll find it was either the Russians or the Germans, who already have their secret intelligence services and who certainly don't want Britain to have one. As nor do I.'

'That's a bit of a long reach, isn't it?'

'All you need is a Russian or a German Melville. I doubt he's the only example of the type. It's just that theirs got a head start on yours.'

The two men stood at a corner, pulled back against a building so as to be out of the onrushing ugliness. Neither spoke for some time, the silence growing so long that Munro said finally, 'Do you think the woman who was killed in the bombing killed the Alken woman?'

'She's as good a guess as any. Are you going to close that case?'

'Not me, but Guillam. I suppose so.'

A minute later, Munro said he had to go. He shook Denton's hand. 'How's Mrs Striker? Better, I hope.'

'The doctor wants me to take her somewhere warm.'

'Might be good for you to get away, too.'

Denton grunted, touched Munro's arm and went off along Oxford Street to join the parade.

Janet was sitting up. It was her first day out of bed, and she smiled in apology when he saw her. She was in an armchair by the window of her sitting room, helped there by the nurse. He had bought her a contraption that had a pivoting arm with a rack like a music stand on which she could put a book. There was a book there now, but it was closed; she had simply been looking out of the window. 'I walked from the bedroom to here.'

'We'll send you back by train.'

'Get Atkins's wheelbarrow, more likely. Oh, please, not more beef tea!' The nurse was approaching with a cup, steam rising from it.

'Does you the world of good. Drink it up.'

'Oh—! It's a threat: if I don't get well, I shall have to drink this stuff for the rest of my life.'

One of her pre-Raphaelite dresses hung on her. The gaudy colours rather mocked her pallor, the severe lines into which her face fell now, the purple crescents under her eyes.

She knew where he had been. She said, 'Was it awful?'

'The choir was nice.'

'Yes, if you want to hear good music when you're dead, St George's is the place.' She took his hand. 'I'm sorry, Denton. I know he was your friend.'

He wanted to shout, *Yes, and I killed him for you! I let him die because I didn't want them to learn about you!* But he couldn't do that. He had wanted to say, *I did it; I lied for you. See how I love you!* But she wouldn't have understood; or, rather, she would have understood in other terms. Love didn't really fall within her understanding.

He said, 'It's wonderful to see you up.'

'I have to get on with things.'

He offered to read to her. They both fell quiet. She looked out of the window. She was quieter since she had been ill, apparently indifferent but perhaps simply weak. Bernat had said that prolonged high fever sometimes affected the brain. Her memory seemed sharp, however, and her comments on what she saw or heard seemed normal. There was simply this underlying indifference, as if the fever had burned away her stronger feelings.

A day or two later, she was gone. So was the nurse; he found that Janet had discharged her. He sent to Bernat's; he sent Atkins to the neighbouring houses, but nobody had seen her. Then in the middle of the morning a cab pulled up and two women in the too-long-worn clothes and the ancient bonnets of poverty brought her up the steps. She had gone to the Isle of Dogs to try to continue her project and had collapsed. Luckily, she had been where she was liked; she could have been robbed and stripped and left in the street.

'It was stupid!' Denton said when she was sitting up that evening.

'All right, it was stupid!' She didn't smile. 'I've known you to do stupid things.'

'Janet, you're hardly over the fever; you could have—'

'Very well, it was stupid!' Her old passion was in her voice. She threw her head back and covered her eyes with her hands. 'God, I hate being *helpless*!'

'Bernat thinks you should go somewhere warmer.' He made his voice level. 'What would you think of Naples?'

She waved a hand, said, 'Why Naples?'

'I've got an idea for a book. About Naples. It would pay for the trip.'

'I've plenty of money.'

'I haven't.'

She shut her eyes and opened them again. 'Leah's bringing Cohan home,' she said. 'He has to go back for more surgery in a month.' She shut her eyes again. 'Better for her if I'm not here. Naples is all right.'

He wondered if Leah were coming home because the woman was gone from downstairs, but of course there was no way she could know that, nor could she know that her 'niece' was dead.

He thought Janet was asleep. He started for the door.

'Denton.'

He turned. Her eyes were open. 'Thank you,' she said. Her voice was gentle, affectionate.

He felt as if his heart had burst in his chest. *She knows!* he thought. *She understands!* It was like a blessing. And then he realized that she didn't mean the lies, the deaths. She didn't know. She didn't understand. She was talking about his taking care of her.

'We need to get you where it's warm,' he said.

He walked to Holborn and then to Chancery Lane. It was a cold, bright day, a few flakes of snow falling from a seemingly cloudless sky. At Fleet Street, he turned and turned again into Bell Yard, then into the mundane doorway of his publisher. Only a tarnished brass plate, and not a very big one, gave any sign of what was to be expected on the other side: *Gweneth and Burse.* No hint of what they did. No hint, either, that Burse didn't seem to exist any more.

Denton went up and found his own way to his editor's crowded office. Diapason Lang was an attenuated man in his sixties, much respected in the tiny world of publishing, always the cause of speculation about his sex, if any. Seeing Denton, he jumped up and said 'Ah!' in a high, somewhat cracked voice.

Denton shook his long, dry fingers. 'I've heard of an actor who said "Ah" after another actor's performance when he didn't dare say how bad it was.'

'Oh, no, no, no! I didn't mean anything like that. Mine was a sound of discovery—of pleasure at unexpectedly finding you here. How's that?'

They sat. Denton said, 'I've come to *schnorr* you.' Lang looked stunned. Denton said, 'The Ghosts of Naples.'

'What? Oh—was that the bad actor's play, you mean?'

'Have you ever heard of Eusapia Palladino?'

'Wait, wait—it's on the tip of my tongue—aha! Peasant woman with remarkable abilities as a medium. Eh?'

'Somebody—Conan Doyle, actually—gave me a book about her. She lives in Naples. Italy. A very old city—established by the Greeks. Ancient buildings. Catacombs. Ruined palazzos. Ancient noble families, inbred and rotten with incest.'

'Oh, dear, I hope not.'

'It's a title, Lang—*The Ghosts of Naples*.' Lang didn't get it: he was putting on the face he used when he pretended to have read a book he hadn't read. 'A *proposed* title, Lang.'

'Ah, I see!' Lang raised his eyebrows, smiled, moved his upper body back and forth. Lang believed that Denton was a horror writer; it was dawning on him that something with 'ghosts' in the title was horror. 'A travel horror book!' He stopped himself. 'But not by motor car this time.' Denton had had a great success with *Motors and Monsters: From Paris to the Land of Dracula by Automobile* some time before. Lang thought that motor cars and the supernatural didn't mix.

'I thought I'd build it around this Palladino woman. People from the Society for Psychical Research are down there now, testing her "scientifically", whatever that means. There must be other mediums there, too. Plus local legends. Blood-curdling ones. I'd find some haunted castles and spend a night in them or something of the sort. And all of this with a lot of the usual stuff about the city. Well?'

Lang reverted to editorial caution. 'When are we going to have a new novel from you?'

'Maybe I'll write one while I'm in Naples. If the advance is big enough.'

Lang frowned. 'You can't write two books at one time.'

'Who says?'

Lang played with a scrap of paper, turned it into a ball, pushed it about his desktop with a pen. 'What would it be like?'

'The travel book?'

'The novel; I see the travel book perfectly well. Good sales on spiritualist stuff just now. *That's* all right.' He looked lip from the paper ball. 'The novel?'

'The working title is *The Secret Jew.*'

'Oh, dear, no.'

'It's about a man who's looking for religion and comes to believe he's a descendant of one of the lost tribes of Israel. Keeps going to religious figures and hitching his wagon to their star for a while—Joseph Smith, the Quakers, the Methodists, maybe somebody like the Amish—then comes to believe that the Eskimos are *the* lost tribe, and goes farther and farther north and finally finds a group who seem to know Hebrew words and other stuff. He moves in with them—a frozen universe, heartless, violent, godless to us but to him the embodiment of God—and, when he dies, the natives put him on an ice floe and drive a cross made out of pieces of walrus tusk at his head, because they think he's a Christian. And he floats away.'

Lang stared at him. His forehead was resting on the long fingers of his right hand. He said in a somewhat strangled voice, 'I never know when you're joking.'

'Granted, I haven't worked it all out yet. I think he may murder his wife and children right at the beginning. It's really about searching for the explanation of guilt. His idea of a god.' He threw his head back. 'I hate talking about my work!'

Lang looked as if he might weep. 'It sounds rather...philosophical. Rather, mmm, *heavy.* I think I'd like to see a more, mmm, fleshed-out something. Mmm? In writing?'

'But you'll buy the travel book.'

'I'll have to trot it past Gwen, of course.' Gwen was the publisher, the Gweneth of Gweneth and Burse.

'Well, trot. I want to start soon. The other one, I've still got a lot of thinking to do. But I like it. I can see it. I don't have a story yet as such, but I can see it.'

'Yes, well, do put something on paper so I can see it, too.'

They chatted for a minute or two more and shook hands, and Denton left the office, not very well pleased but feeling that he'd done as much as could be expected. When he looked up the rackety corridor—a rather undulating floor, walls of crazed horsehair plaster laid up in the eighteenth century, a six-over-nine window whose frame was parallel to nothing else in the building—he saw a shambling figure silhouetted against another window farther down. Seeing Denton, the figure turned and started to shuffle away, but Denton was heading in the same direction.

'Mr Frewn!'

The shambling figure seemed to try to accelerate. Catching up, Denton, who meant only to be polite, said, 'It's good to see you, Mr Frewn.' He was going to pass the old man and go on when Frewn threw himself back against the wall, apparently to let Denton go by, but with his hands raised in front of his chest.

Mr Frewn—he never in Denton's experience had had another name—was something on the money side of the business, perhaps originally an accountant but now something rather greater, nobody could ever explain just what. When Denton wanted his royalties outside the usual six-month cycle, it was Frewn who had to be cajoled and wheedled for the cheque. He was ancient, large, white-haired; the black suit he wore hung on him as if made for somebody much bigger, the worn black fabric looking like some sort of leather, perhaps bat.

'Mr Denton!' he cried. He had a deep voice that nonetheless sounded terrified.

'Mr Frewn. Nice to see you.' Denton was going to pass on when he saw a glint of gold on Frewn's lapel. He stopped. 'You belong to the Brotherhood of Britons, Mr Frewn.'

The note of terror intensified. 'Nothing wrong with that.'

'No. Not—' Denton was thinking about Hench-Rose, felt the now-inescapable pang of guilt. 'Nothing wrong with it unless the other fellow's a foreigner.' He stared at Frewn. Age had pushed Frewn's head forward and down; now, something else pushed it still lower, almost to his chest. Denton said in a thoughtful voice, 'Or a secret Jew.'

Frewn's old eyes flicked left and right, and he muttered, 'I didn't.'

'You didn't what, Mr Frewn?'

'I didn't.'

Denton caught a black lapel between his right thumb and his first two fingers, which pushed the gold pin forward. 'I never thought of you,' he said. He rubbed his thumb over the gold. 'But it makes sense, doesn't it? You're one of the few people who know what my initials are, in fact.' Frewn wrote all the cheques.

Frewn found this bad, not good, news. Still, he found comfort. Coming suddenly to a semblance of life, Frewn threw up a pasty hand in a kind of salute and cried, 'Jews out! Britain for the Britons!'

Denton dropped the lapel. He should have been outraged. Instead, he was merely sad and defeated. 'If I told Gwen, you'd be out of the firm. How could you?'

Frewn looked as if he were going to cry. He whispered, 'I had to do it. To do my part.'

Denton sighed. 'You make me sick.' He walked away. At the end of the corridor, he turned; Frewn was still standing there. Frewn looked like a black stalagmite, obdurate, unchangeable, his little hatreds being added to drip by drip.

'Half a loaf is what's being offered, Mr Denton, and I suggest that it's better than no bread at all.'

'Half-loaves are what I seem to be getting these days.'

'Now, now.' Sir Francis Brudenell looked towards his ceiling and steepled his fingers in front of his chest. 'The government are being rather handsome, after their fashion. However, even they have a limit. We can't get prosecution of the people who abused you, and you can't reveal what you say really happened at this place in Camden Town or they'll deport you. Charrington Street? *Charrington* Street. What an odd location for a government office!'

'They meant it to be secret.'

'Yes, but imagine having to find somewhere to have luncheon in the neighbourhood!'

'And justice?'

'A question in the House is not to be dismissed out of hand. Mr Balfour will take a question that I shall write, something to the effect of "Is there any truth, Mr Speaker, to the allegation that members of the Special Branch of the Metropolitan Police detained a resident foreign national without charge, and that while in their custody, this person was injured?" Then Balfour will answer to the effect that no more than two employees of the police mistakenly detained a foreign resident, et cetera, et cetera, and that in the course of their interrogation excessive zeal was shown and the person was treated somewhat roughly.'

'"Somewhat roughly"!'

Brudenell waved a hand. 'We shall work on the phrasing. Fortune isn't going to come with both hands full on this one, Denton. It's a sign of the remarkable pressures on the PM that he'll go even this far. He'll of course say that there's been a thorough investigation, et cetera, and he has it on the authority of the Secretary of State for the Home Department that the errant parties have been punished. Oh, I know, I know! It's the way government works, Denton!'

'I'm to be "a resident foreigner".'

'They insist on anonymity. I agree, in fact. Publicizing your name would lead to more bother from the press. You're also to get five thousand pounds.'

'Hush money?'

'Compensation for damages.'

'I don't want it.'

'Ah, but I do.' Brudenell's smile was small-boyish, slightly wicked. 'You'll get at least half, of course.'

'Give it to Cohan. He's the one who should be collecting damages.'

'But for a completely different matter. You seem unable to think like a solicitor, Mr Denton. I suppose that's why you're an author.' He tutted over this regrettable quality. 'Now, as for the other matter—' He picked up a copy of *The Command* and held the news-sheet as if it might soil his frock coat. '"Jewganda." How vulgar. But the coinage will be all over London. It will be thought clever.' He looked over his eyeglasses at Denton. 'There's nothing about you in this edition.'

'I know. I read it.'

'Nothing comes of nothing. We can't take an action for libel unless there's a libel. Unless you've changed your mind about being libelled by having been called a Jew——? No. Well, I'm afraid that's that.'

'And they get off scot-free.'

Brudenell tutted some more. He stood, a sign that he was done if Denton was. Walking his client to the door, one hand on his arm, he said, 'Taken for all and all, this affair has turned out not so badly as you seem to think. We've scotched the snake, not killed it, I know, but the government are at least aware that they can't trample on individuals, even foreign ones; the little boxer will get something out of his ruin; the vulgarians have been set back a pace or two, and—what else? Ah—the mystery of the death of the woman found in your garden has been solved. Has it not?'

Denton stopped with the door open in front of him. He was some time in answering. 'Everybody seems to think so.'

The misty cloud had broken up into low, gloomy patches like some sort of scum floating on dirty water. A weak sun sometimes shone, irregular openings of muddy blue at the same time showing through. Denton climbed to his sitting room and fell into his chair, glad to be through with the business of the day, in fact the business of the whole thing that had started that morning at the shooting party with Hench-Rose. The thought of him gave Denton another pang, the death so recent he was still unable quite to believe it. He looked at his post, put the envelopes in his lap but opened none, sat rather with one hand on them, his eyes on the wallpaper. Despite what Brudenell said, none of it had come right. No justice had been done; no resolution had been reached. Half-measures, half-truths or untruths, people let off. He thought about Brudenell's last question. Had the murder of Mrs Alken been solved? The logic that blamed the woman who had been killed in the Charrington Street explosion was attractive, but there was a void in the evidence. Why had she done it? How had she done it?

He decided to take the post upstairs and go through it in a hot bath. His body ached as if he had been working hard. It was his mind that was sore, he thought. He walked to the end of the room and paused, ready to start up the stairs, at the window. The fugitive sun was just then shining, brightening the back of Janet's house and the farther half of her garden. A red armchair sat in the sunlight, next to it a slender yellow kitchen chair, on its seat a washbowl filled with some winter vegetable, mostly dark green leaves, a hint of yellowish white. Turnips? Swedes? As he watched, Leah's head appeared as she came up the stone steps from the Cohans' floor. When she came up another step, he saw that she was carrying her husband in her arms.

She came up to ground level, paused as if to catch her breath and crossed to the red armchair. She bent and put him in it. He said something, nodded. He touched her face with one of his mangled hands.

Leah took the washbowl from the yellow chair and sat with it in her hands. She seemed to be talking to her husband. Her head turned towards him, she picked up the big bunch of vegetables and, taking the roots in one hand and the stems in the other, with one quick twist ripped the stems from the roots. She dropped the stems on the grass beside her.

Denton stared. Abruptly, he threw the post aside and raced down the room for his overcoat, tried to put it on as he thundered down the stairs to the front door, crying, 'I'm going out!'

He left the motor car parked raggedly by the kerb, rear end out farther than the front, and strode to the front door of the Alkens' house in Rutland Road. His ringing brought no answer at first; a second pull at the bell, however, was followed by a muffled thudding, feet on carpeted stairs. After thirty seconds, the door was opened by the same servant, Barton, this time with a coat on but again giving off hints of gin.

'I want to see Lieutenant Colonel Alken.'

'Won't do you no good, will it.'

'What's that supposed to mean?'

Barton stood back, jerked his head towards the interior. 'Might as well come in. Cold out there.' Denton passed him, then waited in the large, cold hall.

'He's had two more strokes, he has. Too much for him, all this about the missus. You can see him if you want, but seeing's all you'll do. He can't talk, can't move but his head, and that only a little, and one arm.'

Denton deflated. 'I'm sorry to hear that. I'd wanted to talk to him.'

'Too late, isn't it.' Barton was looking around, oddly like a shopkeeper looking for something to sell in place of what the customer had wanted. 'You could see them photos again, if you like.'

'No.' Denton remembered tipping him before because of the photographs. 'Well, thanks.' He looked at the door.

'Now, uh—' Barton pinched his nose and sniffed. He moved a half-step closer to Denton. 'If you're interested, there's more photos upstairs.'

Denton was feeling in his pocket for a coin. 'I don't think so.' He held it out. Barton didn't take it.

Barton said, 'These was the missus's. From the old country. Might be something in them for you to see.'

'Where are they?'

Barton looked up the staircase. 'In her bood-war, aren't they?'

'I don't think I should.'

'Now, now... She ain't coming back, is she. As for the house—' He shrugged. 'I'm in charge now, aren't I? After a fashion, I mean. You're a gentleman, I know you won't do nothing improper. Just a matter of me leading you to them, for— half a quid?'

Now Denton looked up the stairs. He had wanted to ask Lieutenant Colonel Alken where his wife had been born. But more photographs as a substitute? To be looked at in such a sordid way? He said, 'You can lead me to them, but I'll decide about a tip for you after I've seen them.'

Barton's lower lip showed a certain truculence, perhaps thanks to the gin. However, after a few seconds of thought, he shrugged again and led the way to the stairs. He was tiptoeing, Denton noticed.

The lower hall was repeated on the first floor; five doors opened off it. One, partway open, let Denton see one post of a bed. A smell of sickness was heavy up here, urine predominant. Barton put a finger to his lips and tiptoed past the open door and went to another beyond it. Opening it, he stood aside, a finger again at his lips.

Denton paused in the doorway.

It was a dressing room. Two Biedermeier armoires stood side by side against the far wall, a dressing table on his right. Mirrored, it reflected the reclining sofa opposite. The pictures on the walls and the furniture, especially the lamps, expressed a taste that was aggressively 'feminine'—ruffles and a good deal of pink—and unconsciously, to use Brudenell's word, vulgar. Barton pointed to a chest of drawers beyond the dressing table. Its top was covered with photographs in gold and silver frames.

As Denton started in, Barton stopped him and pointed at the door in the left-hand wall, which obviously led to the room where the lieutenant colonel lay. Denton shook off his hand.

At first glance, the photographs were a disappointing lot. They were, he thought, Mrs Alken's family, thus relegated up here instead of being with the others in the drawing room. The half-dozen, all slightly red-brown in colour, included three of women, one in a dress of the sixties, the other two in later fashions. They had stern mouths and tight hair: life was serious. One of an older man suggested the same disapproval of the world. He was fat and frowning and self-important, and he had been photographed on the steps of what Denton guessed must have been his house. The boastfulness of his pose had a 'this-is-mine' air about it. The same house, in fact—it took Denton some squinting and comparing to see that it was the same—was in another photograph, a very dark one, as if it had been raining, and not very well composed, the camera too far away so that a lot of flat landscape took up most of the picture. The house looked as substantial as the fat man, with outbuildings beyond it. The last picture was of a boy in a sailor suit and a young girl, posed against a painted backdrop of a balustrade and drapery. The boy looked unhappy, but the girl—his sister?—was smiling. The only smile in the lot.

He thought the girl was Lydia Alken at perhaps fourteen. The clothes were those of the eighties, he thought, maybe earlier. She had a lot of ringlets, the chubby face of early adolescence. The smile was impenetrable: a mask.

That was it. That was what Barton wanted ten shillings for.

Denton studied them again, turned them over, put them back. He saw now that two of the women had been photographed against the same background as the girl and the little boy. All on the same day? The prints had been glued down on grey board, most of which was hidden by paper mat, scissor marks here and there to show the mats were later, amateur work. Denton tried to peer down behind the paper, but on each photo it was held tight. Not bothering to see if Barton was watching, he turned one of the women over and removed the back. He had to cut around the edge of black paper backing with his pocket-knife, then tease out a sheet of thin wood that was held with six tiny, headless nails, really elongated triangles of metal. He caught the edge of the photograph with a fingernail and lifted it away from the glass and the paper mat and turned it over.

He was right. The mat had hidden a gold line around the photograph and, below it, two lines of gold lettering. But not English lettering. He thought it looked Russian.

The other photograph of a woman and the one of the children were the same—same gold band, same gold lettering. He copied the two lines of to him illegible marks on a business card and then did his best to put everything back into the frames.

The nails gave him trouble, but he forced them back into their original holes with the tip of his knife. The black paper from the backs went into a pocket, to be thrown away later. When he was done, the top of the dresser looked to him as it had when he had first walked in. So long as nobody looked at the backs.

Barton was in with Alken and came out as Denton walked out of the dressing room. Barton pulled the door almost closed behind him and went downstairs, beckoning over his shoulder with a finger. At the front door, he said, 'Got what you wanted?'

'I got what there was to get.'

Barton stared at him. He'd had more gin. 'Worth something, I should think.'

Denton felt as if the money was dirty in his fingers. He put four half-crowns into Barton's hand. The servant looked gloomily at them. 'Bleeding little of this in this house any more. You're the first visitor in a week.' He raised puffy, rather bloodshot eyes. 'Coppers came and said there'd been a mistake and the missus's body'd been sent to Liverpool. Liverpool! And she's been cremated and they're sending back the ashes. If she was my missus, I'd sue. But he don't care. Or if he cares, he's got no way of showing it, has he?' He jingled the coins and dropped them into a jacket pocket. 'His sisters is coming on Friday. They'll have him and me both out of here quicker'n you can say Jack Robinson. Then where I am to get a character, I ask you, so I can find another place?'

'Not from me,' Denton said. He reached for the doorknob; Barton got to it first, jerked the door open but stood in the way. 'You know anybody's looking for a butler, you tell them about me, will you?'

'I didn't know you're a butler.'

'Well—more a val-it, maybe. You think I'm low and common because I asked you for money, don't you?'

'I think we're both low and common. Because I gave it to you.'

Denton went out and down the walk to his motor car. He sat in it for some seconds, then went through the irritating routine of starting it by himself and drove away, across the top of the City and then up to Held's house near Maitland Park. The car looked ridiculous among the large houses, cheap and too small. He left it at the kerb.

It was the middle of the afternoon. Still Saturday, still the Sabbath. Denton doubted that Held paid much attention to Sabbath rules; surely he was up to seeing a visitor, at least.

'Mr Held has guests, sir.'

'Oh.' Denton scribbled 'Very important!' on a card and gave it to the male servant who opened the door. 'Give him that, please. I need to see him.'

The footman—he had to be a footman; he hadn't the bearing of a butler—bobbed his head and went away. Denton was left in Held's study. Upstairs, the sound of voices; when he had first come into the house, he had thought he heard music. Ten minutes later, Held came in. *Like going to a Harley Street doctor*, Denton thought.

'I'm very sorry; I have guests.' They shook hands. 'You said it was important.' Denton took this to mean *make it quick*. Held was not trying to sound cordial.

Denton pulled out the card on which he'd copied the characters from the photographs in the Alken house. 'I want to know what these say.'

Held needed only to glance at them. 'They're Cyrillic. I don't read it. Or not well, at any rate. Has this to do with...?' He let it hang; the ellipsis seemed to include everything from Zionism to murder.

'Lydia Alken. The woman who was killed.'

'I see.' Held seemed irritated, as if, now that Herzl was taken care of and the talks with the British government were under way, anything about the murdered woman was an irrelevance, therefore an imposition. 'Well, let me see what I can do.' He excused himself and went out.

Denton sat in a leather chair and pondered the lives of the truly wealthy. Denton knew that to somebody in the East End, he seemed truly wealthy; he knew also that he wasn't. Nor, he thought, was Janet, although she was worth ten times what he was. He tried the old question: Did more wealth bring more happiness? Not in Janet's case, certainly. Nor in his. In Held's? He doubted it. But it had for Hench-Rose, or at least it had brought a kind of boyish delight. Still, why all the fuss about wealth?

He had just got to telling himself that wealth was power, therefore a ladder to a kind of happiness for some, when Held came back, still holding the card. He snapped it with a fingernail and said, 'The top line appears to be a name—Bialys. Polish, we think.'

'A photographer,' Denton said.

'The lower one is the name of a place in the Pale of Settlement. Pilzno.' He handed the card back. 'The Pale of Settlement is where they tried to put the Jews in Russia.'

'I know.'

Held seemed surprised: his eyebrows went up and down, but only slightly. 'You know Pilzno, then?'

Denton shook his head.

Held walked down the room, looking at his books. Now, much farther down the room than he'd found the Zangwill that other time, he stopped, read the backs of several and pulled one out. He returned, leafing through it, then turned to the back, where Denton supposed an index was. He said, 'Pilzno.' Held sighed. 'Pilzno was a town. A famous massacre happened there in the pogroms of 1881. Famous among Jews, at any rate.'

He turned on an electric lamp on the desk and leaned so that the book caught the light. He held the book well away from himself, then fumbled over the desk and found a pair of eyeglasses and put them on—tortoiseshell rims, which made him look owlish and very young.

'The book's in German, so I shall have to translate. "In the summer of 1881, farther south in the Pale—" We don't need that. Mm. And so on, and so on. Ah. "Pilzno, a town of some two thousand with a, mm, sizeable Jewish, ah, component. When it was apparent that the forces of law, not to mention— to say—the government would not impede—not stop—mob action, the Jews of Pilzno felt, ah, justifiably threatened. There was great concern for the children. After two days of mob action, with the normal—no, the usual—beatings and humiliations, including one death by six young—six youths—with axes, gossip came that the next day, Jewish children would be aimed at."' He frowned. '"Would be targets", I think is meant. "Jews concealed their children in cellars, in the nearby woods, and anywhere they hoped the mobs would not find them. Early next morning, the daughter of a wealthy Gentile of the town came to many Jewish houses and said she would hide the children. The mobs would not dare, mmm, visit her father's house. He was a wealthy man and a councillor. Some Jewish families sent their children with her. She took the children to her father's property and put them in an abandoned outbuilding, an unused barn, then locked the door. Only when the catastrophe was finished was it learned that she then went to the mob and led them to the barn and urged them to set it afire. The mob, blessed by their Orthodox priest, did as the girl urged, and thirteen children were burned to death."' Held closed the book and took off the glasses, pulling the bow from one ear, then the other. 'Horrible times, Mr Denton. Eighty-one was a horrible year.'

'Does it give the girl's name?'

'No.'

'What happened to her?'

Held studied the book again. He shook his head. 'She and her family disappeared. They were landowners and could afford to travel.' Held put the book and the glasses on the desk and turned out the light. 'If that's all, I have guests…'

'Yes, of course.' Denton thanked him and went out. At the door, the footman waiting with his overcoat, he looked back. Held was standing at the far end, perhaps showing courtesy in waiting for him to leave. Denton said, 'That's a horrible story.'

The day was closing in, the sky now like a dark cloak being wrapped around the city. Lights were going on in shops and houses, slightly haloed at any distance. Without wind, coal smoke was going up from the chimneys, the smell as rank as the persistent smells of horse and dirt. Soon it would be dark. The cloud, owning the sky again, threatened to press down right to the streets, perhaps to mix with the smoke and become fog.

He drove to his garage and parked the car; then, instead of going home, he started to walk. His mind had leaped through it as he had driven, but now, walking, he could take it step by step. He had no doubt now that Leah had killed Lydia Alken; it was only a matter of seeing it all in order.

Janet had told him that Leah had had a sister killed in a fire in one of the pogroms. It had meant little to him then. Now, he saw it as the explanation for the death of the woman whose body had been found in his garden: old loss, old passion, old hatred. Leah had seen her and had recognized the girl who had taken thirteen Jewish children to their deaths, one of them her sister. She had gone straight to murder, consequences probably never considered.

Lydia Alken had come to Janet's house in search of 'Tania Simonova', almost surely a false name, as was the tale that had been retailed to both Held and to Hench-Rose (as 'intelligence') that she had had a French mother. She had been down in Leah's rooms when Lydia Alken had been let into the house by Annie; she must have fled at once, perhaps only because she heard the woman upstairs asking about a stranger whom Janet had brought home. She had come through Denton's house on the way from Bernat's; now it was to Denton's house that she fled, but Lydia Alken must have seen her as she crossed Janet's garden. Annie had gone to the stairs and called down to Leah to ask about the stranger. Had Leah, looking up, seen Lydia Alken then? Or had she seen her only seconds later when, having run out of the house, Lydia Alken, too, crossed Janet's garden and went through the door into Denton's?

Leah followed. Lydia Alken was in Denton's garden then, perhaps standing by the rear door, perhaps loitering farther back, even against the wall, to study the house. And Leah had twisted her neck as easily as she had twisted the stalks of her vegetables, a woman strong enough to carry a grown man up five steps.

And only then, perhaps, did she think about the consequences. It was then, he thought, that 'Tania Simonova' had
joined her: she had seen the murder, probably from the window
of Atkins's kitchen. And now she understood two things that
she, a woman on the run, a terrorist preparing for a bombing,
could use: a distraction and a victim she could blackmail into
sheltering her. Perhaps she helped to move the body; certainly,
she helped to undress it, but taking the clothes must have been
her idea: she wanted the clothes, and she wanted to leave her own
clothes, which had the same name sewn in them as she had given
to Bernat. She had come to Bernat as Rebecca Shermitz; she
went back into Leah's room as Leah's niece—when she was not
Bernat's illegitimate daughter. Leah, afraid she would be exposed
as a murderer, would have to lie for her.

And after a day or two, with Cohan in the hospital and
Leah there taking care of him, 'Simonova' picked up her suitcase
full of explosive from wherever she had hidden it and brought
it to Janet's house and waited to be told what to do next by a
husband who hated her but needed her. Until she had gone to
Bernat, she must have been in touch with him; belief in their
mission had probably forced her to get back in touch with him.

And Gowarczyk wanted to complete his plan to blow up
Charrington Street. He had visited Denton to get her 'handbag',
but what he had meant was her suitcase. And when she got in
touch with him again, had they fought? Had he beaten her? She
had told him about the abortion, anyway, perhaps out of spite,
even hatred, until, bound by political passion, they had gone to
Charrington Street and he had had his revenge on her.

Denton found himself walking east on Oxford Street. The
street lamps were on, the air thick with moisture now. There
would be fog—indeed, was already a sepulchral heaviness. He
wished he could walk into it, disappear in it. He knew he would
never expose Leah. It was another half-loaf: he had learned what
he wanted to know, but he could not bring justice out of his
knowledge. He would lie for Leah as he lied for Janet, and the
weight of it would be on him.

ᴊers were coming towards him through the
ᴊ saw no pairs, no groups, only single figures, as
ᴊndoned contact with each other. On and on they
ᴊapes in the grey evening, increasingly spectral as the
ᴊ, as if the parade of grotesques he had seen that day
ᴊnro had become a parade of lost souls.

ᴊe had turned around to go home and was walking back
ᴊg Oxford Street when a figure coming towards him seemed
ᴊ know him, signalling with a wave of a walking stick, giving
a mock gesture of astonishment with spread hands. Denton,
wanting, like the other lost souls, to know nobody, groaned.

'Harris, what are you doing here?'

'They allow me to walk on Oxford Street between five and
half-six, so long as I don't assault unmarried women. How the
hell are you, Denton!' Frank Harris would have been a handsome man if he didn't wear that constant look of ferocity, outrage
or lust, sometimes all three together as now, the sum satanic.
Normally seen in a business suit, he was wearing a frock coat and
silk hat, with a black cashmere overcoat slung over his shoulders
but his arms not in the sleeves. His black moustache glistened
like polished wire. He grinned, suggesting a hungry animal. 'You
are looking,' he announced in a loud voice, 'at a happy man.' A
passing woman, her face severe, flinched. 'I've no idea why I'm
happy, but I got up this way—not so long ago, in fact; no matter.
What makes a man happy? Who would know? Perhaps a particularly satisfying evacuation, perhaps nothing more than the first
fart of the day. Will it last? Of course not. Is it to be trusted? It is
to laugh. But while it lasts, it's delirium. You're not glad to see me.'

Harris's gaiety was an added burden. Denton shrugged.

'I am on my way to the Salle Erard to force myself to sit
through a performance of the music of Frederick Delius, a
composer who is without doubt the worst thing to happen to
English music since the harp. I expect irreparable harm to spread
from him like ripples in a mud puddle from a bird's dropping. I
hope to do something outrageous, perhaps chargeable—piss on
the first violinist, or perhaps set fire to the conductor's trousers.

The French do this sort of thing so much b...
sometimes carry fist fights into the streets.'

'I have to be going—'

Harris pulled a gold turnip watch from his w...
glared at it. 'And I have to go off and take a stand f...
music. Why don't you and that wonderful woman of yo...
supper with me at the Royal later?'

'She's been ill.' He had to drag the words from his throa...

'Wonderful creature! Couldn't put up with me for ter...
seconds. I like that in a woman!' He sniggered. He started to
go on, then turned back to Denton. 'What sort of music do *you*
like?'

'John Philip Sousa.'

Harris kept his eyes on him, then opened his mouth; a
sound like 'Ba-ha-ha' came out, then 'Bo-HA-ha-ha,' and this
turned into cascading, cackling laughter. Harris turned away
and, raising his stick like a baton, marched away down Oxford
Street, conducting an imaginary band and da-da-ing a Sousa
tune. Ahead of him, the last shoppers parted to let the parade
pass through, and darkness fell.